Echoes of Lies

Also by Jo Bannister

Changelings
The Hireling's Tale
Broken Lines
The Primrose Convention
No Birds Sing
The Lazarus Hotel
A Taste for Burning
Charisma
A Bleeding of Innocents

M

Echoes of Lies

JO BANNISTER

St. Martin's Minotaur
New York

www.minotaurbooks.com

Library of Congress Cataloging-in-Publication Data

Bannister, Jo.
    Echoes of lies / Jo Bannister.—1st St. Martin's Minotaur ed.
        p.   cm.
    ISBN 0-312-28432-2
    1. Missing persons—Fiction. I. Title.
PR6052.A497 E28 2001
823'.914—dc21   2001041718

First published in Great Britain by Allison & Busby Limited
First St. Martin's Minotaur Edition: December 2001

10 9 8 7 6 5 4 3 2 1

Echoes of Lies

Chapter 1

He'd never heard a grown man scream. Still the sound had a terrible familiarity. In a remote part of his brain, insulated from shock by shock itself, he pondered the enigma.

Despite what was happening there was time. Every second stretched as if racked, leaving space between heartbeats for philosophy. Curiously, the same time was also somehow compressed, the questions hammered at him too fast now to answer or even understand, the pain running seamless as a river, the cries wrenched from him an endless litany of anguish and despair. He had lost track of time. He wasn't sure if this had been going on for hours or days, or if he'd been born to it, spent his whole life ground between unintelligible questions and insupportable pain.

But deeper than the pain and distress, deep in the inner sanctum of his mind, part of him was puzzling how something never before experienced could resonate like a memory. The only explanation was that it came down to him with his genes.

It was a long time since human existence had been like this - a struggle against powerful and implacable forces ending in a flurry of beast and blood - but part of the brain remembered. The cognitive cortex, the intellectual overlay that made Daniel Hood a recognisable individual, was devastated by what was happening to him: throbbing with terror, untouched by comprehension, incapable of resistance, despoiled and defeated and adrift on a killing ocean. But at the core of him, deep in the old brain he had from his forefathers, he knew about dying in agony. The knowledge was instinctive: no previous experience was necessary.

Which was as well, because Daniel had never experienced anything like this. The wantonness of it was almost as shocking as the pain. One moment he'd been letting himself into his flat, the next the floor was coming up to meet him and when he woke it was here, like this - naked, blind, spread-eagle on a table, with men he couldn't see stripping his humanity away an inch at a time.

As the pain mounted he thought they were killing him. But he didn't die. It went on and on, and still he didn't die. His screams faded to sobs, exhausted by the unrelenting brutality. Whimpering like a child he begged them to stop. They said he had to help them first. But he couldn't; so it went on. How long he had no way of judging.

But he knew, even after pain had robbed him of the capacity for rational thought, that he'd come to a place you couldn't walk away from. No one in this room was going to walk away unchanged. Daniel wasn't going to walk away at all.

First they tried threats and then they tried violence. Isolated by his blindfold, he got no warning of it; which hardly mattered since he had no way to avoid it. Blows like cudgels in his face and belly left him gasping for breath and for mercy. But he couldn't give them what they wanted, so finally it came to this. Hurting him. Hurting and hurting and *Please, not again, no more, I can't take any more, why are you doing this? I don't know where Sophie is. I don't know who Sophie is. Please stop.*

But they didn't, and deep down he knew they wouldn't. That they couldn't. They'd gone too far to stop. You could beat a man and dump him by the roadside; you could break his bones and smash his knee-caps. But this ... You didn't do this to someone you meant to survive. You didn't want anyone walking round - or hobbling round, or crawling - knowing you were capable of this. When they were sure, when they were finally and utterly sure that he had nothing to tell them, they would take a gun, or a knife, or an iron bar, and cut loose the knot of suffering humanity that had been Daniel Hood; and the only hope left to him now was that it would be soon.

There were other men in the room with him. One of them had never heard a man scream either, and wavered between horror and a dreadful fascination. Another last heard it twenty years before when an accident with a block and tackle tore a stevedore's hand apart.

And the third heard it all the time, was a connoisseur of men's screams, knew what they meant. "He isn't going to tell you anything. He doesn't know anything."

"That's absurd," said another roughly. The oldest of the three, he was looking at a point midway between Daniel Hood and his tormentor, found it difficult to look at either of them directly. "Of course he knows. He was the look-out."

The interrogator snapped shut the briefcase in which he carried the tools of his trade and straightened with a sigh. "You hired a professional for a job you didn't want to do yourself. Well, my professional opinion is that you got the wrong man."

"No. Try something else."

They were new to this business, they didn't understand. He tried to explain. "Not everyone talks. Whatever you do, whatever you throw at them, there are some people who'd rather take it than talk. They're protecting friends or family, or perhaps a principle. There are people who would die in agony for an idea. But nobody dies in agony for money. If you were right about him he'd have talked long ago. He honest-to-God doesn't know what you're on about."

"I don't believe that." Desperation was audible in the old man's voice. If he was wrong about this ... He *couldn't* be wrong. "He watched it happen, for God's sake! He was part of it, and he can lead us to her."

The interrogator shook his head. "If he was one of those people, who can see their bodies destroyed without saying the words that'll stop it, I'd know."

"You can't give up. If you give up we'll lose her!"

"People who hold out for a principle do it because they're better than the man interrogating them. Stronger, more enduring, above all morally superior. That's what keeps them going. But they need you to know. Once it's too late for lies, they need you to know they could stop you with a word and they're not going to. If you really thought it might be a mistake they'd lose that. Their willingness to suffer rather than betray would never be recognised. Whatever you say, however you treat them, they know they have your respect. They know they're doing something you couldn't do."

11

The third man spoke, for the first time in hours. He had to lick his lips to moisten them. "Have you ... ?"

The interrogator looked at him with disdain, then at the man on the table. "Gone through that? Don't be ridiculous. I don't have any principles worth going through that for."

"So what now?" The old man still didn't believe what he was being told, that it was over.

"Now," said the interrogator briskly, "you put a bullet in him and you take him somewhere he won't be found for a long time. And either you give up and pay up, or you look for someone who really does have some answers."

Polar eyes flared in the lined and weathered face. "I'm not shooting him! That's your job."

"No," replied the other levelly, "my job's interrogation. And it's done, and whether you like it or not I've got out of him all the information he has. I'm sorry it isn't what you were expecting, but it is the truth. Now, to protect us all, you have to finish it. If I do that as well it'll be too easy for you to panic if the police come to your door. If you kill him you'll keep your nerve because losing it would cost too much."

For as long as two minutes the only sound in the room was of racked breathing from the table. But the interrogator wasn't leaving until this was resolved, and he wasn't going to yield. It was too important.

There was more argument, then the interrogator and the third man left together, footsteps ringing on cobbles. It wasn't a room but a stable: after this was finished they'd power-hose the walls and floor, and burn the sturdy old kitchen table, and no evidence would remain of what had been done here.

The old man was left alone with Daniel Hood. He felt no impulse of pity. After a moment he reached out a hooked finger and tore off the blindfold. Daniel blinked, dazzled by the sudden light. His eyes were pale grey, terribly bloodshot, exhausted and devoid of hope.

"You don't fool me," grated the old man. "I know you're part of this. I know you can take me to her. I don't know why you'd rather die."

The whispered reply was too weak for him to catch. He leaned forward. "What?"

Daniel tried again. All through the hurting, when he'd have given anything to lose consciousness, his senses had remained crystaline. Now it was over the darkness was crowding in. He struggled to make himself understood. "Why? Why me? Why *this*?"

The old man shook his head impatiently. "There's still time. I can save you. Tell me where she is."

"Sophie," whispered Daniel.

"Sophie."

"Please. I can't ... "

"I'll protect you. Whoever they are, I can protect you from them. Tell me how to find her. I'll look after you."

Daniel's voice was a breath from the abyss. "I don't know who you're talking about."

The old man struck him in the face. As if someone who'd come through so much might in the end be unmanned by the sting of a hand on his cheek.

It might only have been another sob, but the old man thought it was a chuckle. He hit him again. The ravaged face turned unresisting under his hand. Daniel Hood was finally safe from him.

A moment later tyres rumbled in the yard and the others returned. A moment after that the sound of a gunshot echoed and re-echoed between the brick walls.

Chapter 2

Detective Inspector Jack Deacon was looking at the photographs when the front desk called. A woman to see him; claimed to know something about the Hood business.

When he put the phone down he fanned the pictures out and regarded them impassively. It was nine-thirty on Tuesday morning, he'd had twenty-four hours to come to terms with what they showed. But even as revulsion subsided, anger had grown. People had no right to treat one another like this. People who thought they could had to be found and stopped. Deacon put the photographs back in the file, speaking to them as if Daniel Hood were there in person.

"It's not over yet, lad," he said softly. "Somebody knows what happened to you. Maybe she's at the front desk right now."

He went downstairs to find out.

Quite close friends thought her first name was Brodie. But because this was official - so official it could end up on a charge-sheet - she'd announced herself in all her glory: Elspeth Brodie Farrell. They could call her whatever they liked, right now she had more important things to worry about. She paced the floor. Framed by a cloud of dark hair, her face was so pale it was almost luminous.

There was a chair but she couldn't sit still. Her agitation was the first thing Deacon saw when he entered the room. He noted that she was tall, aged in her early thirties, smartly dressed; certainly striking, possibly even beautiful though he wasn't an expert. He was interested in what she knew, not how she looked.

He noticed the long dark hair, curly as a gypsy's and tidied away behind a bandeau, and the brown eyes, deep-set under narrow knitted brows, but mostly he was aware of her distress. She wasn't crying, but tears would have been superfluous. Every line of her body, every movement she made, spoke of disquiet.

Deacon felt a small hope stir behind his breastbone. Something

14

had upset Elspeth Brodie Farrell profoundly. Maybe she did know about Daniel Hood.

He took her to his office. They might end up in the interview room, but that would mean tapes and solicitors and all the paraphernalia of impending prosecution, and he didn't know yet if that was appropriate. Maybe she was just here to help him with his inquiries. God knows, he thought, I could use some help.

He steered her to the chair facing his desk. "All right, Mrs Farrell, what's this all about?"

She knew what she had to say. Still it took her a moment to get it out. He saw dread holding her like a net. "I think I've been part of a conspiracy to murder."

The policeman felt one eyebrow climbing, scarcely managed to stop it before it disappeared into his hairline. He peered at her face, but nothing he saw there suggested it was a joke. "Don't you know?"

She nodded. "Yes, I'm afraid I do. *Now* - I didn't until this morning. Until I saw this."

She had a copy of the morning paper. She put it on the table and removed her hand quickly, as if it might burn.

Deacon had been studying pictures of this man for twenty-four hours, but none of them looked like this. They were forensic photographs, documenting the damage. Right now Jack Deacon knew the body of Daniel Hood better than his mother did. Right now Daniel Hood's mother wouldn't recognise him.

This was not a forensic photograph but a snapshot. When he first saw it in the paper Deacon thought it had been taken by a friend. It seemed to offer a peephole into a moment's intimacy: Hood was laughing, glasses pushed up so he could wipe his eye on his wrist, and the wind had made silken tangles of his fair hair.

But when he checked with the paper Deacon learned that the photograph had been taken by a thirteen-year-old with a throw-away camera during a school outing. Hood had taken his class up onto the Firestone Cliffs to teach them the principles of trigonometry. For some reason that troubled the policeman. He'd got some comfort from thinking that, before his life deteriorated so abruptly, Hood had

15

been enjoying the days of his youth with someone who made him laugh like that. He was sorry when it turned out to be only one of his pupils; as if Hood had been robbed of his past as well as his future.

So far as Deacon could establish there was no significant other, no close friends. He'd been in Dimmock less than a year. Everyone who knew him agreed that Hood was a pleasant young man, likeable and easy to talk to, but no one pretended to know him well. His principal said he was a good teacher. The general concensus was shock at what had happened to him.

He was twenty-six. But he'd been one of those people on whom time sat lightly: the photograph made him look about eighteen. When he was genuinely eighteen he'd have had trouble getting served in pubs; as late as last week he could have made use of student discounts. This week, though, the years that had been turning a blind eye suddenly remembered and dropped on him from a great height. When Daniel Hood was found in a rubbish skip with a bullet in his chest and the marks of abuse all over his body, he looked like an old man.

"Do you know him?" asked Deacon.

"No. Well - yes. Sort of." Brodie swallowed, tried again. "We've never met. But the moment I saw that picture I recognised both the name and the face."

Deacon waited a moment but she was going to need prompting. "How?"

She took a deep, shaky breath. "Thursday. That's when it began; at least, my part in it. On Thursday afternoon a woman came to my office."

* * *

It wasn't a big office. There was room for a desk, a couple of filing cabinets and a small sofa. She liked the sofa, it put clients at their ease. Also, it took up less space than two chairs, and if she ever finished unpacking space was going to be a problem. There was no reception desk and no waiting room, but that was all right because she couldn't afford a secretary and never got clients more than one at a time.

The little office in Shack Lane, a hundred metres from Dimmock's shingle shore, had two major advantages. It was cheap and it was on the ground floor. The card in her window could be read by those heading for the antiques shops, craft shops and second-hand book emporia packed into The Lanes as if with a shoe-horn, and among the hundreds who passed were a handful who were indeed looking for something.

That was what she'd called the business. *Looking For Something?* Her name was there too, on a classy slate shingle. But Brodie Farrell could be anything: a solicitor, an architect, an estate agent, even a discreet hooker. *Looking For Something?* both caught the eye and hinted at the nature of the service she offered.

People called in on spec; or they noted her number and phoned later. Invariably they began with the words: "Have I got this right - you find things?"

*   *   *

"What kind of things?" asked Jack Deacon.

Brodie lifted one shoulder in a distracted shrug. "Anything one person needs enough to pay another to find. I used to work in a solicitor's office" - she wondered about elaborating, decided against - "and half my time was spent looking for things. Legal searches, property conveyancing; researching case law for relevant judgements; looking for disappearing clients and witnesses who really didn't want to testify. I got pretty good at it. The internet added a whole new dimension: there's a world of information out there for someone who knows how to look."

"You can make a living like that?"

Brodie sniffed. "If I can't I've wasted good money on an office."

"What sort of things do people pay you to find?"

She was growing impatient. This wasn't what she was here to talk about. She was a Londoner, the idea of a finding agency wasn't as bizarre there as it seemed to be here on the south coast. "China.

People break bits of Grandma's tea-set: they can't go into a shop and buy some more, they ask me to find replacements. Missing pairs. A pair of anything is worth more than twice as much as one: people give me photos of what they've got and ask me to find another. Houses. They know what they want, they aren't getting anywhere with the estate agents, they ask me to help. Locations for television and film work. Costumes and period cars for same; or for weddings or parties. Horses. People sell them, then a couple of years later they wish they hadn't but they've gone through too many hands and they can't trace them. Books. An out-of-print favourite that got lost: can I find another? Paintings. Great Aunt Martha was once sketched by Modigliani ... "

"I see," said Deacon before she could cite any more examples. "And five days ago a woman came to you - looking for what?"

Brodie glanced down at the newspaper and quickly away again. "Looking for him."

* * *

The woman in red tapped on her door and said, "Have I got this right - you find things?"

Brodie nodded. She'd been tidying up: she hid a feather duster behind her back.

"People? Could you find him?"

Brodie had traced missing persons often enough for the legal profession. But she wanted more information before she would do it for someone who came in off the street. "What can you tell me about him?"

The woman snorted. "I can tell you he's a liar! The name I knew him by, the address where he claimed to live, were both invented. He's a con-man, and he's made off with fifteen thousand quid of mine. I don't like being made a fool of, Mrs Farrell."

"Surely it's a police matter?"

The woman looked at her sidelong. "I suppose it is, strictly speaking. He got the money under false pretences: that's theft or fraud or something. But ... "

18

Brodie prided herself on her ability to read between the lines. "But you'd rather avoid a court case."

The woman nodded. "I don't need to see him in prison. I want my money back, and I'd like to give him a piece of my mind, but I can't afford to make a big issue of it." She glanced down at the gold ring on her left hand.

On the whole people were easier to find than first editions. Brodie reminded herself that she didn't have to get involved in any unpleasantness: all the woman wanted was a name and address. "Twenty percent."

"What?" As well as red, the woman wore rather a lot of make-up, and thought it made her look younger than her forty-odd years.

"That's what I charge. If I succeed; if I don't all it'll cost you is two hundred pounds. For that I'll start the search: if I don't think I can get anywhere I'll let you know and there won't be anything more to pay. If I think I can find him I'll continue at my own risk. If I succeed you'll owe me three thousand pounds less the start-up fee."

"Three thousand pounds is a lot of money," the woman said doubtfully.

Brodie nodded. "Twelve thousand is a lot more. That's what I may be able to save you."

She thought about it but not for long. She took money out of her handbag, counted out two hundred pounds.

Brodie blinked. "A cheque would do."

The woman shook her head crisply. "I don't want my husband to know about this." So it wasn't just her money the man in the photograph had taken.

Brodie studied it. It was a terrible likeness. "Did you take this?"

The woman shook her head. "He had it in his wallet. He said it was for his mother but I asked him to give it me instead." She didn't blush: she looked up, defiantly.

"It's not very clear," said Brodie, sticking diplomatically to business. "Do you have any other pictures?"

The woman shook her head. "He hated cameras. Now, of course, I understand why. I think he had that grainy little thing specifically to fob me off with. He must have thought it would be no help to anyone wanting to trace him. Was he right?"

Brodie sucked on her teeth. "It certainly makes it harder. On the other hand, a photograph's usually better at confirming someone's identity than finding that person anyway. Tell me what you know about him."

"I know his name isn't Charles Merrick and he doesn't have contacts in the bloodstock industry. Weatherby's had never heard of him, nor had any of the big sales. I think now he wouldn't know a Dubai Cup prospect from a dray-horse, but that was the story - that he was putting together a syndicate to buy an undervalued two-year-old."

"You know something about horse-racing?"

The woman scowled. "Not enough, obviously. He was plausible, I'll give him that. He'd done his homework. He seemed absolutely genuine. We spent two days together, planning the campaign. Then he went off to buy the colt, and I never heard from him again."

"You called at his address?"

"A dog-food factory on the Brighton Road."

"The money you gave him was cash too?"

"For the same reason."

Brodie looked again at the photograph.

The one thing all con-men have in common is that they look respectable. They don't wear kipper ties and pushed-back hats, they look decent and honest and trustworthy. Oh yes: and charming. Most people wouldn't lend money to even a respectable stranger. To succeed, the con-man has to circumvent his target's natural suspicions, charm his way under her guard.

The man who wasn't Charles Merrick was a lot younger than the woman in red. She'd found his attentions flattering. And though he wasn't particularly good-looking he had that soft-focus boyishness that some middle-aged women find hard to resist. Oh yes, he'd seen her coming, all right.

"Can you tell me anything that might help me find him?"

"Not much. If I'd known where to start I'd have gone after him myself."

"Where did you meet?"

"Up on the cliffs. You're supposed to be able to see the French coast: I'd taken my binoculars to give it a try. He asked to borrow them; from glasses he steered the conversation onto racing; you can guess the rest."

"When was this?"

"Sunday morning. He was clever, I'll give him that. He didn't just throw the bait at me. He was rather diffident: I had to squeeze it out of him. At least, I thought that's what was happening. When pressed he said he wondered if I might be interested in a sporting proposition."

She chuckled, without much humour. "By then I'd have been interested in a collection of dirty postcards if it meant seeing him again. He told me about the horse. He said thirty thousand pounds - no, guineas, he said - was a steal, but he couldn't find it all himself. We met again the next day, talked about it over lunch; and on Tuesday he took me to Newmarket to watch the thing on the gallops."

"He introduced you to the trainer?"

The woman shook her head. "No, we watched from the road. He said he didn't want to push the price up by showing an interest. *Now*, of course, I realise he didn't *know* the trainer - he just spotted a likely looking prospect on the gallops and pointed me at it.

"I fell for it like a fool. Fifteen thousand quid? - I'd have mortgaged my soul if he'd asked me to.

"He set off with the money yesterday morning, promised to call me within a couple of hours. He didn't. When I tried to call him there was no answer. I made some calls but nobody knew him. This morning when he still hadn't phoned I went to what was supposed to be his home address. Right enough, they knew about racehorses - they were canning slow ones. So I went to the police station." She fell silent.

It didn't take a leap of intuition. "But you didn't go inside."

"I sat in my car for an hour; then I came here. I realised if they found him it would eventually become public knowledge and my husband would find out. I remembered seeing this place. I thought,

21

if I hired you I'd have more control of the situation. I might get my money back without it costing me my marriage."

Brodie said, "If you decide to go ahead, I'll do what you want me to do and stop when you want me to stop; and whether or not I find him, no one'll ever hear about it from me."

"That's what I need."

Brodie nodded. "Did he tell you anything about his background? Where he went to school, where his family come from? People he'd worked for, places he knew?"

"Nothing! I see *now* how evasive he was being. But he said the deal had to be put together quickly and quietly or somebody'd get in ahead of us, and I believed him."

"Of course you did," said Brodie kindly. "That's how he makes his living - by making lies sound like the truth. He'll have taken a lot of intelligent people for a ride before he tried it with you. But maybe this time he picked the wrong person."

"I do hope so," said the woman fervently. "What do you think - is there a chance?"

"There's always a chance," Brodie said firmly. "Give me a day or two to look into it and I'll be able to say how good a chance."

"Quicker is better. I'd like that money back in my account before my husband misses it."

It might have been impossible. There were people who came to Brodie with quests so plainly futile she wouldn't take their money. But there was something in the photograph that just might help. She didn't want to draw attention to it: too much honesty could cost her three thousand pounds. She'd get the magnifying glass out after the client had left.

She lifted a pen. "I'll need your name and address."

The woman's eyes flared. "Is that necessary? I'll be paying cash."

"I'm sorry, it is necessary. But don't worry, I really will treat the matter with absolute confidence."

"Oh, very well. *Mrs*" - she emphasised the word just slightly - "Selma Doyle, 57 River Drive, Dimmock."

"You won't want me calling you," said Brodie. "Call me here tomorrow afternoon. I should be able to tell you then if I can help."

"I take it you could," said Jack Deacon.

"Oh yes," said Brodie Farrell bitterly. "Helpful is my middle name."

"How? With just a bad photograph?"

"I was right," said Brodie, "there was something else in the picture. When I put it under a magnifying glass I could see what it was."

* * *

It was a telescope. Quite a big telescope: as tall as the man, with an aperture as broad as his fist.

Brodie faxed a copy of the photograph to the Astronomical Association in London. Though it was a bad picture to start with and would be worse by the time they saw it, they might still be able to identify the subject.

And so they did. "Your photograph shows a 100-millimetre skeleton reflector of Newtonian design, apparently home-made. Suggests the owner is a serious amateur. This is about the largest telescope that would be conveniently portable: anything bigger would be on a permanent mounting."

So the man she sought, the man who wasn't Charles Merrick, was serious about astronomy. He would be known in places where stargazers met.

The "Yearbook of Astronomy" alerted her to three forthcoming meetings within a thirty mile radius of Dimmock. Brodie took the grainy picture along to the first, a lecture in Eastbourne that evening.

There she learned his name. Daniel Hood wasn't present but people who recognised him were. Or rather, people who recognised the telescope. Faces seemed to be just so much wallpaper to them, but a 100-mm skeleton Newtonian reflector, well, you don't see one of those every day.

"Where would I find him?" she asked.

They weren't sure. They only ever saw him at gatherings like this. They supposed he had a home and a job somewhere, but those were things that took place in the daylight and astronomers mostly come out at night.

Armed now with a name, she trawled the membership lists of astronomical societies across southern England until she found him. And where she found him was only quarter of a mile from where she was sitting: a flat converted from a netting loft on Dimmock's shingle shore.

She was less than honest with the club secretary. She claimed they were cousins, she'd promised to look him up when she moved to the area only she'd lost his address. "What does he look like? I'd hate to fling myself at the wrong Daniel Hood."

The secretary thought for a moment. "Mid twenties, small, fair. Terrible eyesight, which is a major problem to an astronomer. You need your glasses to find what you want to observe, then you take them off to use the eyepiece. But the finderscope isn't lined up, so you put them back on to adjust it. Then you take them off to look through the telescope again. And it's dark, you see, so if you put them down you have to remember where ... "

"Oh yes," said Brodie with certainty, "that's cousin Dan." The bottle-bottom glasses had been clear even on that photograph.

A scant twenty-four hours had passed. When Mrs Doyle phoned immediately after lunch Brodie was able to pass on the good news; and on receipt of the fee the name and address of the man who cheated her. And she thought that was the end of it.

* * *

"Then this morning," Brodie said, and both her voice and the hand she pointed shook, "I saw that."

Her first desperate thought was that it was a coincidence. But even then she didn't believe it. She grabbed the phonebook; the Doyle family weren't listed so she hurried out to her car. But the River Drive houses ended at number 56.

"Then I knew," she whispered. "I don't know how much of what she told me was true - maybe none of it. But she wanted him for something, and she used me to find him. I never suspected! I swear to you, I never guessed she meant to do anything like - like ... " She hadn't the words. She folded in her chair, defeated.

The telephone rang. Detective Inspector Deacon answered it. The other party did most of the talking; Deacon said "Yes" and "I see" a couple of times, and once he said, "Right." Then he put the phone down and turned his attention once more to Brodie Farrell.

"Well now," he said, and waited for her eyes to come up before going on. "Is there anything else you can tell me? About this Mrs Doyle, for instance."

"I met her twice, for perhaps thirty minutes in total. I have a good picture of her in my mind. If I could work with the E-fit people ... ?"

"Yes, I'll organise that once you and me are finished. I'll also want a statement from you. But let's be sure, first, that we've covered everything you'll want to put in it."

She knew what he was suggesting: that she'd been less than frank. "Inspector, if I knew any more - about Selma Doyle, about any of it - I would tell you. I've nothing to hide. I'm ashamed of my stupidity, appalled by what I've been a party to, but I never guessed how the information I gathered would be used. I don't think I've committed an offence, although right now that isn't much comfort. What happened to Daniel Hood would have been impossible without my help. I don't know if he did what the woman calling herself Selma Doyle said he'd done, I'm not sure it matters. Nothing he did could have justified what was done to him. I'm here to help find the people responsible."

"People?"

"The only one I had any dealings with was Mrs Doyle," said Brodie. "But Inspector, surely to God you don't think that a middle-aged woman who'd lost her money and her dignity to a toyboy would hit back like this? Torture him, shoot him and dump him in a skip?"

"Hell hath no fury ... " murmured Deacon.

"Perhaps not, but she was a plump forty-year-old woman, not Arnold Schwartzenegger. She couldn't have lifted a man's body into a skip. She must have had help."

"Yours, for starters."

Tears started to Brodie Farrell's eyes. She wanted to throw the words back in his face, but they were true. She dipped her head. "I didn't know what I was helping her to do."

"You really thought she was just going to give him a piece of her mind? And that, as a result of that, he'd return her money?"

"I suppose so. I didn't give it that much thought. I did what I was paid for, it was up to her how she used the information." She heard how that sounded and flushed. "I never expected her to use it like that!"

Deacon wasn't sure what to make of her story. There were things he didn't understand, things he'd want clarified. But he didn't have the sense that he was talking to a cold-blooded killer, and if she wasn't that then perhaps her account was true.

He stood abruptly. "Mrs Farrell, will you come with me, please."

She looked up, took a deep breath. "If you're going to charge me I'll want to call my solicitor." Her eyes were full of misgivings, but still the threat of prosecution didn't seem to disturb her as much as knowing what she'd contributed to.

"I'm not charging you; not yet. I want you to come to the hospital with me. There's something I want to show you."

Chapter 3

She had no idea what to expect. But she was familiar enough with Dimmock General Hospital to know that the mortuary was in the basement. Detective Inspector Deacon parked at an unmarked rear entrance and led her upstairs. At least she was to be spared the ultimate humiliation of seeing what her unthinking cleverness had led to. All the way over here she'd been afraid he wanted to show her the body.

He knew where he was going, twisted and turned without hesitation until a shut door blocked their way. A policeman sitting in the corridor rose to his feet. "Sir?"

"I'm letting Mrs Farrell in on our little secret," said Deacon heavily. One hand pushed the door open while the other, firm in the small of her back, pressed Brodie inside.

Inside were all the trappings of intensive care but only one bed and one nurse who looked up at the sound of the door. She recognised Deacon and nodded a greeting.

"Any change?" he asked.

"Not a lot."

"That's good? Bad?"

She shook her head. "I'm sorry, Inspector, I can't tell you anything more than the doctors already have."

The bed was occupied but Brodie could see almost nothing of the patient. High-tech medical equipment clustered around his head like old women gossiping about what had put him there. Tubes ran up his nose, down his throat and into his veins, and his eyelids were taped shut. On a dark screen a blue line described a series of peaks and valleys. A monitor ticked off every heartbeat with audible relief.

Heartbeats. Shallow, irregular, the sort of pulse to make an insurance assessor blanche, but heartbeats for all that.

Brodie Farrell turned to DI Deacon with fury in her eyes. "You animal!" she cried. "He's alive! He's alive, and you didn't tell me."

Jack Deacon had been called worse with less reason. He bore her anger stoicly. "Mrs Farrell, you're only here because I don't think you're responsible for this. If I did I'd have let you go on believing that the paper got it right and Daniel Hood died of his injuries.

"That wasn't careless reporting, it's what I told them. There'll be hell to pay but I don't care. I don't want whoever did this to know he's still alive. If they think he's dead he's safe, and maybe he'll get well enough to tell me who they were and what it was all about. If they knew he was alive they'd come back. They were professionals; the evidence is written all over him, and I don't want my officers risking their lives against professional killers if there's an alternative."

Brodie hardly knew what to think or how to feel. She thought she'd helped strangers to murder a man she'd never even met, for money. She hadn't guessed that was what she was doing, but for the last two hours it was what she believed she had done. Now it seemed no one had actually died; at least not yet.

But why had they come here? Why was Detective Inspector Deacon taking such a gamble? "Inspector," she managed, "what do you want from me?"

"What we talked about: a statement and an E-fit."

"We can't do either of them here. What am I doing *here*? What is it you want me to see?"

Deacon debated with himself for a moment. What he was contemplating wasn't nice but it might be helpful. It was reason enough. He stepped over to the bed and, before Brodie could anticipate what he intended or the nurse protest, threw back the sheet. "This."

If he'd expected her to faint he was disappointed. But she did, finally, cry. She knew Daniel Hood had been tortured before he was shot; but *The Dimmock Sentinel* was a family newspaper and hadn't wallowed in the gory details. So Brodie wasn't ready for what Deacon wanted her to see: a young man's body so pock-marked with burns that his doctors had had trouble finding enough undamaged skin to tape their monitors to.

There wasn't a critical injury among them: the treatment he'd received, which seemed to consist in part of wrapping him in cling-film, was already bearing dividends. By the time the bullet-wound healed the lesions spreading like an obscene rash across his body would be shrunk to mere fingerprints of shiny pink skin. But there were so many of them. They represented hours and hours of agony.

The tears streamed down Brodie's cheeks. So this was what it looked when one person really wanted to know what another really didn't want to tell. The urge to turn away was strong, but she owed him better than that. Grief welled under her breastbone, and she cried silently for the horror and the hurt.

Jack Deacon had meant to shock her: it was why he'd brought her here. He hoped that when he confronted her with what she'd done she'd go weak at the knees, slump on his shoulder and tell him everything, even the bits it had seemed politic to forget. But she didn't even look away. After a minute Deacon began to feel himself diminished by her courage. He took out his handkerchief, offered it gruffly. "Here."

Brodie looked at him, her eyes enormous. "*Why?*"

"I'm still hoping you can tell me that."

"And you thought this would *help*? You thought, unless I saw this I wouldn't try hard enough?"

"I had to impress on you how serious it is." Even to Deacon it sounded like an apology. "It isn't just his life at stake, it's yours too. The people who did this know who you are. And you're the only link between them and him.

"So far as I can make out, they took him the same afternoon you gave them his name and address. No one saw him between leaving school at quarter to five on Friday and turning up in a builders' skip at eight-fifteen on Monday morning. The doctors reckon he was there most of the night, so these people had him about forty-eight hours. They wanted something from him - wanted it badly. But they didn't get it."

"How do you know?" Brodie's voice was a whisper.

Deacon shrugged. "Look what they did to him. If he could have stopped it he would have done. He couldn't. But it was two days before they'd accept that. They must have really wanted what they thought he could give them. They only shot him when all hope was gone.

"The man interrogating him was a professional, but the man who shot him wasn't. A pro would have shot him in the head, and the chances of the bullet missing anything vital would have been just about zero. Also, a pro would have made sure he was dead. But they shot him in the chest, didn't even notice that the bullet had travelled along the ribcage and out through his armpit - there was a lot of blood and they thought that was what mattered. They dumped him in the skip and reckoned they'd done enough.

"With any luck at all they'd have been right: he'd have bled to death before he was found. But it was a cold night. The paramedics have a saying: They're not dead until they're warm and dead. When they warmed Danny up he was still alive.

"So that's two mistakes they've made. They thought he was dead, and they thought you'd keep quiet. Real pros would have done a proper job on him and then come for you. But they thought the damage you could do them was minimal - the woman you met was probably just a go-between, she won't know much more than you do. Anyway, the chances of you ever seeing her again are remote. You didn't see anyone else, you don't know anything else.

"And they thought you'd be too scared to report the little you do know. Why risk being treated as an accessory to murder when there's so little you can say? They thought you'd keep your head down and your mouth shut. If they find out they underestimated you, Mrs Farrell, the next bullet will be for you, and this time they'll wait long enough to take a pulse afterward. I needed you to understand that. Not just to hear it but to understand. Now you do."

Brodie was slowly shaking her head. "No. That's part of it: the part that sounds defensible. But mainly you hoped to shock me into saying something I wouldn't otherwise have said. You thought I was holding something back; at least, you weren't sure I wasn't. This was a way to find out. You thought I'd see - this - break down and confess all. You thought you could achieve more in five minutes this way than with three hours of patient questioning."

She lifted her head to look Deacon in the eyes. He was a big man, with strong features and an air of repressed violence about him like a prize fighter. He was forty-six years old, and a detective inspector, and he was still the first person everyone at Dimmock Police Station thought of when there was a brawl in the front office.

The expression in Brodie Farrell's gaze scourged his cheeks. "Well? Was it worth it? Did you find what you were looking for? You upset me, you used him - but it would be worth it if you know something now that you didn't when we left your office. Do you?"

"As a matter of fact," he said, hard-faced, "I do. I know there's nothing more you're going to tell me. Either you can't, or you've too much to lose to blurt it out.

"So I'm going to assume I was right first time and you really weren't involved. But if I'm wrong, I should warn you I'm not a good loser. If I find you were in deeper than you've said, or you know more than you've said, you're going to pay for it. I'll see you in prison if I can. And if I can't - well, there's more than one way to skin a cat. If I think you bear any responsibility for this, I'll destroy you."

Having rearranged her patient's sheets the nurse was watching open-mouthed, scarce able to believe what she was hearing. But Brodie had spent much of her working life with police officers, sometimes on the same side, sometimes not, and she knew that even the best sailed close to the wind at times. When their actual powers were unequal to the task before them, sailing close to the wind was the only way to progress.

She wasn't afraid of DI Deacon, she didn't even resent his threats that much. Except for the man in the bed, no one had a better reason than her to hope he'd find the truth. She just hoped he was now convinced of her innocence. He was entitled to think she'd been stupid but she didn't want him wasting time persecuting her.

He couldn't prove she was responsible for this in any legal sense because she wasn't. But he could squander valuable time trying, time in which cruel and violent men would be covering their tracks. So it mattered that he believe her. If her reaction to the brutalised body of Daniel Hood had helped then what he'd done was, if not justified, at least forgivable.

She breathed steadily. "Inspector, I'm not lying and I'm not holding anything back. I'm as horrified by this as you are. Maybe more -

you may have seen things like this before but I haven't. We're on the same side. If there's anything I can do to convince you of that, tell me. If there's anything I can do to help, tell me."

Finally Deacon believed her. Believing left him free to be a little ashamed of himself, though not to admit it. He growled, "Help? How?"

Brodie shrugged. "Information is my business. I may be able to ask questions you can't."

Deacon shook his head. "Stay out of it, Mrs Farrell. This isn't an intellectual exercise: if the people who hurt Hood have any reason to come back I could lose both my witnesses. I don't want them thinking you're a threat to them. Leave it to me. I'll find them; and when I do they won't come after me with a cigarette-lighter."

He turned and headed for the door. "There's nothing more we can do here. Let's go back to the station and complete the formalities."

But Brodie was still looking at the unconscious man. "A cigarette-lighter? Is that what they used?"

Deacon frowned, not understanding why she needed to know. "Some of the time. And some of the time, presumably for a bit of variety, they used the cigarettes."

She made herself look long enough to see the distinctive small, perfectly round lesions that made daisy-like patterns on his weeping skin. Whoever did this had been bored enough to doodle. More shocked by that than anything that had come before, Brodie said faintly, "It hardly seems very professional."

Deacon disagreed. "You think he should carry stainless steel instruments in a black leather bag? And maybe wear a black velvet hood with the eye-holes punched out. So the first time he's stopped by a zealous wooden-top for breaking the speed limit or going through a red light, and he's asked to open the bag, his only choice is between shooting his way out and trying to explain why he's equipped like an extra from *The Rocky Horror Show*. No, Mrs Farrell, real professionals don't need props. It's not about inspiring terror, it's about inflicting pain, and a few domestic implements such as you'd find in any kitchen or garage will do that every bit as well and much more safely. The man who did this can open his bag for every

32

policeman, customs official and security guard who asks. If he couldn't, he'd be behind bars by now."

Brodie stared at him. "You mean, this isn't the first time ... ?"

Deacon shook his head. "This is how he makes his living. People will pay him ten thousand pounds a throw to do it. He probably does it all over the world."

"You have to catch him! Stop him."

Deacon gave a weary chuckle. "I intend to try. But Mrs Farrell, we have to be realistic. If he's been doing this for years and nobody's caught him yet, it can't be as easy as deciding we ought to. Looking for him may not be the best approach. It'll be easier to find the person who hired him."

Brodie glanced uncertainly at the bed. "If he wakes up."

"That would be a big help," agreed the policeman. "But even if he doesn't we may be able to work it out. There can't be *that* many people sufficiently pissed off with him to do this."

"The *Sentinel* said he was a teacher."

"Grounds," admitted Deacon, "but possibly not grounds enough. He must have been pissing people off in his spare time."

Brodie's eyes sharpened. "You think he really is a conman?"

"Maybe."

"Then what Mrs Doyle said ... "

It wouldn't have cost much to let her think so. But Deacon had never salved his own conscience with convenient lies and saw no reason to let anyone else. "About the racehorse? A cover story, designed to gain your sympathy and explain why she was telling you instead of me. If it had been true Hood might have ended up shot but nobody'd have tortured him first. If he had the money he'd have given it back; if it was gone they might have beaten him up, they might even have killed him, but that? No. It was about something bigger than money."

They left the same way they came in. Outside the rear entrance he held the car door for her. Jack Deacon would have thumped anyone who accused him of being a gentleman, but a part of him his mother would still have been proud of thought Brodie Farrell was a lady.

She paused in the open door and regarded him hesitantly over the top. "Inspector - will it be all right if I visit sometime? Just to see how he's doing? If he's supposed to be dead I can hardly ask at Reception."

"You can call me," said Deacon. "Good news or bad, I'll tell you." Then with a sniff he relented. "But yes, if you want to bring him a Get Well card I don't see why not. Be discreet, I don't want people wondering what you're doing here with half the flower shop. If it gets out that he's still alive I'll know who to blame. But if you're careful it won't do any harm. I'll leave word that if you turn up alone you're to be admitted."

"Thank you," said Brodie.

Chapter 4

Finishing at the police station in mid afternoon, Brodie returned to her office. There was still the post to deal with. She'd abandoned it when she opened the newspaper. There might also be a queue of impatient clients awaiting her services, though she doubted it.

It was early days yet. But what, as a sideline, had seemed to occupy an inordinate amount of her time and provide a comfortable extra income was proving erratic as a full-time job. A steady trickle of work kept her head above water, but the better jobs that represented her profit margin were like buses: either there were none or they all came at once. It hadn't mattered when she could afford to turn some of them down. Now *Looking for Something?* was it: what it didn't pay for didn't get bought.

There was no queue, no messages and nothing much in the post. So she resumed the search for a cranberry glass épergne to grace the other end of Mrs Campbell-Wheeler's three metre dining table.

She phoned the antiques dealers who clustered along the south coast from Bournemouth to Brighton, but although there were épergnes aplenty, and no shortage of cranberry glass, no one had what she needed. She made sure they each had her number and made a note in her diary to try again before the weekend. Mrs Campbell-Wheeler was getting tetchy, but even Brodie couldn't find what wasn't there. And after today's events it was hard to get excited about a Victorian ornament. If the woman had wanted a pair she shouldn't have bought one in the first place.

Then she phoned a horse dealer in Newmarket, on the trail of a Welsh pony called Flossie. She'd been loaned out two years ago while the family waited for their younger child to get bigger; and loaned on again when the child of the second family lost interest; and somehow there'd been a misunderstanding. When the child of the third family broke her arm, Flossie was sold.

Now Brodie was trying to track one fifteen-year-old white Welsh pony among thousands, with no guarantee that if she found her the new owner would be prepared to sell her back. She was promised her own fee if she found the pony, whether or not the complexities of ownership could be resolved, and the eight hundred pounds they'd agreed on was probably as much as the pony was worth; but she was part of somebody's family and you can't put a price on that.

The news was good: the dealer thought he knew where Flossie was and could buy her back. If the family that sold her would pay him as the price of their mistake, and if the family getting her back would pay Brodie, and if the family that loaned her on without permission would reimburse half of that, everybody would be satisfied - even if it meant that middle-aged pony had ended up costing as much as a decent hunter.

She phoned Flossie's owners and fixed a time for them to inspect the pony, and accepted their tearful gratitude as if it was a lost child she'd found for them, and then moved on to the next item on her list: a navy-blue Ford Anglia in showroom condition for a young man who'd been unwise enough to take his mother's pride and joy to a rave.

Between phone-calls and e-mails, most of them fruitless but some worth following up, Brodie kept herself occupied until seven o'clock. Then all at once she'd had enough, and she shut up the office and headed home. Flossie would pay some bills and restock the larder, and tomorrow was another day.

It had come as a bit of a culture-shock, having to worry about bills. All her life she'd been financially secure; even now she could be if she hadn't let pride come between her and her dues. She'd accepted John Farrell's provision for his daughter; but the house was his family home, she didn't feel entitled to half of it, proposed instead a settlement which bought her a comfortable flat in a Victorian merchant's house with enough left over to start the business. The courts might have given her more; John offered her more; but she didn't want his charity. There was more pleasure in denying him the opportunity to be generous. Leaving him in her debt salved her angry soul better than a new car and a dress allowance.

But now she was having to pay for her pride. Almost with every post, it seemed. For the first time in her adult life she had to set priorities: a Sunday roast or a night out, new shoes or new brake-shoes. But she'd gone into it with her eyes open and wouldn't reopen negotiations at the first sign of hardship. For one thing she wouldn't let John think she couldn't manage on what she'd asked for. For another and better reason, self-respect demanded that she succeed at something soon. Her marriage had failed; and she'd long ago abandoned her career, which was clerking for the man who was now her ex-husband. Her self-confidence needed a boost.

She'd thought that running her own business would do that; and so it might, if she could get through the difficult start-up period. She hadn't expected it to be so uncertain for quite so long. Six months. Of course, in a seaside town the winter was always going to be harder than the summer. The seasonal influx brought extra work for everyone, not just the cafés and trinket-sellers. It was March now: in two months The Lanes would be full of people, and some of them would have need of her services. *Looking for Something?* was a good idea, she knew she could make it work. The money situation would improve if she just kept at it.

Money! Dear God, she hadn't until that moment wondered what to do with Mrs Doyle's three thousand pounds. She'd already lodged it in the bank but it couldn't stay there. It had been earned - heaven knows it had been earned! - you could argue that it had been earned honestly. But much as she needed it, Brodie knew she couldn't touch a penny. She could hand it over to the police. If he recovered she could offer it to Daniel Hood - and stand there while he slapped her face. If he died, or if he wouldn't ease her conscience by accepting it, it could go to charity. She'd bankrupt herself before she'd take blood-money.

She collected Paddy from Mrs Szarabeijka upstairs and tried to put the affair to the back of her mind, at least until the child was in bed.

But Paddy Farrell was the daughter of a lawyer and a woman who made a profession of being inquisitive, and though she was only four years old she knew that something was wrong. "Bad day, Mummy?" she asked with heart-rending solicitude.

"Rotten day," Brodie said feelingly, holding the child tight against her until they both needed to breathe. "Getting better now."

While Paddy was there, under her feet as she did some desultary housework and prattling about her day with Marta Szarabeijka - "We went shopping and then we went to the park. There was a dog chasing the ducks. Mrs S swore at it in Polish and it ran away. Then she swore at the ducks" - it was possible to distance herself from what was already feeling like a bad dream.

Last year Brodie Farrell was so typical a middle-class housewife and mother she could have starred in the adverts. Good family, good education, satisfying but not overly demanding job, marriage to a professional man; gave up work to have her child and look after her nice house in the better part of Dimmock and go to coffee mornings and charity lunches with other women who were exactly like her.

But even then she hadn't lived in an ivory tower. In seven years working for a solicitor she'd met every kind of criminal - and people who struck her as even less desirable, people she'd have climbed five storeys rather than share a lift with. But the sight of Daniel Hood's injuries had shocked her to the core. She hadn't known there were people capable of such atrocity. Now she'd seen it and still couldn't quite believe it. While Paddy was splashing in the bath and swearing in Polish at the yellow plastic duck it was almost possible to think she'd imagined it.

When Paddy was clean, dry, bundled up in her pyjamas and tucked, improbably angelic, into her bed, still Brodie put off the moment when she would be alone with her thoughts by reading not one but two stories from the *Big Book of Dragons*. For the child of two essentially conventional people, Paddy Farrell had shown an early streak of individuality. Not puppies and kittens but dragons; not dolls but tractors. She knew the difference between a John Deere and a Massey Ferguson three fields away. Kind people on trains who noticed her interest in "the big twactors" were apt to get a lecture on the subject.

But whatever her mental age, her body was just four and she was asleep before the second dragon had found a way to palm the nagging princess off on a gullible knight. Brodie went into the living room and tried to watch television. Unwanted images drifted between her eyes and the screen. She went into the kitchen to make a cake. She wasn't a serious cook but she did rather pride herself on her marmalade cake.

She weighed, she measured, she sifted, she rubbed. The necessary precision of the mundane activity occupied her mind. She scorned the mixer and buried her hands to the wrists, rubbing and blending until her shoulders ached. She made so much mixture she wasn't sure she'd have enough baking tins. It hardly mattered. The cakes were the end-product but not in fact the purpose of her industry.

The last scrapings shoe-horned in, she began to load the oven as carefully as if the cake had been Minton going into a kiln. That was her undoing. In thinking about the logistics she forgot the fundamental rule of cooking: ovens are hot. She burned her hand.

It wasn't a bad burn. She hissed, shoved the last tin in any old way and put her hand under the cold tap. After a minute she pulled if out to see if it was working. Heat mounted immediately in the red spot on the back of her hand. More cold water and she tried again; same result.

Then she thought of the burns on the body of Daniel Hood. All the little burns, not one of them life-threatening but each of them the source of more pain than this was giving her. And no cold running water to take the worst away; and not even the knowledge that time alone would eventually bring relief. For Daniel Hood, time had just brought more little burns - dozens of them, she hadn't counted but there had to be dozens of them, scores of them, jostling for space on his cringing skin, spreading like a pox. And it wasn't an accident, the unhappy result of a moment's carelessness. Someone had *done* this to him: done it hour after unbearable hour.

Brodie burst into tears, sobbing into her arms on the kitchen table as if her heart would break.

When she regained control she let herself quietly out of the flat and went upstairs.

Marta Szarabeijka was watching television. A music teacher by profession, she had remarkably eclectic tastes. Sometimes when

Brodie came up here she was listening to the Berlin Philharmonic, sometimes she was watching *Emmerdale*. Brodie suspected this was where Paddy got her taste for tractors.

Tonight it was a game-show. Beside herself with excitement, Marta waved Brodie to a chair. "Sit down, sit down - one more inflatable reindeer and he gets to go to Lappland!"

Brodie remained standing. "Marta," she said faintly.

Marta Szarabeijka knew a real crisis from a show-biz one even in the sound of a word. She turned off the television and put her arm about Brodie's shoulders in the same fluid movement. She was a tall, bony woman in her fifties, as strong as a mule and about as obstinate, and Brodie's life would have been poorer with almost anyone else living upstairs. Marta was her child-minder, her signer-for-unexpected-parcels, her confidante, her friend. The generation separating them was no obstacle: they enjoyed a kind of pick-and-mix relationship that was partly that of sisters, sometimes more like mother and daughter, most often that of a couple of college girls. They laughed together, complained about men to one another, dried each other's tears when the need arose.

Marta peered into Brodie's red-rimmed eyes with real concern and said quietly, "What happened? Is Paddy all right?"

"Paddy's fine," Brodie nodded. "Though I'll have to get back. I came to see if you've got anything for burns." She held out her hand. The red spot was barely visible but the word destroyed her. She fell on her knees on the carpet, hugging herself and rocking, and crying and crying and crying.

Marta dropped beside her, folding her in long bony arms, talking softly into Brodie's hair. "Is all right," she crooned in her oddly gruff and accented voice, "is all right. Marta's here. Cry as much you want. Then we go downstairs and you tell me what this is all about. A little burn like that? - I don't think." But before they left her flat she collected a jar from the bathroom cabinet.

Brodie had got her breath back enough to start feeling guilty. "What about the reindeers? Come down when it's over."

"Fock the reindeers," said Marta Szarabeijka briskly, shutting her door.

Paddy was still asleep, dreaming of combine harvesters. They tiptoed back into the living room and Marta turned her attention to Brodie's hand. "You want to tell me what happened?" She pronounced her Ys like Js.

Brodie wanted desperately to tell her what happened. But DI Deacon's warning echoed in her ears. She'd have trusted Marta with her life, but she'd given her word and wouldn't break it to get a little sympathy.

"I can't tell you much," she mumbled. "I promised, and someone's safety could depend on it. But I did something in good faith that helped someone else do something terrible." She looked down at her hand, comforted by Marta's potion. "Somebody got burned. I was trying so hard to rationalise it - I didn't know, there was no way I *could* know what they intended. And then I did this, and somehow it didn't matter who was to blame, what I knew and didn't know, only the pain. They couldn't have found him without me, and when they did they hurt him so much ...

"Oh Marta," she moaned, "I'm saying too much now, don't breathe a word of this outside, only I can't bear it. This - it's nothing but it really hurt. And him ... And I didn't even know him. I just did it for the money. It was a job: you give me some money, I find who you're looking for - and it's hardly my fault if you nearly torture him to death, is it? Only it is. They couldn't have done it without me. It's my responsibility. And I don't think I can bear it."

"Listen to me, darling." Her Gs came out like Ks. "You're not responsible for what you can't prevent, and if you didn't know what they intended you couldn't stop them. Don't crucify yourself. There's no need: there's always a queue of people waiting to do it for you.

"Now tell me. Are the police involved? Do you need - what, an alibi? Tell me what I should say."

Torn between tears and laughter, buoyed as always by the generous, anarchic nature of her friend, Brodie shook her head. "The police know all about it. I don't need protecting from them, though thanks for the offer. I just - I needed to tell somebody - "

Marta regarded her with compassion. "Brodie - you don't think maybe you should tell John?"

"John?" That really did take her by surprise. "Why?"

"Because he's a lawyer. Because whoever did what to who and however little of it was your fault, the police are involved and you may need legal advice. Better he knows now than you phone him in the middle of the night with them hammering down the door." Marta's opinion of the police had been influenced by the circumstances in which she left Poland.

"If I need a solicitor, it won't be John."

"Why not? Because he fell in love with someone else? Bad taste, I grant you, but he's not a bad man. He was always straight with you, Brodie. Be straight with him. Is best."

She didn't think so, but Marta was an astute woman, Brodie would always give her opinions serious consideration. "Honestly, Marta, I'm not in any trouble. Or only with my own conscience." She took a deep breath. "Is this making *any* sense to you?"

"Not a lot," confessed Marta cheerfully. "But then, you don't want me to know what happened, do you, only how you feel about it. And I can see how you feel. Now you have to decide what to do about it."

"Do about it? What can I do?"

"The man who got burned. He's alive?"

Brodie hesitated. But Marta wasn't going to betray her. "He's in the hospital. I don't know if he'll recover. It wasn't just the burns: when they'd finished with him they shot him. They dumped him in a skip." Tears welled again.

"Not a lot of respect for human life, hm? Well, I tell you. Whether he lives or dies, what you need is to make your peace with him. Go to the hospital. Now: I'll stay with Paddy. Tell him they tricked you, that you didn't know. Tell him you're sorry."

She clearly hadn't understood. Brodie shook her head, the dark cloud of her hair tossing like a storm. "If I thought he'd understand ... But he was unconscious. He could be dead by now. Even if he isn't, he wouldn't know I was there."

Marta gave a Slavic shrug. "This doesn't matter. Him hearing it isn't what it's about. You saying it: that's the reason. Confession and forgiveness." She smiled sombrely. "This he can do with his eyes shut."

Brodie was neither a Catholic nor a church-goer, so the quest for absolution that made perfect sense to Marta left her doubtful. But if it was only an empty gesture, even a gesture was better than nothing. Perhaps when she'd confessed she could begin to forgive herself.

So an hour later Brodie parked her car behind the blockhouse architecture and dingy white concrete of Dimmock General and let herself in by the route Deacon had shown her.

There was a different constable outside the door, but when she gave her name he nodded her through. It was also a different nurse. Neither of them asked her business, which was as well because Brodie would have found it hard to explain.

It was twelve hours since she was here before and changes were apparent. Most of the tubes were gone so more of Daniel Hood was visible. Tentatively, Brodie walked closer and stood looking down at him.

She wouldn't have recognised him: not from the photograph Selma Doyle had given her, not from the one the newspaper had carried. This wasn't because his tormentors had concentrated on his face, because they hadn't. They'd wanted to hurt him without dulling his wits. There were bruises and his lip was split, but they were minor injuries predating those under the sheet. They had achieved nothing and no one had expected they would. Whoever inflicted them knew they wouldn't be enough and had no time to waste on self-indulgence.

But a few cuts and bruises weren't why he looked so different. He looked different because he *was* different. When the photographs were taken he was a young man at the peak of his health and strength, with a career, with a future. Now he'd been through hell and emerged into a vacuum. Nothing in his life before this week was of any consequence. Nobody he knew, nobody he cared about, nothing he wanted and worked for, nothing he aspired to then had any reality this side of the event horizon. If he lived he'd have to reinvent himself, or for the rest of his days he'd be haunted by his

43

lost persona, by the feeling that if he could just make contact with who he used to be things would go back to how they used to be, things would be all right. And they never would.

No one comes through trauma unscathed. Euphoria, depression, anger, guilt and bitterness are all hurdles to be negotiated on the way back, and a person familiar with these extremes of human emotion is not the same as one who is not. Whoever Daniel Hood was a week ago, today he was someone else, as different to the man who had yet to live his nightmare as was that man from the boy who preceded him. Already, before awareness had begun to flutter his eyelids, the change was apparent, and irreversible.

Apart from the everyday facts of his life, like his name and where he lived, Brodie Farrell knew three things about this man, and one of them might have been a lie. He liked watching the skies. He might or might not be a liar. And for that or some other sin, actual or perceived, he'd suffered unimaginably.

There was a chair by the bed. Brodie drew it uncertainly towards her and sat down.

Plainly taking Brodie for a friend or relative, perhaps even his wife, the nurse said kindly, "He's doing better. He'll be all right, you know."

Brodie looked at her, hope constrained by fear. "Really?"

"Really. He'll be awake tomorrow." She stood up. "I'm going for a coffee. Can I bring you one?"

"Thank you." But Brodie wanted privacy more than the drink.

"I won't be long. If you have any problems" - she pointed - "hit that button."

Brodie had no idea how close the nearest coffee machine was, but she couldn't count on more than a few minutes. She bit her lip, wondering how to start.

"You don't know me," she said softly. "I don't know much about you. But I've done you a terrible wrong. I suppose I'm here to apologise."

Even as she said them the words sounded hollow and meaningless. If he was going to be awake tomorrow she should come back and say them then. Trying to shift her burden of guilt onto an unconscious man was an act of cowardice. But Brodie was afraid that if she left now she'd never return. Better a flawed apology than a shirked one.

"She said you'd stolen money from her. I found you for her. I had no idea what she meant to do. If I had, I swear I'd have had no part in it. Try to believe me. I can't offer a single good reason why you should, but if you don't ... "

She was going to say, I don't know how I'll live with it. She was going to say, I'm going to be stuck in a nightmare with no waking. Then she remembered who she was saying it to, what she'd seen below the sheet, and it sounded trite and self-pitying. She was asking for Daniel Hood's help? For his understanding? Didn't she know he'd be fully occupied managing his own emotions, living with his own ghosts? People had treated him like meat on a slab. She was worried about bad dreams? How was he ever going to shut his eyes again when people like that could be out in the darkness waiting? Her selfishness mortified her.

If there'd been anyone to see the colour rising through her cheeks she'd have covered them with her hands and made a rapid if undignified retreat. As it was she steepled her fingers in front of her mouth, her eyes wide with remorse, her breathing unsteady. "Oh Daniel," she whispered, "I'm sorry. I'm talking about my feelings when I should be thinking about yours. You know why, of course. Because I'm ashamed. I'm ashamed of the harm I've done you. I'm talking about what happened to me because if I think about what happened to you I'll break down.

"I'm not a brave person, Daniel. I've never had to be, I never learned how. If it's any comfort, I have never felt so inadequate in all my life."

She managed a shaky laugh. "I don't think I'm cut out to be a Catholic. Confession isn't doing my soul any good at all. I've done you a dreadful wrong, and there's nothing I can do about putting it right, and the longer I sit here talking the clearer that is to me. I'm going to go now. If you woke up and found me here you'd be very, very angry and I have no right to put you through any more. Inspector Deacon knows where I am. If you want to see me when

45

you're feeling better, tell him and I'll come. I can't think why you would, unless you want to tell me what you think of me. But that's all right. If calling me all the names under the sun will help, even just a little, do it."

She had a hand on the back of her seat, ready to rise. She looked up - at the ceiling, at nothing - blinking away tears. Her other hand was on the edge of the bed.

A cool touch made her start almost out of the chair, banged her heart against the inside of her ribs and drove a wordless gasp between her teeth. Brodie looked down in alarm; but there was nothing to be afraid of. Daniel Hood's slender hand, the one with the canula taped into the back, had crept over her own, lay cupped over her knuckles, the grip of his fingers as frail and stubborn as for twenty-four hours his hold on life had been.

Brodie tore her gaze away from his hand and looked at his face. His cheeks were still pale, his lips bloodless. But his eyes were open. Pale grey except where the whites were muddied with blood, half-hooded as if the effort of opening them wide had defeated him, uncertain and unquiet, they found Brodie's face and fastened on it like a child clinging to its mother's skirts.

A breath of a voice lay on his lips. "Please," whispered Daniel Hood. "I don't know where I am."

Chapter 5

Brodie went on staring, more in horror than delight. She'd come here, opened her heart to him, in the belief that his physical presence was all she'd have to deal with. Confessing to an unconscious man hadn't offered the catharsis she'd sought but it was all she was prepared for. If she'd known he was awake she wouldn't have come; if she'd known he was about to wake she wouldn't have stayed. Now she was trying desperately to remember how much she'd said, how much of that he might have heard.

Daniel Hood woke in a place he'd never seen before, surrounded by instruments he couldn't identify, under the appalled gaze of a woman he didn't recognise. It was an unreassuring renaissance for a man who'd lived a terror and died in blood. White lips in the white face trembled. "Please ... "

With a jerk like slapping her own face Brodie pulled herself together. Whatever her regrets, right now his needs took precedence. "You're in hospital," she explained quietly. "You were hurt but you're getting better. Everything's going to be all right." Which was a little sweeping but kinder than the unexpurgated version.

"Who are you?"

She hesitated a moment. But her name was the least of what she owed him. "Brodie Farrell. We haven't met before. I came to see how you were." She smiled carefully. "You look better than you did this morning."

Daniel was getting left behind. "Hospital?"

Brodie nodded, wondering how far this was going to go, how much she'd have to tell him. She wouldn't lie to him, but in the pit of her soul she was praying she wouldn't have to tell him the truth. Let Deacon do that; let a doctor, let a priest. Not her. Let her not have to watch his face as she told him what had been done to him, and whose fault it was.

"You've been here a couple of days. You're on the mend now. Are you in pain? - shall I call the nurse?"

He had to think about that for a moment, then he shook his head. Or rather, lacking the strength to lift it, turned it on his pillow. The fair hair made a halo around his face. His lips moved again. "My chest ... "

"Yes. You were - " She hesitated. She wasn't sure she should tell him. But he was bound to find out sooner or later, and evading his questions could only increase his anxiety. "You were shot. But you're on the mend now. Listen, it's late. Go back to sleep. You'll feel stronger tomorrow. Someone will tell you the whole story tomorrow."

Even this abridged version was more information than Daniel could take in. "Shot?"

Brodie looked at her trapped hand, aching to be free. There wasn't enough strength in his fingers to hold a butterfly against its will. But to pull away would be to take advantage of what had been done to him, and she would not benefit from the actions of his tormentors even to that degree. She suffered his touch to keep her there. Raising her other hand she dropped a featherweight fingertip to the dressing on the left side of his chest. "There. Don't worry, it'll heal before you know it. You're sure you don't want the nurse?"

"I feel - strange."

"You've been unconscious. The best thing you can do is sleep it off."

But he was afraid of sleeping, aware at an instinctive level that the last time he went down that road he'd had trouble getting back. His brow creased, the grey eyes anxious. "No. I need - " His breath was coming quicker, ragged in his throat. "I need to know what happened."

The easy thing would be to call Deacon, make him wait till the policeman arrived. But if Brodie Farrell didn't consider herself a brave person she had too much pride to be a coward. If he needed to know she would tell him. "Where shall I start? What do you remember?"

He tried to think, to make sense of the snap-shot images twisting in his mind like dust motes at a window, now bright, now gone. "I don't know. Maybe nothing. Or - " His eyes flew wide, galvanised by flashback. "God! Was that real? A dream?"

She could have fobbed him off, agreed it was probably a bad dream. But she'd have left here feeling like a worm. She folded her free hand over the top of his. "I'm afraid not. Daniel, I can't tell you everything, there's still so much we don't understand. We're hoping you'll be able to tell us what it was all about. But what happened is" - she took a deep breath - "someone hurt you. Burned you. Then they shot you and left you for dead. I'm sorry."

His eyes had filled with tears and he was gently nodding. "I remember. Dear God! - I thought I dreamt it. I thought it was a bad dream and I couldn't wake up. I couldn't move. And it went on and on ... "

She tightened her hand on his, ashamed of her inadequacy. She knew that what he needed was what Paddy needed when the night terrors came· holding, hugging. Partly concern for his injuries, but more a fear of trading on his ignorance when she knew the link between them and he didn't, made her reluctant to offer any more than her hand and a banal reassurance. "It's over now. You're safe."

But Daniel didn't feel safe. Even unconsciousness had been scant defence: awake he felt his vulnerability eating at him like acid. If the dreams were real, waking was no respite. "I don't understand," he whispered. "Who were they? Why would anyone do that to me?"

Brodie bit her lip. In her heart, and in her head, she knew that Selma Doyle wasn't real and probably nothing she had said had been real either. But while any possibility remained that a genuine grievance lay behind the atrocity, that Daniel Hood had in some measure contributed to his own tragedy, Brodie would not entirely give up hope. If he was only a little guilty then she was a little less so. "Something to do with a racehorse?"

She knew, before he said a word, from the bewilderment in his eyes, that that last hope was illusory. Whoever tortured him, it wasn't a vengeful woman from whom he'd stolen more than her money. It was all a lie.

"What racehorse?" he mumbled.

Brodie shook her head and tried to smile. "It was just a thought. I don't know why. The police are looking into it. They'll get you some answers."

49

His meagre strength was failing, the bruised lids drooping over his eyes. He wasn't taking in what she was saying. "Who did you say you are?"

She told him again. He nodded, but she knew he wouldn't remember. There was no point trying to explain further, he couldn't stay with her long enough. She'd have to leave it to Deacon or whoever spoke to him next. She squeezed his hand. "Just remember you're safe now. Nobody can hurt you any more."

He was already asleep. She slipped out of his grasp, careful not to rouse him, but then stayed a moment longer looking down at him. It was an odd sensation, watching a stranger sleep. Lovers apart, generally you only ever see other adults when they're awake and vertical. Unaware of her scrutiny, fragile and dependent, Daniel Hood looked like an exhausted child.

Brodie waited until the nurse returned and explained what had happened. Then she went home. She wasn't sure what her visit had achieved. But she slept, and no nightmares came.

* * *

Jack Deacon got the message as soon as he arrived at his office the next morning. He didn't take off his coat: he went straight round to the hospital.

He found Daniel Hood, propped up on pillows, studying the marks on his body as though he might read there the story of his misadventure. He looked pale and weak, but it was clear that he was going to live. He was going to talk.

Deacon introduced himself, curt in his impatience. He thought he was seconds away from understanding, perhaps only minutes from a resolution.

So Daniel's first words came as a bitter disappointment. "Can you tell me why?"

Deacon shook off his raincoat, pulled up the chair. He studied the young man's face, looking for signs of dissemblance, but there were none. Daniel was watching him as intently as he was watching Daniel, waiting for an answer. Never mind, Deacon told himself, this was only the start. This time yesterday he hadn't known if the boy would recover. It was too soon to expect a full and rational account from him. "How much do you remember?"

"Inspector, I remember everything." Daniel's voice wavered. His hands, rigid at his sides, were knotted in tight white fists. "Everything that happened. They asked me questions, and they hurt me when I didn't know the answers. But I don't know who and I don't know why."

"What questions?"

"Where is she?"

Deacon blinked. "Who?"

"That's what they asked: where is she? Where have you taken her? I said, I don't know who you mean, and they hurt me." A shudder ran the length of him and his eyes strayed once more to his daisy-mottled skin, drawn by a compulsion he could not resist. His voice fell, half reproachful, half apologetic. "She said you'd find out why."

But not the same she. "Who did?"

"The woman who was here last night. I don't know who she was."

Warning signals rang in Deacon's head. But if they'd found him they'd have killed him. "Describe her."

"About thirty. Tall, slim; brown eyes. A lot of dark curly hair."

The inspector let out his breath in a sigh of relief. He should have thought of Brodie Farrell: he himself had told her she could return.

Now he debated with himself how much to say. The brutal truth or discretion? The first might cost him the woman's co-operation, for what it was worth. Perhaps more to the point, he wondered if Daniel was ready for the whole truth. He was hanging onto his equilibrium by his finger-nails: anything that added to the burden could break his grip. Then the doctors would sedate him and it would be days before Deacon could talk to him in any meaningful way.

He opted for tact. "Mrs Farrell. She's been helping us. What else did she say?"

"I don't know. I couldn't stay awake. Something about a racehorse? I didn't understand."

Deacon shook his head. "I wouldn't expect you to. The racehorse was a red herring. The people who hurt you ... Mrs Farrell was given to understand ... There was this woman, who said ... " It was too difficult: he gave up. "I'll explain when you're stronger. But the racehorse wasn't real. Mrs Farrell just hoped it was."

Though Daniel struggled to make sense of what Deacon was saying, talking was helping to clear his mind. For the first time since the floor of his flat came up to hit him he felt like more than a helpless bystander at his own fate.

He'd been at other people's disposal - one lot of faceless unknowns hurting him, another healing him, neither of them giving him a say in what they did - for so long he'd all but forgotten there was another way. But he wasn't tied and blindfolded now, he wasn't unconscious or drugged, and the only thing keeping him in this bed was his own weakness. It was time to start asserting himself.

"Explain it now," he said softly. "I need to know what it was all about."

Taken aback, Deacon sniffed. It was like giving someone the kiss of life only to have them complain about your mouthwash. "So do we, Mr Hood. So do we. I'm sorry if Mrs Farrell gave the impression that we know more than we do. I was hoping you could tell me what happened."

"I can. I can't tell you why it happened."

"Do you a deal," offered Deacon. "You tell me what, I'll try to find out why."

Daniel wrestled the memories into some sort of order. His problem was not their paucity but their overwhelming power: when he tried the door they flew at him. Deacon saw him wince but said nothing. It was a door that, sooner or later, he had to force open and go through, and it might be easier now than after his mind had thrown up barricades around the hurt. He waited.

Somehow Daniel weathered the hailstorm of images and sensations, and found his way back to the start. Beads of sweat broke on his lip and his brow furrowed with effort. "They were waiting when I got home. Friday evening. What's today?"

"Wednesday. You've been here since early Monday. We think they shot you on Sunday night."

Daniel swallowed: "Two days. It went on for two days?"

"Didn't you realise?"

He didn't know how to answer that. "It felt like my whole life. At the same time it was just *then*, there was nothing else. It might have been two hours or two weeks. Then they said they weren't getting anywhere, they were going to kill me. I heard them arguing about who should do it."

Deacon's voice was hard. "And who did?"

A fractional shake of the yellow head. "I don't know. I don't know who any of them were."

"Come on, Daniel," growled the policeman, "you must know something. They had you for two days. They tortured you for two days - and they didn't tell you why? They didn't tell you what they wanted?"

"I told you. They were looking for someone. They thought I knew where she was. But I didn't. I don't even know who she was."

Daniel's breathing was growing distressed. Deacon found himself watching the dressing that ran at a rising angle from below his left nipple into his armpit. At the first spot of blood he'd have to stop this and call for help.

"She - a woman? What was her name?"

With everything else that was acid-etched on his brain, that he couldn't remember. "I did know. Every time they asked they said it - 'Where is she? Where's ... ?' Sonia? Sylvia? I can't remember. Dear God, I can't remember! Every time they asked they hurt me, and I can't remember her name!"

His voice soared out of control. Deacon grasped his shoulders with strong hands, anchoring him in time and space. "Easy, Daniel. Take your time, it'll come."

More than the pressure, the unexpected kindness wrung his heart. Tears welled. He dashed them away with the back of his wrist in the gesture Deacon recognised from the photograph. "But it's so stupid! The one thing I could tell you that might cast some light on this, and I can't remember. Why not? What's wrong with me?"

53

"Nothing's wrong with you. At least, nothing that won't heal. You've been hurt. You've been frightened and hurt, and your mind couldn't deal with it any more. It started shutting down, and what hurt most it shut down first. It associates that name with what was done to you, and thinks if you can't remember you can't be hurt any more.

"But you're right, the name is important. I need you to remember as much detail as you can. I want these bastards, Danny. Whatever it was about - a racehorse, a woman - whatever you did to provoke it, I won't have them running an inquisition in my town. The only one who conducts interrogations in Dimmock is me."

Another tremor ran through Daniel's narrow frame. Even the word hurt. "Inspector, I didn't do anything to provoke it. Nothing they said made any sense. I never understood what it was they thought I'd done."

"Tell me what happened. From the start."

* * *

It started on the Friday, after school. He walked home across town, let himself into his flat a little after five.

"Except I didn't have to turn the key. The door wasn't locked. I thought, 'That was careless' - but that's all I thought. That I hadn't shut it properly that morning. I never thought there was someone waiting for me."

But there was. Though he didn't feel the blow that felled him, there was a moment in which he knew something shocking had happened, that he was falling and couldn't seem to stop himself. Then the darkness took him.

He woke to a voice saying his name, a hand flicking his cheek, but no face. He thought he was blind. When he tried to raise a hand to his eyes he couldn't. He had no idea how long he'd been unconscious. His head ached, he felt muzzy, but at that point he wasn't badly hurt.

He was, however, afraid. This wasn't a prank that had gone too far. He didn't know what it was instead, but he knew it was deadly

54

serious. He knew he'd been kidnapped, that he was bound and blindfold, and from the cold along his skin that he was naked. He didn't know what was coming next. He whimpered like a frightened child. "Who are you? What do you want?"

As time went on he came to realise it was not just the two of them in the room. But most of his dealings were with the man who spoke then. "Where is she? Where have you taken her?"

He swore he didn't know. The man didn't believe him. He was part of it; he'd been seen. Where was she? The more Daniel protested his innocence, the rougher the questioning became. He was struck in the face and, more persistently, in the belly, measured rhythmic blows that he could neither avoid nor absorb, that seemed to turn him inside out. He hadn't even the freedom to curl around the hurt. He vomited blood.

Of course he knew, the man said, his voice breathy with effort. He was the look-out. Where had they taken her? He'd talk in the end, he might as well save himself some grief and do it now. But he couldn't.

At length the voice changed, stopped hectoring and took on a note of regret. He'd tried to avoid this but Daniel had left him no choice. What happened now was his own fault. He could stop it, but only one way.

Daniel tried to say that he couldn't, he didn't know the missing woman or where she was; but half way through the sentence pain like he'd never imagined seered his breast.

Even after what had gone before it came as a shock. He screamed and his body convulsed. Patiently the voice repeated its questions. Daniel gulped for breath, stammered an apology - he was sorry, he was sorry but he didn't know, truly he didn't know ... This time the unseen flame tongued his navel and he screamed again.

So it went on, for a period Daniel had no way of measuring. The same questions that he couldn't answer; the same response that somehow managed to be shockingly different each time. He never learned to anticipate or to brace himself. Every mark on his body was a little savagery as devastating as the first. There were breaks, not for his benefit, then it started again.

Finally he grew aware that it had stopped; that a discussion was taking place and that he wasn't part of it or the decision it was leading to. A door opened and footsteps receded; he was left alone with one of the men. Not the man who'd asked the questions: by the voice, an older man.

He recounted to Inspector Deacon every word that passed between them. The man slapped his face. His consciousness was sinking fast then, but he heard the footsteps return and the first voice - the voice he'd never forget, fading now into the background - say, "Do it." And the world stopped.

* * *

"Danny - Danny! It's all right. You're safe here. There's nothing to be afraid of."

Broad and strong, Deacon's hands reached him through the burgeoning panic and brought him back to the present. He blinked in the light as if he really had been blindfold a moment before. He looked around, confused. Somehow he'd found the strength to push himself up the bed and hard against the wall.

"They shot me," gasped Daniel Hood. "Oh Christ. Oh Christ. They shot me."

"You were lucky." Jack Deacon watched the young man with compassion and hardly registered the absurdity of what he'd just said. "If they'd known you were still alive they'd have finished it. They took you to a building site and left you in a skip. The builders found you on Monday morning. Sunday night was frosty: the cold kept you from bleeding to death."

Daniel hugged himself. The room was hot and stuffy but the memories were like ice. "And you don't know why."

Deacon shook his head. "I'll find out."

"Will they come back?"

That was the big one. But the answer depended on why they'd come in the first place and was thus far unknowable. "They think you're dead," said Deacon. "That's what I told the papers. If they learn otherwise they may come back. Or not, depending on why they wanted you in the first place. We'll do our best to protect you.

56

But I'd be lying if I said we could keep you safe indefinitely. The best way to do that is to put them behind bars."

"But if you don't know who they were ... ?"

"Exactly," nodded Deacon. "Well, I have one good witness, somebody who was there throughout. Maybe something you heard or saw will help - something that hasn't come back to you yet but will do. If anything occurs to you, whether or not you think it matters, call me."

"I've told you everything."

"No you haven't," said Deacon without rancour. "No one ever does. You've told me everything you've remembered so far. But there is more. There has to be. There's a reason for what they did, and somewhere behind those mental barriers you know what it is. You must do. Whether or not you understand why, you're the key to all this."

"I think they made a mistake," murmured Daniel. "I don't think it was me they wanted."

"They didn't think they'd made a mistake."

"They thought I knew something about this Sylvia or Sophie or whoever." His brow cleared suddenly, his eyes surprised. "Sophie. The woman they were asking about - she was called Sophie."

"There you are," said Deacon approvingly, "that's something we didn't know five minutes ago. And it won't be the last thing. Keep thinking about it. I'll get onto the Police National Computer and start looking for a missing Sophie. In the meantime, is there anything you want?"

Daniel considered for a moment. "An explanation. Catch them if you can, but I'd settle for knowing why. And ..."

"Mm?"

In the circumstances his smile was unbearably tender, like the first blink of spring sunshine, the first tremulous birdsong. When Deacon first saw Daniel Hood he thought he looked like an old man. Cleaned up, warmed up, fed, healing and with his pale face lit by that unexpected smile, he looked not just younger but oddly ageless. And androgynous. Ambiguous.

Daniel said, "And, for none of this to have happened. I want to be

57

who I was a week ago. I liked my life then; I liked me. Now I don't even know who I am."

Deacon's gaze dipped, hiding his confusion. He wasn't a man who was easily touched by other people. He was pragmatic and objective, and many people thought him hard. It was how he saw himself. He was startled by the feelings this young man stirred in him.

There was nothing wrong with them. Even by his own rather narrow terms of reference there was nothing wrong with feeling compassion for someone who'd suffered as Daniel Hood had. He just wasn't used to responding to people on an emotional level. He dealt in facts, in evidence, in forensics. He was disturbed to find himself empathising with someone he didn't know, didn't need to know, only needed to do his duty by.

He stood up, turned away and headed for the door. "I'll try and get you the explanation, anyway."

Chapter 6

The computer had nothing helpful to offer. Deacon was appalled by just how many people were missing nationwide. But though there were a handful of Sophies of various ages being sought by their families, none was a recent disappearance and none came with the sort of baggage that might explain what happened to Daniel Hood.

Two scenarios occurred to him, though he knew there could be more. Sophie might have been abducted or she might have run off with someone. In either case the moving force was someone close to her - a father, a husband, a lover; jealous or distraught.

Jealous? Someone had spent two days torturing a young teacher out of jealousy? Perhaps. An abduction would appear on the computer but a girl leaving one man for another wouldn't. Had Sophie fallen for another man? Not Daniel - Romeo wouldn't have taken two days like that for Juliet - but someone he might be expected to know about? Then why didn't he? Maybe he couldn't help, however desperately he wanted to, but he should at least have known what he was being questioned about.

Could he have been a victim of mistaken identity as he claimed? It wasn't totally impossible. Deacon had been a police officer for half his life, he knew that jealous angry people make more mistakes than calm rational ones. They misread situations, lay the blame in the wrong place, crave vengeance out of all proportion to the harm they've suffered. They kill people they love - wives, husbands, children. They maim them, scar them for life, do things that can never be forgiven. Oh yes, jealousy could certainly have been the motive.

This was the second man: not the man who tortured Hood, the one who paid. The one Deacon had a chance of finding. The one who, when Sophie disappeared, threw large sums of money and no morality at the problem. He paid Brodie Farrell to find Hood and the interrogator to pick him up. Deacon knew the pro was on the team by then from the way Hood was taken, the way he was kept blindfold even though there was no intention that he would escape with his life.

A keen amateur might have thought of these points as he laid plans in the calm and quiet of his own sitting-room, but he'd have made more mistakes carrying them out. In the panic to get Hood under cover at the start, and later on when the mayhem he'd nerved himself to commit failed to have the desired effect. Most rages would abate over two days, most jealousies subside. But whoever did this continued for forty-eight hours despite the fact that he was getting no answers, the growing certainty that he would get none. Not for anger, or jealousy, or revenge. He stuck at it because he was being paid.

But the man paying him was also there. Hood had heard him giving the orders; he'd even seen him, in a manner of speaking, right at the end when in a fever of frustration he ripped the blindfold away. But Hood couldn't describe him: partly because he was by then palpably close to collapse, but mainly because he didn't have his glasses on. Deacon shook his head in weary incredulity. Sometimes he believed in God simply because there had to be someone up there messing him around. If Daniel Hood hadn't been as blind as a bat wearing sunglasses in a cellar at night, he might have made an arrest by now. Instead of which he was hunting through the PNC for missing Sophies and earlier occasions on which someone had extracted information from unwilling communicants by means of a few simple items purchased from a tobacconist.

Well, Deacon couldn't start arresting smokers. Maybe the money was the significant thing here. Whoever wanted Sophie back had spent a serious amount of it. He'd hired the woman in red to approach Farrell, Farrell to find Hood and the interrogator to rip the truth out of him.

"But you couldn't tell them what they wanted to know," murmured Deacon; not exactly to himself, he had the forensic photographs spread on his desk again. His brow made a little frown as if he thought they were holding something back. "I know you're telling me the truth about that, Danny - you must be. If you'd known where Sophie was you'd have talked; and if you'd talked this" - one finger flicked at the prints as if he still couldn't credit what they showed - "wouldn't have gone on for two days. Of course, *if* you'd talked sooner they might have been in less of a hurry to wrap it up and you mightn't still be alive. Funny old world, isn't it?"

The money. Whoever ordered this paid Farrell three thousand pounds; maybe he paid the woman in red another thousand. But two days' torture would have come pricier; probably dearer than murder. The man Sophie had fled - if that was what happened; Deacon had to remind himself that he didn't know that yet - had the resources, both of money and of anger, to spend fifteen or twenty thousand pounds to get her back. Other deserted husbands and lovers might care as much but have to settle for an advert in the personal column of *The Dimmock Sentinel*. This wasn't just an angry man, he was a rich one.

And more than that, he had contacts that the average millionaire-next-door didn't. The go-between might just have been an out-of-work actress, hired over the phone and paid with a manilla envelope under the door, but the interrogator was a professional in a highly specialised field. His number wasn't printed in *The Yellow Pages* or pasted up in phone-boxes; probably the only way to find him would be through personal recommendation. The man who hired him, the man with the money, knew the kind of people who knew *this* kind of people. He wasn't just rich and angry: he was rich, angry and dirty.

"What are we talking here," Deacon asked himself softly, "the mob? Drug money?" It would go some way to explaining what happened, but not why it happened to Hood. Someone had run off with a Mafioso's squeeze? - well, reckless but not impossible. But someone had run off with a Mafioso's squeeze and there was reason to think a comprehensive school maths teacher knew where they were? That really was straining the bounds of credulity. They were two worlds that hardly ever collided.

He needed to see Hood again. There had to be a connection, however tenuous, between him and someone with that kind of power. If he knew about Hood, Hood should know about him. He couldn't possibly know so many rich, angry, ruthless men that he wasn't sure which of them had had him turned inside out.

Breathing heavily, Deacon filed away the photographs. "Either you're being dim, Danny, or you're being deceitful. Let's have another little natter, see if we can work out which it is."

But though he spoke to Hood three more times over the next thirty-six hours, he still wasn't sure.

* * *

A point comes in any convalescence where recovery seems to stall. The better you get the worse you feel. Daniel reached that point when he'd been in hospital for four days. Physically he was making good progress: the burns were healing, the hole in his chest was closing to a scar and he was gaining strength visibly.

But the mending of his body was not matched by a healing of his spirit. At first just staying awake was an effort, when he had energy to spare for thought he didn't get much further than amazement at what he'd survived. He had neither the physical nor mental resources to dwell on those responsible: when Detective Inspector Deacon made him try he found his thoughts glancing off, like shot deflected by armour. It was too hard, too painful, and he didn't persevere. Almost he was resigned never to knowing who they were or why they used him as they did.

By Thursday, however, he was able to think about his ordeal in greater depth, and the relief at being safe gave way to a fury that filled him to bursting-point. Anger wasn't a natural emotion for Daniel, so it overwhelmed him easily. When the flash-backs came, which they did increasingly, hatred raced through him like nausea. The calm man who hurt him. The angry man who could have stopped it and didn't. The third man who watched and hardly spoke until the end. He wanted to kill them. He was a gentle man, a teacher, a man who respected other people and their ideas. And he wanted to take something heavy and smash their unseen faces to pulp. He lay on his bed, lungs pumping and heart pounding, and thought he was going mad.

When the rage abated, leaving him shaking and with sweat pooled in the hollows of his eyes, he searched desperately for an anchor to cling to when the tempest returned. But nothing offered. He had no family to speak of; he had friends but none he could share this with. He'd always been happy: until now he hadn't realised how essentially alone he was.

Even if there had been someone he could call it might not have helped. Perhaps no one who'd known him before could help him now. He'd come a long way this last week from where and who he'd been: nothing from that past had any rôle to play in this present. Daniel was surrounded by people, all of them well-meaning yet none of whom seemed apt to help. The detective who called at intervals to ask if he'd remembered anything new had no answers, only more questions, and Daniel had suffered enough questions for a lifetime.

Then he remembered the woman. He still wasn't sure who she was, thought she must work in the hospital. Mrs Farrell. He remembered her as someone kind, who'd sat with him when the mere presence of another human being was what he needed most, who'd listened when he needed to talk and answered when he needed answers. He was a private man, self-contained, but now he needed contact with someone and Mrs Farrell's had been the first kind voice he'd heard, the first gentle touch he'd felt, since before this began. He dared to wonder if she could help him now.

* * *

Brodie had finally found a cranberry glass épergne. It was a good match, a good price, and it was hers if she could be in Worthing before the shop shut.

She was on her way to the door when the phone rang again. She picked it up in flight, meaning to take a number and call back. The sound of his voice stopped her dead. She lowered herself onto the desk and took a moment to answer him. "Mr Hood. Of course I remember you. What can I do for you?"

Incredibly, he sounded embarrassed. "I wondered - I mean, not if you're busy - but if you have the time ... It's just, my head's full of stuff and there's nobody I can talk to. The nurses are interested in my temperature, the doctors in my wound, Inspector Deacon in a whole bunch of things I don't know, and I just need to *talk* to somebody. But if you're busy ... ?"

"I'll be there in ten minutes." The cranberry glass épergne was going to have to wait.

* * *

Daniel looked both better and worse than Brodie expected. He was out of bed, wrapped in a towelling dressing gown, curled in a chair. A little colour had seeped back into his face and he rose to greet her without much difficulty. Two days earlier he couldn't lift his head.

The biggest difference was the addition of a pair of large circular wire-rimmed spectacles. Through them he was able to focus on her as he had not before. The people who took his clothes, his dignity and almost his life had not thought to throw his glasses into the skip with him when they were finished. Someone had been to his home for another pair. Brodie might have thought of that. After all, she knew where he lived.

But his physical progress was not mirrored in his mental state. He was troubled, restless and ill at ease. It was no wonder, but it turned the knife in Brodie's heart. This too was her responsibility. It didn't end when Daniel woke up, wouldn't end when he went home. The nightmare never going to be entirely over, for either of them.

She drew up a chair beside Daniel's. She owed him a smile. "I'm glad you called."

Immediately his eyes dropped. "Inspector Deacon thinks I could tell him more about this if I tried. I can't. I *have* tried: there's nothing more."

Brodie shook her head dismissively. "Inspector Deacon can ask his own questions. I'm not his gopher."

"Then ... ?"

She shrugged. "I was just glad to hear from you. I kept wondering how you were."

"I wasn't sure I should call. You must be busy."

"Daniel," she said firmly, "you're the most important thing any of us has to deal with right now. Sure I'm busy, but if you want to talk we'll talk. You want to play snakes and ladders, we'll do that. If I can help, in any way, I want to."

He blinked behind the thick lenses. Belatedly, Brodie wondered if maybe that wasn't what he needed either. Maybe he'd been the centre of attention long enough and what he really needed was the resumption of normal services; which in the case of a comprehensive school maths teacher probably meant being ignored for much of the time.

She sighed. "I'm overdoing it, aren't I? The caring bit. It's just, this whole situation is way outside my experience. Tell me what you want me to do."

He wasn't as tall as her and the roomy dressing-gown emphasised the slightness of his frame. But his hands were a size bigger than expected, as if he still had some growing to do. They sketched a gesture of impatience before he could fold them tightly across his chest. "I don't know! I'm sorry, I shouldn't have called. I don't know what I want. I don't know what I'm doing any more. This place is driving me crazy!"

"Daniel, you're not crazy," Brodie said quietly. "You've been through hell. You nearly died. Of course your emotions will be in tatters for a while. You're right, you need to talk. I can find you a professional in the field of victim support" - she saw his face fall, changed horses in mid stream - "or you could talk to me. I'm not a bad listener. Yell, stamp, bang the table if it helps. You've every right."

The look he threw her glanced off into a corner of the room. His voice was thick with feelings he didn't know how to express. Nothing in his life before had given him either the practice or the vocabulary. "No, I just want to talk. Only, I don't know what it is I want to say."

Brodie considered. "You want to say you're angry."

"Yes."

"Then say it. You have nothing to be ashamed of. Not your anger, not your pain. You have the right to express them. It's not an imposition, asking someone to listen."

Daniel nodded, the Adam's apple bobbing in his thin throat. "That's how it feels. Like I'm - trading on it. Like I'm droning on and on when good taste and simple good manners say it's time to drop it. That I've become a bore and an embarrassment, like someone's aunt who's always on about her operation."

Brodie's chuckle was rewarded by a flicker of wry humour crossing Daniel's face. It was a pleasant face: not handsome, not striking or distinguished in any way; just the nice, amiable, honest face of someone it would be easy to spend time with. A face to inspire more friendship than passion, but the kind of friendship that can last longer.

A face someone had spent big money finding and two days reducing to a gaunt mask. It was still incredible to her. What could a man like Daniel Hood have done to incur such wrath?

She said softly, "I don't think the rules of polite conversation apply. I think if you try to put this out of your mind you really will go crazy. What happened to you was too big. Rules designed for normal social interactions are no help when the sky's fallen in. You're hurting, you need to grieve."

She heard herself then, the women's magazine philosophy, and the colour raced up her cheeks. "Oh Daniel, I don't know enough to advise you. I'm talking as if you were a friend whose marriage was in trouble, whose kids were going off the rails. But this isn't something we can fix over a cup of tea. I shouldn't even be here. You need a proper counsellor."

Daniel's lips pursed on a question mark and his fair brows knitted. The distress swilling behind his eyes was not enough to mask the fundamental intelligence of his gaze. "But I thought ... Isn't that ... ?" He swallowed, almost as if he had a premonition what the answer would be. "Mrs Farrell, if you aren't a counsellor - or a psychiatrist or something like that - who exactly are you?"

Brodie's mouth opened and closed twice and nothing came. She had to tell him. She couldn't lie, not about this. But she couldn't find the words. Or rather, the only words that would serve seemed likely to destroy them both.

66

It was too late to turn back. She couldn't leave him unknowing any more than she could lie. She took a deep breath and told him. Who she was, where she fitted in; what she'd done.

She watched the fragile new strength that had been growing in him turn to ashes in his face. The faint new colour in his cheeks fell in seconds to the bleach of bones. Behind the glasses his eyes grew huge and smoky with anger, and the breath sawed in his throat.

Brodie hoped he'd turn away, or order her from his sight. He must want to. But he went on regarding her fiercely, the grey eyes at once stunned and implacable, refusing to release her until the worst was told. When she'd finished, with the silence between them stretched until it seemed something had to rip, with the bath of his gaze seering her skin like acid and her mind screaming for him to say something - something harsh, something hateful, anything would be better than this dearth - finally he sucked in an unsteady breath and rasped, so low she could hardly make him out, "I don't know how you have the nerve to come here."

"Do you want me to go?" she whispered.

"I didn't say that."

They went on sitting, a metre apart, eyes on one another's faces. If Daniel had struck her it would have broken the tension. Brodie ached to be away, dismissed in her shame; but she wouldn't leave unless it was what he wanted. She owed him the chance to tell her what he thought of her. She went on sitting, hands knotted in her lap, and didn't notice when the filling of her eyes spilt onto her cheek.

Daniel said, "You didn't know what they intended?"

"No."

"Is that the truth?"

She blinked, spilling another tear. "*Everything* I've told you is the truth. Dear God, you think I'd make this up? You think there's something worse I could be hiding?"

He went on looking at her. Eventually he shook his head. "No."

She nodded, unsure whether to be grateful. "I wish..."

He stopped her with his eyes. "Please. Just ... don't say anything for a minute."

Hunched in misery she obeyed. The silence folded them.

Suddenly Daniel stood up and moved to the window, looking across town towards the silver line of the Channel. He drew the dressing gown tight around his bones. "They *hurt* me!" he cried.

"I know," Brodie murmured.

"You helped them. They couldn't have done it without you."

"Daniel, I know! I'd give anything to turn the clock back and change things, but I can't. Not my stupidity, and not the price you paid for it. I know I can't make amends with an apology, but I don't have anything else to give you. I'm sorry."

He turned and stared at her again. Every breath shuddered through his body like a spasm. His voice cracked. "It's not enough!"

"I know that too." The tears were streaming down her cheeks now but she would not hide from him. "But then, what could be?"

Daniel's brow furrowed as if she were some kind of conundrum, a puzzle he couldn't fathom, another question he couldn't answer. He cupped his hand across his mouth, his eyes burning over the top of his fingers. The silence returned.

At length he drew another deep, shuddering breath and let it slowly out. If he'd found some kind of an answer, Brodie could only wait to be told what it was.

"All right," said Daniel, his voice thin. "I won't pretend I'm OK with this. I'm not. I thought, whoever they were, they were history and I was never going to have to deal with them. I thought, if I treated it as something like an avalanche or lightning, something impersonal, then I could get past it and go on. There's no point stoking your hatred for an Act of God.

"Now - what you're telling me - that makes it personal. Now I have a face to put on it: yours. And suddenly hating seems the appropriate response again." He blinked, seemed to see her tears for the first time. Astonishingly, there was compassion in his eyes. He shook his head. "And that isn't fair either. It wasn't your fault. You couldn't have guessed what they meant to do. You thought you were helping someone who'd been cheated and humiliated. You couldn't know it was a lie."

"I could have checked," stumbled Brodie.

Daniel shrugged towelling shoulders. "We take things on trust. We have to: we can't cross-check everything, life's too short. Unless you've reason to think otherwise you assume people are telling the truth. Hindsight's a great invention, it's easy to be wise after the fact, but I don't think you did anything you should have known was wrong. I don't think I have any right to hate you. Them, yes. But you're not part of them."

Brodie buried her face in her hands. Now she understood. This was what Marta had sent her here for: the agony of confession, the relief of absolution. Catharsis. It closed a door on the past, made it possible to open one on the future.

When finally she lowered her hands her voice was a reed. "You have no idea what that means to me."

Daniel's expression was rueful. "There's not much satisfaction in hating the wrong person."

"People do it, all the time. When hating the right person would be too difficult or too dangerous."

A ghost of a smile touched his lips. "I'm a mathematician," he said simply. "I like things to add up."

* * *

With the unspeakable thing between them confronted, now Brodie felt no great urge to leave. She waited for some cue from Daniel that he was finished with her. But he came and sat down again. "Tell me again what it is you do."

So she did. She told him about Mrs Campbell-Wheeler's cranberry glass épergne, about Flossie the pony, about the relatives lost touch with and the paintings sold and the vintage Hispano-Suizes that would make or break a television serial.

"It must be interesting," said Daniel. "Never knowing what's coming next."

"Up to last week it was. Now I think I'll go back to clerking."

Daniel frowned. "Give up the business? Because of me?"

"Because of what happened to you, yes."

"You were unlucky," said Daniel, quite without irony. "It was a fluke, a chance in a million. You can't give up something you've worked for because of that."

"I don't think I have a choice," said Brodie softly. "I can't do the job if every time someone comes through the door I ask myself whether they're lying, what they really want from me, what they're going to do with the information I give them. I won't risk this happening again."

He didn't dismiss her fears but thought for a moment. "You can't eliminate all risk from life."

"There are risks and risks," said Brodie tightly. "I'll take my chances with the occasional careless driver and iffy curry, but I don't ever again want to feel the way this has made me feel."

"Me neither. I just don't think it's a basis on which to live your life. Do you know what probability math is?" She shook her head. "It's a means of estimating the likelihood of an event based on the ratio between its occurrence and the average number of cases favourable to its occurrence taken over an indefinitely extended series of such cases."

Daniel recited it like a mantra; then he saw her face and his smile lit the room. "Sorry. It's a way of predicting the mathematical likelihood of something happening. Mathematically, you're more likely to be kicked to death by a donkey than get involved in anything like this again. You don't know where things are going to lead. You can't. You take reasonable care, and then you get on with it. You don't give up something you're good at because of one bad experience. You made a mistake. You'll make others, but you won't make this one again."

Brodie felt her heart swell at his generosity. "What makes you think I'm good at it?"

Daniel smiled. "If you weren't we'd never have met."

Chapter 7

Deacon phoned her at the office the next morning. "You've been talking to Daniel." It was half a question, half an accusation.

Brodie saw no need to apologise. "That's right."

"Twice."

"I was there when he woke up. Yesterday he wanted to see me again."

"Why?"

"He needed to talk to somebody. He had the idea that was my function."

"And did you tell him what your function in all this actually was?"

Brodie didn't like his tone. One of those people with more skill, and possibly more goodwill, than good manners, this seemed to be how the policeman reacted to anything he couldn't immediately categorise: with hectoring aggression. As if making people defend themselves was a short-cut to finding out who they were and what they knew.

A couple of days ago she'd have been upset. But now Brodie had faced her demons, and making her peace with Daniel left her strong enough to cope with Inspector Deacon. "As a matter of fact I did," she said calmly. "No one else had put him in the picture so I did. I told him everything I know."

Whatever Deacon was expecting, it wasn't that. Her honesty put him off his stride: it took him a moment to recover. "And how did he feel about that?"

"He was shocked and he was hurt," said Brodie. "And then he thought about it, and how it had happened, and he forgave me. I'm sorry, Inspector, but if you were hoping to keep playing the guilt card you should probably have kept us apart."

There was a long pause, then a harsh barking laugh. "I'll say this for you, Mrs Farrell - you have guts. So what did he say?"

She frowned. "About what?"

"About what happened! What did he tell you?"

She looked at the telephone as if she'd dropped it in something nasty. "Inspector Deacon, I'm not your spy. I didn't ask him about what happened, and he didn't volunteer. And if he had I'm not sure I'd be reporting our conversation to you. Daniel Hood isn't your suspect, he's the victim. If you want to know what it was all about, ask him."

"I did," said Deacon gruffly. "He said he didn't know."

"Then why don't you believe him? If he knew who'd treated him like that, don't you think he'd want them caught? What reason could he possibly have to protect them?"

Deacon gave a disparaging sniff. "I won't know that until I know everything else."

"Well, it's no use thinking I can help you. Daniel didn't tell me anything new."

"So what *were* you talking about?"

Brodie took some satisfaction in her reply. "Probability math."

* * *

Having got nowhere with Brodie, Deacon returned to the hospital. He was startled to find Daniel dressed and packing his belongings into a carrier bag. "Where do you think you're going?"

"Home," said Daniel.

"You can't."

Daniel didn't look round. "Funnily enough, that's what the doctor said. He was mistaken too."

Deacon breathed heavily. "Daniel, we've been through this. If you go home, they're going to know you're alive. They tried to kill you once, they may do it again."

"Sometime I have to take that risk. I'm not spending the rest of my life running from shadows."

Jack Deacon was coming to realise that the man before him was not at all who he appeared to be; except that he looked exactly like a teacher. He also looked callow, unformed and malleable, and Deacon had thought he would be easy enough to bend to his

72

bidding. That he'd be grateful to be told what to do and when to do it in return for the policeman's protection.

But beneath the damaged exterior and even the gentle, bruised spirit lay buried a sliver of adamant. Perhaps Deacon might have guessed. Hood was a mathematician: he thought things through to their logical conclusions, which he then invested with a kind of sanctity.

Numbers aren't like words: they always mean the same things. It makes mathematicians at once scrupulous and unbending. No amount of argument would persuade Daniel Hood that one and one could make anything but two, or that any other conclusion he'd reached by pure logic should be subject to external variables. Like doctors and policemen telling him what to do. Like the possibility of murderous madmen hunting him. It wasn't exactly courage, more a kind of intellectual obstinacy.

Deacon chewed his cheek for a moment and forebore to comment. Then he nodded. "You're right. Who the hell are they to tell you what to do? You stand up to them, dare them to do their worst. It'll make a terrific epitaph."

Behind the round glasses Daniel's eyes widened and then narrowed to a smile. "You're saying, it's not worth risking my life for a principle."

"Yes," said Deacon.

"You wouldn't."

"No ... " He saw the trap just too late.

"Inspector, we both know that if that door burst open now and armed men rushed in, they'd have to go through you to get at me."

Deacon didn't deny it. "That's different."

"Not really. The bottom line is, if decent people take the path of least resistance, violent people win. You resist them your way, I'll resist them mine."

"Your life is a high price to pay for self-respect."

Daniel nodded. "It would be. I very much hope it won't come to that. But Inspector, I'd rather take the risk - I think I'd even rather pay the price - than settle for the crumbs of an existence they left me." His expression softened. "With all your questions, you haven't

73

asked one thing. Who they were, what they looked like, what they said, what they wanted, what they did. But not how it felt."

"I can imagine how it felt," Deacon said in a low voice.

Daniel shook his head; not with reproof but as if being honest mattered more than being polite. "No, I don't think you can. I don't think anyone could. Maybe, just maybe, the pain - we all know what pain feels like, we can just about handle the concept of pain for its own sake, deliberate and unrelenting.

"But it wasn't just the pain. It was how they made me feel. Like nothing. Like I was so worthless they had a right to treat me like that." A tear trembled on the lip of his eye. "But they hadn't. They were wrong: I'm worth more than that. I might have to keep reminding myself, but I *know* it's true."

Deacon still didn't understand. "You're going to risk your life to prove it?"

"No. I'm going to *live* my life to prove it. I'm going home, I'm going to get well, I'm going back to work and I'm going to achieve something. This is not going to shackle me for the rest of my life. I'm not going to be their victim forever. For two days they used me like they owned me, but they're not going to rule my existence for the next ten, twenty, fifty years."

"How about the next fortnight?"

Daniel gave a wry grin. "I could almost go for that. But if I did, and at the end of a fortnight you still hadn't got them, I'm not sure I'd ever get past that door."

Jack Deacon was like any other police officer: for every collar he felt he lost two. It was a reality of the job he'd long come to terms with, though he still found it offensive to watch a criminal head down the police station steps. He told himself that he'd catch up with them some day, and very often he did. If it wasn't exactly philosophical it was pragmatic.

But he also knew when he was fighting a battle he wasn't going to win. He couldn't hold Daniel Hood against his will any more than his doctor could. He nodded. "My car's outside."

* * *

74

If he'd thought Daniel could match the deeds to the words he might have been slower to take him home. He thought they'd get to the flat over the drying sheds - to the place where it had begun, to the door which he'd last opened onto mayhem - and he'd turn away, grey and shaking, and Deacon could take him back to the hospital.

The flat was once a loft where fishermen knotted their nets. It was approached by an iron staircase up the outside - in pre-Building Regulations days it had been wood - and you had to look twice to know someone lived there. The door was tarred and weathered like the rest of the shed, but there were curtains at the windows and two milk bottles at the foot of the steps.

For a moment Deacon thought they weren't going any further. With his hand on the rail Daniel slowed to a halt and swayed. Deacon stood ready to catch him if he fell. But then sheer willpower stiffened his back and his hand knotted white-knuckled on the rail, and he went up.

His keys had been lost. Deacon had some made to facilitate the investigation. He used one now, pushed the door open, and waited.

Daniel barely paused on the threshold. Deacon followed him inside, shut the door behind him, looked round for somewhere to put the bag. He found a bedroom, dropped it behind the door.

He turned in time to see Daniel's cheeks blench paper-white, the pale grey eyes roll behind the thick lenses and his knees go to string; he folded with a sigh, and it was all Deacon could do to reach him before he hit his head on the hearth.

"Easy, Danny," whistled Deacon, sinking to his knees and pulling the young man safely into the compass of his arms. "It's all right, I've got you. Sit still a minute and get your breath back."

The grey fog cocooning him left Daniel no choice. He lay passive against the older man's chest and felt a little of his strength percolate into him. His lips twitched. "Sorry."

"Will that do?" asked Deacon quietly. "Have you had enough now? Can we go back?"

But Daniel was shaking his head. "I'm staying."

"You can't. Damn it, just walking through the door was enough to make you faint!"

"I'll be all right in a minute. It was just ... "

"The shock."

"Yes."

"Brought it all back."

"Yes."

"Daniel - brought *what* back? What was it in aid of? Who's Sophie? What is it you're not telling me?"

Daniel Hood squirmed out of the policeman's embrace and, kneeling on the hearth-rug, stared at him in rank incredulity. "Nothing! I've told you everything I know. Why won't you believe me?"

Deacon clambered roughly to his feet. "Because if I did I'd have to leave it at that. Because you are the only lead I have. Because if you really have told me all you know, if there really isn't anything else, I might as well move onto some case I can conceivably solve. Pirate videos, maybe, or lost dogs. If you can't tell me anything more I have nowhere else to look. What they did to you: they got away with it."

"Don't say that ... "

"Then help me!"

"I can't!" Tears were swimming in his eyes. "Can't you see - this is what they did? Asked me questions I had no way of answering, and hurt me, and told me it was my fault. It wasn't then, Inspector, and it isn't now."

Shame turned a knife in Jack Deacon's gut. He turned away and stood breathing heavily by the door. When he had his emotions under control he said gruffly, "I can take you back to the hospital if that's what you want. I don't think there's anything else I can do for you."

Still on his knees, Daniel surveyed the granite set of the policeman's shoulders. Tiny waves of regret, of anger, of disappointment broke across his face. But he was too protective of the shreds of pride left to him to beg. "I'm staying."

Chapter 8

Brodie shut the office at four-thirty, with the dusk creeping down the Channel. She'd negotiated a stay of execution on the cranberry glass: leaving Shack Lane she turned left towards Worthing.

Most south coast towns have tourist attractions, tourist traffic and one-way systems: the east-bound road is a block inland from the esplanade. Dimmock, however, had the fag-end of a fishing industry, a shingle beach, no marina, no amusement park and no shopping mall. It did have a by-pass to speed the tourists on to where they might actually want to stop. Consequently it didn't need a one-way system, and Brodie drove east along the sea-front, past the netting sheds.

The tide was out, the shingle sloping abruptly where the fishing boats used to haul out. Now a single hulk rotted unglamorously on its side. The long vista was deserted, except for two boys throwing stones for a collie dog and, down at the water's edge, a solitary figure in a hooded parka.

She never afterwards knew how she recognised him. The afternoon's light was fading; he had his back to her; his bright hair was covered by the hood, his slight frame muffled by the parka. Also, she'd never seen him dressed. But she knew the lonely figure as Daniel Hood in an instant; and in another instant realised he had no business being there, in full view of anyone who passed. On Tuesday morning she'd been ushered into the hospital in deepest secrecy, warned that an indiscretion could cost his life. Now it was Friday and he was wandering around the seafront within a stone's throw of his home. Short of wearing a sign reading "I'm Daniel: kill me" he could hardly make a more tempting target of himself.

She parked by the sea wall. Dimmock didn't need many yellow lines either.

Daniel must have heard the crunch of steps behind him. But he didn't, as Brodie expected, turn to see who was coming. He seemed rather to freeze, to hunch in on himself, to take root there, stubborn and defenceless.

With a hand on his shoulder she spun him to face her. Fear for him blazed in her eyes like fury. "Do you *want* to die?"

The tension went from him in a little pant and his shoulders dropped. "It's you. Er - no. Oddly enough I don't."

"Then what are you doing here? Where anyone looking for you is bound to start? Why aren't you still tucked up, warm and anonymous, in a hospital bed?"

Daniel chewed ruefully on the inside of his cheek. "I discharged myself."

"You've gone AWOL? What's Inspector Deacon going to say when he finds out?"

"He knows," Daniel said. "He brought me home - admittedly, under protest. And he said pretty much what you did."

"But he left you here?" Brodie's scowl was more puzzled now than angry.

"Not here - at my flat." Daniel waved a vague hand. "He's - er - "

"What?"

He sighed. "He's given up on me. He thinks I could help him solve this if I tried. More than that, he thinks I'm holding something back."

"Are you?"

"No. It makes no sense to me either. I don't think it ever will. I think all that's left now is to try and pick up the pieces."

"And hope there's nobody out there thinking that all that's left now is to silence you."

He nodded. "I thought - when I heard you coming ... "

"I know what you thought," Brodie said roughly. "You thought I was coming to kill you. And you stood and waited."

"I'm a lot better," he said defensively. "But I couldn't outrun a bullet just yet."

"Then why aren't you at least inside, out of sight?"

The eyes he turned on her were haunted. "I was. I couldn't stay there. I told Mr Deacon I could, but I couldn't. It was like it was starting again. My hands were shaking, the sweat was pouring off me. I tried to phone you but I couldn't stay there long enough. I thought, if I came out here for ten minutes, got some fresh air into my lungs and calmed down, I could go back."

"When was this?" asked Brodie softly.

"Oh ... " He glanced at the sky. "About one o'clock." He'd been on the beach almost four hours.

The decision made itself. "Come on," said Brodie, folding an arm briskly through his, "come with me."

"Where?"

"Well, you can't stay here, you can't go back to your flat and you won't go back to the hospital. Come home with me."

They went the scenic route, via Worthing.

*　*　*

Daniel was very tired. Brodie sat him down in the living room while she went to make up the spare bed; when she got back he was asleep. She sighed and stripped the bed again, easing the pillow under his head and tucking the duvet round him. He might wake stiff but he wouldn't be cold. She went upstairs for her daughter.

While Paddy was getting her things together, Brodie acquainted Mrs Szarabeijka with the latest development. Marta's eyes widened dramatically. "You brought him here? To your home? Your child's home?"

"What else could I do with him? Anyway, he isn't going to do Paddy any harm."

"I don't expect he is," agreed Marta. "But what if these people come after him? What if they find him here?"

"She's a child, Marta! They're not going to hurt a child."

"How can you *say* that, when you know what they've done already?" She thought for a moment then nodded decisively. "Leave Paddy with me. Then it's only your own stupid neck you're risking."

Brodie prided herself she could take a hint. "You think I'm wrong, don't you? Bringing him here. Getting involved."

"I think you're crazy," Marta said honestly.

"He needed somewhere to go, someone to be with. He looks so - alone."

"He needs to be in hospital, with a police guard. You're neither a nurse nor a policeman."

"No. But I owe him more than they do."

"Not your life! Not your daughter's life."

"I think the danger must have passed," struggled Brodie. "Or why would Deacon take him home?"

Marta shrugged. "It's a hell of a gamble."

People who knew her before the divorce mostly thought of Brodie Farrell as a nice woman. But she'd never been that nice, and now she had to fight for what she wanted she could be downright devious. "You want me to send him away."

"I think it would be sensible, yes."

"All right, I will. Come downstairs with me and we'll tell him."

The older woman recognised the trap being laid for her. But Marta Szarabeijka had never refused a challenge in her life. She marched downstairs and threw open Brodie's front door. "You. You're putting these people in danger. Get out of here."

But Daniel no more than stirred in his sleep, the fingers of one hand plucking at the duvet. Brodie had put his glasses on the coffee table: without them he looked as she had first seen him, frail and impermenant.

By the time Brodie caught up with her Marta was in full sock-knitting mode. "Send him away indeed!" she exclaimed in *sotto voce* indignation. "How can you talk of such a thing?"

* * *

When Deacon, heading home after nine, went to check on Daniel and found the door unlocked and the flat empty, his first thought was that the unknown people, for their unknown reasons, had returned for him and this time he was gone for good.

His second was of Brodie Farrell.

He didn't announce himself when she answered the phone. He demanded, "Do you know where he is?"

Brodie recognised both the voice and the manner, and knew at once who he meant. But Deacon himself had stressed the need for caution. "Who's speaking, please?" she asked coolly.

"Detective Inspector Deacon," he said in his teeth. "You do, don't you? Where is he?"

"Can you prove that you're Detective Inspector Deacon?"

She could hear him fuming. His warrant card was useless over the phone: Brodie waited calmly while he thought up an alternative.

"Yes, I can. It was me took you to see him in the hospital. We went in the back way. When we were leaving you asked if you could go back sometime and visit him."

"Good evening, Inspector," Brodie said politely. "You understand, we have to be careful."

Deacon understood exactly what she was doing, and it wasn't being careful. "He isn't where I left him. Do you know where he is?"

"He's here."

"He's all right?"

"He's fine. He's asleep."

Deacon fell silent, thinking. If it wasn't the ideal refuge it was at least better than his own flat. No one in their right mind would look for Daniel Hood in the home of the woman who sold him to his enemies.

"All right," he said after a moment. "Will you keep him there?"

"As long as he wants to stay."

"Good. Keep him out of sight if you can. I realise," he added ironically, "this may not be as easy as it sounds."

Brodie gave an unseen grin. Awkward, irascible and offensive as he often was, she harboured a secret liking for Jack Deacon. She wasn't sure his gruff exterior hid a heart of gold, but she suspected there was a heart of some sort in there, somewhere.

"I will." She cleared her throat. "Inspector ... "

"What?"

"He said - He has the idea you've given up on this case."

Deacon sounded more tired than defensive. "I haven't given up, Mrs Farrell. But the reality is, in the absense of new information we may never make any more progress. I know Daniel thinks I've been bullying him; I dare say you think I've been bullying you. But you two are the only people I'm aware of who know anything about what happened, and so far neither of you has given me enough to get an investigation rolling.

"Oh, we've got an Incident Room, I've got people trawling the computer for similarities and others stopping passers-by on the seafront in case they were there last Friday night as well and saw something odd. It's what we describe as Pursuing the Usual Avenues. The point about avenues, though, is that most of them are dead ends. To date, nobody has been able to add one iota to what you told me on Tuesday and Daniel told me the day after. And everything I have isn't enough to tell me what to do next. I need more information."

"You need a good night's sleep," Brodie said kindly. "Go home, Inspector. Things may look brighter in the morning."

* * *

The phone, or perhaps their voices, penetrated his sleep. Daniel sat up, feeing for his glasses. The rest had done him good. "Inspector Deacon?"

"Just making sure you're still alive."

"I should have told him where I was."

"He knows now."

Daniel's smile was puzzled round the edges. "I can't make you out."

Brodie was genuinely surprised. "Me? There's nothing complicated about me. What do you mean?"

"I don't think you're who you seem to be. This - mother, home-maker and businesswoman: you're all those things, I know, but they aren't you. There's a whole that's more than the sum of the parts."

Brodie shook her head, unsure whether or not to be flattered. "You're mistaken. What you see is what you get."

But Daniel wasn't persuaded. "I heard you talking to Deacon. He terrifies me - but he doesn't frighten you, does he? He gives you a hard time, you give him one back. And coming to the hospital, telling me what you did - that took real courage. Most people could-n't have done it. Most people wouldn't even have tried."

"It was the lesser of two evils. It was eating away at me, I had to do something. I thought, if I talked to you ... " She smiled wryly, "And then, I wasn't expecting you to wake up."

She made some supper. As they ate Daniel's eyes roved the living room.

"What is it?"

"My coat. What happened to it?"

It was damp, she'd put it by the stove to air. In his socks he padded into the kitchen, came back with a bottle of pills. He shook out two and washed them down with tea.

Brodie's eyebrows sketched a question-mark. "Painkillers," Daniel explained briefly.

She looked as if he'd slapped her. Remorse widened his eyes. "It's all right," he said hurriedly, "it's not bad. It just needs the edge taking off for another few days."

Brodie swallowed. "Do you need ... I mean, I could probably change a dressing or something ... ?"

Daniel shook his head. "There's no need. I was just worried I'd forgotten the pills. But I wasn't home long enough to take them out of my coat pocket, and the coat was the one thing I grabbed on the way out."

"I can fetch you some things if you'd rather not go back to the flat yet."

"Maybe tomorrow."

They sipped the tea. Daniel looked up shyly. "Can I ask you something?"

Brodie steeled herself. "Anything."

"How did you find me?"

It had to come. She couldn't expect him to forget as well as forgive. He was entitled to know everything she could tell him. "From a photograph."

"But how? Without a name or address or any information about me. How do you set about finding someone from just a photograph?"

"You can't always. But sometimes there's something in there besides the subject that gives you a frame of reference - a time or a location or somewhere to start. In this case it was the telescope. I went to a star-gazers' meeting and showed the picture round."

"Someone recognised me?" Daniel sounded pleasantly surprised.

She was sorry to disillusion him. "Well - the telescope, actually. But it was enough."

Daniel was thinking. "This photograph. Where was it taken?"

"Hard to tell. You were leaning on a stone parapet with the telescope beside you. Ring a bell?"

He nodded slowly. "Yes. The monument in the park - I hauled the telescope up there last Wednesday. Sun-spot observations: I'd been watching a good group back in February, I didn't want to miss their reappearance just because it was a school day. So I took the telescope over to the park at lunchtime. It's really too big to lug around like that, but the detail it gives is phenomenal. For some things, bigger really is better."

Brodie was eyeing him with disbelief. "Daniel - you can see the sun from all over Dimmock! From your flat, and from the school. What's so special about the monument?"

"You want the sun high so you're observing through the minimum amount of atmosphere: before school was too early, after school was too late. And there's nowhere at school that's high enough off the ground."

"You were trying to get closer?"

His gaze was level on her face. He knew she was quizzing him: if he minded it didn't show. "There's a lot of pollution at ground level. It distorts the image. A telescope can't filter out the garbage: the bigger the magnificiation, the bigger the distortion. You have to get above the dust layer. A mountain's perfect, but the monument's high enough to improve the view significantly."

She nodded. Dimmock had never had much time for the Clean Air Act. "I thought astronomers only came out at night."

Daniel smiled solemnly. "Bit hard to watch sunspots in the dark."

"Ah." She went to return the smile; and then she realised that Daniel had known what she was doing before she did herself. She was trying to catch him in a lie because a part of her still hoped this was his fault. That he'd brought it on himself. Sunspots? - yeah,

84

right. But if it wasn't true, then he was up the monument with a telescope for some quite different purpose. And she didn't know it, and Deacon didn't know it, but perhaps the people who hurt him did ...

Daniel held her gaze. "It's all right," he said, his voice low.

Brodie shook her head angrily, the flying hair masking the colour in her cheeks. "No, it isn't, it's pathetic. It's stupid and it's cruel, and more than that it's cowardly. I'm desperate to shed some of the blame, and if I can't find anyone else then you'll do. It's like blaming the woman for getting raped. Damn it, Daniel, I'm stronger than this!"

"I know you are," he said softly. "But it's enough to be strong most of the time. You're allowed time off for good behaviour."

She laughed at that; it came out half a sob.

Daniel leaned back in his chair. "So the photograph was taken at lunchtime a week last Wednesday. And the people who kidnapped me had it. Why? What possible interest could me and my telescope be to them?"

"Did you see anyone?" He shook his head. "I expect you were too busy with your sunspots. And they were some distance away: the picture was taken off a video and enhanced within an inch of its life."

"Someone was filming me? That's crazy."

"Daniel, it's all crazy! Never mind the video: why would anyone want to hurt you like that?"

His voice was a murmur. "They were looking for Sophie."

"But you say you don't know anything about her. Why would they think you did?"

Daniel shrugged. "At first I thought they'd made a mistake - grabbed the wrong man. But that makes no sense either. They had a picture of me on top of the monument with twenty kilos of optical equipment. Who the hell could they have mistaken me for?"

He was right, the odds against had to be - well, astronomical. Brodie felt her chest tighten, her eyes grow wary. "No, that wasn't a mistake." She pushed herself away from the table, away from him. "And if it wasn't then they got the right man. Who are you, Daniel?

85

What have you done that made someone want to kill you an inch at a time? Deacon was right. What is it you're not telling us?"

Five days ago he was at death's door. Since then his young body had concentrated all its resources on healing; but the burns and the bullet-wound were not his only injuries, and psychological scars remain livid long after physical ones have faded.

Post traumatic stress disorder can show itself in depression, alcoholism, drug addiction, violence, marital breakdown, asthma, eczema, psoriasis and diabetes. Daniel was at the very start of the process, with any or all of them ahead. For now the clearest sign was the way tears sprang too readily to his eyes. He recoiled from her barrage as if she was throwing not questions but crockery at him. "Please don't shout at me. I can't think straight if you shout at me."

Brodie bit her lip. With the possible exception of DI Deacon, the last people hammering questions at him had punished his failure to answer with fire. In tears? - it was a tribute to the resilience of the human spirit that he wasn't in a strait jacket. "I'm sorry. Daniel, I'm sorry ... "

"It's all right. I'm just a bit ... shaky still. I'm all right; really I am."

Brodie came back to the table and sat down, capturing his hands with her own. "No, you're not. There's no way you could be. And no reason you should be - not here, with me. I know what you've been through. You don't have to pretend for me."

"I know," said Daniel. "I'm just ... trying to deal with it. Only every time I think I'm winning I find myself crying again."

Brodie shrugged. "So cry. It's what you do when you're hurt."

"If you're a man you're not supposed to."

She sniffed. "Men do lots of things they're not supposed to, most of them more harmful than crying."

He gently reclaimed his hands. There were pink lines on his wrists where the straps had cut him. "To answer your question," he said quietly. "I haven't done anything that would explain what happened. I am exactly and only what I appear to be. I'm not holding anything back. I don't know why they took me, or why they filmed me." He blinked. "Have you still got the picture?"

Brodie had given it to Inspector Deacon. But before that, before she'd known there was anything sinister going on, she'd scanned it onto her computer. She'd been working at home that evening so the picture was in her PC in the spare room.

It was strange, studying it together. Though poor it was innocuous enough: it showed Daniel Hood, his telescope and the stone parapet on top of the monument. But it was the start of everything.

Daniel knew it too. His voice was unsteady. "We should be able to work out where this was taken from."

Brodie nodded, keeping her eyes on the screen. "We know when you were up there so the shadows will tell us which way you were looking. If we follow that line till it reaches either the ground or another building, that's where the camera was."

He didn't reply. After a moment she looked up and found him watching her. "I was right. You are good at this."

"Not bad," she admitted. But it wasn't just a compliment: there was something odd in his voice. She waited for the other shoe to drop.

"Finding things - finding people - that's what you do."

"I told you that."

"I know. I'm just thinking ..."

She got there before he could say what he was thinking. "No!" she exploded. "No. Never. Forget it."

"All right "

"I mean it, Daniel." She screwed round to look him square in the face. "They nearly killed you. They know who you are - they know who I am. We're not rattling any cages! It's Inspector Deacon's job to find them, not ours."

"Deacon's given up. I'm not ready to."

"We'll tell him about the photograph."

"He's *got* the photograph! He's got all the information we have - if he was going to use it he'd have done it by now."

"Maybe he has, and it didn't get him anywhere."

"And maybe he hasn't, because he hasn't the incentive I have. His life goes on whether or not he ever finds out what happened. I'm not sure mine will."

Only the lethal mixture of sympathy and remorse kept Brodie

from switching off the computer there and then, going to bed and telling Daniel to do the same. She looked at his face and saw it pinched with anguish. "I suppose ... "

"What?"

"I suppose it wouldn't do any harm to go to the park and look. If we could work out where the video was taken from, telling Deacon might be enough to kick-start his investigation again."

Daniel nodded, painfully eager. "Now?"

"It's dark! We'll go tomorrow. Or I will - maybe you should stay here."

"I'll stay in the car."

Brodie nodded. "All right; tomorrow. Now, let me make up this bed again and then let's get some sleep. It's been a busy day."

He had nothing to sleep in. She found him some joggers and a T-shirt printed with the slogan "Solicitors do it in triplicate". It was an old T-shirt.

She left him to undress. In the doorway, though, she paused and looked back. "Daniel, there's one thing you should consider before we go any further with this."

"Yes?"

"If we start searching for these people, we just might find them."

Chapter 9

Daniel slept and dreamt of waking.

Brodie roused him. The cloud of dark hair was loose, framing a smile. In his dreams he was not short-sighted.

"Rise and shine," she said.

She reached under the cover for his left hand, gave it a friendly squeeze and laid it on the pillow beside his head. Then she did the same with his right hand. She smiled again and, languidly, he smiled back.

Then she pulled down the cover briskly, and pulled up the witty T-shirt, baring his chest. "Ready when you are," she said to someone out of sight behind him; and when Daniel tried to move he found his wrists were tied to the headboard.

His cry of terror woke him, Brodie, and quite possibly the rest of the house.

Brodie hurried through from her own room, snapping on lights as she went, to find him huddled against the wall, the bedclothes on the floor, John's T-shirt - wringing wet - clinging to his ribs. His eyes were wide and staring.

"Daniel. Daniel!" She knelt quickly in front of him, gripping his shoulders. "It's all right. It was a dream, that's all. You had a nightmare. Wake up now, it's over."

She saw uncertainty creep into his eyes as he ventured the gulf between sleep and awareness. When he recognised her he flinched, which upset her more than his cries had done.

"Daniel, it's all right. You're safe here. It was just a dream."

When he believed her he shut his eyes for a moment and panted softly. "I'm sorry," he whispered. "I'm sorry."

"It's all right," Brodie said, still holding him. "It's only to be expected. Was this the first time?"

"I think they gave me something. In the hospital." He managed a wry, transient smile. "I suppose that's one of the reasons they wanted me to stay."

"Do you want to go back?"

"No." He shook his head, droplets of sweat spraying from the rat-tails of his hair. "What time is it?"

There was a clock on the wall. Brodie passed him his glasses. "Nearly eight," she said. "I'll make some breakfast. Why don't you have a shower?" Her face fell. "Oh - can you?"

Daniel smiled. "A careful one."

The phone went. It was Marta. "Is everything all right?"

"Fine. Oh - you heard Daniel. He had a nightmare."

"You want me to come down?"

"Come for breakfast if you like. Bring Paddy. It's time you all met."

"Give me ten minutes," said Marta. "To beat out some of the wrinkles. We don't want I should give him another nightmare."

Brodie found some clothes Daniel could use - a rugby shirt and a sweater she'd bought for John then reclaimed because he never wore it. It would drown Daniel, but that was better than fitting too snugly over his tender skin.

Dressing took him time. Marta and Paddy arrived first. Marta looked round the living room with an interrogative shrug, and Brodie gestured towards the spare room.

Paddy was more direct, demanding in her piercing four-year-old voice, "Where's Mummy's boyfriend?"

Brodie could cheerfully have strangled her. She leaned down and hissed into the child's face, "Daniel is *not* Mummy's boyfriend. He's a nice man who's had a bad week and needs somewhere to stay for a few days. All right?"

Paddy thought about this for a moment. "That's what Daddy said about Julia." Marta succumbed to a coughing fit.

When Daniel found the living room full of people his first instinct was to retreat. But he pulled himself together. They were two women and a child, for heaven's sake! - if he couldn't face them he'd better look for a hermitage.

Brodie ushered him to the table. She nodded at the sweater. "Coral is you." She performed introductions.

They breakfasted half in an awkward silence and half in a

90

budgerigar twittering that was a desperate attempt to talk about anything except why Daniel was here. They were all profoundly grateful when the teapot was empty.

Brodie tried not to work at the weekends. Usually she and Paddy did the week's shopping on Saturday morning. But generous as ever, Marta cast a significant glance at the visitor and announced that she was going to the supermarket, she might as well take the child and Brodie's shopping list as well.

Brodie knew what she meant and was grateful. She got Paddy dressed and handed her back to her friend, along with her house keeping purse. "Get a taxi back," she said. "You'll have too much to carry, and it's the least I can do."

"I was going to," Marta said airily.

After they'd gone Brodie made a last effort at dissuasion. "Are you sure this is what you want?"

"I'm sure."

"Then, will you stay here while I go to the park?"

"You've been very kind," said Daniel, "but you can't pick up the pieces for me. I have to do it myself."

"You don't have to do it today. We could leave it till tomorrow. Or next week."

"Or sometime, or never." He smiled ruefully. "Mrs Farrell, I can't hide forever. I have to get back to the real world. I have to stop cowering in corners and listening for footsteps. This is as good a time as any. I'm not fooling myself, if that's what you think. Finding where the video was shot isn't going to solve the mystery. It probably won't even help. No one'll be there now: it's ten days too late to catch them in the act.

"I'm not doing this because I think I'll find the men who hurt me. I'm doing it for my own self-respect. It took a beating, it's not up to much right now, but until I stop behaving like a victim it won't get any better. I have to stand on my own two feet again, and the longer I leave it the harder it'll be. That's why I have to come with you, and we have to go now. If I start thinking there's an alternative I'll never do it."

"You want to be doing something," said Brodie. "I understand

91

that. You want to do something because before there was nothing you could do. But exposing yourself to more danger can't be a good idea."

"Too much time has passed. If they were still interested in me they'd have found me by now."

"They think you're dead! They won't go on thinking that if you start wandering round in broad daylight."

Daniel shook his head. "I don't think they care any more. If they know I'm still alive they also know I can't harm them. If I could, Deacon would have had them out of their beds before now."

Brodie thought about that for a moment, then shrugged. "It's your call - if you want to do it, we'll do it." She paused in the doorway. "One condition."

"Yes?"

"Call me Brodie. I may be older than you, but I'm not old enough to be your mother."

* * *

She'd printed a copy of the picture off the computer. Brodie parked as close as she could - Daniel still found walking difficult - and they strolled over to the monument and then round it, looking where the shadows fell and calculating where they would fall shortly after midday.

"Here," said Daniel, coming to a standstill. "But that doesn't work either. The angle's wrong. If it was taken from down here all it would have showed is the underside of my chin. The camera must have been higher up."

They turned away from the monument, seeking a vantage point. But unless someone had shinned up a tree with a video camera under his arm, the park offered none.

"So he was outside the park." Brodie nodded to where the town began to climb towards the Firestone Cliffs. Three hundred metres away the buildings were already as high as the monument. It was a typically Dimmock-sized folly, a stumpy tower like the castle in Chess, no taller than a three-storey house, commemorating an obscure triumph of the Boer War.

She looked at the steps and then at Daniel. "Are you up for this?"

He thought he was. His clothes were chafing and his feet were sore where the flame had licked the insteps, but he could bear the discomfort. He went to lead the way. But nearing the bottom step he found his breath coming faster and the sweat breaking on his brow. When he made himself continue an electric tremor invaded him, starting at his knees and working up his spine.

Defeated, he leaned one shaking hand against the stonework. "You go. I'll stay down here, tell you when you're in the right place."

It wasn't Nelson's Column but the monument afforded good views across Dimmock, south to the channel, east to the green swell of the cliffs. Brodie circled the parapet slowly.

Ten metres below Daniel shouted, "Left a bit. No - my left. There. Now: what can you see?"

She raised her binoculars, scanning a narrow band up the rising town. "A couple of rows of houses, then there's a red-brick building. In Pound Street, maybe? The top floor might have the right sort of view. I think the houses are too low. And beyond the red-brick building you're getting a long way for photography. I know it was a bad picture but I doubt it was taken from half a mile away."

Daniel nodded. "So let's find the red-brick building."

Someone followed them back to the car.

It could have been a coincidence. It wasn't a very big park. There were only four paths radiating from the monument, everyone crossing it would use one of them. The man in the fawn tweed jacket could have been anyone using the park as a short-cut. Brodie gave him a long hard look, enough to be sure that she'd know him if she saw him again, then got into the car.

The man in the tweed jacket crossed the road to a café. Brodie vented a tiny sigh of relief. Coincidence, after all. She pulled away from the pavement.

Pound Street was two right turns from the park. A red fastback came up behind her as she made the first, was still there after she'd made the second. The red-brick building came up on her left: Brodie drove past at a steady twenty.

Daniel looked at her in surprise. "Wasn't that - ?"

"We have company."

He went to screw round; Brodie grabbed his sleeve. "*Don't* look back. I don't want him to know he's been spotted."

She was thinking fast, trying to work out the quickest route to the police station without leaving the main roads. She took a left turn, then another. The fastback stayed with her.

Then all at once it was gone. She stopped at traffic lights, her heart in her mouth, but the red car didn't stop behind her and when she looked to see where it had got to it was turning into a yard on the right. It hadn't emerged by the time the lights changed and she moved off.

"So he wasn't following us," said Daniel, relief audible in his voice.

"Or he was doing it well."

The police station or Pound Street. She pictured Deacon's expression if she told him she'd been followed through three junctions by a stalker who vanished when she was forced to halt, and immediately Pound Street looked the more attractive option. "We'll drive round for a minute to make sure."

She went on turning at random and saw nothing. Then she made a mistake. There were road-works in Dalton Street: she saw the sign but didn't think quickly enough. The road was blocked, she had to turn round. In doing so she found herself bumper to bumper with a red fastback driven by a man in a fawn tweed jacket.

Dalton Street was a narrow residential road, there were cars parked on both sides. Maintaining a flow of traffic always required the co-operation of other drivers. But the man in the fawn tweed jacket stopped in the middle of the road and got out of his car, striding towards them.

The last time Brodie had felt this helpless was when her husband told her he loved someone else. Her life had crashed in flames and there had been nothing she could do to stop it. This was like that; and again there was nothing she could do. If she reversed the car would drop into a hole, making sitting targets of them. If she drove forwards she'd ruin two perfectly good cars and still not win clear. If this man intended murder he was going to succeed. Her heart raced, her breathing stopped.

The man went to the passenger side, staring at Daniel through the windscreen. He gestured but Brodie kept the window tight shut. He leaned closer, shouted through the glass. "I know who you are."

Daniel moistened his lips. "Yes?"

"You're supposed to be dead!"

Daniel didn't recognise the voice. That didn't necessarily mean he was safe. "You're mistaken."

"I *told* people you were dead!" insisted the man. "Detective Inspector Deacon told me you were found dead in a skip."

Brodie didn't know what the hell was going on, who he was, but he didn't seem to purpose murder. She lowered her window a crack, as much to draw him away from Daniel as because she wanted to talk to him. "You know Inspector Deacon?"

"Of course I know him," snapped the man. "I'm Tom Sessions, I work for *The Sentinel*. I wrote the front page lead for our Tuesday edition. 'Local teacher murdered: body dumped in skip'."

"Ah," breathed Daniel. So he wasn't going to die; or not now. Still the situation was a tricky one. Denial wouldn't work. He wasn't sure what would. "Reports of my death were greatly exaggerated?"

Sessions looked as if he'd quite like to put that right, as if it might be more fun than running a correction. "What happened?"

"I can't tell you," said Daniel.

"Well, *someone's* going to tell me," snapped Sessions. "I put my name to a lie. That's not something I make a habit of. If I don't hear a damn good reason in the next thirty seconds, you're going to be front page news again." He straightened up. "And will you get out of the damn car? You're giving me back-ache."

Slowly, Daniel did as he was told. He straightened with a wince that was not lost on the reporter. "When you wrote that story, actually it was only a slight exaggeration. It could have been true by the time *The Sentinel* hit the streets. Someone tried to kill me. I don't know who and I don't know why. Inspector Deacon thought they'd try again if they knew they'd failed. I'm sorry he lied to you. He was trying to protect me."

Tom Sessions was still breathing heavily. But he was an intelligent man: his eyes took in the pallor of Daniel's skin, the marks still visible on his face, the way he moved. He didn't like being used but nor did he want to put anyone in danger.

Brodie saw him vacillate and stepped swiftly into the breach. "I know you want to put the record straight. But if you do, among all the people who ought to know they were misinformed are a handful who mustn't. Who must be prevented at all costs from knowing. If they find out he's still alive, they'll come back and they'll kill him.

"You want to know what happened to him? I'll show you what happened." She'd sidled between the bonnets of the two cars while Daniel was speaking, now she was at his side. Before either man could guess what she intended she reached for a handful of Daniel's sweater and tugged, baring his chest with its burden of hurts. The worst were covered by dressings, the rest in plain view.

The reporter's jaw dropped. But it wasn't the horror in his eyes that stabbed at Brodie's heart, it was the pain in Daniel's. "I'm sorry," she muttered, letting go, not looking at him.

Daniel said nothing, quietly straightened his clothes. He didn't need to yell at her to underline the extent of her trespass: Brodie knew. For the same good reasons she'd done what Deacon had done: used his abused body to get what she wanted. At least Deacon only did it while he was unconscious.

Sessions licked his lips. He was a man in his mid-thirties, he could have been working in London for ten years if he hadn't decided this was more important: writing for a small town newspaper where fifty thousand readers believed what he said. He slumped down on the bonnet of his car. "And you don't know why?"

"No," said Daniel.

"And Deacon doesn't."

"No."

"But he does know you're alive."

"Yes. He's the reason I'm alive. Him and you."

Sessions flicked him a worried look. "You're going to ask me to keep this quiet, aren't you?"

Daniel smiled. "No."

Brodie had no such scruples. "Well I am. Listen, Mr Sessions, I know you feel used. I was used too. You were used to protect him - I was used to hurt him. Believe me, it isn't the same thing."

"How long?" asked the reporter. "How long am I supposed to pretend I still believe what I wrote?"

Brodie shrugged. "Ideally, until these people are behind bars. But that may not happen. How about, until someone else notices?"

Sessions went on regarding her, without much affection. Finally he nodded. "All right. I don't want anyone's life on my conscience. But it's my career if this blows up in my face.

"This is the best I can do. I didn't see you in the park and I didn't follow you here so I have no idea that Daniel Hood is still alive. If someone else sees you, or brings their suspicions to my editor, I'll do what I'm paid for - I'll write the truth. I won't be able to keep your secret then."

"I understand," said Daniel. "It's as much as I could ask."

It wasn't as much as Brodie could have asked, but she recognised it as all she was going to get. She nodded. "Thanks. If the shit hits the fan I'll make sure people know why you helped us."

"If the shit hits the fan," said Sessions grimly, "you'll have your work cut out keeping your head above it."

Chapter 10

When the red fastback had gone, clearing the way, still Brodie looked at the road ahead. The alternative was looking at Daniel. "I'll take you home - my home - then I'll pick up some things from your place. Clothes, shaving gear - anything else?"

Daniel said, "What about Pound Street?" His voice was thin and level.

It could have been worse. He could have asked her to explain why shocking Sessions and humiliating him had seemed like a good idea.

"This has to stop," she said unsteadily, "right now. That man's put his career on the line to keep you safe. Deacon did the same. You can't go swanning around town waiting for someone else to recognise you."

He thought about that. Obligation was something he took seriously. "If I'm spotted," he said slowly, "I'll call Sessions so he can break the story before anyone else does."

"Fine," gritted Brodie. "Unless the person who spots you is the one who wants you dead."

"We've been through this," Daniel said quietly.

"We haven't resolved it, though."

"I'm not going to hide," he said, with the stubbornness of a man drawing a line in sand.

"Why not?" she demanded. "What's so wrong with looking after yourself? Deacon lied for you; from now on that reporter's going to be lying for you; why do you have to go round flaunting the truth?"

Daniel's composure cracked, and his voice with it. "You really don't understand, do you? You keep saying you understand, but you don't at all. You think I'm trying to prove a point - to them, to you, to myself. I'm not. I'm trying to keep my life together. I'm this close" - she couldn't see through the gap between his fingers - "to losing it. I want to stick my head under the blankets and never come out again. I want to shut the door, and lock it, and put the key in a box and lock that too. I'm afraid every moment I'm awake; and when I sleep the fear turns into things hunting me. Eating me."

Brodie stared at him in stunned compassion. "I had no idea! You seemed to be getting over it so well."

"Of course you hadn't," he panted. "Every ounce of courage I have left - and there wasn't that much to start with, there was even less by the time they'd finished with me - has gone into keeping up the pretence. I thought, I still think, you can cope with more than you think by pretending to be more than you are. First you convince other people, then you convince yourself. It starts by being an act, ends up being the truth.

"But I can't keep fighting this same damn battle! I can't keep persuading you that this is what I want to do, what I have to do, only for something to happen half a mile down the road that makes you want to argue it out all over again. I'm too tired. Brodie, either help me or let me get on with it alone. I can't keep having this same conversation."

She didn't know what to say. He was breaking her heart. It wasn't that she'd forgotten what he'd been through, more that it had suited her to believe what he'd wanted her to believe. The swifter his recovery, the less reason she had to punish herself. But someone with less to lose would have known it was - no, not a pretence, there was nothing phony about the courage it took, but a screen, a shield. Partly to protect his wounds, but mostly so that the blood didn't show.

She folded her hands over her mouth and thought carefully about what she said next. "Since before I knew you I've been doing things that hurt you. It wasn't from malice, it wasn't deliberate, but that's how it worked out. And I'm still doing it, and I didn't even know. I was trying to look after you. I didn't mean to drop mountains in your way."

Daniel flicked her a tiny smile and nodded. "I know."

"Saying I'm sorry doesn't begin to cover it. I am, I'm desperately sorry for all the bad decisions I've made, but it doesn't change a thing. Tell me what you want and I'll try to remember I promised not to argue."

"I want to go to Pound Street. To look at the red-brick building. Depending on what it is, I may want to go inside."

"You don't suppose whoever's behind this is still there?" Her instincts screamed, I'm not taking you within half a mile! Sheer force of will kept her from saying it aloud.

"No. They might have been, once, but not now. Whatever the building is, I think it's a dead end and no one there will know about me or Sophie or a video-camera. In a way, that's what I'm hoping. That there'll be no leads left to follow. That any search I can make will end there. If it does, I can walk away knowing that I tried, that I wasn't too scared to try. If it ends in Pound Street, I may be as relieved as you."

Brodie sniffed. "Don't count on it." She hesitated a moment, wondering whether she dared make another request. "All right. We're going to Pound Street, and depending on what the red-brick building is we're going inside. You have to do it for your peace of mind. Will you do something for my peace of mind?"

He looked wary. "What?"

Brodie rummaged in the back of the car, came up with a bobble hat. "Put that on. If it makes you look like an anorak, so much the better. And take your glasses off."

Daniel pulled on the hat, and covering his bright hair made him instantly less recognisable. But he drew the line at removing his glasses. "I might as well not go for all I'd be able to see."

As she drove, Daniel looked at himself in the mirror. He sighed at what it showed. "I *am* an anorak," he said mournfully. "Even without the bobble hat. I teach maths in a comprehensive school and make my own telescopes. That's a textbook definition of anorakdom."

* * *

The red-brick building in Pound Street was also a school. A sign on the gates announced it as St Agnes's Preparatory School. It was

Saturday morning so there were no classes, but twenty little girls on bicycles were solemnly negotiating obstacles chalked on the asphalt playground. A banner tied to the railings announced: "Cycling Proficiency Training Day".

Brodie and Daniel exchanged a puzzled glance. *"Janet And John Hire A Contract Killer?"* ventured Brodie.

Daniel snorted a little chuckle. "I think we've come to the wrong place."

But Brodie was peering at the wall above the school entrance. "Maybe not. What's that?"

"Security camera," said Daniel. "Closed Circuit TV. So?"

"And CCTV uses - ?"

"Video." Daniel stared at her. "You think ... ?"

"I don't know," said Brodie quickly. "But look where it's pointing. Back at the park." She turned in her seat, looking over her shoulder. "There are gaps between the houses. If the top of the monument's visible through one of them ... "

She didn't finish the sentence. She didn't need to.

Daniel's lips pursed as he confronted the real question. "But - *why*? What would someone at an upper-crust primary school want with me?"

"They wanted to know about Sophie."

"But I don't know who Sophie is!"

"Maybe someone in there does."

They sat in silence for what seemed like a long time.

Brodie was thinking that it wasn't possible, it couldn't be that easy: it couldn't be that forty minutes' intelligent application had achieved more than Detective Inspector Deacon with all his resources had in a week. It was a coincidence. Security cameras were springing up everywhere, even Dimmock wasn't immune to progress. Brodie thought that if St Agnes's head teacher was in her office, using the quiet of a Saturday morning to catch up on her paperwork, and Brodie asked about the CCTV, her answers would be entirely unhelpful. But she thought she had to ask anyway.

And then she was going to have to come back and tell Daniel, and watch the disappointment pool in his eyes. He claimed he could let it go now, be satisfied that he'd done his best; but Brodie knew it wouldn't be easy. She was going to take his last hope of understanding what happened to him and dash it in his face.

Daniel was thinking there were two possibilities. One was that it *was* a coincidence, the video had been taken from somewhere along the line-of-sight between St Agnes's and the monument, one of the intervening houses, even a carefully parked car, and this was where the trail ended.

The other was that the people who'd reduced him to a quivering, whimpering knot of abused humanity and then shot him were just metres away behind a red-brick wall. If they were, the answers were there too: who they were, who Sophie was, who they thought he was, why they acted as they did. His limbs turned to jelly. He didn't think he could get out of the car and take one step towards the wrought-iron gates.

Minutes passed. One of the little girls completed her run successfully, another fell off and cried.

Finally Brodie cleared her throat. "Sitting here isn't getting us anywhere. Do we go in or not?"

Daniel said nothing. When she looked at him he was staring straight ahead, his lip caught between his teeth. So he'd finally run out of courage. With everything he'd pushed himself to do, this was going to defeat him.

She'd promised to help. She wouldn't fail him now. She said quietly, "I'll see if I can find the principal. If there's nothing to learn here there's no point staying."

Daniel said softly, "I can't."

"I know. Stay here: if I'm not back in half an hour, call Inspector Deacon."

"If it's them in there ... "

"It won't be. It's a school. We've come to the wrong place."

"Then why go inside?"

"I suppose, because there's always the outside chance. I ought to make sure."

"Fifteen," said Daniel.

"What?"

"I'm not waiting half an hour while they could be hurting you. Be back in fifteen minutes."

* * *

The children barely spared her a glance as Brodie crossed the playground and let herself into the school. A minute's wandering round and she found the door with "Principal: Miss Winifred Scotney" on it. She rapped with her knuckle and a faintly surprised voice called, "Come in."

Brodie gave her name and her most winning smile. "I don't know if you'll be able to help me, Miss Scotney, but I see you have a closed-circuit TV camera above the door. I need to know what the field of view is."

Miss Scotney smiled too, not so winningly. She was a woman of about fifty, as tall as Brodie and twice as far round, a headmistress in the old mould. Formidable was the word that sprang to mind. "And why do you need to know that, Mrs Farrell?"

She could lie, she could tell the truth, she could tell part of the truth. The whole truth belonged to Daniel; and while there was any possibility that St Agnes's was involved she wouldn't risk betraying him to his enemies again. And Miss Scotney looked as if she habitually flogged liars during milk-break.

"I was given a photograph and asked to find someone. That's what I do: I find things. But my client lied to me and now I'm looking for her. The picture might have been taken by your security camera. I wondered if you knew anything about it."

So far as she could judge Miss Scotney was genuinely astonished. "What client? You're not accusing me ... ?"

Brodie shook her head. "Of course not. I met her, I'll know her again if I can find her. I just need to know if the picture could have been taken by your camera. And what happens to the tapes."

On careful consideration Miss Scotney saw no reason not to answer. "The camera is primarily a deterrent. I glance at the monitor occasionally, but mostly to keep an eye on what the children are up to. Most tapes are reused without ever being played."

Brodie sighed, torn between disappointment and relief. She'd have left then, except that she felt the burden of Daniel's hopes. "There's been nothing - unusual - going on here?"

"Like what, for heaven's sake?"

"I really don't know."

Miss Scotney was a busy woman working on what was supposed to be her day off, and her supply of patience was running low. "Mrs Farrell, if you don't know the questions, how am I supposed to know the answers?"

Brodie gave an apologetic shrug. "I'm scraping the bottom of the barrel. Something happened to the man in the photograph, and I'm trying to find out who's to blame. Even if the picture didn't come off your tape, it's possible your camera saw something that would help explain matters."

"In my playground?"

"In the park."

Miss Scotney shook her head crisply. "We can't see the park from here. The camera shows the playground and the street outside. It's there for the children's protection."

"Not even the top of the monument? I thought maybe, between the houses ... " Brodie tailed off lamely.

The principal of St Agnes's frowned. "The monument? I suppose it's possible. I've never thought to look." She reached a strong hand towards the monitor on her desk and the playground emerged from electronic snow.

Brodie leaned forward, brows knit, getting her bearings. Ignoring the cyclists she peered into the V-shaped gaps between the roofs.

And there it was. Distant but quite distinct: the crenelated parapet atop the monument. If someone had been standing now where Daniel Hood had stood ten days ago, looking the way he'd been looking, Brodie would have got the same view of him as the picture showed of Daniel.

It was a long shot, enlarging it to provide a recognisable image

104

must have taken skill and expensive equipment. But whoever did this wasn't pressed for money.

Brodie grew aware that Miss Scotney was eying her oddly and started breathing again. "You said you reuse the videos?"

"Mostly they just show the children playing. When you've seen one game of hop-scotch you've seen them all."

"I think my picture was taken a week last Wednesday, a little after one. Is there any chance that you've still got the tape? Or that maybe someone else got hold of it?"

"They're not the Crown Jewels, I don't keep them under lock and key. But why would anyone steal them? Who, anyway? - one of the children?"

"I doubt it."

More in sorrow than anger the principal said, "Mrs Farrell, if you want me to help you're going to have to be a little more forthcoming."

But there was nothing more Brodie could say; and anyway, she thought she'd got all she was going to. She didn't believe Winifred Scotney was part of any conspiracy. The picture of Daniel Hood might or might not have come from St Agnes's CCTV, but even if it did the most casual thief could have taken the tape and it would never have been missed. If the trail came through here, here was where it ended.

Brodie stood up. "I'm wasting your time. I'm sorry. Thank you for seeing me."

But Miss Scotney was still thinking, her broad brow corrugated. "Wednesday lunchtime, did you say? Ten days ago?"

Brodie's blood quickened. "Between one and one-fifteen. Why?"

"There's just a possibility we kept that tape." She opened the drawers of her desk, one after another, without success. "Now, what did I do with it?"

"You didn't recycle it?"

"No. At least, not at once. I put it on one side while we sorted out what was happening."

"What was?"

Miss Scotney gave a chuckle without much mirth in it. "One of the parents was trying to give me heart-failure. Oh, he didn't mean to - he said he'd sent a message but I didn't get it. I can't make them understand that the children are only theirs during out-of-school hours: nine to three-thirty they're my responsibility." She sighed. "This job would be a sinecure if all the children were orphans."

Brodie sympathised, but this wasn't what she was interested in. "So you did keep the tape?"

"For one dreadful moment I thought the police would need it. Then I managed to get the child's father on the phone and it turned out there'd been a misunderstanding. The family were going on holiday, the chauffeur had picked her up. The father thought I'd been informed. But I wouldn't have forgotten. It's something we have to be terribly careful about. You do with any children, but these in particular. We have some wealthy families, abduction is always a possibility."

Momentarily, irritation distracted Brodie. "It's worse when rich kids get abducted?"

"No," said Miss Scotney. "But it is more likely."

Brodie dipped her head in apology. "But in fact the child was safe?"

"Quite safe - she was with her father when I phoned. They're in the Caribbean for a month."

Envy stabbed momentarily. Brodie wouldn't have minded a month in the Caribbean. She'd have settled for a fortnight in Wigan if it had started a fortnight ago. "So you still have the tape."

"Wait a minute," said the principal, remembering. "No ... but I know who has. Mr Ibbotsen asked if he could have it. I suppose it's a family joke by now - 'This is Sophie being abducted.' But it felt deadly serious at the time. If he hadn't answered his phone I was calling the police." Her brow furrowed again. "Mrs Farrell? Are you all right?"

Brodie's face was as stiff and grey as concrete. She genuinely hadn't seen this coming. Her eyes stretched until they watered. "Sophie?"

Chapter 11

It had been more than fifteen minutes. Daniel hadn't called the police, but as Brodie hurried out of St Agnes's she met him coming in. No pupil ever entered a school more reluctantly: every step seemed to cost him blood. But he was coming.

She hadn't time to appreciate his courage. She swung him round and towed him with her. "Back to the car," she said tersely. "We have to talk."

Brodie marshalled her thoughts as she was getting her breath back. "All right," she said, gripping the steering wheel as if it might try to get away. "There was an incident here. A week last Wednesday, during the lunch break. A little girl went missing and when the staff checked the CCTV tape it showed her being led away by someone they didn't know. Since that's when you were watching your sunspots, and the camera picks up the top of the monument, you would have been on the same tape."

Daniel cast Brodie a fugitive glance. He knew what was coming "Did you get her name?"

"Sophie Ibbotsen. And she hasn't been in school since. The principal thinks she's on a Caribbean cruise."

"Sophie." His voice was barely a whisper. "They were looking for a child. They thought I'd abducted a child?" His eyes were hollow, desolate.

Brodie nodded sombrely. "They treated you like an animal because they thought you were one."

"The family? These - Ibbotsens?" He was having trouble putting the words together. "It was them?"

"It figures. They have the tape of the incident. When the stills were blown up they showed you with a telescope looking towards the school. The Ibbotsens thought you were watching the kidnap. Maybe they thought you were supervising it."

Almost, he didn't want to believe it. He'd been just about ready to let it go, to accept that he would never know who or why. Now he had a name and a reason, and the refuge of ignorance would be forever denied him. Brodie had warned him about this. If we search for them, she'd said, we just might find them. But he hadn't realised what it would mean.

He forced a shaky laugh. "Do I *look* like a master criminal?"

Brodie had worked for a solicitor for seven years, she knew that criminals come in all shapes and sizes. But still ... "It wasn't a very good picture."

Another thought struck Daniel, rocking him. "And Deacon? What did he take me for? He hammered questions at me until my head was ready to explode, and all the time he *knew*! He knew what it was about so he knew who'd done it. My God! - they bought him off?"

Brodie slowly shook her head. "I don't think so. I don't think he knows anything about it."

"A child abduction? He must know. I gave him her name: he must have made the connection."

"Think about it. He's only going to know if somebody tells him, yes? The school didn't tell him - they were assured that the child was safe with her family. And if her father lied to them, why would he tell the police? I don't think Inspector Deacon knows that one of Dimmock's leading families is being blackmailed for the return of an abducted child."

"Then we have to tell him!"

"Perhaps." Brodie was still trying to get the facts into some sort of order. "Or maybe not. Hold on a minute, let's think this through. Why hasn't Ibbotsen reported this? - because the blackmailers threatened to kill Sophie if he did. He doesn't want the police involved. He wants to get the money together and get his little girl back unharmed. If we tell Deacon, we could put her life at risk."

To his eternal credit, Daniel managed not to say what he was thinking. That these people had forfeited any right they might have had to his sympathy. That their agony was the only currency capable of redeeming his. His voice was low but his own again. "This happened ten days ago, it must be over by now. For good or ill, it must be finished."

"No," said Brodie with certainty. "If they'd paid up and got her back, Sophie'd be back at school. And if they'd killed her Deacon would be running a murder hunt and the time for secrets would be past. It's still going on."

Daniel's eyes creased in puzzlement. "Do blackmailers do that? Hold onto people for weeks while their families wonder if they're worth the money?"

Brodie flicked him a troubled smile. "I'm not the national expert on blackmail, you know. But yes, I think it always takes time. Having money isn't the same as having it on tap. If you want your target to be discreet, you have to wait while he liquidises some assets. Then you have to work out a mechanism for the exchange."

"How old is this little girl?"

"Five." Brodie had wondered that too.

"A five-year-old child's been in the hands of her kidnappers for ten days, and we're the only ones who know?"

Brodie shuddered. "I think so."

"Well ... if we're not going to the police, what *are* we going to do?"

She swivelled in her seat to look straight at him. "Daniel, this isn't my decision. It's yours. Whatever his reasons, however dreadful his dilemma, Ibbotsen nearly killed you. You don't have to forgive that. You don't have to excuse it. Forget what I just said: we can take what we know to Inspector Deacon and let him sort it out. That'll get him off your back. He may even consider it recompense for my stupidity.

"And maybe it's the best thing for Sophie. If this has gone on for ten days it may mean the family can't sort it - even with their money, even with the kind of help they can buy. It may be the best thing all round. It may be the only way it can be brought to an end."

Daniel Hood was by no means recovered from his ordeal. His body was rigid in the seat beside her, the parchment skin tight over the bones of his face, his eyes the colour of bruises. Even so, Brodie realised with some surprise, he was not at the end of his resources. Beneath the fragility, deep down where the corrosion of fear and pain and humiliation had never entirely penetrated, his soul was entire. Around its glowing ember was drawn a tight knot of resolution.

"That isn't what I want," he said in his teeth.

"I understand," said Brodie softly. "You want him to pay for what he did. So we go to Deacon. There's nothing for your conscience to struggle with. If he intervenes it's because he judges it best; if he wants to hold back until Sophie is either safe or beyond help, he can do that. He's the professional. Put it in his hands and leave it there."

But she'd misunderstood, again. Daniel shook his head fitfully, groping for the words. "I mean, it's not vengeance I want. Oh, in a way it is - it's only human, isn't it, someone hurts you, you want to hurt them back. But ...

"Look, I'm a teacher, yes? I teach maths, and science if pushed, but mostly what we teach - what we all teach - is living. We take children and try to turn them into people capable of behaving well in a difficult world. We call it growing up; but some kids have it at ten, some don't get it till they're twenty and some never get it. They spend their whole lives relating to other people as they did when they were eight: hit me and I'll hit you back, steal my apple and I'll steal your satchel. Make me cry and I'll tell my mum.

"I think - I hope - I've learned something since I was ten. I think I've grown beyond that. I hope I can stand back, even from this, and make decisions that I'll be able to defend after the scars have faded. If a little girl died because I wanted to punish her father for hurting me ... Brodie, how could I live with that? I couldn't go into a classroom again. I couldn't presume to tell anyone how to behave if I valued my revenge above a little girl's life."

Brodie detached her hands from the steering-wheel and prayer-folded them before her, breathing his name through the apse they made. "Daniel ... you're a good man. A gentle man. You're the last man in the world who should find himself in this position. Someone who thought with his gut would be on the phone to Deacon right now, because that's the visceral response. Someone who thought with his head would do the same because it's the intelligent thing to do.

"But you think with your heart. You try to do the right thing. You don't hide behind the law, or practicality, or the frailty of human nature - you strive to do what's right. And you'll get hurt every time."

"You think I'm wrong?"

Brodie shook her head. "No, I think you're right. I'm just afraid that, if you won't consider your own needs, no one's going to."

She started the car. Clearly they weren't going to the police station, at least not yet. She headed for home where they could discuss their next move in comfort.

"Ibbotsen," Daniel said again as she drove. "You know the family?"

"Well - of them. I don't move in their social circle. They're in shipping: everything from coasters to cruise liners. Serious money. Though Lance Ibbotsen's supposed to have started as an apprentice on a Cape Horner."

Daniel's eyebrows rocketed. "Sailing ships? How old is he?"

"About seventy, I think. It may be apocryphal but that's the story."

"This isn't Sophie's father we're talking about then."

"No, grandfather. The father would be his son David."

"They live in Dimmock?"

"The big house with white columns up on the Firestone Cliffs. *Chandlers* - you can see it from your loft. It's worth as much as the rest of the town put together." Brodie glanced at him. "I can't believe you haven't heard of them. It's like living in London and not knowing about the Queen."

Daniel shrugged apologetically. "I haven't been here long. I'd noticed the house but I never heard who lived there. I never expected to have any dealings with them." He thought about that, then said the word again, softly. "Dealings."

She drove him to the netting sheds to collect some clothes. From the shore they had a panoramic view of *Chandlers* up on the hill.

Daniel couldn't take his eyes off it. "Do you suppose that's - where - ?"

Brodie bit her lip. "I don't know. I don't think it would do you any good *to* know."

Still his gaze was held by the house with the white columns, a mile away across the bay. "Maybe we've got this wrong."

"What makes you think so?"

111

"I don't know. Do decent people behave like that?"

"No. But sometimes rich ones do." She glanced covertly at him. "It must be a pretty weird feeling, knowing who it was at last."

"It is. I thought, if I knew what happened I could draw some sort of a line under it. But it's not that simple. Now I know who was responsible I have to make a decision, even if the decision is to do nothing. It was easier when there was nothing I could do." He gave a pale smile. "And that's a textbook definition of moral cowardice."

"No, it's just you expecting too much of yourself," said Brodie. "Listen, we can talk this through when we get home. You don't have to decide anything here and now. Collect what you need and let's get back. Oh." She glanced up at the loft. "Can you? Or do you want me to?"

"No," he said quickly. "No, I'm fine. I won't be five minutes." He climbed the iron stairs carefully but didn't hesitate at the top.

"There's no rush," Brodie called after him. "While we're here I'll stick my head into the office. Pick up the post, see if there are any messages. I'll leave the car here in case you're finished first. Play the radio if you get bored."

The post was mostly bills but there were messages on the machine. One offered her a job if she could return the call before midday. It sounded a good job so she called.

The client was Arthur Burton, managing director of a family-owned cider bottling plant in Somerset. An extraordinary general meeting had been called for Wednesday morning to consider merging with a big multi-national. He was trying to contact his cousin whose shares, as the numbers currently added up, gave her the casting vote.

Brodie stared at the telephone. "The meeting's on Wednesday? And you call me on Saturday?"

Mr Burton sounded rueful, but mostly he sounded worried. "We thought we had it wrapped up. More of the family wanted to keep the business independent than wanted to cash it in. But now my uncle Edwin's had a stroke and it's thrown the whole deal back into the melting pot. Yesterday I didn't need Cora's votes; today I do."

"And she lives in Dimmock?"

"I don't think so; not any more."

Brodie was confused. "Then why ... ?"

"Her last known address was in Dimmock. She moves around a bit. She's a painter, she's always lived like that - taking short-term lets and moving on after six or nine months. Eight months ago she took a cottage on the Bramwell estate, but when I called last night there was a new tenant and neither he nor the estate office had a forwarding address for Cora. I'm not worried about her, we'll hear from her in a week or so with her new address - but by then it could be too late to save the firm. I have to find her quickly, and I don't know how to but I'm hoping you do."

Brodie's mind raced. Any other time she'd have jumped at the job, set a price reflecting the value of the company and had cousin Cora found by close of play tonight. But today Daniel needed her services even more than Arthur Burton.

Perhaps he didn't need her every minute of the next three days.

"All right, Mr Burton," she said, "I'll need two hundred pounds up front, and another eighteen hundred at noon on Tuesday if I've found your cousin by then. Whether she votes with you or not."

He didn't question the price, which made Brodie suspect she'd pitched it too low. Too late now. It still wasn't bad for a few hours' work. "Done," said Arthur Burton.

Brodie took all the details he could give her. Mindful that Daniel would be waiting, she didn't start phoning round there and then but put the notes in her handbag, meaning to run the search from home. She'd already been longer than she'd said. Still, two thousand pounds was two thousand pounds. She locked up the office and hurried back to the shore.

When she reached the car the radio was playing, there was a bag on the back seat, but Daniel was gone.

Chapter 12

The shock caught Brodie under her ribs like a boot. She found herself looking again, as if she might have missed him. But he wasn't there, and only the radio still softly playing and the bobble hat on the floor by his seat said he ever had been. Daniel Hood had come into her life without warning, filled it for a week, and now it seemed he'd vanished the same way.

Her first instinct was to call Deacon and tell him that the people who'd tried to kill Daniel once had found him again, and only taken him somewhere quieter to complete the task. At least she could give him a name now. Whether he could act quickly enough to prevent a tragedy was another matter.

Half way through dialling another thought came. Daniel had packed what he wanted and brought it down to the car. Could he have remembered something else then and returned to the flat, and be there still? - having lost track of the time, perhaps, or maybe curled in a corner somewhere, overwhelmed by the same storm of emotions that drove him onto the shore the previous day. Brodie hurried up the steps, her feet ringing on iron. But the door was locked and there was no answer to her urgent knock.

As she turned at the top of the steps, her mind swamped with grief and fear, the white house on the cliffs caught her eye. She'd always thought it a handsome house; now it seemed to squat there like an albino toad, watching her in return, the columned portico sketching a half-smile.

If David Ibbotsen had found Daniel, that house was the last place she should go.

But, actually, had Sophie's father any further interest in him? He must know now that he'd made a mistake, that Daniel wasn't involved. Even if he believed the man could have kept his silence through what was done to him, even if he remained unconvinced by the newspaper reports, the kidnappers must have been in touch in the intervening week. Didn't he think it odd that they never mentioned their missing colleague?

All Ibbotsen had to fear from Daniel was the possibility that one day they'd meet, or Daniel would see a photograph, and he'd recognise his tormentor. But he was blindfold most of the time, and it wasn't Ibbotsen but his hired man asking the questions. Snatching Daniel from a car in the street was surely riskier than doing nothing.

So maybe, thought Brodie, Daniel wasn't snatched. Maybe he was on business of his own. She raised her eyes once more to the brooding presence on the cliffs.

He couldn't be so stupid! Even if he was safe on the street, going up to *Chandlers*, alone, was entirely a different matter. In view of the stakes, knowing his earlier error would not stop Ibbotsen from dealing with him the simplest, most direct way. He was not a man to let common decency stand between him and his own best interests.

Brodie checked her watch, doing swift calculations. Thirty minutes since she'd left Daniel, enough time for him to walk up to *Chandlers*. At least, it would have been a fortnight ago. But Daniel only left hospital yesterday, getting from the car to the monument had drained him: a walk he might normally do in half an hour would be entirely beyond him at present. He might have found a taxi, or he might have ground to a halt within a few hundred metres. It was too soon to give him up for lost. Brodie threw her car into the traffic, ignoring the honks of protest around her.

Despite its name, Shore Road made no attempt to cling to the chalk bluff of the Firestone Cliffs, cutting inland instead. The handful of properties on top of the cliff were served by a private avenue surfaced with pale gravel. The houses sat in expansive grounds, growing grander as they climbed towards the cliff. *Chandlers* was the last house: a hundred metres of the road was its own personal driveway, guarded by iron gates.

They were closed. Brodie stopped the car. Her heart leaden, she reached for her phone.

In doing so she almost missed him. He'd got this far but no further. He was sitting on the verge, his back to someone's brick wall, his arms around his knees and his face buried. A stone eagle atop a gatepost was sneering down its beak at him.

He didn't look up, even at the sound of the car or her quick footsteps. She couldn't tell if weariness had beaten him, or pain or fear, or if he'd suffered some new harm. She dropped to her knees beside him. "Daniel? Daniel, speak to me!"

He lifted his yellow head and regarded her myopically. His glasses were on the grass beside him. "Brodie? What are you doing here?" He sounded tired, nothing more.

Fear began to wane, anger to wax. "I'm here to save your stupid neck, you stupid man!" she raged. "Whatever did you think you were *doing*? If Inspector Deacon knew about this he'd have you committed. Doctors would be lining up to section you."

He put the glasses on but avoided her gaze. "I couldn't do it," he murmured. "Someone in a van gave me a lift to the end of the avenue, all I had to do was walk out to the house. Getting this far took me forever. I couldn't get any further."

At the disappointment in his voice, the slump of his shoulders, Brodie's anger dissolved. "You're not ready for route-marches yet."

It was an adequate explanation. But Daniel Hood had the kind of reverence for the truth that the Holy Inquisition had for Christianity: it didn't have to matter if it hurt. He shook his head. "That wasn't it. I was afraid to go on. Afraid of him. David Ibbotsen." There was an audible tremor in the words.

"This surprises you?" Brodie asked softly. "Daniel, the man almost killed you. Of course you're afraid of him. *I'm* afraid of him. We need to get away from here."

She offered her hand but he didn't take it. He looked from her to the gates and back. There was regret in his voice. "I didn't want to involve you in this."

"You didn't. Ibbotsen did; and I let him. An error of judgement involved me in this. Let's not talk about it here. Get in the car and we'll go home."

"I wanted to see him," said Daniel. "To talk to him. He isn't a monster, he's a man. A man who was as scared and confused as I was, and maybe hurting as much."

116

"What were you going to do? Forgive him?" Astonishment made Brodie say it as if it were the height of absurdity.

"Maybe. I don't know. I thought I'd know when I met him." He looked again at the gates. If anything they seemed to be receding.

"Daniel, he's not interested in your forgiveness, only your silence. If you go in there you won't come out."

"So I should pretend none of this ever happened? That I don't know what it was about or who was responsible? I can't put the genie back in the bottle, Brodie! It's too late to walk away: the only way now is through. I don't want to be afraid of this man for the rest of my life."

"Then let Deacon deal with it. He's a desperate man, Daniel, and a vicious one. You *know* what he's prepared to do to get his daughter back."

"I'm not a threat to her."

"You're a threat to him! Have you seen what lies on the other side of that house? A hundred metre cliff. It's a garbage shoot to oblivion."

"He has no reason to hurt me now."

"Ten years' imprisonment is a pretty good reason!"

For someone who'd promised not to argue with him any more she was close to persuading him. She saw doubt in his eyes as he looked again at the wrought iron gates. He knew he wasn't walking through them. He couldn't win the internal conflict: his body refused to do what his heart asked of it. In another minute she'd have got him to his feet and taken him home.

Instead he said, "Ah," and his voice was paper-thin.

Brodie followed his gaze. It was too late. It had taken too long to find him, and they'd spent too long sitting on the verge discussing it. A car had come down from the house and the gates opened to let it through.

It stopped beside them and a man got out. A man too old to be Sophie's father, probably too old to be the family's chauffeur even if they didn't mind him wearing a cardigan and a glacial stare. A man just about old enough to have sailed on the last of the Cape Horners. Brodie stood up. "We took a wrong turn. We were just leaving."

Lance Ibbotsen ignored her. His blue diamond gaze was fixed on the white face of Daniel Hood. "My God."

The collision of their eyes was silent but shook the air nevertheless. Daniel swallowed, forced out the words. "I believe we've met."

* * *

The stunned silence lasted perhaps ten seconds, which is a long time with so much to be said and three people saying none of it. Nor was it merely an absence of speech. The cold breeze fell still; the traffic seemed to pause on the busy main road; if Daniel had taken a measurement now he might have found that the sun itself hesitated in its orbit for those ten pregnant seconds.

Ibbotsen broke the spell. Hands that suggested he had been, in his prime, a much bigger man fisted in Daniel's clothes and hauled him to his feet as if he were a child. Hands that have worked acres of heavy canvas, stiff with spray, and mastered miles of cordage rough with salt never lose the habit of strength. Madness flared in the old man's eyes.

"I knew it!" he hissed in Daniel's face. "The others thought it was a mistake, but I knew who you were. I knew you could help if we just made it hard enough for you to refuse."

All the fear in Daniel's eyes was not enough to mask the incredulity. "You think you didn't?"

Lance Ibbotsen was too angry to trade words, even bitter ones, with his enemy. He'd believed the man was dead. He'd believed, despite what he'd been told, despite what he'd read in *The Sentinel*, that Daniel Hood had been part of a conspiracy to kidnap his granddaughter for ransom, and that he'd paid for that mistake with pain and death. Now here he was again, demonstrably alive and watching the house. All the rage, the frustration, the fear of the past ten days welled up in him in a moment, and he abandoned words and reacted with force. He struck Daniel across the mouth with the back of his fist, hard enough that he didn't so much stagger back as fly.

The hedge caught him. Disorientated, he twisted in its spiny embrace, seeking something solid to hang on to. But the hedge only

118

shook and bellied, trapping him and offering no support. He couldn't free himself.

Lance Ibbotsen freed him, with another blow that wrenched him out of the hedge and sprawled him full length along the verge. The impetus carried the old man after him, already aiming the toe of a heavy boot at Daniel's jaw.

Overt violence has a paralysing effect on normal people. It had taken Brodie seconds to react, time in which Lance Ibbotsen was committing murder before her eyes. She doubted neither his desire nor his ability to do it.

Sheer determination forced her brain to act, her muscles to respond. She dived for Ibbotsen's head, snatching off her coat. The first thing she did was blind him with it; the second was wrap the sleeve round his throat and tug until he had to abandon his attack on Daniel to deal with the attack on him.

When she had his attention Brodie said fiercely in his ear - or where his ear ought to be under the fabric - "You're wrong, Mr Ibbotsen. You misjudged him, and you misjudged me, and I really don't need any more incentive to rip your frigging head off!" She probably couldn't have done it. But she was in the mood to try.

She felt the tension of his long muscles ease slightly as he stopped fighting her and stood still. Muffled by her warm coat he said, "Mrs Farrell?" If he'd seen her before he hadn't recognised her. She wasn't sure he'd seen anything but Daniel.

"That's right," she said, yanking the sleeve for emphasis. "Now, you know I'm not part of any conspiracy against you. And I'm telling you that Daniel Hood isn't either. And if you don't believe me, perhaps you'll believe Detective Inspector Deacon when he gets here. He's already on his way."

Of course it was a bluff. But in a sense it didn't matter. Even if he thought Deacon was coming, Ibbotsen might decide he had nothing to lose by tearing Daniel limb from limb and enjoy the experience while he could. Though she seemed to have wrested the upper hand for the moment, Brodie wasn't sure she could stop him if he set his heart on it.

"Get this off me," he growled through the coat.

"Oh sure!" snarled Brodie.

"Get it off! I'm not talking to anybody through three layers of wool worsted!"

Brodie thought fast. He no longer sounded like a homicidal maniac. And perhaps it was better to free him than to let him free himself and know for sure he was stronger than her. "Daniel, get in the car. Lock the doors."

Daniel's eyes were still vague from Ibbotsen's fists. But Brodie didn't think concussion was why he made no attempt to get up. He knelt on the grass, softly panting, watching the man and woman frozen in their uncompleted struggle. "Let him go."

"Daniel - !"

"Please. Let him go."

After a moment Brodie shrugged and took her coat back. Raw fabric poked where some of the stitches had given way. It was never designed to be used as a weapon.

Lance Ibbotsen didn't even turn to face his adversary. His eyes were locked on Daniel's. "I don't believe you."

"Fine," spat Brodie. "You tell the police what you think he's done, and I'll tell the police what I think you've done. And he'll walk away, and you won't."

"He kidnapped my granddaughter!"

"No. He didn't."

"He was seen! He was watching through a telescope."

"He's an astronomer. He was making observations."

"In the middle of the *day*?"

"Sunspots," Daniel said quietly.

Ibbotsen went on staring fiercely at him. But there was doubt in it too. "You're saying it was - a coincidence? My granddaughter was abducted from her school, he was watching through a telescope, and it was a coincidence?"

"Yes," said Brodie. "Exactly that."

"Then why didn't you go to the police?" demanded the old man, his body bent like a bow with the desire to get his hands on Daniel again constrained by the knowledge he must not. "Happens a lot, does it? - you go to watch sunspots and see a crime in progress? You used to report them but you got bored? One kidnap's pretty much like another? You're lying. The only people in this whole town who could have seen that and *not* called the police were those involved."

"I don't lie," said Daniel firmly. "And I didn't see anything."

"With a telescope that size? Of course you did!"

Daniel thought for a moment. "You were a seaman, Mr Ibbotsen. You've used binoculars. Can you remember who showed you how to use them?"

Ibbotsen frowned. "As a matter of fact I can."

"What was the first thing he said?"

The old man grinned with no humour whatever. "He said, 'If you see a swastika, run.'"

"Even before that," said Daniel.

Ibbotsen thought. "He said, 'Find yourself a patch of shade.'"

"Exactly. Because if you start tracking something and find the sun you're going to burn your eyes out. Well, my telescope's a lot more powerful than your binoculars. There are only two ways to make solar observations. One is not to look through the telescope at all but to project the image onto a screen. The other's to fit a good sun filter in the eye-piece. It's very dark, and it cuts out so much light that the sun's the *only* thing you can see through it. Everything else is brown fog. My eyes are nothing to write home about, but they're still the only ones I have: I use the thickest filter you can buy. A scuffle in a playground quarter of a mile away? - I wouldn't have seen *The Hindenburg* sail over the park and moor to the monument."

Finally Lance Ibbotsen believed him. Finally he had to acknowledge the truth he'd been avoiding: that he'd made a mistake. A simple mistake, easy to make, understandable in the circumstances. The facts before him had seemed to add up, he simply hadn't considered the possibility of coincidence. Now he had more facts he could see how it had happened: how innocent actions had given the appearance of guilt.

And how, because of that, he'd watched an innocent man suffer two days of agony.

Brodie saw the understanding condense in the sharp blue eyes until it was heavy enough to sink through the man's expression and on down through his heart and stomach. Whatever his reasons, this was not a small thing to him. He knew what he'd done. He'd thought it was justified. Now he knew it was not.

She waited for him to try, however lamely, to apologise. She waited in vain. Ibbotsen's gaze never left Daniel's face, but his next words were addressed to her. "The police are coming?"

Her nostrils flared in disgust. "That's what I said."

"Then there isn't much time. I won't pretend I didn't do what you know I did. But I want you to understand why. And then I want you to do something for me. Will you come up to the house?"

"Do we *look* stupid?" exclaimed Brodie incredulously.

Daniel just said, "We can talk here."

Lance Ibbotsen was too old for sitting on kerbstones. He leaned back against his car and drew a deep breath. "I thought you were dead."

"You had every reason," said Daniel, watching him.

Ibbotsen nodded slowly. He was tall, narrow and angular, with skin salt-tanned to hide. His voice was like gravel. "I don't expect you to care, but I'm glad. What I did: I thought you could return my granddaughter. I thought it was worth your skin and my soul to save her."

"Sophie."

"Sophie," nodded Ibbotsen. The polar eyes that had never filled for Daniel filled at her name.

"Is she safe now? Did you get her back?"

The old man shook his head. "No." Then his brow gathered and he looked from Daniel to Brodie and back. "You *knew*, didn't you? About Sophie being abducted. That's why you're here. *How* did you know?"

"We worked it out," said Brodie. "From the questions you asked Daniel and the photograph you gave me. Neither of us could have found you alone."

"Tell me about Sophie," Daniel insisted quietly. "You haven't made the exchange?"

Ibbotsen shook his head. In his eyes was an ashy despair more plaintive than tears. "I think she's dead."

"Are they still asking for money?" inquired Brodie. The old man nodded. "Then she's alive. They'd kill her rather than be caught with her, but they wouldn't contact you again."

Ibbotsen stared at her. "How do you know?"

"I worked for a solicitor for seven years. He defended a kidnapper once. I read up on the subject. It isn't a spur-of-the-moment crime: people plan meticulously, cover all the contingencies. What they'll do if this happens, what they'll do if that happens. Even when they intend to kill the hostage it's the last thing they do. No one pays out for a dead hostage."

"Is that what happens?" breathed Ibbotsen. "They kill the hostage?"

"Not always. It can depend on how good a witness they'll make. Young children don't remember much, and can't always recount what they do remember. Sophie may well be safe." Against her will Brodie found herself wanting to reassure him.

Daniel said, "You do know, don't you, that I wasn't involved?" The words were considered but his voice shook.

After a moment the old man dipped his head. "I do now. I believed you were involved when we took you. I believed it, absolutely, every minute that you were here. I swear it."

Daniel said nothing.

The old man filled his lungs and squared his shoulders. "I presume the police are coming here to arrest me. I can't blame you for that."

Daniel's voice was low. "You said you wanted me to do something for you. What?"

Brodie interrupted before Ibbotsen could answer. "It doesn't matter what he wants, Daniel. He's no right to ask anything of either of us."

"Maybe not. But I want to know." He looked at the old man, his chin coming up. "I won't lie for you."

Ibbotsen shook his head. "I don't expect you to. I know you want revenge for what happened to you. What I want - what I need - is for you to understand is that it was my responsibility. David had nothing to do with it."

"No?"

"No."

"There were three ... "

Ibbotsen leaned forward suddenly, caught his wrist in a bony hand. "If the police arrest us both there'll be no one left to negotiate. The kidnappers will kill her. She's five years old and they'll kill her if there's no one left to sign a cheque. Please: I'm begging you. There were two."

Daniel freed himself with an effort; then he rose and stood swaying slightly. His breathing was ragged. "Mr Ibbotsen, what I understand is that only one thing matters to you right now. Getting your granddaughter back safely. Well, I have news for you: right now that's the only thing that matters to me too." Before Brodie could stop him he went on: "The police aren't coming. They don't know about you or Sophie. If it'll help we'll keep it that way, for now."

"For Christ's sake, Daniel!" exploded Brodie. "Now he can kill us both with impunity!"

Somewhere Lance Ibbotsen found a grim chuckle. "Not in front of the neighbours. That kind of thing plays havoc with property values. Will you come to the house now?"

"Where the neighbours can't see?" There was the ghost of a smile on Daniel's lips.

Ibbotsen nodded. "Also, I need a drink. If my word's worth anything" - he looked at Brodie - "you're free to leave any time you want."

"That makes all the difference," she grunted gracelessly. "The word of a torturer."

Lance Ibbotsen shuddered as if she'd slapped his face. Without another word he got back in his car and turned it.

Brodie and Daniel stood for a moment at the kerb.

"We could just go home," she said. "Wait and see what happens. If it ends in tears, at least none of it will be our fault."

"We might be able to help."

Brodie shook her head dismissively. "A man like that can buy any help he needs. And the sort of help he buys we don't want to mix with.

"Daniel, you've done what you set out to do. You've found the man who hurt you and talked to him about why. You're right, he's not a monster - but he's not somebody you'd want to spend much time with either. Walk away. He isn't big enough to haunt you. When this is over we'll talk to Deacon together, and then neither of us need waste another moment thinking about these people. It's not the past that's a foreign country, it's the monied class. They're the ones who do things differently."

"But they hurt the same. It's a little girl, Brodie. It's not her fault her grandfather behaves like Genghis Khan. It's not her fault he has enough money to make kidnapping her worthwhile. Maybe there's nothing I can do, but if I don't try I'll never know. I want to see it through. If you'd rather go home I'll walk. I'll call you later."

Brodie knew that any further argument would be futile. Gentle and adamantine, when he decided what was right he was immovable. She got into the car, Daniel got in beside her and they followed Ibbotsen up to the house. The wrought iron gates closed behind them.

Chapter 13

Ibbotsen drove round the back of the house and Brodie followed, crossing a courtyard of empty stables. Daniel shuddered.

Even the back door to *Chandlers* was of epic proportions. Ibbotsen parked beside it and waited. "Come inside." Brodie wished she knew what he was thinking. But then, she wished she knew what Daniel was thinking too.

Ibbotsen led them not to one of the grand public rooms poised above the Channel but a family-scaled sitting room overlooking the side garden, upholstered in worn chintz and smelling of dog.

But nobody sat. They stood around awkwardly, tense behind crossed arms. They were here to talk, but it wasn't an easy conversation to begin.

Finally Ibbotsen accepted his obligation as host. "What do you want to know?" he asked Daniel. "Where do you want me to start?"

Daniel said, "Have you paid the ransom?"

Lance Ibbotsen stared at him, the ice-blue eyes all but lost in their deep creases, perplexed. "The ransom?"

Daniel moistened his lips. "What did you expect me to ask? Why you abducted me? - I know. Why you tortured me? - I know that too. I know you put me through hell because someone was doing the same to you. I don't know if that's an excuse, and right now I'm not detached enough to work it out. I want to know if Sophie's safe. Have you paid the ransom?"

Ibbotsen dropped into a chair as if all the strength had drained from his limbs. "What kind of a man are you?" he whispered hoarsely.

Incredibly, Daniel managed a laugh. "Flesh and blood - but you know that, don't you?"

"You've come for an apology?" Ibbotsen's voice soared till it cracked.

"Don't you think he's entitled?" hissed Brodie.

Blue fire spat at her. "Of course. If it means anything at all coming from me, he has it. But I was afraid he'd take it as an insult. If it had been me ... "

"Oh, me too," said Brodie with certainty. She picked a chair at a distance from Ibbotsen's and seated herself with cat-like fastidiousness. "But then, Daniel doesn't think like other people. Daniel doesn't do anything like other people."

That note of irritation was not lost on Daniel. He flicked her a tiny smile and lowered himself carefully onto the sofa midway between them. "Not an apology. I don't want to be in the position of having to forgive you."

"I understand that. Then what?"

It was something Daniel felt in his heart, that didn't easily translate into words. He struggled to explain. "What passed between you and me, there's time to sort out. It matters that the balance sheet adds up at the end of the day, but you have to get the receipts in first.

"I don't want to do anything to make Sophie's situation more dangerous. I can wait. If you're negotiating with the kidnappers on the basis that the police aren't involved, I won't bring them in until you're finished."

Brodie said tersely, "Deacon's not a fool. He won't charge in mob-handed while a little girl's in danger."

"Inspector Deacon has his job to do," Daniel said quietly, "and other needs to consider. What he can do may be governed by policy beyond his control. It isn't only Sophie he has to think about, it's all the children who'd be at risk if kidnapping was an easy way to make money. I'm sure if he knew about this he'd do the right thing. But it might not be right for Sophie."

Ibbotsen hardly knew what to say, and hardly had a voice to express it. "She's right," he managed at last. "You don't think like other people."

"Is that a yes?"

Ibbotsen nodded. "Yes. Thank you."

Brodie was watching Daniel. His hands were steady and a little colour had crept back into his face. This meeting with the man who'd abused him, that he'd pursued against all reason with an obstinacy that made a credible substitute for courage: had he been right about it all along? What Brodie had taken for obsession: had it in fact been a legitimate - or even the only - way to deal with his demons? Face them and dismiss them, like other bullies? He'd gambled present safety for a future unencumbered by fear, and it looked as though he was going to win.

If he'd taken her advice, none of that would have been achieved. Meeting Lance Ibbotsen, talking with him, had cut the monster down to size. He was only a deeply fallible human being after all, one who made mistakes, who had regrets, whose wealth had bought him comfort but also more pain than most people would ever know. Behind the horror was the banality of a man with enough money to fund all the wrong choices.

Daniel said, "Then how far have you got with paying the ransom?"

Ibbotsen didn't answer directly. His gaze moved across the room. "Within twelve hours of this beginning I'd consulted experts in every aspect of kidnapping. They told me that prompt payment isn't always the best response. It's what the kidnapper wants, but from the hostage's point of view it can help to spin it out. There's always the possibility that the kidnappers will be found. Even if they aren't, the difficulty of keeping a frightened hostage safe day after day may incline them to be more reasonable. They also get to know the hostage, which makes it less likely that their final act will be murder. Children in particular are harder to kill, safer to leave alive."

Brodie had heard the arguments before, wasn't sure what Ibbotsen was telling them. "So you kept them waiting?"

"And then," said Ibbotsen, off at a tangent again, "we thought - I thought - I had a picture of one of the gang. From the tape taken by the school camera. I thought, if I could find ... well, you ... "

"*What* did you think?" demanded Brodie. "That they'd swap a child worth - what? What did they ask for?"

"Half a million pounds."

"That they'd swap a child worth half a million pounds for a dozy look-out who couldn't keep his own face off a security video?"

"Maybe not," growled Ibbotsen. "But then, if we knew where she was by then it wouldn't matter. I didn't expect to have so much trouble getting the information. Two days after Sophie was taken I thought I had my hands on one of the kidnappers. You were here soon after five o'clock. I expected to know everything you knew by six."

"You did," murmured Daniel.

The old man nodded slowly. Even now he was having to make himself believe it. "I didn't allow for that. For the possibility that you knew nothing."

"So two days had passed," said Brodie. "Had you heard from them by then?"

"We heard from them before we heard from the school. They must have called as soon as they had Sophie in the car. No demands then, just that if we called the police they'd kill her. Ten minutes later St Agnes's rang to say she hadn't gone into her one o'clock class, they'd searched and she wasn't in the building. When they looked at the tape it showed a woman they didn't recognise taking her away in a car.

"The headmistress was about to call the police - we had to lie, quickly. David said he was taking Sophie on holiday, that our new driver had picked her up, that he'd called to let the school know but the message must have gone astray." He gave a grim smile. "I never credited my son with that much imagination. It's amazing what you can do when your child's in danger."

"So instead of calling the police you asked St Agnes's for the video tape," prompted Brodie.

Ibbotsen nodded. "As a reminder to be more careful in future, I said."

"And when you played it," said Daniel in a low voice, "you saw me apparently watching through a telescope."

"I took the tape to a photographic analyst. He made the image Mrs Doyle gave to Mrs Farrell. Of course," he added, looking at Brodie, "that isn't her real name."

"Another expert?"

"An actress. I told her what to say. She didn't know anything."

"You used her to get to me, and me to get to Daniel." Brodie felt the anger rising until it met an enigma. "Why me? I'm good at what I do but I'm not world-class. You could have hired the best."

"I wanted someone local. I thought local knowledge might be worth more than international expertise. And I wanted someone on the job immediately. It was a gamble. It seemed to pay off."

"Oh yes," ground Brodie, despising him. "I know one thing: I didn't charge you enough."

"I'll give you more if you want it," Ibbotsen said, and the disdain in his voice was almost too much to bear. Brodie clenched her fists at her sides to keep from hitting him.

Daniel was regarding them as if they were bickering third-formers. He raised a finger. "Enough," he said; and even without raising his voice there was sufficient force in that one word to make both of them subside into the upholstery. "Mr Ibbotsen," he said, "you still haven't answered my question."

"Which one?" That was dissemblance: plainly he knew.

Daniel's patience had been tempered in the flame of comprehensive school maths teaching. It was a fine thing, honed and polished, with just enough give in it to stop it shattering. "The one about the ransom. They asked for half a million pounds. Have they got it yet?"

Ibbotsen took a deep breath. "It was midnight when she called again. A woman - I suppose, the woman on the video. She must have thought that if she let us sweat a while we'd do anything she asked. It wasn't a long conversation. She asked for half a million pounds in used, unmarked notes from a variety of sources. She said she'd call again in twenty-four hours with further instructions.

"I said I wouldn't do anything until I'd talked to Sophie, but she'd already rung off. The whole call couldn't have lasted a minute."

"Any idea who this woman is?" asked Brodie.

"I don't think it's anyone I know. We taped the call; a voice analyst said she was probably around thirty and came from the south east of England. That didn't mean anything either to me or to David."

"Why did you speak to her?" asked Daniel.

Ibbotsen frowned. "She asked for me."

"Why? You'd expect Sophie's father would be keenest to get her back.

Ibbotsen raised his head, glaring down his beaky nose. "When you're old enough to have grandchildren, young man, you'll know

130

they're as precious to you as your own ever were. She knew that."
He sniffed. "She also knew that I hold the purse-strings."

"I see." Daniel's tone was ambivalent. "So you spent Thursday visiting various financial institutions, filling a suitcase with notes, and at midnight they called again."

Lance Ibbotsen nodded. His gaze went between Daniel and Brodie and then off to the window. "Sort of."

Brodie blinked. "Either they did or they didn't."

Daniel was looking at Ibbotsen's face. The weathered skin was drawn tight over the high bones and the thin lips were clamped shut. It was the face of a man under a lot of stress - a desperate man, a man who could react with unpredictable violence. Daniel already knew that. But there was something else, something he couldn't put his finger on. Anxiety, fear and ... guilt? It wasn't for what he'd done to Daniel: he regretted his error but not the choice he'd made. What could he possibly have done that was worse than that?

And then Daniel knew. The knowledge crashed through him, bruising his heart, wrenching his gut, leaving devastation in its wake. His eyes widened, bottomless with disbelief. The healing that had begun in the last half hour was undone by the knowledge of the choice Ibbotsen had made next. "Oh, you bastard," he breathed.

Brodie stared at him, stared at Ibbotsen. "What? Daniel, what?"

His voice was a whisper. "They called. No one answered."

* * *

"You don't understand," mumbled Lance Ibbotsen. Everything about him suggested he was more accustomed to shouting than mumbling; now he was too ashamed to raise his voice.

"You're mistaken," said Daniel distinctly. "I understand perfectly. Your granddaughter's life was worth burning the skin off me. It was worth inflicting the kind of pain you can only end with a bullet on someone you didn't even know. But it wasn't worth half a million pounds of your money."

"It wasn't about money," gritted Ibbotsen. "I'd hired every expert I could find, I had to listen to them. They told me paying the ransom could hasten Sophie's death. When there was no reason left to keep her it would always be safer to kill her than to send her home."

"You thought they were more likely to return her safely if you refused to pay up?" Midway through the sentence Brodie heard the wonder in her voice and replaced it with disgust.

"I thought they'd try to persuade me. Which they could only do if they could reach me. I thought if I avoided talking to them they'd have to keep her safe. Even a few days might be enough to find them."

"Enough to find me, anyway."

Brodie looked at Daniel in concern. All the colour had gone from his face again. He looked as if the draught from an opening door would knock him off the sofa.

Ibbotsen wouldn't look at him. "Once we had you, I thought we'd have Sophie within hours. But the hours turned into days - and then I was told it was all a mistake, you didn't know anything after all."

"So you decided to kill him?" snarled Brodie.

"I had no choice," said Ibbotsen, almost plaintively. "The people you hire for jobs like that, they make the rules. He wouldn't leave you alive. He said his own security depended on it."

"But it wasn't him who shot me. Was it?"

"Mr Hood," the old man said, finally meeting Daniel's eyes, "there is nothing in the whole of our association that I don't regret bitterly. Shooting you? - yes, certainly; and what was done to you before. But most of all, I regret that you weren't the man I took you for. If you had been, my granddaughter would be safe now."

It may have been luck, it may have been instinct, but honesty was a weapon against which Daniel had no defence. It was the one thing guaranteed to earn his respect.

He bit his lip to still it. The shakes had returned with a vengeance. "Mr Ibbotsen, I don't know how I feel about you. I hate everything you've done, and not just to me. I hate the kind of advice you buy, and the way that, having bought it, you feel you have to follow it. I hate the way you make big, important decisions with your wallet.

"If I could hate you too, maybe I could pick up your phone and call the police. You hurt me, Mr Ibbotsen. You spent two days hurting me, and then you left me to die in a rubbish skip. I really want to hate you for that, and if I thought you'd done it to save yourself some money I would. All that's stopping me is the possibility that you genuinely believed Sophie would be safer if you refused to communicate with her kidnappers."

"I did," said Ibbotsen simply.

"What if you did?" demanded Brodie roughly. "What difference does it make? You tortured a man to get information he didn't even have, but when you had the chance to buy the child's safety you turned it down. That's the bottom line, and nothing you thought then or say now will alter it."

But Daniel was shaking his head. "What if his experts were right? What if Sophie's alive now because her kidnappers haven't got what they want? It *does* alter it, Brodie. Just because I couldn't do the same thing, just because you couldn't, doesn't mean he was wrong. If Sophie's alive because his experts gave good advice and he had the strength to follow it, doesn't that justify what he did?"

"To you?" Brodie's voice soared. "*Nothing* justifies what he did to you. And we don't know if his experts were right. All I know from the bottom of my heart is that *he* was wrong. He gambled with a child's life, and he did it to save himself half a million pounds."

She couldn't get past the money. She couldn't forgive Ibbotsen for having the means to finish this and not doing. To Brodie the issue was not what the kidnappers did but what Ibbotsen had done.

But Daniel was a mathematician, he had to accommodate all the factors. He couldn't ignore an inconvenient one because it spoiled a neat equation, and he couldn't get past the possibility that if Sophie Ibbotsen had been his child or Brodie's she'd be dead now but because she was David Ibbotsen's she might still be alive. If she was then her grandfather had made the right decision.

Daniel wiped a dew of sweat from his upper lip. "I'm sorry: I can't give either of you what you want from me. You" - he looked at Brodie - "want justice, but a justice that's a hair's breadth from vengeance and I daren't go down that road. If I started thinking these people could pay for what they did to me, I think it would cost me my soul. I didn't leave here with much: I don't want to end up with even less. And you" - his gaze switched to Ibbotsen - "want absolution, and I can't do that either. Time will tell if you were right. If you were, you don't need my forgiveness; if you weren't it won't help.

"All I can do is keep my promise. I said I wouldn't go to the police till this was finished, and I won't. But there is a price."

Ibbotsen was staring so hard he forgot to blink until his eyes started to burn. He nodded. "How much?"

Daniel shut his eyes for a second. When he opened them he was very faintly smiling. "You keep doing that, don't you? Trying to buy us off. First Mrs Farrell, now me. The only people you won't give money to are the only ones who actually want it."

A tic thumped above Lance Ibbotsen's cheekbone. "Think what you like of me. It doesn't matter: all I care is that you keep your silence. So let's agree that I'm stupid and obsessed with money, then tell me what it is you want."

"I want what you want. I want to see Sophie safe home, and I don't trust you to get that done. What's happening right now? Have the kidnappers been in touch again?"

"They tried. The calls are being screened - neither David nor I talk to them."

"Who does?"

"A professional negotiator. All my calls are going through him.

Daniel licked his lips. "What about ... ?"

Brodie knew what he wanted to know and couldn't bring himself to ask. She asked for him. "And your ... interrogator? Is he still on the payroll?"

Ibbotsen shook his head. "No. That was - a mistake. I didn't know what would be involved. I went along with it because I was desperate, and I kept thinking it would be over soon. I thought that for two days, then I was told we'd got it wrong - there was no information to be had, and because of that ... " The horror of those two days was still keen after a week. It was a physical effort to control his breathing. "I did what I thought was necessary. But I couldn't have done it again, not even for Sophie. I paid him and he left."

Daniel could only cope with this by focusing on the core issue. "Are you *any* nearer to getting Sophie back?"

134

Ibbotsen's glance was haunted. "I don't know. He doesn't talk to me - the negotiator. That was what I wanted, that was the deal - everything would go through him. The family would not be involved: if at some point he advised us that paying the ransom would bring her home we'd do it but not until he was sure. So far he must think she's safer if we do nothing."

"You don't *know*?" Daniel's voice cracked. Brodie thought his heart had too. "You're not even talking to him?"

Ibbotsen stared him down. "If I knew what was going on, what was being said, I'd take over. And I'm too close, too involved - we both know my judgement isn't reliable right now. I have to stay out of it, for Sophie's sake. I've bought the best help I could find: I have to trust that whatever can be done will be done."

Daniel blinked and then nodded. "I see that. So all I can do to help is keep quiet." Brodie heard regret in his tone, as if he'd hoped otherwise. As if helping save Sophie might ease the memory of what her abduction had cost him.

Lance Ibbotsen seemed to understand. There was an unlikely gentleness in the gravel of his voice. "I don't believe so. But it is the most important thing. If the police become involved, whatever's been achieved so far will go for nothing. I have no right to ask you for favours. But if I had, that would be the one."

Daniel managed a tired smile. "You have it. Until it's over: then I'll have to talk to Inspector Deacon."

"I understand that."

"You'll keep me informed? Do you have my number?"

Ibbotsen winced and his voice was so low as to be barely audible. "Yes."

But there was no point him phoning Daniel's number when Daniel couldn't go home. Brodie said briskly, "Daniel will be staying with me for a few days. You have my number as well." She stood up. "I don't think there's any more we can do here." She headed for the door, Daniel in her wake.

On top of the back steps, though, she paused and looked at Ibbotsen once more. "Good luck. Whatever's happened ... between us ... there's still a little girl out there who needs to be with her family.

She doesn't deserve what's happened to her. Actually, neither do you."

Astonishingly, Ibbotsen's eyes filled. "Thank you. And - I'm sorry."

"Let us know when there's some news."

"I will."

He went inside then. Brodie started the car.

But before she even had it in gear he was back, hurrying down the steps faster than was sensible for a man of his age, his face livid with fury. "You said you hadn't called them. You said you *wouldn't* call them!"

Daniel and Brodie exchanged a puzzled glance. "What? Who?"

"The police!" snarled Ibbotsen. "You promised you'd keep silent until Sophie was safe."

Brodie shrugged and Daniel answered. "We haven't called the police?"

"Then how come there's a detective inspector at my gates right now?"

Chapter 14

Detective Inspector Deacon was not a quitter. In his own way he was as stubborn a man as Daniel. It was a long shot, but where the PNC had failed his policeman's memory had dredged up a possibility. He knew of someone who had a daughter called Sophie, and the money to do something if she went missing, and the kind of morals to use someone who could help him find her as Daniel Hood was used.

Driving up the gravel avenue onto the Firestone Cliffs, Deacon reflected sourly that the possession of conspicuous wealth was no guarantee of civilised behaviour. He wondered how many of these modern manor houses with their manicured demesnes had been built with blood-money by men who should be behind bars.

Another thing about wealthy people was that they didn't put numbers on their gates. Deacon drove along, searching, until he was stopped by wrought iron. He thumbed the button on an intercom, announced himself and said who he was looking for.

A woman's voice directed him along an elegant sweep of gravel drive to a porticoed front door and a flight of steps Scarlett O'Hara would have killed for. Deacon trudged up them stolidly, giving his shoes every opportunity to shed any mud they might have collected on the way.

The housekeeper answered his knock and showed Deacon into the library to wait. Sophie's father was at home, then; which made the minutes that passed more than a little galling. Wealthy people always thought they had the right, if not the duty, to keep a public servant waiting. At the end of town he was more familiar with Deacon would have twiddled his thumbs for thirty seconds and then gone looking. But though he believed in one law for rich and poor alike, he couldn't ignore the reality that behaviour which was grudgingly tolerated on the Wellington estate might, if duplicated here, reach the ears of the Chief Constable. He ground his teeth and glared at the Channel.

Finally the door opened again and Deacon turned to see a face he used to know framed by a collar he used to dream of feeling. He nodded, expressionless, flicked his gaze around the room. "Terry. You've done well for yourself."

"Not bad," said Terry Walsh with obvious content, "not bad. Mind you, Jack, neither have you. Chief Inspector, is it?"

"Inspector," ground Deacon.

"Oh well," said Walsh breezily, "that's Sheehy for you. You'll probably go straight to Superintendent."

"You could help," said Deacon. "You could confess to everything we both know you did to afford this house."

Walsh laughed, the deep-bellied laugh of a man with either nothing to hide or the confidence that his secrets are safe. "I don't know where you got this idea that I'm a leading light of the criminal underworld. I make paper: you know that. You've seen the factory; damn it, I'll take you to Norway and show you the woods if you like!"

It was a genuine offer: Deacon knew that if he accepted Walsh would whisk him off by private plane for an away-day among the fjords to watch great stands of timber being harvested by equipment with the man's initials on it. It altered nothing. Jack Deacon knew Terry Walsh when they were boys in the East End of London, when his only use for paper was rolling reefers. The fact that Walsh had always managed to evade the long arm of the law didn't alter Deacon's conviction that his primary interest was still in drugs. All that had changed was the scale: he didn't sell reefers on dancefloors any more, he shipped cocaine wrapped in tons of newsprint.

"That's all right, Terry," Deacon said bleakly, "it's not how you make your money I'm interested in today. It's how you spend it."

Walsh not only had more money than Deacon, he also had more hair. It wasn't as black as Deacon remembered, but if anything it was curlier. It danced when he shook his head, apparently perplexed. "Sorry, Jack - spend it on what?"

Deacon sniffed. "Far as I remember it, the East End didn't produce many intellectuals. We mostly spent money on having a good time and looking after our families." He raised an eyebrow, seemed to change the subject. "You still smoke, Terry?"

Walsh shook his head again, firmly. "Gave it up, Jack. Costs too much. And then I heard this rumour" - he looked round his library - "that you can't take it with you. So I want to put off going as long as I can, just in case."

Deacon nodded, trying not to smile. Walsh had always had this effect on him. Even when you knew how he made it, even when you'd give your pension to see him banged up, it was hard not to like someone who so enjoyed the fruits of his labours. The neighbours must consider him deeply vulgar. But Deacon had a soft spot for honest-to-God vulgarity.

On top of which, he was already thinking he was on a fool's errand. Terry Walsh was too happy to see him. If he'd tortured a man, shot him and dumped him in a skip less than a week ago he'd be cagier than this. They didn't get together to chat about the old days so often that he would think that was why the policeman had come.

Still, he had to make sure. "What about the family? You've got a daughter, haven't you - Sophie?"

"And a son, Simon. Yourself?"

"Nah." Deacon pursed his lips. "Tell you why I'm here, Terry. It's about your Sophie. She's all right, is she?"

In an instant Walsh's expansive face tightened in fear. "What's happened? Jack, tell me - for the love of God - !"

Deacon took pity on him. "It's all right. Nothing's happened - at least, nothing you don't know about. Somebody's Sophie is in trouble, but she has been for a week or more - if you've seen her recently it's not your daughter."

The man looked slightly reassured. "You're sure? I can call her - she drove over to the stables where she keeps her horse an hour ago, I can get her on the mobile if there's any chance she's in trouble ..."

"Call her if it'll make you happy," said Deacon, "but there's nothing to worry about. At least, there is, but it's somebody else's problem. It involves someone called Sophie, a lot of money and a fair bit of brutality, so naturally I thought of you. Where were you last weekend?"

139

Walsh didn't have to think. "I was in Norway until Saturday; Sunday I played golf. You can check if you need to."

Deacon nodded. He would, but he didn't expect to learn any different. "How about Sophie? Where was she last week?"

"Working. She's PA to the proprietor of an art gallery in Eastbourne - I'll give you his number so you can check that too." He did. "Jack, whatever is this all about?"

"I'm barking up the wrong tree, I think. Something's going on, something that nobody's telling me about, and I thought maybe something had happened to your Sophie and you were on the warpath because of it." Deacon sniffed. "I'm glad I was wrong."

"You thought we were in trouble and you came to help? Jack, I'm touched." Amazingly enough he seemed to mean it.

Deacon shrugged. "Partly that. And partly, I might have had some new charges to throw at you."

Walsh laughed aloud. "Sorry to disappoint you." A thought occurred to him. "Have you tried Ibbotsen at the end? His granddaughter's called Sophie, I think. Mind you, she's only a tot, I don't know how much trouble she can have got into."

"The house with the gates? I went there looking for you. You want to put a number up sometime."

"Jack - anyone I want to see knows where I live."

Deacon squinted at him. "Ibbotsen the shipping guy? I doubt he'd fit the bill. I know he has money. But I'm looking for someone with dirty money, and the morals to go with it."

Walsh grinned. "What do I have to do to convince you I'm not like that? I'm a businessman, that's all."

Deacon smiled too; it looked like a crocodile smiling. "Terry, I've been a policeman over twenty years. I've known you since we were at school. I know when you're lying. Ask me how."

"How, Jack?"

"Your lips move."

* * *

Even after Detective Inspector Deacon was seen driving away up

140

the avenue, Ibbotsen wanted them to wait. "I can't risk you being seen leaving here."

Brodie answered with a negligent shrug. It would have suited her very well for Deacon to see them leaving: she wanted this subterfuge to end. She believed the day would come when she'd regret keeping secrets from Deacon.

She gave Ibbotsen five minutes then started the car again. "I'm not moving in with you just to avoid being seen leaving." But Deacon was long gone and no one else was interested.

Exhausted by the morning's revelations, Daniel fell asleep in the few minutes it took them to get home. Brodie couldn't throw him over her shoulder and carry him inside the way she did with Paddy: she tapped his arm. He started with a sharp intake of breath.

"Sorry. We're here."

"What time is it?"

"Just after twelve."

Upstairs Marta Szarabeijka had a pupil: one who thought a piano was like a bicycle, the harder you pedalled the better it went. The sound crashed through the window and splintered in the front garden.

Brodie opened her door. "I'll make some lunch."

Daniel hesitated in the hallway. "You don't have to do this."

"Make lunch?"

"Look after me. I can go home now. There's no one waiting for me - there's *going* to be no one waiting. Or I could go to an hotel."

"Do you want to?"

"Not much," he admitted.

"Then come inside and shut the door. It's no hardship putting you up for a few days. Now we know there'll be no repercussions Paddy can move in again. An extra place at the table: that's all the trouble you are. Go home when you're ready, stay till you are."

He followed her into the kitchen, watched her peel potatoes. "How much longer can it go on?" he asked. "It's been ten days: how much longer before the kidnappers decide they're not going to get what they want and ... "

"And what?" Brodie looked at him over her shoulder.

Daniel swallowed. "That was my next question. What will they do when they give up on the money?"

She peeled steadily. "If there'd been no contact for ten days I'd be afraid for that little girl's life. The kidnappers might have waited two or three days and tried again, but if they really couldn't make contact with the family they'd cut their losses. Either they'd leave her somewhere to be found, or they'd leave the body.

"But that isn't the situation. Ibbotsen's negotiator has been talking to them for a week. Since ... well."

"Since they decided they weren't going to find her through me," supplied Daniel. When she looked at him the ghosts were quiet.

Brodie nodded. "That's quite a long time too, but if she's somewhere safe and they're somewhere safe maybe they're not too worried. Snatching her was risky; collecting the money will be risky; talking on the phone really isn't. Not if you know what you're doing.

"The first thing the negotiator would say is that the money is available - that it isn't the money but Sophie's safety which is the issue. So the kidnappers are thinking not if but when. They believe she's worth half a million pounds to them.

"What both sides have been doing for the last week is laying the foundations for a deal. It must seem a hell of a long time to both Sophie and her father, but actually the old man was right. It doesn't matter how long it takes if it ends in success."

"All right," said Daniel, "suppose they agree on how to do it, and where and when and all the safeguards. Will they keep their word? Or will Sophie come home in a box?"

"Employing a professional negotiator was a good move. He'll deal with more of these things in a year, working all over the world, than Scotland Yard does in five. He'll break it down into stages. You do *this*, we do that; you do *this*, we do the next thing. He'll try to ensure that they can't get away with the money until Sophie is safe. Of course, the kidnappers will be trying to ensure that the Ibbotsens can't get Sophie until they've paid for her. That's what takes the time. As long as nothing unexpected happens, they'll find a way."

She looked at him sidelong, wondering how much truth he could handle. What he'd been through had taken him to the limit, physically and mentally: if it turned out to be for nothing, she was afraid for him. The hope that Sophie Ibbotsen would come home safe was holding him together.

Daniel caught the look and frowned. "What?"

"The negotiator will make sure the kidnappers play fair. Who's going to make sure Ibbotsen does?"

"You think he'd risk her life?"

"No. But he might think he could do it without much risk."

"I couldn't bear it if she died," Daniel said softly.

Brodie nodded. "All we can do is wait. And pray, if you've a mind to."

Daniel shook his head. "I'm a mathematician. I believe that two and two always make four. They can't make five however much someone wants them to."

Finished with the potatoes, she leaned back against the counter. "So mathematics is the death of wonder?"

He did his heart-stopping smile. Brodie had known professional charmers, men who could gauge to the split second when to turn it on and how long to leave it running; and though like any woman with twenty-twenty vision she could appreciate a goodlooking man she had never been much impressed by expensive orthodontics.

Daniel Hood was different. He wasn't a professional, the smile was his own. And he had no idea how affecting it was, how it got under her guard. It would have been captivating on anyone at any time. On someone who'd come through what he had, it was devastating.

"On the contrary, mathematics is the perfect tool for exploring wonders," he said. "No man has been further than the moon - on the universal scale that's like moving up the sofa. But we know about the chemical processes in the hearts of stars on the far side of the galaxy, and mathematics is how. We know about other galaxies on the far side of the universe. We're able to understand things whose physical structure is so bizarre we couldn't describe them in any language except mathematics.

"Do you know about Spin Half?" Brodie shook her head. "The

143

universe is made up of some particles that look different depending on which way you look at them, and others that don't. In the same way that a sphere always looks the same from every angle, and a bow-tie would look the same upside down, but you'd have to walk right round a person to get the same view. With me so far? Particles like that are responsible for the forces operating in the universe: they're described as having spin nought, one and two.

"Particles of matter are described as having spin half. Turning a particle like that through three hundred and sixty degrees isn't enough to make it look the same. You have do it twice."

"That isn't possible," said Brodie with conviction.

Daniel beamed. "It is; but we can only confront the idea through mathematics. Paul Dirac cracked it in 1928 in the first theory that was consistent with both quantum mechanics and special relativity."

Brodie was at once puzzled and amused. Every time she thought she was getting a handle on him, understanding who he was and how he thought, he did this to her: changed the basic perameters of their relationship. She talked to him as if he were a child; and quite without resentment, possibly without noticing, he replied in terms that would have stretched a Nobel physicist. It wasn't a put-down: it was just that, behind the ordinary face and the mundane job, he was very, very clever. She wasn't sure he'd noticed that either.

She changed the subject. "Talking of confrontations. How do you feel after yours?"

The pleasure that had animated his face stilled. He thought about it. "Weird. But - better."

"I thought you were crazy wanting to talk to that man," said Brodie. "But you were right: it was what you needed."

"I've never been brave," confided Daniel. "Violence frightens me, even when I'm not the target. You know the seven-stone weakling in the chest-expander ads? - that's me. All my instincts are to kick sand in my own face to save bigger guys the trouble.

"But you miss a lot by going through life like that. You back away more and more, quicker and quicker. You start by avoiding thugs on the beach, you end up staying indoors on sunny days. Once you start to run, somehow there's no stopping.

"But you can make yourself stand still and face what's coming. It's hard at first, but it gets easier every time you think you're going to die and don't. Facing your fears doesn't mean you never get hurt, but at least you learn who poses a genuine threat and who doesn't. You still get sand in your face sometimes, but not every time someone walks past. And you do get to go on the beach."

Brodie shook her head, her regard for him growing. "You're a strange human being, Daniel Hood. But I'll say this for you. You know what you want, and you have the guts to go for it. That makes you braver than nearly everyone I know."

* * *

First thing on Monday morning she drove him to the hospital to get his dressings checked. "Call me when you're done and I'll pick you up."

"I'll get a taxi."

"Call me."

The doctor was still offended at him discharging himself. But when pressed he admitted that Daniel had come to no harm, that his injuries were healing, that more of the clingfilm could be dispensed with

Daniel came out of the treatment room, tender and pink under his shirt, to find Detective Inspector Deacon waiting for him. Surprise froze him momentarily in his tracks.

"Daniel," said the policeman non-committally. "You're looking better."

In the couple of seconds it took to detach his feet from the linoleum Daniel had made two decisions. He wasn't going to tell Deacon about the Ibbotsens, and he wasn't going to lie. If need be he'd stand there all day trying to reconcile the two. "I'm a lot better," he said.

Deacon nodded. "Good. Now let's see if your memory's improved too."

"There never was anything wrong with my memory," Daniel said quietly. "I told you everything I knew. I don't know why you didn't believe me."

"Well, I'll tell you," said Deacon expansively. "It's because when

145

people are telling the truth, it adds up and makes a kind of sense. When it doesn't add up and it doesn't make any sense at all, nine times out of ten somebody's telling porkies."

"I haven't lied to you. I just didn't know the answers to your questions."

"That's right," remembered the detective. "You don't like liars, do you? 'Tell the truth and shame the devil' - it's a good epitaph. I'll have it inscribed on your tombstone."

Daniel felt his skin crawl. "What do you mean?"

"I'm only being realistic." Deacon put an arm around his shoulder and, if he noticed the younger man wince, pretended he hadn't. "The people who chucked you in the skip thought you were dead. I lied - sorry about that, I know you won't approve - I lied to the press to keep them thinking that. And now here you are, walking around in public and staying with a woman they also know about. Whoever they are, whatever it was all about, they must know by now that they left the job unfinished. It can't be long before they decide to rectify that."

He cocked his head, waiting for Daniel to reply. But Daniel said nothing. Deacon smiled his crocodile smile. "I have to hand it to you, Danny, you're a braver man than me. That's a good quality in a teacher, though it's not the first thing that springs to mind. You think of teachers and you think cardigans, long holidays, pay disputes and whingeing on about not getting the respect they're entitled to. You don't immediately think of people brave enough to stand in front of a loaded gun just to prove that they can."

Daniel knew he was being goaded and dared not respond. "Inspector - what is it you want from me?"

"I want to know what you know," Deacon said forcibly. "I want to know why all at once you feel safe wandering round a public building where a week ago I had you hidden away under a false name with a guard on the door. Something's changed. Something's happened, or you've remembered something, but anyway you know something now that you didn't then. Tell me what it is."

"I can't tell you anything," insisted Daniel. "All I can do is repeat what I said before: I got tired of hiding. It's not bravery, or stupidity - I think the danger's passed. Maybe it's time you called *The Sentinel*

146

and put the record straight. It'll come out sooner or later - when I go back to school if not before. It would be better coming from you than someone else."

Deacon regarded him speculatively. "Daniel, do you hate me?"

Daniel stared. "Of course not."

"Then why are you trying to sabotage my career? What I did to protect you I will get away with, just, if I can make an arrest. Without that I'm just another fascist pig with no respect for the public, lying to cover my own failure. I went out on a limb for you. I knew it could break. I *didn't* expect to turn round and find you sawing like crazy behind me."

"I'm not! Inspector Deacon, I'm grateful for everything you've done. But I still can't answer your questions."

"Can't? Or won't?"

Daniel Hood lost his temper. He didn't shout or throw punches when he was angry, but his eyes crackled like embers. "The last people who thought I was lying to them burned me with cigarettes. After two days I still couldn't help them. I can't help you either, and I don't know what you think you can do that'll be more persuasive than what they came up with."

Jack Deacon had seen most things in his time on the force. He'd seen things done to the human body that made Daniel Hood's injuries pale into insignificance. And he'd been at the centre of a staring crowd more often than he could remember. He wasn't easy to shock, impossible to embarrass. And everything Daniel did and said reinforced the conviction in his gut that the young man knew things that he wasn't sharing.

"I know what was done to you," he said wearily. "I saw it when it was worse than it is now, when I thought you were going to die. And when I thought you were an innocent victim. Now I think you're in this up to your eyeballs. I think you could tell me the whole story if you wanted to.

"But if you don't want the people who hurt you to pay for it, damned if I know why I should. Sort it out between you. You think you don't need my help any more? Well, if they kill you next time we'll know you were wrong."

He turned on his heel, left Daniel standing flushed in the middle of Reception and almost walked over Brodie Farrell. "I should have known you'd be here," he said nastily. "When you've got Superman, can Lois Lane be far behind?" He stalked out through the swinging doors into the car-park.

Mystified as she was, Brodie refrained from comment until she'd ushered Daniel away from the fascinated gaze of the packed waiting room. Then she said, "What was that about?"

"Mr Deacon still thinks I'm holding something back."

"Well - you are, aren't you?"

Daniel nodded mournfully. "*Now* I am. I wasn't last time I talked to him."

She hadn't much sympathy for him. Most of what he'd suffered had been someone else's fault but this he'd brought on himself. She'd tried to warn him what finding his enemies would mean, and about joining their conspiracy of silence. He hadn't understood that keeping secrets mostly means telling lies.

"Well, you've got two choices - you do what Deacon wants or what Ibbotsen wants. You can't do both. It may be, in the end, you won't be able to do either."

"I gave my word," murmured Daniel.

"I don't think Jack Deacon's a man you want to annoy."

He stared. "Meaning that Lance Ibbotsen is?"

Brodie breathed heavily. It was getting just a little irksome the way he used his pain as a kind of trump card, an answer to every argument. "Meaning," she said, getting into the car, "that you'd better pick a side and stick to it. And if it isn't Ibbotsen's, we'll go round to the police station right now and tell Deacon everything."

Daniel's expression was stubborn. "I gave him my word. I won't go back on it."

"Then get in the car. They want us up at *Chandlers*."

Misgivings clouded his face. "What's happened?"

"I don't know," Brodie said tersely. "I got a phonecall from David Ibbotsen ten minutes ago. He wants to see us right away. He wouldn't say why."

Fear bloomed in Daniel's eyes and his voice was hollow. "Oh no."

Chapter 15

As Brodie turned off the Shore Road towards *Chandlers,* suddenly Daniel stiffened beside her. "Stop the car."

She pulled in quickly. "What is it?" But he was already bailing out, stumbling across the verge and throwing up in a hedge.

She said nothing, simply waited until he came back, white and shame-faced. "Sorry."

"Daniel - why are you doing this to yourself? Let's go home. I'll ring them and say we're not coming."

He shook his head. "I told them to call if there was anything I could do. They called. I can't just go home."

"Of course you can. Just because an Ibbotsen yanks our chain doesn't mean we have to jump. We owe them nothing. And any help they need they can buy."

"They know that too. They must think there's something we can do for them that the experts can't."

With no answer to his logic, Brodie appealed to common sense. "But we're getting in deeper and deeper. That family's problems are not our concern. You've already helped more than they had any right to expect. I don't like the way you've been manoeuvred into lying to - all right, misleading - the police. You don't want Detective Inspector Deacon as an enemy."

"I don't want *any* enemies," protested Daniel. "But a choice between irritating one person and letting another get hurt, or maybe killed, makes itself. What did he say when he called you? Has something happened?"

Brodie looked away. "I don't know. He was upset, he wasn't making a lot of sense. He said something about the post."

Daniel jolted visibly. "He's got something from the kidnappers. Something to stir him into action. But if Sophie was dead he wouldn't have called us, he'd have called the police. He must think we can do something. We have to find out what."

"No," she said forcibly, "we don't. He shouldn't be asking, and we shouldn't consider it. Daniel, listen to me. If the child is already dead, then it's a tragedy but there's nothing for us to reproach ourselves about. If we get drawn into Ibbotsen's machinations and she dies tomorrow, that may not still be the case."

His eyes were as clear as ice. But ice is deceptive. It only looks fragile: actually it's hard, and it burns. "What if there's some way we can help and we're too scared to try? We're not going to reproach ourselves about that? You know how I feel about cowardice - it terrifies me."

Brodie looked at him, troubled, and saw the tiny smile. It would have been easy to give in to him. But there was too much at stake. "Daniel, if this is what you want, I'll do it. Not for David Ibbotsen, or even his daughter, but for you. I owe it to you. But I believe it's a mistake.

"I was afraid that if we found these people it would be the end of everything. Well, we found them; and now I'm afraid this is just the start. We're going to get so mired in this whole sorry business there'll be no escaping the consequences. We'll be powerless to prevent what's going to happen but too close to avoid the fall-out. The Ibbotsens can't keep the police at bay forever. When Deacon finds out that a child was kidnapped and nobody told him, and that we knew about it, he's going to come after us with a meat-cleaver."

"We haven't done anything wrong! Helping a man get his daughter back isn't a crime."

"Withholding evidence is. I don't know what Deacon can do to you - maybe in the circumstances he'd feel pretty silly trying to arrest you. But he'll drop on me like a ton of bricks. He doesn't even have charge me with anything: he can put me out of business just by deciding to. I don't work for crooks - at least, not knowingly - but I do work for a lot of people who rely on my discretion. If Deacon starts taking an interest in what I do, half my clientele will vanish overnight.

"David Ibbotsen isn't the only one with a child to think about. I have a four-year-old daughter. I don't want to raise her on Family Credit."

Daniel's gaze was compassionate. "I don't want you to do anything

150

you're uncomfortable with. You may have owed me something a week ago but not any more. Go home, I'll walk from here."

"You said that yesterday."

"You could have done it yesterday. Today it'll be easier: you know now nobody wants me dead."

But death wasn't the only conceivable disaster. Brodie steeled herself. "I know what you're thinking, Daniel. That bringing that little girl home will change how you feel about what happened. Replace terrible memories with something better. But what if she doesn't come home? What if it all goes wrong? Can you face the possibility that Sophie Ibbotsen is going to die because of some decision you'll be a party to?"

She saw him think about that, the idea carving at his heart. "I don't know. But if I walk away, if I refuse to help and Sophie dies, I know how I'll feel then. I'm twenty-six years old. I don't want to spend the next fifty years wondering if she'd be alive if I hadn't been too scared to go up there today.

"Sometimes trying to cover all the angles is just too difficult. You have to do what you think is right and hope for the best."

"The road to hell is paved with good intentions," said Brodie.

"No. The road to hell is paved with fear. With the echoes of lies, and the ghosts of good deeds stillborn because people were afraid of the consequences."

Brodie had no more arguments to offer. She started the car again. "Then let's do it."

* * *

Lance Ibbotsen met them at the back door. "David's in the sitting room." His voice was so low as to be barely audible, his face stiff and grey.

Brodie needed to know what to expect. "What's happened? I couldn't follow what he was saying."

"No. He was upset. I offered to call, but we weren't sure you'd come for me."

"Something came in the post. Is that right?"

151

"The kidnappers must have decided things were taking too long. They sent us a go-faster message."

There was a box on the coffee table, the sort designed for posting flowers. It had been opened but it was closed now. Surreptitiously Brodie checked the bottom corners. At least it wasn't leaking.

David Ibbotsen dragged his eyes away from it long enough to offer her a thin smile. It was the first time they'd met. "Thanks for coming. I couldn't think who else to call."

She nodded at the box. "What's in it?"

David Ibbotsen jerked one hand in unsteady invitation. Like Daniel, he seemed to be clinging to the edge of the abyss by his fin-ger-nails. The only difference was that every day brought Daniel a little healing. Every day was another mountain between this man and his child, another nail in the crucifixion of his hopes. Every minute that passed could be the last before he learned of Sophie's death. If the phone rang, if the doorbell chimed ... Brodie imagined herself in his position and found it too painful to continue. Every second that she didn't know where Paddy was or if she was safe would be like vitriol on raw flesh.

The man needed help. Daniel was right: whatever he'd been a part of, they couldn't leave him to suffer. Brodie set her teeth and reached for the box.

Lance Ibbotsen saved her that at least. He lifted the lid. "It's her hair."

As golden as sunshine, as fine as spring rain, it filled the box in tumbling profusion. As if a phoenix had been lining a nest for the chick it would never see.

Brodie breathed in and out for half a minute, letting her heartbeat steady. Then she said, "What does your negotiator make of this?"

David looked quickly at his father. He wasn't the least bit like him, or even as he must have been at thirty-five. The bones were thicker, neither so long nor so angular, and better covered. He was a good-looking man, or would have been when his cheeks were not sunken nor his eyes red with rubbing. He looked as if he hadn't slept since this began and was at the end of his strength. "Tell them."

Ibbotsen nodded, once, crisply. "He's gone. The kidnappers refused to deal with him any more. I don't know why - they must have thought he was spinning things out, that we'd settle quicker with him out of the picture. They said they wouldn't talk to him again, that if we couldn't talk direct they wouldn't waste any more time. They said they'd kill Sophie and disappear, and it would be our fault."

Brodie frowned. It seemed the sort of thing that would be said at some stage in every hostage negotiation. "And because of that your negotiator left?"

Ibbotsen sniffed. "Not exactly. He said they were just trying to up the stakes. He said we shouldn't fall for it. He also said, of course, that the final decision was ours."

"And you gave him his marching orders." The one thing they'd done right they hadn't been strong enough to abide by.

"Call me a cynic," growled the old man. "But he had less than us to lose and more to gain by making it last. We weren't getting anywhere. I paid him off."

"You're wrong," said Brodie. "He had his reputation to lose, and that may have meant almost as much to him as Sophie does to you. If he loses a hostage he may never get another client. He makes a lot of money doing this, but only because he's successful. You lost an ally."

Lance and his son traded a quick glance. "We didn't think of it that way," mumbled David. "I'm not sure it would have mattered if we had. They threatened to kill her. Sophie: my daughter. They threatened to *kill* her! You can't call a bluff like that."

"*You* couldn't," said Brodie. "A professional negotiator could." Still, the deed was done. The negotiation was compromised, he wouldn't come back on board now if they asked him. "When did the box arrive?"

"Forty minutes ago, just before I called you." David passed a hand across his mouth. "One of the neighbours brought it round. It had been left on his doorstep by mistake."

"That wasn't a mistake," said Brodie. "They knew they couldn't get to your front door without being spotted. Your neighbour: does he have a security camera?" These were all valuable properties, serious security would be the order of the day.

"No, he has Rottweilers." Which might have been even more of a deterrent but wouldn't be able to give a description.

"Was there a note or are we still waiting for them to call?"

"There's a message in the box."

A sheet of computer listing paper nestled in the golden hair.

> This is between us. It can only be resolved between us. Do as we say and you'll have the rest of your grand-daughter back inside twenty-four hours.
>
> We won't tolerate any more delays. Buy the child's life or we'll return her dead body free of charge. Find a go-between to bring us the money and return with the child.
>
> We'll call tonight and tell her where to go.

"Her?" Brodie's voice was ribbed with presentiment.

Ibbotsen shrugged. "Obviously they'd rather deal with a woman. If that's what they want, that's how we'll do it. I'm not fighting them any more. They can have everything they want, including the money. Will you take it to them?"

Disturbed as she was at the idea, the glance she cast Daniel carried a certain wry humour. So it wasn't his help they needed, it was hers. He didn't return the look, or even seem to notice it. All his attention was on David Ibbotsen. Of course, it wasn't the first time they'd met.

"Will you?" asked David. "Please. We'll pay you ... "

"My God, you're at it again!" exclaimed Brodie. "I never knew a family with such rotten judgement when it comes to money! Yes, I'll help. And no, I don't want paying. And so help me, if either one of you flashes his chequebook at me again, I'll deck him!"

Having gained their full attention, she took a seat. "Now. If you'd kept your negotiator on the payroll he'd have told you that the contents of that box change everything."

"I don't need him to tell me that," growled Ibbotsen. "I don't need *you* to tell me that."

"I think you do. You seem to think Sophie's in more danger today that she was a week ago. Well, I'm not convinced she's in danger at all. Not today or for the immediate future."

The three men stared at her as if she'd thrown off her clothes and commenced a fan dance on the coffee table. She found their interest gratifying, was in no hurry to move on.

Finally, more or less in concert, Daniel said, "Are you sure?" and David said in anguish, "That's my daughter's *hair!*" and Ibbotsen growled, "You want to explain?"

She answered them all. "Yes, I'm pretty sure. I don't think Sophie's in danger because that box contains the one bit of her that came off without hurting and will grow back in a few months. It could have been her ear, or a finger, or any one of a dozen body parts that can be removed without endangering a little girl's life by anyone brute enough to do it. But it was her hair. Not a drop of blood, not a tear, was spilt. Ask yourselves why."

"Because there's a limit to the depths even kidnappers will sink to!" cried David in distress. "They didn't need to maim her to gain our co-operation, and they knew that."

"Actually," said Brodie, "there are no limits to the depths kidnappers will sink to. People who like children don't abduct them - except in certain circumstances where money isn't the issue. We'll come back to that in a minute. And after the last twelve days they could be forgiven for thinking they'd have to do something pretty extraordinary to get your co-operation. This was it - her hair?"

"No," whispered David. His eyes were afraid. He'd thought Brodie was here to help him. Instead she was raising fresh obstacles to the safe recovery of his child. "This was just the start. If this doesn't work either, maybe she'll come home a piece at a time."

"For God's sake!" snarled Ibbotsen; but he couldn't stop the picture imprinting behind his eyes. "Look, it's over. They've won. I want you to take them the money and hopefully come back with my granddaughter."

Brodie shrugged. "It's your money, spend it how you like. But I doubt it'll bring Sophie back."

The Ibbotsens, father and son, stared at her as if she was threatening to kill the child herself.

Daniel said softly, "You said there are times when money isn't the issue. You said you'd get back to that."

She gave him an appreciative nod. At least somebody, besides her, was still thinking. "Yes. Children aren't always kidnapped for ransom. Sometimes they're kidnapped because someone wants a child. Either that child, or any child."

Ibbotsen said, uncertainly, "Like women who take babies from hospitals?"

"Well, that's one example," said Brodie. "Though at five Sophie is probably too old for that. They want a baby they can pass off as their own."

"Then what *are* you talking about?" demanded David, desperation contorting his features like fury. "White slavery?"

"I'm talking about tug-of-love children," said Brodie calmly. "Mr Ibbotsen, who is Sophie's mother?"

Chapter 16

Ibbotsen said, "Marie?" and his voice was incredulous.

David said sharply, "Don't be absurd."

"Why absurd?" asked Brodie. "Clearly from your reaction Sophie's mother is still alive. Why couldn't she be trying to get her daughter back?"

David was looking at her as if she were mad. "Because of the ransom demands. Whoever did this doesn't want Sophie - they want half a million pounds."

"That's certainly what they said," nodded Brodie. "Sometimes people lie. Tell me this. If you thought Marie had snatched Sophie from the playground, what would you have done?"

Ibbotsen didn't hesitate. "Called the police."

"And she'd have been picked up within minutes. But you didn't do that, did you?"

"Of course not. They said - " Understanding was like a crack growing in the ice-field eyes. "You mean, the ransom thing could have been a smoke-screen?"

"Where does Marie live?"

"In Brittany."

"Is she French?"

"Oh yes," said David feelingly. "But - "

Brodie cut him off with a wave. "Let's just follow this through. You married a French woman, you had a daughter, and then you separated."

"Divorced."

"She went back to France?"

"This is nonsense," insisted David in growing desperation. "It has nothing to do with Marie."

Ibbotsen answered for him. "It was the best thing."

There was plainly a sub-text. Brodie raised an enquiring eye-brow.

"She needed drying-out. It made more sense to use a clinic close

157

to her parents' home. The marriage was over by then, there was no affection left between them."

"Your daughter-in-law was an alcoholic?"

"*Is* an alcoholic," said Ibbotsen. "You can stop drinking. You can't stop being an alcoholic."

"And did she? - stop drinking."

He avoided her eyes. "I'm not sure. She left the clinic - I know because I paid the bill. I have no way of knowing if that was the end of her drinking or if she went back to it later. We haven't seen her for three years."

Brodie's eyes grew stalks. "Three years? She hasn't visited her daughter in three years?"

"Don't look at me like that, it's perfectly legal," growled Ibbotsen. "The court agreed she wasn't capable of caring for a child. It said she could visit Sophie once a month but wasn't to take her out of this house unless accompanied by my son. In fact she never came. Perhaps she felt it was better to make a clean break."

Brodie had to make a conscious effort to blink. For a moment she was entirely lost for words. Then she said slowly, in wonder, "Men. Stupid, ignorant, arrogant bloody men. For twelve days you've been worried that Sophie was kidnapped by strangers, for ransom. You've avoided the police; you've spent big sums of money on experts in something that hasn't happened; you perpetrated atrocities on someone who never did you any harm and finally you damn near committed murder. Because you thought David's ex-wife wanted a clean break from her daughter!"

Her venom had knocked all the expression off their faces. Ibbotsen was the first to recover. He said carefully, "I take it you think that's unlikely."

"Unlikely," echoed Brodie. "That the mother of a five-year-old child, denied the right to raise her by an addiction plainly induced by living with you two, should decide to write off this daughter and hope for better luck next time? Should go back to the land of her birth and never hop on a EuroStar to visit her little girl? Should go through the trauma of detox and never ask herself if she was now fit to look after her again? Oh yes, Mr Ibbotsen, I'd say that's pretty unlikely, wouldn't you?"

"When you put it like that," said Ibbotsen, tight-lipped. "I just never considered it. Marie? She never asked to reopen the custody issue."

"She wouldn't have succeeded, would she, not against you. But she would have alerted you to how she was thinking, and the possibility that she might take more extreme measures."

"Like kidnapping her own daughter?"

"Exactly like that! Mr Ibbotsen, it's not that rare. And this is a classic case. The estranged parent is a foreign national who's returned to her native land. There's a history of mental instability and a sense of grievance. She thought she had only to get Sophie back to France and they could disappear. All she had to do was stop you calling the police for a few hours.

"And she knew how to do that. She knows the pair of you pretty well, after all. She knew you wouldn't risk Sophie's life. But she also knew you wouldn't pay good cash money without a fight. She guessed you'd stall for time and mount a counter-attack. She wanted time too. A few hours would see her safely across the Channel; a few days would let her disappear so completely she'd be safe even when you realised who you were looking for. A few phonecalls and some lurid threats kept you thinking this was a hostage situation while she hid Sophie away.

"Finally she pretended to lose patience and sent you the box of hair. Hell, maybe she's in the mood by now. Maybe she thinks she can have Sophie and your money as well. Maybe she thinks she's earned it."

"This is crazy," moaned David. "Crazy! It's nothing to do with Marie. We *know* what it's about: half a million pounds. Dad, I'm begging you, please don't listen to this. I don't doubt Mrs Farrell knows what she's talking about, and I'm sure she's trying to help, but she's wrong. If you let her persuade you that Marie has Sophie so there's time to sort this out without paying the ransom, God knows what's going to happen.

"My little girl's with people who look at her and just see a pile of money. They've had her for nearly a fortnight - she hasn't seen a friendly face or heard a kind word for a fortnight. She must be scared out of her mind. She's only five years old: she has no idea what we're doing, doesn't realise that these things take time - she must think we've abandoned her.

"And maybe that's pretty much what they think too - the kidnappers. We know they're tired of waiting. They cut off her hair; but they won't stop at that if we do nothing. Please, Dad, don't change your mind again. Pay them, and let's get her home."

He was almost in tears. But Ibbotsen looked at him not with compassion but irritation. Then he looked back at Brodie. "It wasn't Marie on the phone."

Brodie shrugged. "She hired some help. You can get someone to do anything for enough money; as you know. What about the video?"

"What?"

"The video of the kidnapping. It was a woman who took Sophie away, wasn't it? Could that have been Marie?"

David shook his head miserably. "It was nothing like her."

But Ibbotsen turned on the television and the VCR. The tape was already loaded: of course, no one in this house had been watching anything else. "I never thought of Marie," he said by way of explanation. "I didn't recognise the woman, but perhaps if I'd been thinking of Marie ... " They watched the children play, the traffic pass.

A car pulled up beside the railings: a big, smart, dark car for people who thought limousines a tad flash. When David Ibbotsen told Miss Scotney it was family transport she would have believed him.

There were two people in the car. The camera showed nothing of the driver, only picked up the passenger as she walked to the school gate. She was wearing a dark suit with a calf-length skirt, high heels and a brimmed hat. She never looked at the camera, either because she didn't know it was there or because she did. The face of Daniel Hood, fiddling with his telescope on top of the monument five hundred metres away, could be enlarged and enhanced until there was a recognisable image, but the kidnapper the camera was there to capture remained resolutely anonymous.

160

"I'm telling you, that isn't Marie," insisted David.

Ibbotsen nodded in reluctant agreement. "No, I don't think it is." He went to turn the television off.

Brodie hadn't seen the tape before. Its existence was responsible for her involvement in these events, and for Daniel's. They'd been able to infer what it must show, but this was the first time she'd seen it. "Let it run," she said, and Ibbotsen stood back.

The woman entered the playground and made for a knot of little girls dressed in identical claret uniforms and playing some kind of clapping game. There was no soundtrack.

She knew which of the children she wanted, dismissed the others. Long fair hair spilling down her back identified the girl as Sophie Ibbotsen. For a couple of seconds she and the woman seemed to speak. Then the woman took her wrist, led her to the car and got into the back seat with her, and the car drove away. The whole episode had taken less than a minute.

Brodie took the remote and wound the tape back; looking for something.

Daniel frowned. "What is it?"

"I'm not sure. Maybe I imagined it. Let's run it again."

"What am I looking for?" But she wouldn't tell him.

She restarted the tape as the woman led the child towards the car. She played it for a few seconds before stopping it again. "There. Did you see?"

Daniel nodded. "Yes."

Ibbotsen, who hadn't, grew impatient. "What? What did you see?"

Brodie played it again. "Sophie doesn't want to go with this woman. Either she doesn't know her or she doesn't like her. She's hanging back so the woman's practically dragging her.

"Now look. Sophie reaches the point where she can see inside the car, and now she isn't reluctant any more. She moves towards the open door. Would Sophie recognise her mother?"

David Ibbotsen was watching the tape closely. "No. She was only two when Marie left."

The old man disagreed. "Of course she would. Marie never sends her a birthday card or a Christmas card or anything else without enclosing a photograph of herself. She doesn't know her mother but yes, I think she'd recognise her."

"And want to go with her?"

Ibbotsen thought about it. "I imagine most children with only one parent would want to meet the other."

Brodie nodded. "I think so too. Put your money back in the bank, Mr Ibbotsen, it won't bring Sophie back. What you need now are a French private detective and a specialist in French law."

Daniel said softly, "You're saying she's been safe all along?"

For a moment Brodie couldn't bring herself to answer. If she was right he'd suffered for nothing. But lying wouldn't alter that, only devalue the pain. "I think so. I think she's been enjoying a jolly holiday travelling with her mother through the French countryside. I think if Mr Ibbotsen paid the ransom, what he'd get in return would be a happy snap of the two of them together.

"I think France is a big country, and it's full of people whose first loyalty is to other French people rather than their English ex-husbands. I think Sophie's fine, but it could be a long time before she's back in England. Possibly not until she's old enough to buy her own ticket."

There was silence in the room, each of them coccooned in private thoughts.

Brodie thought she'd solved the mystery, and if it wasn't the ideal solution there was at least a certain natural justice to it.

Daniel was feeling guilty because he'd felt better when he thought Sophie's life was in danger.

Ibbotsen was trying to decide how he felt, because he didn't want to lose either his granddaughter or his money but he really didn't want to be robbed of both.

David Ibbotsen alone was unequivocal in his feelings. Any match between his father's money and his daughter's safety was a no-contest. This alternative scenario suddenly produced like a rabbit from a hat by a woman who had only the most peripheral involvement with the family, who didn't know either Sophie or Marie, who'd been picked out of a phonebook to serve a particular function and should have subsided into anonymity again once her task was done - it wasn't so much that he doubted her, more that he *knew* she was wrong. He *knew* it was about money. He knew Sophie couldn't come home until the money was paid.

He looked at Brodie with deep resentment. "For ten days we had one of the best hostage negotiators in the business on the case. He didn't think he was talking to Sophie's mother."

"He probably wasn't. We know there was another woman involved - he was probably talking to her. Marie would be pretty crazy to phone you herself. She involved a friend and let her do the talking."

Ibbotsen was nodding slowly, remembering. "He did say - our negotiator - there was no rush. That Sophie wasn't in any immediate danger. That the woman he talked to wasn't panicking to get her off her hands."

"Of *course* he said that," snarled David, "he was being paid by the day! These people are professionals too, they can afford to take the long view. What they can't afford to do is waste time on people who've made it clear they're never going to pay up. That box of hair that no one else is taking seriously: that's a warning. They're running out of patience. If we don't deal with them now, today, they'll hurt her; and after that they'll kill her. You're going to let them kill Sophie for less money than it takes to antifoul an oil-tanker!"

"Sonny," growled Ibbotsen, "you have no idea what it costs to antifoul an oil-tanker. I have. That's the difference between us, and that's why it's my money they're after, not yours."

In despair David turned to Brodie. "He trusts you. You gave him value for money. Tell him you could be wrong."

Brodie squirmed in the urgency of his gaze. "Of course I could be wrong. Anyone can be wrong. I gave you my honest opinion, based on a certain amount of experience. It's still my opinion. But yes, I could be wrong."

"Now tell him that if you're wrong my little girl's going to die!" The emotion was packed so tightly into David Ibbotsen's voice that it vibrated.

Brodie couldn't deny it. She was good at what she did, she trusted her instincts, but she'd never had to gamble a life on her judgement before. Would she have been so confident the missing child was safe, that the money could be retained without penalty, if it had been Paddy they were talking about? Just asking herself the question was enough to stifle the answer in her throat.

Daniel leaned forward, the scant bulk of his body coming between David and Brodie as if to protect her from something more physical than the truth. He didn't raise his voice, but there was that iron note in it that made people sit up long after they were old enough to ignore him. "Mr Ibbotsen, we're here because you asked us to come. You asked Mrs Farrell for her professional opinion and you've had it. If you don't like it, if you think she's wrong, fine, we'll go. But don't blame her for this. She wouldn't be involved if you hadn't involved her. Neither of us would. We'll help if we can, but we won't be your scapegoats."

David stared at him as if something unexpected had happened: as if one of the staff, or even one of the fire-dogs, had answered him back. Then he blinked rapidly, and passed a hand in front of his face and exhaled. "I'm sorry. You're right: I'm behaving badly. I'm just ... so worried. I'm so scared we're going to get this wrong.

"An hour ago, when I called, I was scared then too but I thought we were on the last lap. They'd told us what to do, the only thing we could do that was acceptable to them, and my father and I had agreed we were all out of options. I thought all we had to do was follow instructions. They wanted a woman to bring them their money? - OK, we could do that. We could do it today, this morning, and just maybe have Sophie home for lunch.

"Then you arrive and instead of doing what we ask you rake over it again. Putting it in a different light. Offering new alternatives. Putting the whole thing back in the melting-pot. It's been going on for twelve days, and I'm cracking up with the fear, and now you tell me she's never coming back?"

Brodie felt the pang of his fear like a small knife under her ribs. She was no longer convinced it was warranted, but she believed he thought it was which made it just as real. "David - "

But he didn't want to listen. He didn't want anyone to listen to

164

her talking down the risk. He hurried on. "If I believed you it would be difficult. I'd have to get used to the idea that it could be months, even years, before I saw Sophie again. But at least I'd know she was safe - that when we finally got it sorted out, she'd come home safe and well.

"But I *don't* believe you. I'm sorry, Mrs Farrell, I know you're doing your best, I'm sure what you say makes sense. But you don't know Marie and I do, and I'm convinced that you're wrong. And that means my little girl is still in deadly danger, and I can't get any of you to understand! I'm sorry if I upset you. But you're a mother - you know how you'd feel in my position. With the greatest respect, Mr Hood, you don't."

Daniel breathed lightly. "You're mistaken. I know exactly how much your daughter means to you. You were willing to kill for her; perhaps you'd be willing to die for her. But maybe what she needs from you most is that you keep your nerve."

David regarded him with a dislike that, in the circumstances, had a certain nobility about it. But his voice was level. "You offered to leave now. I'd take that as a kindness."

From the depths of his chair Lance Ibbotsen growled like a bear. "This is my house, David, if anyone's to be thrown out I'll have the pleasure of doing it. If you can't deal with this rationally, go for a walk and leave it to me. I happen to think Mrs Farrell's contribution has been profoundly helpful. Or perhaps you reckon I don't care enough about Sophie to have an opinion either."

"I think you care about your money more!"

A more hurtful riposte could hardly be imagined. There may have been some justice in it; whether or not, the man could be forgiven for the tattered state of his emotions. But either way it threw a monkey-wrench into the discussion. There was no ignoring it and no getting past. Lance Ibbotsen rose slowly to his full height.

"Care about money?" he rumbled. "Damn right I do! I started with nothing, I've worked for every penny I have. First I did it for me, then I did it for you, now I do it for Sophie. Half a million? - chicken-feed! I'd set fire to the whole damn lot if I thought it would bring Sophie home. To start with I didn't pay up because I was afraid it might get her killed. Now I'm not paying up because I think Mrs Farrell's right: that box of hair isn't the act of someone who's prepared to hurt her. But whether I pay or don't pay, sonny, it's my money and my decision.

"I'll take the blame too if I have to, but if there are mistakes to be paid for they'll be my mistakes, not yours. My judgement is good. I've had to gamble everything on my wits before this; you never have. Everything you've ever had was served to you on a plate. I don't begrudge you that, but don't think it qualifies you for an equal say in business matters. You haven't the talent, the skill or the experience. Half a million pounds won't break me, but it does put this into the big league. And you're not a big league player, David, and you never will be."

David was on his feet too. But there was nothing he could say to change the brute reality that he hadn't the means to defy his father even in this most personal of crises. His eyes filled and his lip trembled, and he turned and stumbled out of the room without a word.

Chapter 17

Ibbotsen made no effort to follow his son. He lowered himself back into his chair like a pteradactyl folding its wings.

Brodie regarded him with disbelief. "How can you claim to love someone else's child so much and show so little respect for your own?" She left the room in David's wake.

She expected to find him in the hall, possibly kicking an effigy of his father kept specifically for the purpose. But the hall was empty, and there were six doors and a sweeping staircase he could have used. She scowled. She couldn't search the house for him, and doubted he'd answer if she called.

A faint fairy tinkling drew her eye to French windows leading from the rear of the hall to a terrace overlooking the sea. They were shut, but a wind-chime of tiny bells was shivering gently, stirred by a recent draught of air. She let herself out onto the terrace.

The view was spectacular: across the sapphire sea all the way to France on a clear day. But she wasn't here for the view. She walked around the terrace until she found David Ibbotsen, hunched on a Lutyens bench. With his chin on his chest and his eyes closed he almost looked to be asleep.

Brodie said nothing. She sat on the bench beside him. He didn't lift his head, but one eye opened and regarded her laconically. "Welcome to the House of Ibbotsen," he drawled. "Half Greek tragedy, half Hammer Horror."

"Pretty much like everyone else's, then," she said.

That made him chuckle. He shook his head. "The thing about serious wealth is that it opens the door to genuine hatred. People who need one another never get much beyond dislike."

"He's an arrogant man," said Brodie. "I suppose he thinks, having made all this, he's entitled to be. But he does care about you. You and Sophie both."

"No," said David quietly. "It's one of those comforting fallacies. Like women who spend every Saturday night in Casualty saying,

'He's always sorry afterwards.' No, he isn't. If he was he wouldn't keep doing it. If my father gave a damn about me or my daughter he'd have paid up as soon as he got the ransom demand, and worried about getting even after Sophie was safe."

"There was some logic in what he said," murmured Brodie. She wasn't sure why she felt moved to defend the old pirate. Perhaps for David's sake: perhaps it would be less hurtful if he understood that it wasn't a clear choice between the child and the money.

"Would you have handled it that way? If you'd been in our shoes?"

She wouldn't lie to him. "No. But that doesn't mean I'd have been right."

"Maybe it's not a question of right," said David Ibbotsen softly. "Maybe decency comes into it too. If I get Sophie back without the old man having to stump up, you'd have to say that what he did was right. But it wasn't decent."

Brodie couldn't argue with that. "There really is no such thing as a free lunch, is there? The people who envy you all this - this house, the family business, the lifestyle that goes with it - don't appreciate that you pay a price for it. You must dream sometimes of having a nice little semi and a job in a building society."

David chuckled weakly. "He's right about one thing - I do have an easy, comfortable, privileged life. But if I had that semi I'd still have my daughter safe at home."

"And your wife?"

He looked at her then away, shrugging. "I don't know. I doubt Marie would have married me in the first place. But maybe someone would."

"What's she like? - your wife."

"Ex-wife. She's - volatile. Emotional. Everything's triumph or disaster with her. When she's happy she's the best company in the world; when she's sad she plumbs the depths of despair. So you ask why, and it turns out it rained when she wanted to go sailing. You say, 'Go tomorrow' - and she bursts into tears because she's surrounded by insensitive louts. I loved her for two years. The third exhausted me, and after that I honestly couldn't wait for her to go."

168

"It wasn't her drinking that ended the marriage then."

"The drinking was a symptom, not the cause. We weren't well enough suited, and I was too infatuated to see it." He gave a rueful sniff. "And she thought marrying money would be a lot more fun than it turned out to be. Unfortunately, to enjoy my father's wealth you have to take my father as well. She thought she could change that. When she couldn't she started drinking."

"David, everything you say about her fits my theory. Why are you so sure she isn't behind this?"

He bit his lip, made himself answer rationally rather than emotionally. "Because she hasn't the patience. Whoever did this spent time planning it. Marie might have snatched Sophie off the street if she'd seen her out walking with the housekeeper. She'd never have waited three years and then hit us with something as smooth, as calculated as this. She's not a cruel woman. I think she's a disappointed woman."

"We know there were at least two people involved. Maybe the woman on the tape - whether she's a friend or hired help - set it up. Or there may be someone new in Marie's life. Someone who does think long-term, and who expected a share of the proceeds."

"I suppose it's possible," he conceded reluctantly. "But you're asking me to wager Sophie's life on your guess-work. What if you're wrong?"

Brodie gave an apologetic shrug. "I'm not here to talk you into anything. She's your daughter, it's your money - the decision has to be yours."

At that his eyes flared bitterly. "If it was, this would have been over ten days ago."

"Can't you raise the money yourself?"

David shook his head. "Institutions that would prostitute themselves to lend to the Ibbotsen Line would show me the tradesmen's exit. The old man's right: I'm not an equal partner. I'm not any kind of partner, just a handy conveyance for his genes."

She wouldn't believe that. "If it hadn't been Sophie who'd been kidnapped, if it had been you - "

"He'd have called the police," David said flatly.

Brodie felt terribly sorry for him. Maybe he wasn't the man his father was, but maybe he shouldn't have to be. He was entitled to be himself. Living in the old man's shadow had gift-wrapped a future for him, but it had also robbed him of the chance to make his own. It had undermined his marriage and now he believed it had taken the one thing that was of his own making, his child. If there was room to criticize David Ibbotsen, there was reason enough to sympathise with him too. "If you want us to butt out, Daniel and me ... "

"I don't think it would make any difference. He'll do what he wants to do; if you hadn't given him an excuse he'd have invented one. Don't blame yourself, Mrs Farrell: I don't blame you and I shouldn't have said what I did. The whole mess is more to do with the Ibbotsen family than any outsider. We don't need anyone's help to tear each other apart."

Brodie was trying to think. "When you called Marie to say that Sophie was missing, was she there? Did she answer the phone?"

David's eyes dropped, but not quickly enough to hide his embarrassment. "I didn't call her. It seemed - best."

Brodie looked at him levelly. "You're telling me Marie doesn't know that her daughter has been missing for twelve days."

He winced. "You'd understand if you met her. Marie is an hysterical personality. If we'd told her it would have been on the internet the next day. Keeping it secret meant keeping it from Marie."

But increasingly Brodie believed that Marie knew well enough. "Phone her now. You don't need to talk to her - if she answers, put the phone down."

He frowned. "What will that achieve?"

"It'll tell us that she's at home. If she has Sophie, she won't be. She has to be aware you might work it out, and if you do she'll have the gendarmerie knocking at her door. She'll be somewhere they don't know to look."

They went inside. David had to look up the number.

The call was taken by an answering machine. He left no message. "What does that tell us?"

"Not a lot," admitted Brodie. "She could be there or not; she could be close enough to drop in and collect messages, or the far side of the country and phoning for them. Someone has to go there."

"How will that help?"

"You'll know then if she's still living there, if she's visiting at intervals or if she's done a runner. The neighbours will know if she's still around, the local shops will know. The wonders of modern technology can take you just so far. After that you have to start knocking on doors."

"You're talking about a private detective. A French private detective."

Brodie understood his misgivings. There are good inquiry agents and there are bad ones, and it can be hard enough to distinguish between them in one's own language. "I'll go if you like."

David stared at her. "You'd do that? After everything?"

"You need an answer quickly. I can do it quicker than anyone else. Or you, of course."

His gaze fell. "If I go I leave my father to man the phone and make any decisions that have to be made alone. I don't trust him to make the right ones. If you're offering I'll accept, gratefully. If Marie can convince you she's not involved, maybe you can convince the old man."

"All right," said Brodie. "I'll go now. Give me Marie's home address, and her parents' address if that's different, get me on a plane - "

"We have a Lear jet," said David. "It'll be ready inside an hour. Do you want to go home first?"

"I need my passport. And I'll drop Daniel off." The sound of his name brought a question to her mind. She wasn't sure she wanted to hear the answer but she needed to. "Will you tell me something? Honestly, without worrying if it'll upset me? I'll go to France whatever the answer."

"What?" But it was in his eyes that he already knew.

"For two days a man hired by your father tortured Daniel Hood for information he didn't even have. To what extent were you part of that?"

There was a long pause before he answered. "I only knew about it when it was almost over. I knew they were questioning someone: I didn't realise what that meant. Maybe I didn't want to. When I saw what they'd done I threw up. My father looked at me as if I'd let him down again."

Brodie nodded. "Tell him what we're doing. I'll be ready in twenty minutes."

* * *

David picked her up in the Range Rover, stowed her bag and passed her an envelope. "That's Marie's address in Quintin, and the address of her parents' home on the coast at Étables fifteen miles away. We're flying you into St-Brieuc and there'll be a car to meet you."

"I'll start at Marie's," said Brodie. "I doubt if she'll be there; but if she is, either Sophie'll be with her or she won't know anything about this." She looked at him sideways as he drove. "You understand, don't you, that even if I find Sophie I won't be able to bring her home? You'll have to get your solicitor onto it: he'll contact the Home Office and they'll liaise with the French authorities. I don't want you to be disappointed when I get off the plane alone."

In profile, David smiled. "Brodie, if you can find her - if you can tell me she's safe with her mother - I'll be eternally grateful. It doesn't matter how long the paperwork takes. Of course I'll get impatient, but the only thing that counts is Sophie's safety. Right now I believe she's being held by kidnappers who're prepared to hurt her, to kill her, for half a million pounds of my father's money. And since he'll do anything, say anything, convince himself of anything rather than pay up, I'm scared sick. If you can tell me I needn't be, that she's all right where she is however long it takes, I'll be in your debt forever."

"But you don't believe it, do you?"

He shook his head. "No. I'm afraid." He drew a deep, steadying breath. "But the sooner you find Marie and we know for sure, the better. If you tell the old man that money's the only answer, he'll pay. I believe that. I have to."

Stone walls clad in ivy and a lane of cobble setts led to what had been a small farmhouse. But unless the French had found a way of house-training them, no cows had crossed the yard in years. A small garden rumoured the spring and the pale sunshine picked out pastel paintwork. Marie Ibbotsen - or Soubriet, she had reverted to her maiden name - had been part of the nineties' land-rush, when city-folk decided the country was the new town, stocked up on Laura Ashley, and immediately started complaining about the smell of slurry and the noise of roosters.

The driver stayed in the car when Brodie got out. It occurred to her, perhaps a little late, that if Marie was part of an extortion racket she might be unwilling to discuss it calmly. If she or an accomplice produced a weapon, Brodie thought she'd leg it rather than waiting for the stout Breton in the Renault to defend her.

The Wedgwood blue front door boasted both a bell and a knocker. Brodie availed herself of both and waited. No one came. She tried again with the same result.

She looked around. No close neighbours: a farm cottage where this lane left the Quintin road was nearest, she could ask there as they left. First, though, she'd have a nosy round.

A timber gate, painted to match the front door, led down the side of the house to an orchard full of apple-trees. An A-frame ladder leaned against a white-washed outhouse. Climbers that should have been pruned back in the autumn had the rustic pergola in a strangle-hold.

Shading her eyes against reflections, Brodie peered in at the back windows. Though it was fully furnished there were no signs of life.

Continuing round the house Brodie came to the back porch. Her heart missed a beat when she tried the handle and the door swung open, but the kitchen door was locked. The boots in the porch could have been there for years.

Which was, after all, what she was expecting to find: the house quiet, the occupant gone. Brodie nodded knowingly to herself. She'd talk to the neighbours, then she'd go to Étables and see the parents. She might get a lead on Marie's whereabouts and she might not, but unless they could prove she was in hospital having her appendix out Brodie would believe she'd got to the bottom of this. She might not have resolved it but at least she could set David's mind at rest. Now he'd need more experts to find Marie, and different ones to get Sophie back.

She turned on the back step to find someone watching her from the pergola. She thought at first it was a boy but it was a girl, in denims and boots and a corduroy coat, her brown hair in a gamine crop. She eyed Brodie warily but raised no challenge to her trespass, waiting for an explanation.

Resorting to schoolgirl French, Brodie stumbled, "Pardon, mademoiselle. Je cherche la maison de Madame Soubriet. Est-ce que je suis perdu?" She was quite pleased with that. It may not have been fluent but she was making herself clear. There was no call for the girl to respond as she did.

"I speak English," she said.

Brodie sniffed, mildly offended. "I said, I'm looking for Marie Soubriet."

"I know you did. But English people are better at speaking French than at understanding it."

It was quite true: the first French phrases Brodie ever used outside the classroom were "Lentement, s'il vous plaît" and "Voulez-vous répéter cela?" She dipped her head in acknowledgement. "Your English is certainly better than my French."

"You are looking for Marie?"

"Is she here?"

The girl gave that stereotypical Gallic shrug that can mean anything from "Perhaps" to "Mind your own business", and ruder things than that. "Have you looked?"

"I just arrived. There was no answer at the door."

"And in England, when there is no answer at the door, you wander round the back garden?"

Stung, Brodie scowled at her. "I've come a long way. I didn't want to miss her just because she was out back feeding the chickens."

The girl - or woman, rather, Brodie saw now she was in her

174

mid-twenties - considered her speculatively for a moment longer. Then she stepped into the porch and, kicking her boots off, reached under a flowerpot for the key. "Pig," she said calmly.

Brodie blinked. "I don't think that's called for!"

"I was feeding the pig. I am Marie Soubriet. Come inside."

Brodie's mind whirled. She'd found the woman she'd come looking for. But - didn't that mean Marie wasn't the one she was looking for after all? Now she had to decide how much to tell her. And should she attempt to search the house? She could not discount the possibility that Sophie was here. Perhaps Marie had disdained to flee, had brought her daughter home trusting in her countrymen's support and the old enmity as defence enough against the claims of perfidious Albion.

Then, other people were involved: if she talked too freely she could find a shotgun in the small of her back. Or if she was wrong about Marie the woman would scream for the law the moment she heard the word "abducted". For the first time Brodie understood the dilemma the Ibbotsens had wrestled with these last twelve days. There were more ways to get this wrong than right.

But she had to start somewhere. If she left now she could tell David nothing. He would believe that finding Marie at home must mean she wasn't involved. And that might be the case, but Brodie wanted to be sure. At least she wanted to talk to the woman long enough to get a feeling for who she was, what she might be capable of.

She introduced herself, gave an abridged version of what she did for a living. Marie curled herself cat-like into an armchair. "Who asked you to find me?"

"Your ex-husband."

That didn't come as a surprise. She arched and then lowered one eyebrow. "David knows where I live. He doesn't need a private detective."

"I'm not a private detective. After I find things, sometimes people want me to negotiate for them."

The expression, contained before, now froze on Marie Soubriet's face, becoming utterly unreadable. "And what could I possibly have left that David might want?"

Brodie chose her words carefully. "He wants to talk about your daughter."

"*Ma* fille?" Anger jerked her back into her native tongue. Her eyes spat fire. "When did the Ibbotsens start thinking of Sophie as *my* daughter? Since the day of her birth Sophie was David's daughter, and more than that Lance's grandchild - a new generation to add to the Ibbotsen line. He didn't want her baptised, he wanted to break a bottle of champagne over her head."

Brodie chuckled, without much humour. "I haven't known them long but they are a bit overwhelming, aren't they?"

"Overwhelming." Marie tried the word and found it wanting. "Bastards. It is a house of bastards. My child is being raised by bastards."

"They do love her, you know," said Brodie, not so much for David's sake as to reassure the woman before her. She hadn't seen her child for three years and thought she was in the hands of bastards. Of course, that was true. "Both of them - David and his father - think the world of her."

Marie shook her head. "They value her, as a possession. You don't deprive a child you love of her mother."

Brodie knew she was walking into a minefield. "They say you could visit Sophie. That that's what the court decided."

"Court!" She controlled, just barely, the urge to spit. "They had money, I had a drink problem. The court did its duty."

Actually, Brodie thought it probably had. "Why haven't you been to see her? You wouldn't have to go alone, you could take your mother or a friend. You wouldn't have to spend any time with the Ibbotsens. As long as Sophie doesn't leave the house, you're entitled to some privacy with her."

Marie Soubriet considered. What it was she was considering, Brodie wasn't sure. "David described me to you, yes?"

"Not well enough for me to recognise you."

Marie smiled tightly. "Oh yes, David described me to you."

If Brodie lied Marie would not admire her discretion but judge her the Ibbotsens' mouthpiece. "He described you as volatile."

"Hysterical."

"That too."

"It's not a kind thing to say," said Marie, "but it's not wildly inaccurate. You know the French - we cry a lot, we wave our hands in the air. Well, even the French think I'm emotional. I get upset. I don't want to be in tears every time my daughter sees me. We write, I send photographs, she sends me drawings. Maybe I should start visiting. The divorce was difficult but I'm stronger now: maybe soon I'll be able to visit my daughter without upsetting her and making a fool of myself."

Brodie nodded encouragement, but her heart was leaden. It would be wilful to go on believing this woman had kidnapped Sophie, for ransom or any other purpose. Everything she said, every eloquent gesture of hand and body, argued against. She didn't know the child was missing.

Which left Brodie in a quandry. If Marie heard what had happened she would panic and the carefully preserved secret would be out. Later she might regret that; particularly if it transpired that Ibbotsen had been right all along about how the matter should be handled; but by then it would be too late.

When the world's press learned that a millionaire's granddaughter had been kidnapped, it wasn't going to agonise over the ethics of the situation like the man at *The Sentinel*. It was going to pick up the story and run. The people who had Sophie were already restless: that could be the final straw. Brodie had been wrong about the hair and David had been right - it was a last humane warning. Marie Soubriet didn't need to live out her life knowing that her panic attack had led to her daughter's murder.

Marie said, "Is that what they wanted to discuss? Me visiting Sophie?" Her face was puzzled. "I thought they never wanted to see me again."

Brodie took a deep breath. "Marie - there's been an incident. I believe Sophie is safe and well, but there's a possibility that she's in some danger. Try not to be too upset and I'll tell you everything I know."

Marie heard her out almost in silence, with just a little whimper of animal fear. When Brodie first said the word "kidnap" she clamped both hands tight over her mouth and went on listening while her eyes grew enormous with terror. When the tale was told and Marie lowered her hands, there was blood where she'd bitten her lip.

"Your head must be buzzing with questions," Brodie said quietly. "I'll answer all I can."

The only answers Marie really wanted were the ones she knew Brodie didn't have. Where is my daughter? - is she safe? - when will she be home? She managed to suppress them long enough to think. "The police have not been informed?"

"The kidnappers insisted. Mr Ibbotsen thought it best to go along."

"But he hasn't paid them yet?"

"The money's ready. He's been afraid to hand it over in case they took it and never returned Sophie."

"So - what is he doing?"

She couldn't say, He's waiting to hear if I was right and you staged the kidnap. "Waiting to hear from the kidnappers again. They have to arrange a hand-over. As soon as there's some news I'll call you. I just need to be sure that you understand something. Sophie's your daughter: you have the right to involve your police. But that could jeopardise the negotiations in England. If you can bear to, nothing is the best you can do for Sophie right now."

Marie Soubriet was coping better than Brodie had expected. Three tough years had taught her more than how to do without alcohol. They had matured her, given her a resilience that was absent when David knew her. Brodie found herself wondering whether, if he met her now, he would fall in love with her again.

"Lance is handling the negotiations?"

Brodie nodded. "It's his money and the kidnappers know it. No agreement they reached with David would be worth half a million pounds."

"That's right." Marie was nodding too, mechanically. "If he says he'll pay, he'll pay. He may be a monster, but he is at least an honest monster."

"So you'll wait?" prompted Brodie. "If the police step in at this point, I don't know what the consequences might be."

178

"I understand." Marie wiped the blood off her mouth onto the back of her hand. "I understand."

Brodie stood up. "When this is over and Sophie's safe, you have to get the question of custody looked at again. I don't believe any court in England would deny you the right to bring your daughter home now."

Marie's eyes widened again. "You work for them! You shouldn't be saying this."

"I don't work for them," Brodie retorted tetchily, "I'm trying to help Sophie. And I think she'd be better with you than with the Ibbotsens. This wouldn't have happened if she'd lived with you."

Marie walked her back to the waiting car. "You'll call me as soon as there's some news? Good or bad?"

"I promise."

Chapter 18

Lance Ibbotsen met her plane - well, his plane - and brought Brodie up to date. It didn't take long: no word had been received from the kidnappers in the five hours she'd been away. Then he wanted to know how she'd fared. "Were you right? Don't tell me David was?"

Brodie shook her head, defeated. "I felt so *sure* ... But no, Marie isn't part of this. I'd stake my reputation on it."

Ibbotsen stared at her as if he couldn't credit what he was hearing. "You mean - everything you told me - you were *wrong*? Sophie isn't with her mother - isn't with anyone who loves her and cares what happens to her? We've wasted another day because what you told me was wrong?"

Brodie was troubled too, or she'd have pointed out he was in no position to lambast her mistakes. "I don't understand. It makes no sense any other way." She heard then the echo of what he'd said and her pointed chin came up ready for battle. "But don't blame me for wasting time. If the kidnappers haven't contacted you since I left there's nothing you could have done whether I'd gone to France or not."

He was reluctant to let her off the hook. But finally he looked away and nodded, starting the car. "I suppose not," he said gracelessly.

They made the short drive from the airport in silence.

* * *

"*Now* do you believe me?" demanded David. "Now will you accept that the only way we're going to get Sophie home is to do what we're told?"

Avoiding one another's eyes, Brodie and Ibbotsen both nodded.

"Can we give them the money?" David was looking at his father. The old man nodded again. David turned his gaze on Brodie. "And will you do as they ask? Will you take it to them?"

180

"If that's what you want," she said, subdued.

"Thank you."

She'd come inside with Ibbotsen but she didn't sit down. "You have my mobile number. I'll keep it with me until I hear from you. When I do, I'll be here in ten minutes."

David seemed surprised. "You aren't staying?"

"I want to get home and see if Daniel's all right."

He said nothing. He had one eye on the phone as if expecting it to ring any moment.

"Look," Brodie said reasonably, "they haven't called since they sent that packet. They're letting you fret about what it means. Try not to worry: they won't do anything more until they've spoken to you again."

"I suppose not. No, you're right of course. I'm sorry." He forced a smile. "I'm not thinking straight any more. Of course you should go home. You have a little girl to think of too." But he didn't want to leave the phone long enough to drive her home. He called her a taxi.

* * *

It was tea-time. Marta had set places for everyone and Daniel was upstairs. There was a note on the hall table so Brodie wouldn't think she'd lost him again. She dumped her coat but kept her bag with the phone in it and went to join them, entering her friend's flat without a knock.

She walked in on a scene which shocked her to the core.

They'd been making pancakes. Daniel was good at working out the quantities but not particularly deft with a whisk and he'd covered himself in batter. Marta found him a clean T-shirt.

"If I keep wearing women's clothes," he said ruefully, "people will talk." He stripped off his spattered shirt.

Brodie arrived at the worst possible moment. A minute before and she could have got Paddy tactfully offside; a minute after and it would have been too late to intervene. But she saw him about to bare his ravaged body in front of her four-year-old daughter and the protest was out of her mouth before she could consider the implications. "Daniel, for heaven's sake!"

The exclamation startled everyone and for a moment the tableau froze. Paddy, puzzlement holding back the pleasure at her unexpected arrival; Daniel, surprise turning to understanding and then shame; and Marta, dear reliable mercurial Marta, angry with her, seeing what her delicacy had done to the bruised soul in her keeping.

Brodie bit her lip, sorry to add to his burden of hurts. But Paddy was her first responsibility and the child shouldn't have to see the consequences of her mother's stupidity.

It was too late for anything but regrets. If she'd said nothing Daniel would have had the shirt on by now: as it was her horror had paralysed him. He fumbled for the sleeves and failed to find them, all the while feeling her eyes lashing on his raw flesh.

Marta threw the spattered shirt aside and reached to help him. But Paddy got there first. Four-year-olds have perfect instincts, they cut right to the chase. This isn't always convenient but it saves a lot of time that adults waste on tact.

Her eyes widened and she moved in for a better look. She pointed with one small forefinger: Brodie was dreadfully afraid she was going to poke the lesions to see what happened. But she stopped just short. "What's that?"

While Brodie was struggling for an explanation suitable for a small child, Daniel told her. He was used to children's questions, including the embarrassing ones, invariably found honesty served best. It was part of what made him a truth junkie. "I got burned," he said quietly.

"I got burned once," said Paddy, remembering. "Mummy said, 'Don't you dare play with matches you stupid infant.'"

"It was good advice." Daniel had finally found the sleeves of Marta's T-shirt and slid into them.

"It really hurt," said Paddy. She went on peering at his chest, taking in the scale of the damage. "I bet that hurts too."

"It did," nodded Daniel. "It's almost better now."

"Good." Satisfied, Paddy went back to help Marta at the kitchen table.

Brodie put down her bag. She said softly, "I'm sorry."

"I didn't mean to upset anyone," mumbled Daniel. "I wasn't thinking."

"You didn't upset Paddy, and I had no right to be upset. It was stupid and unnecessary."

Daniel looked up nervously. "Is it that bad?"

"No."

"The truth. I've got used to it, but if it's so grim I ought to keep it out of sight I need to know. I don't want to go through life making children scream and old ladies faint."

Brodie smiled. "Daniel, I promise you, it's not that bad. It's better now than when I first saw it, and it'll be better again in another week. I don't know why I reacted like that. Motherhood messes with your brain, you start seeing problems where none exist. Never mind me, you saw how Paddy reacted. She didn't scream. She was sorry you'd been hurt, that's all."

Daniel managed a smile too. "She's a nice kid."

"She is, isn't she?"

On the floor beside them Brodie's handbag warbled.

* * *

Half a million pounds worth of gold is solid and heavy and looks like exactly what it is. Half a million pounds worth of diamonds sparkle like the night sky. But half a million pounds in banknotes doesn't look particularly impressive. It fitted into a suitcase that wasn't heavy enough to trouble her, and Brodie had to keep reminding herself it was the most money she'd ever have her hands on. It might have been Monopoly money, or the cut-down newspapers with which master criminals are so easily fooled on television.

But it wasn't: Brodie checked. She checked every bundle, refusing to be intimidated by Lance Ibbotsen's glacial stare. "I'm going to be closer to these people than you are. I'm not doing it without knowing exactly what it is I'm carrying. You can risk your neck for a week's worth of the *Financial Times* if you want to, but not mine."

"I wouldn't dream of it," he said distantly. It was, of course, a lie. He'd done more than dream about it: he'd given it serious consideration, only dismissed the idea when he couldn't find a way of getting it past Mrs Farrell. He'd known she would want to see the ransom, had even expected she might check it. It didn't make him any happier about standing there while she riffled every one of the twenty-five bundles under his nose. There aren't many ways to humiliate a seriously rich man, but she'd found one.

"All right," said Brodie when she was satisfied. "What do I have to do?"

"Drive west along the Shore Road," said David. His voice was level but only because he was working on it. His face was tense - with hope, fear and deep anxiety - and the muscles across his shoulders were rigid. "They'll phone you with instructions."

"That's it?"

"Pretty much. They want you to go alone; they want you to use your car; and they want the money on the front seat beside you."

"In the suitcase?"

He blinked. "I presume so. They didn't say."

Brodie nodded. "At some point they'll want it open, but it won't do them much good if I'm robbed before I get out of Dimmock. Did they put Sophie on the line?"

"Yes," nodded David, "I insisted. Only a couple of words, but it was her and she sounded all right. In return ... " His voice petered out, the sentence unfinished.

"What?"

"In return," growled Ibbotsen, "they had him put me on the line."

Brodie understood. They'd wanted confirmation that the money was coming from the only source where it could be raised. They wanted to deal with the organ-grinder, not the monkey.

She avoided David's eyes. "All right," she said tightly, "then let's get it over with." She managed not to add, "One way or the other," but the sentiment hung in the air.

"Be careful," murmured Daniel.

She'd wanted to leave him at home but he refused. He couldn't come any further with her, but this was where the first intimations of success or failure would come and he wanted to be here when they did.

Even though it meant being alone with these people. Before they left home Brodie had made sure he'd thought about how that would feel. She wasn't sure if he was coping with all that had happened or if he was still pretending, and she didn't dare ask. If it was self-defense, an incautious word could break him between one moment and the next.

He'd answered with his shy, stubborn shrug. "Difficult. But the rich have more bathrooms than normal people: I'll never be too far from somewhere I can throw up."

Now she looked at him and nodded. "Count on it. I won't forget that Sophie's life is at stake."

"So's yours," said Daniel. "You don't have to do this, Brodie. Not for them, and not for me."

"Perhaps not," she said, just the hint of a shake in her voice, "but I have to do it for me. I don't think I'm in any danger. They want my help too - they asked for it. And no one's trying to cheat them."

David bit his lip. "He's right. We're asking a lot. If it goes wrong, if you find yourself in danger, walk away. No one will blame you. We'll make another chance."

Brodie knew what it had cost him to say that. Through the turmoil under her breastbone she felt compassion for him, and respect, and something that was more than both. In other circumstances, when he didn't have the weight of dread hanging round his neck, this could be a kind, intelligent, likeable man.

"It's hard to make promises when we don't know what's going to happen," she said softly. "But I'll do the best I can. If it's within my power at all, I'll bring Sophie home."

Chapter 19

For the first mile Brodie drove with infinite care and didn't quite know why. When understanding dawned she was disgusted with herself. She didn't drive like this when she had Paddy in the car, but she treated half a million pounds on her front seat as if it were cut glass. Shame-faced, she picked up speed and followed the setting sun.

She had no idea how far they would want her to go. She might be driving all night to a rendezvous in Cornwall: there was simply no knowing. For ten minutes she glanced at the phone as often as she checked her mirror, willing it to ring. But it didn't, and gradually she accepted that it was going to take longer than that.

The Shore Road began to veer inland. She passed the signs for Bognor, Selsey and Chichester. She checked the mirror repeatedly, but if anyone was following her they were doing it well. The phone stayed resolutely silent.

When it finally rang, somewhere between Chichester and Hayling Island, Brodie jumped so hard she hit the seatbelt.

She let it ring while she pulled over. It was in no one's interests that she wreck the car at this point. "Yes?"

"Who are you?" It was a woman's voice. No particular accent, certainly not a French one.

"Brodie Farrell. I'm acting for David Ibbotsen."

"About time, too," said the woman shortly. "You know who I am?"

"No. But I know what you want."

"Have you got it?"

"Yes."

"All of it?"

"Yes. I checked."

"Good," said the woman. "Finally we're getting somewhere."

"Tell me where to go."

* * *

She did as she was told - exactly as she was told, including not phoning *Chandlers* to pass on the directions. Not that anyone had asked her to. At long last all those involved were agreed that the time had come to get Sophie home.

The route she was given took Brodie inland. Every few miles another call redirected her. In the darkness she drove up country lanes overhung with trees and through fly-speck villages clinging to the edge of the South Downs. She knew where she was to within three or four miles, but after the third phonecall knew she'd never be able to retrace the route exactly. When she had Sophie - if she got Sophie - she'd have to keep driving until she picked up a sign.

People whose knowledge of the South Coast is limited to Brighton, Portsmouth and Southampton always think it's more densely populated than in fact it is. A lot of the towns are quite small, and five miles inland are stretches of not very much at all. It wasn't necessary to send Brodie off into the West Country in order to get her lost. An hour's reconnaissance had given the kidnappers everything they needed, including somewhere for the exchange to take place.

The phone rang again. "There's a crossroads up ahead. Wait there."

There wasn't even a signpost, and no other vehicle in sight. Brodie pulled over, switched down to sidelights and waited.

After five minutes someone tapped on her window and she hit the seatbelt again.

It was the nearside window. She lowered it enough for voices but not hands to pass through. She could see the figure outside but not a face or any other distinguishing feature. A man's voice said, "Is that it?"

"Yes."

"Show me."

Brodie hesitated. If they chose to break the car window, take it from her and vanish without leaving the child in its place, she couldn't stop them. All she could do was make it awkward. She lifted the suitcase onto her knee and opened it.

"I can't see."

She switched on the car's interior light. The bulb was brilliant against the night, diminishing further her chances of seeing clearly the man she was talking to. She let her hand hover over the bundles. "Which one?"

"That one."

She picked it up and opened it, fanning it like playing cards. Then she put it back and closed the case. "The child."

He had no instructions to wrestle the money from her. "Turn left. Drive a quarter of a mile till you see a forest park sign. There's a track on the left: drive up there. Wait at the footbridge and someone'll meet you."

Brodie took a deep, unsteady breath. She didn't want them to think she was making difficulties but she had to be careful. They'd expect that. "I'm going to lock the money in the boot now. I won't get it out again until I've seen Sophie."

"All right. Drive to the footbridge and wait."

She drove on a hundred metres before stopping the car to do as she'd said. They could force the boot and get the money without her co-operation if they had to, but it would take longer than smashing the window.

The sign loomed out of the darkness and Brodie followed it. Through the crack of the window came the sound of water; a moment later her headlights caught the rustic filigree of a footbridge springing across a deep ravine. She stopped the car beside it. At intervals she had to remember to breathe.

A minute passed. Then the wooden bridge creaked, and by degrees a solid form coalesced out of the darkness at the limit of Brodie's vision. She couldn't tell if it was a man or a woman, only that it wasn't a child. It advanced to the apex of the bridge's curve and stopped there.

Brodie waited, breath abated, heart hammering in the cage of her ribs.

A woman's voice was raised over the clamour of the sunken river. "Get out of the car and come up here."

Slowly Brodie did as she was bid. She didn't think they meant to hurt her: as long as she did as they said it wasn't in their interests.

But she wasn't taking any unnecessary risks. She stepped onto the bridge but stopped well short of the waiting figure.

"Closer," said the woman. "You won't be able to see from there."

"See what?"

"Come closer."

But Brodie wouldn't step within snatching range. The keys to the car were in her pocket: if they grabbed her now they could have both the money and the child. The bridge could be a trap: they only had to block each end to make her captive.

But no one grabbed for her and no one emerged from the darkness to block her retreat. The woman spread her arms in a not wholly convincing gesture of goodwill and stepped back.

Brodie took her place at the highest point of the bridge. "What am I supposed to be looking at?"

"The rope."

It was thick and strong, and tied loosely around the handrail. Confused, Brodie followed it with her torch. Down at her feet it was tied, much more firmly, in a complex knot around one of the heavy trestles. Taut then, it went down another two metres. Brodie started to say, "I don't see ... " and then she did.

The rope held a cage suspended above the stony torrent. It might have been a travelling crate for a big dog. Through the slats as she moved the torch around she could see something curled on the floor, wrapped in shiny red fabric. It wasn't a dog. It might have been a child bundled up in a sleeping-bag.

Brodie battened down all the rage that might have clouded her judgement and turned towards the other woman. "Sophie?"

"Sophie." The woman had a knitted hat pulled down over her head while a scarf inside the upturned collar of her coat masked the lower part of her face. Brodie knew she could meet her in broad daylight tomorrow and never know.

"She's dead."

"Of course she isn't dead." She put out her hand. "Give me the keys."

"Not till I know she's alive."

"I could take them."

Brodie had them in her hand, held out over the ravine. "Not as quickly as I can drop them. It would take you all night finding them, and you haven't that much time. If they don't hear from me soon the Ibbotsens will call the police."

She could almost hear the woman thinking. How soon? She wouldn't risk compromising the exchange with success so close. But every minute increased the danger. She had to get the money and leave the area before any search could begin.

"All right," said the woman tersely. "You can talk to her, in a minute. First I want you to understand the situation. The rope's tied in a slip-knot: it won't free itself, but one good yank and she drops like a stone. I doubt she'd survive the fall; even if she did, she'd drown before you could get to her. All right? You understand that?"

Brodie nodded fractionally. "I understand."

"Good. Now, while I'm standing by this rope I have her life in my hands. When I walk away, you have. If you can't pull her up she'll be perfectly safe until you can get help.

"In a minute, when you're satisfied she's alive, you're going to fetch the briefcase from the car. You're going to open it and show me the money, then put it down beside you. Then I'm going to leave the rope, walk past you, pick up the money and leave. You'll stay on the bridge for five minutes. Then you can go for help, phone for help, anything you like. It's over."

"All right," said Brodie.

The woman regarded her keenly. "Don't think you can grab the child and come after the money. It'll take you minutes to pull her up even if you can do it alone, and by then we'll be gone. But if you leave the bridge before then, the last thing you'll hear will be the first barrel of a double-barrelled shotgun. The last thing Sophie'll hear will be the second barrel."

"I've no intentions of doing anything heroic," gritted Brodie. "I'm not here to make this harder, I'm here to get it done. How do I talk to Sophie?"

"Loudly," said the woman. "She's sedated - nothing heavy, just so she's too sleepy to be scared. Call her name, she should hear you."

190

Directing the torch once more through the bars of the crate, Brodie leaned over the handrail and raised her voice. "Sophie? Sophie! Your daddy sent me to fetch you. Are you all right? Sophie, tell me you're all right."

For the longest time there was no response of any kind. From thinking the drama was as good as over, Brodie was beginning to fear that the situation had taken the worst possible turn.

Then the faintest movement of the red nylon maggot on the floor of the crate indicated the presence of life. With a surge of hope Brodie redoubled her efforts, shouting the child's name as if she were on the far side of a football pitch. Finally she was rewarded by the emergence of a blonde head from the sleeping-bag. The new haircut and bleary expression made her unrecognisable from the little girl in the video, but she was about the right age and Brodie needed only a little reassurance to believe it was the right child.

"Are you all right?" she asked, dropping her voice a little now she had the girl's attention. "Has anybody hurt you?"

"'M cold," the child mumbled plaintively. "Wanna go home."

"What's your name?"

Learned by rote, it came out parrot-fashion. "Sophie Ibbotsen, *Chandlers*, Firestone Cliff, Dimmock," David's daughter chanted sleepily. "Can we go home now?"

"Yes, we can." Brodie no longer had any doubts. It was exactly how Paddy would have responded, drummed into her at the same time as not talking to strangers and asking to go to the bathroom before it was too late.

She turned to the woman and nodded. "I'll fetch the money."

From there it proceeded as planned, the transaction completed within a couple of minutes. The woman took the suitcase, crossed the bridge and disappeared into the trees. The sound of a car engine, a wash of headlights through the branches and they were gone, leaving her alone with the ransomed child.

Who was still dangling above a river on the end of a rope.

The first thing Brodie did was to take the loose end and tie it very tightly to a sturdy piece of the bridge. Then she took a moment to think.

Unsure where she was, she could call for help but not direct it here - it could be some time before anyone would find her. And now the child was awake, and she was cold and she was going to get frightened.

She was a year older than Paddy, heavier but perhaps not that much heavier. The crate was designed for transporting animals, for which it needed to be strong but lightweight. Brodie was no fitness freak, found her everyday life energetic enough that she didn't feel the need to pump iron as well; but she'd always thought of herself as strong enough for most eventualities. If it had been Paddy on the end of that rope she'd have got her up somehow. Somehow, she would do as much for David's daughter. She gripped the rope and began to haul.

It was harder than she expected, and took longer, and because of that she had to dig deeper into her reserves of strength and fortitude and sheer determination than she would have believed they stretched. But she kept hauling and resting, hauling and resting, and ignored the broken fingernails and the bloody palms where the rope got away from her for a moment and went through like sandpaper, and after a little while she could see the child's face, white between the bars, watching in fear. Lacking the breath to call encouragement Brodie nodded a greeting and kept hauling until the crate jammed against the handrail and would come no further. Brodie tied the rope to hold it there.

She waited another minute till her heart stopped thundering and her lungs slowed, then she swung a long leg over the rail and leaned down until she could reach the door of the crate. She just had time to think, If it's padlocked we're stymied, before her fingers found a plastic clip. She opened the door carefully and reached inside.

Then Sophie Ibbotsen was in her hands, and a moment later she'd swung her up and over the rail and was kneeling on the damp timber, hugging her - sleeping-bag and all - to the warmth of her body, sobbing into the sharp new haircut with exhaustion and relief and happiness.

When she had her breath back she carried Sophie to the car. The child was asleep again before she got the door closed.

There was one thing more she had to do - well, two, but one more important than the other. She took out her mobile phone and dialled Marie Soubriet's number. Only when she'd finished reassuring Sophie's mother, laughing and crying with her often at the same time, did she call *Chandlers*.

Chapter 20

She had to keep saying it again, to all three of them. Obviously they were passing the phone between them, and every new voice began, "Is she really all right?"

"Yes," said Brodie, again and again, "she's fine. She's a little sleepy. They gave her something so she'd doze through the scary bits. Talk to her. Just don't be alarmed if she nods off mid-sentence."

She gave Sophie the phone. The child said, "Hi, Daddy," as if she hadn't seen him since lunchtime, and yawned, and fell asleep curled round it, ignoring the increasingly agitated questioning.

Brodie sighed and extricated the mobile from the little girl's grasp. "She's gone back to sleep. It's the best thing. With any luck I'll have her home before she wakes up again."

"But she is all right?" It was Lance Ibbotsen. "She doesn't need a doctor?"

"I'm as sure as I can be that she's fine. But if you want your medical adviser to give her the once-over, I'll be with you in about an hour."

David this time: "We'll come and meet you."

"Don't do that. I'm not sure where I am, we'd end up missing one another on the road. David, she's fine, and she's coming home. We'll be there in an hour."

* * *

The sitting room at *Chandlers* was a tip. Every surface was covered with cups half-full of cold coffee. As if waking from a trance the three men looked around them, seeming almost puzzled to find themselves there. David made a vague effort to tidy up, but didn't keep at it long enough to achieve anything.

"I suppose - Mrs Handcock - in the morning?" He lifted one shoulder in half a shrug and sat down again, unable to organise a coherent sentence let alone an archaeological excavation.

194

Lance Ibbotsen rumbled, "She didn't say anything about the money."

David just looked at him. "It's gone, Dad. That's *why* Sophie's on her way home. That's what it bought. I'm sorry. I will pay you back. It may take a little time."

The old man dismissed that with an irritable gesture. "That's not necessary. It's not about the money; it never was. It's about stopping people seeing us as an easy mark." He stood up stiffly, easing painful limbs. "I'll call the police."

David stared at him. "You can't."

Ibbotsen frowned. "Why not? Sophie's safe."

"Yes. But we're not."

Daniel moistened dry lips. "He means, if you report this, Detective Inspector Deacon's going to charge you with attempted murder."

There was a long silence. Then: "Only if you tell him to. Which is, of course, your right. No one would blame you for wanting your pound of flesh now."

Daniel lurched to his feet, padding unhappily round the room. He ended up at the window. The curtains were open but the view was limited to a couple of metres of garden; beyond that was blackness. The night was easier on his soul than this room.

He rested his brow against the cool glass. "Damn you, Mr Ibbotsen," he said, his voice low. "This is not my fault. None of this was my doing. How dare you blame me for the consequences?"

"He's right," growled David. "He isn't responsible for what happened to us. We *are* responsible for what happened to him."

Ibbotsen's look set hooks in Daniel's back. "It could end here. All he has to do is keep his mouth shut."

Goaded by his tone, Daniel spun to face him. His eyes burned. "Why don't you offer me some money, Mr Ibbotsen?"

The old man thought about it. But he'd learned that lesson at least. "Because you'd spit in my face."

Daniel gave a wild little laugh. "Well, at least we've got that straight. Now let's see if we can make the next great leap of understanding.

"Nothing I say or don't say will make any difference. If you tell the police about the kidnapping, no power on earth will stop Jack Deacon from realising that your granddaughter is the same Sophie I was questioned about. That I was tortured and shot because of. Ten minutes after you make that call he'll be on your doorstep, and he won't be one bit interested in getting your money back for you."

Ibbotsen's eyes were glacial with comprehension. "You could lie."

Daniel could have said, "Deacon would know better." He could have said, "Why should I lie for you?" He could even have said, "I want to see you pay." Instead he said, "I don't lie." Just that, a bare statement of fact that left Ibbotsen staring at him more in bewilderment than anger.

David stepped quietly between them. He turned his back on his father. "What if we don't call the police? Will you?"

Daniel felt the weight of their hopes as a physical burden, crushingly heavy. "I don't know."

Ibbotsen snorted derisively. "I'll take that as a yes, shall I?"

But David shook his head. "I will never understand how a man can be so successful in life without learning *anything* about other people," he said bitterly, swinging on his father. "Have you forgotten what was done here? He almost died. He must have wished he *would* die. And you want him to pretend it never happened, because that way we get away scot-free.

"And the amazing thing is, he's actually considering it. Oh, not for you; and not for me either, and why should he?" He looked once more at Daniel. "You're thinking about Sophie, aren't you? You're thinking that bringing her home will be a hollow victory if everyone she cares about is behind bars."

The turmoil in his heart frayed Daniel's breathing. The decision had troubled him when he'd faced it before. He'd deferred it until Sophie was safe, but it wasn't any easier now. He'd spent time with these people, shared their fears and their hopes and the glorious, unmanning moment when the phone rang and it was Brodie reporting success. Now he had to choose. Either he let go of the pain and the anger, let them float away unacknowledged, or he redeemed them at the cost of two men's freedom and a little girl's happiness.

"I don't know," he said again. Behind the thick lenses his eyes began to fill.

David saw and turned away. "All right," he said quietly. "This isn't something we can settle now. Dad, if you phone the police you're mad. You'll go to prison, and so will I. Forget the money. If Daniel goes to the police you'll have a lot more to worry about than half a million pounds.

"Also if he doesn't. Because there's a debt there. We owe him. We know what he thinks of your chequebook so I don't know how we'll set about paying it, but somehow we have to. It's going to be hard enough looking at one another over the breakfast table from now on: if we don't even try to make things right I think it may be impossible.

"Thank God we're getting Sophie back," he said. "But the price wasn't just half a million pounds: it was every shred of honour either of us possessed. I don't know about you, Dad, but I'd quite like to salvage just a little — just a few rags to keep myself decent. Daniel, can we maybe talk about this again, when the dust's settled? If you won't take something for yourself, maybe we could set up a charitable trust of some kind - something to help people in trouble?"

"You spending my money again, son?" rumbled Ibbotsen softly.

"You'd sooner go to jail?" demanded David. "Fine - I dare say that's Daniel's preferred option as well. You call the police, I'll pack us a bag each."

"Please." It was Daniel. Now the tears were coursing openly down his cheeks. "Please, don't shout. I don't want anything from you. Not your money, not your promises, not five minutes of your time let alone five years. I'm glad Sophie's safe. Maybe if you'd done things differently she wouldn't be. Maybe that's what - what you did - bought. I'm going to think so. I don't need revenge. Just call me a taxi, I want to go home."

They stared at him for a couple of minutes before they could bring themselves to believe it. Generosity was not an Ibbotsen family trait. They seemed nonplussed by it. But there was no catch, no hook beneath the bait; Daniel added no conditions or qualifications, and nothing they knew about him suggested he'd change his mind once he was away from here.

Lance Ibbotsen cleared his throat. "Aren't you going to wait for Mrs Farrell?"

Daniel shook his head. "Tell her I went on. If you like, you can tell her what I said."

The old man went on regarding him for a moment longer. Then he nodded. "I'll drive you."

"I'd rather have a taxi."

* * *

This was an occasion. Brodie drove straight to the front door, gravel crunching under her wheels. They heard her coming: the door flung open and David raced down the steps, his father following in his wake.

Nothing she could say would be worth hearing. She opened the rear door of her car and stood back, and David Ibbotsen swept his child up into his arms without even waiting to see if she was awake.

Sophie blinked and looked over his shoulder at the familiar scene around her. Every light was ablaze, the forecourt as bright as day. "Home," she mumbled, a note of satisfaction in her little voice. Then she went back to sleep, and no amount of rocking and hugging and stroking would disturb her.

David carried her upstairs to bed. The family's doctor went with them but ten minutes later he was on his way, satisfied the little girl had suffered no ill-effects and would wake in the morning none the worse for her adventure.

Lance Ibbotsen made some fresh coffee. He took Brodie through to the sitting room and poured. "Tell me everything."

But she looked around, frowning. "Where's Daniel?"

"He went home. He waited till we knew that Sophie was safe, then he called a cab. He was tired. Don't worry about him, he's fine."

Brodie nodded. Suddenly reaction was making her tired too: she sat down before her knees gave way. "It was nothing to do with Marie. It was a straightforward ransom for money. In the end they played it by the book." She recounted everything that had taken place.

When David came downstairs she went through it again.

He listened in silence until she was finished. Then he leaned forward and took her hand. "Brodie, I said this to Daniel before he left and now I'm saying it to you. I don't know how we can ever repay you. For your help, or how we got you involved in the first place. But I'd like to try. We can't hope to recompense Daniel, and it won't be a lot easier to make things right with you. But if there's any way we can make you feel a bit better about what's happened, we'd welcome the opportunity."

Brodie shrugged and shook her head, but she didn't shake off his hand. "David, I don't - I can't - Look, I just can't think about it now. If you want to we can talk about it another time. Right now, I'm just so glad it's over and you've got your little girl back safely." She paused and gave a tiny smile. "I bet that's what Daniel said too, isn't it?"

David answered with a sombre smile of his own. "Pretty much. Except he didn't want to talk about it another time."

Brodie nodded. "That doesn't mean he won't be glad of a friend sometime."

Lance Ibbotsen was watching her like a hawk. She frowned. "What?"

"Hood said he wouldn't go to the police about this. What about you?"

"Dad!" David exclaimed in dismay; but the old man wanted an answer.

Brodie let him wait; enjoyed letting him wait. Then: "*Is* that what Daniel said?"

"Yes."

"You know I'll see him when I go home, that I'll ask him?"

David nodded. "It's what he said. Unless he changes his mind."

"Oh, he won't change his mind." Brodie gave an exasperated chuckle. "Rivers change their courses, continents change their outline but Daniel Hood never changes his mind! If that's what he said, you can count on it. And I won't go against his wishes. If that really is what he wants, you've nothing to fear from me."

199

Ibbotsen nodded brusquely. David let out a long sigh. "Thank you. For everything."

"That doesn't mean," she went on, "you have nothing to fear. Jack Deacon doesn't strike me as the sort of man to give up on his job when it gets too difficult. He won't find you through me, but if he gets to you some other way you're going to be in trouble. Daniel won't lie to protect you, and if you deny his account I will tell the truth."

David nodded slowly. "If it gets that far, we won't deny it. Dad?"

Now Ibbotsen let the silence stretch. But finally he nodded too. "I said I'd pay the price if we could just have Sophie back, and I will. If I have to."

They sat a little longer, drinking coffee and hardly talking. Twice David tiptoed upstairs to check that Sophie was where he'd left her; the second time Brodie went with him. The child was sound asleep with a little smile touching her lips.

She caught David looking at the cropped cap of golden hair. "It'll grow," she whispered.

He looked round with a smile. "I think I rather like it."

For a moment Brodie almost told him it made Sophie look like her mother. But she stopped herself in time, aware that wasn't what he most wanted to hear.

She was ready to leave. She saw him wondering whether to say something, and then he did. "Listen. This isn't what we were talking about earlier - trying to make things right. It's just something that, well, might be nice anyway ... " He swallowed and tried again. "I'm going to take Sophie away while we get over this. We told the school we were going to be cruising in the Caribbean, I think that's what we'll do. I wondered, would you come? You and your daughter? The girls would be company for one another, and - and I'd like it too."

Brodie went on staring at him, dumbfounded. Whatever she'd been expecting it wasn't this. She didn't know how to reply. After a moment, the fact that she didn't dismiss the idea out of hand struck her as deeply significant. "I can't just shut up shop and disappear to the Caribbean! I have obligations, work to finish."

"I appreciate that," said David. "But it doesn't have to be tomorrow. Sophie should probably have a few days to get her breath back anyway. If we left it a week, could you clear your desk by then? Finish what you can, not start anything new? I realise it's asking a lot. The business is important to you, you can't neglect it. But suppose I hire a temp? Someone to man the desk, field phone-calls, make appointments for when you get back. People would just think you were busy and take it as a good sign. Nobody wants to hire someone that nobody else wants to hire."

He seemed to hear himself babbling and broke off with an embar-rassed grin. "I'm sorry, I don't mean to press you. It would mean a lot to me if you could manage it, but if you'd rather not ... "

She wasn't sure she could; she wasn't sure she should; but Brodie was fairly sure she wanted to. "What about Daniel?"

David looked doubtful. "I didn't think he'd want to spend any more time with the Ibbotsen family."

Brodie thought so too, but that wasn't what she meant. "I should-n't leave him. Not yet. He's still - very raw."

David ducked his head but not quick enough; she saw him wince. "Well - would you think about it? Things might look different in a week."

"I'll think about it," she promised.

Chapter 21

In her heart of hearts, Brodie was annoyed with Daniel. She knew he was still weak, she understood that the waiting and then the news must have wrung him out like a wet rag. Even so, she thought he might have stayed to celebrate her triumph. The Ibbotsens' gratitude was one thing: that she'd earned. But she hadn't done what she'd done for them. She'd done it for Sophie and for Daniel; and one of them had slept through most of it and the other had gone home. Anti-climax made her tetchy.

It also made her more inclined to accept David's invitation than she might otherwise have been.

When she got home there were no lights in her flat, only in Marta's. "Is Daniel here?"

Marta shook her head. "I haven't seen him since you both went out. What happened?"

There was very little of the story that her friend didn't already know so Brodie told her. Told her all the thoughts that had been chasing through her head, all the things that could have gone wrong, everything she did to keep the show on the road. Told her about meeting the kidnappers, and how she'd made them prove the child was alive before parting with the money. Told her about hauling the crate out of the gorge though it took all her strength to do it.

Told her, in fact, all the things she'd expected to be telling Daniel. Marta exclaimed in wonder, in horror, in admiration, in all the right places; but it wasn't the same. Marta was her friend, she'd have done that however poorly Brodie had performed. If she'd got everyone killed Marta would have thought she'd done OK. But she'd done better than OK, and she'd looked forward to hearing Daniel say it. She felt let down. Marta fussing over her, anointing her sore hands with salve, was no substitute.

Paddy was asleep in Marta's spare room. Brodie didn't disturb her, except to look at her the way David had kept looking at Sophie, to reassure herself she was still there and all was well. Then she kissed Marta goodnight and went downstairs.

Daniel wasn't there either. Brodie hadn't really expected him to be. He'd said he was going home, and that wasn't here. So she'd served her purpose and he was done with her. Perhaps he didn't owe her any more. But she'd begun thinking of him as a friend, and friendship brings its own obligations.

She reached for the phone, to check that he'd arrived safely, then she put it down again. Why wouldn't he be safe? The people who hurt him before had no interest in him now. He'd been a hunted man for a week; now he was just a comprehensive school maths teacher again. She went to bed.

Bone-tired as she was, sleep was a long time coming.

* * *

She was in her office in Shack Lane before eight. She had a day to find Cora Burton and acquaint her of the crisis facing the family business which her shares could resolve. Brodie had expected to have this wrapped up yesterday, but once again the Ibbotsen drama had intervened.

So Cora was a painter. If she lived on her work she must sell it, presumably through galleries. Brodie started with the Yellow Pages, moved on to the internet, then started making phonecalls.

Within half an hour she'd found two galleries - one in Brighton, one in Hastings - which had sold paintings by Cora Burton. But neither of them had seen her within the last few weeks and both still had her Dimmock address.

Brodie tried to put herself in Cora's sandals. This was a woman who lived quietly. She didn't own a house, or even take a proper lease. She rented surplus farm cottages for a few months at a time. She barely saw her family, only visited galleries when she had something for them to sell.

This was not a woman who took any pleasure in other people's company. Dimmock had probably seemed like a city to her; Brighton must have seemed like Las Vegas. She went there only when she had to.

So when she had to, she would do everything she could only do somewhere like Brighton. She would buy things there that she couldn't get in country post offices, or even in Dimmock.

"What's the name of your nearest artists' supplier?" she asked the man at the gallery.

And when she phoned the supplier, they did indeed see Ms Burton every few months - every time, so far as Brodie could make out, that she took work to the gallery round the corner. She bought canvases, brushes and paint; sometimes she had them frame something for her.

"Did you know she's moved?" asked Brodie.

"Again?"

"I mean, from Dimmock."

"Oh yes," said the girl, "I knew that. About three weeks ago. She bought some canvases last time she was in: they were too big for her to take with her so she asked us to keep them until she moved and then deliver to her new home."

Brodie nodded, feeling smug. "You have the address?"

"Oh yes. Do you want the phone number too?"

Brodie called Cora, explained the situation and asked her to phone Arthur Burton immediately. To make doubly sure Brodie also phoned him herself. "You'll be hearing from your cousin Cora any minute. But just in case you don't, this is her number."

She could almost hear the cider bottler mopping sweat off his brow. "I didn't think you'd find her in time."

Brodie indulged in a bit of boasting. "It's only the impossible that takes a little time. The merely difficult I try to do at once."

Burton chuckled appreciatively. "I won't forget this, Mrs Farrell. I'll gladly recommend your services to anyone I think can use them."

They parted with mutual expressions of satisfaction. Brodie leaned back in her chair, well satisfied, and glanced at her watch. Ten-fifteen: time for elevens. She thought she might nip out for something. Down to the seafront, perhaps.

As always, Daniel's loft looked little different from the other five that still held rotting nets, old oars that had lost their partners, lobster creels, lengths of cordage too short to reuse but too good to throw away, and seaboots with holes in them. The only signs of occupation were milk-bottles on the bottom step and curtains at the high windows.

Brodie parked by the kerb and crunched across the shingle. As she climbed the iron steps *Chandlers* came into view on the hill. Somehow it no longer looked like a toad.

She thought Daniel wasn't going to answer her knock. She was about to leave when the door finally opened. She'd clearly got him out of bed. It was mid-morning, but then he did still have a hole in his chest.

"I'm sorry," she said, and meant it. "Go back to bed. I'll see you later. I'll pop across at lunchtime if there's not too much happening."

Daniel shook his head, the yellow hair tousled from his pillow. "No, come in. I'm awake, I just haven't got going yet." But his glasses were on crooked and the eyes behind them were bleary. She thought he was only awake because she'd woken him.

She followed him inside. The flat surprised her. It was both more stylish and more homely than the natural habitat of the single twenty-six year old male. There wasn't an empty beer-can in sight and the floor was not being used as a laundry box. Unless he'd come home late last night and immediately started tidying up, this was how he lived. Perhaps it figured: chaos could have scant appeal for a mathematician.

"I wanted to see if you were all right," said Brodie. "Last time you were here ... " She left the sentence unfinished, wished she hadn't started it.

He shrugged the green dressing-gown closer around his bones. "It wasn't too bad. Of course, knowing there was nobody waiting behind the door helped. Sit down, I'll make some coffee." He left the kitchen door open, talking through it. "I'm sorry I missed you last night. I had to get out of there."

"That's all right," said Brodie off-handedly, as if she hadn't given it a thought. "I suppose it was asking a lot, for you to sit down with the old thug. Is it right what he said - that you're not going to shop him to Deacon?"

"Is that what he told you?"

"Pretty much. It isn't true?"

Daniel sighed. "I suppose it is. I said I wouldn't lie to the police, but I wouldn't send them round with a Black Maria either." He smiled gently. "They don't have Black Marias any more, do they?"

"Not in your lifetime," grinned Brodie.

"She was all right?" It wasn't a non-sequitur: it was the only thing worth talking about, everything else was just conversation. And it was only half a question: he wanted reassurance more than information.

Brodie nodded. "She's fine. Like I told you last night."

Daniel brought the coffee. "I should have waited. I - they - It was difficult."

"I can't get over the old sod asking you to cover for him," snorted Brodie. "The way he was talking yesterday morning, if he could just get Sophie back wild horses wouldn't keep him out of Jack Deacon's office."

"I suppose the richer you are the less attractive prison looks. When Sophie was safe he could afford to worry about himself."

"David said - " She thought better of it. "They were both keen to offer any kind of recompense they thought you'd accept."

"I know." He looked at her. "I'm really not interested in their money."

"I know that." Conscience pricked and she tried again. "David wants me and Paddy to join them on this Caribbean cruise."

Daniel made no reply. He sipped his coffee.

"You think it would be a bad idea," prompted Brodie.

"I didn't say that." His grey eyes caught her gaze and held it. "You like him, don't you? David."

"Maybe." She considered some more. "Yes, I think I do. Not enough to excuse what he was part of, but ... Daniel, he swore to me he was only aware what was happening when it was almost over."

"Yes?" Daniel returned his attention to his mug.

"I wouldn't go," said Brodie, "if I thought you'd be hurt."

"You don't need my permission."

"I know."

206

"Or my blessing. And if you want an unbiased view on whether it's a good idea to accept Ibbotsen hospitality, you've come to the wrong place for that, too."

Brodie turned away, obscurely disappointed. Of course he wasn't going to wish her luck. She didn't need him to: she was a grown woman, she made her own luck and her own decisions. What she was hoping, she realised with a twinge of discomfort, was for Daniel to make one more sacrifice in someone else's interests. To tell her it was all right, it didn't matter, he didn't mind. And that wasn't reasonable. Of course he minded. He was just too decent to say so.

"Well, I don't have to decide today," she said, finishing her coffee and getting up. "I must get back to work. And you should get some more rest."

He said, "I thought I might go in to school."

Brodie's eyebrows rocketed. "Daniel, you're not ready! It could be weeks before you're fit enough."

"Not to work," he said. "Just to show my face. And there's something in the library I want to check."

"Can't it *wait*?"

"I've nothing else to do. I can't spend all day in my dressing-gown. I need start getting back to normal."

* * *

She never afterwards knew what made her return to the loft when she shut the office at one. She bought some sandwiches, told herself she was making sure he kept his strength up, but that was only the excuse. From midday on she felt a mounting unease that no amount of common sense would quash.

That sense of something amiss sharpened as she climbed the steps to find the front door unlocked. She didn't even knock: she threw it open and hurried inside. "Daniel?"

"In here."

She found him in the kitchen. The sink was full of cold water; his sleeves were rolled up and his face and forearms were wet. Without his glasses he looked as she had first seen him, white and vulnerable.

"What's happened?"

He reached for a towel. He tried to smile but didn't pull it off. "Going back to school," he said in a thin voice. "Not a good idea."

* * *

At first it had seemed so. The stolid unchangingness of the place had been reassuring. A week be damned: he could have been away for a year and it would still have felt utterly familiar as he opened the door. The smell of disinfectant hiding the smell of something worse; the clatter of feet, the thump of falling books; the groan of unslammable doors being slammed anyway; Charlie Monroe standing in the corridor outside the principal's office.

He'd timed his visit carefully. Apart from Charlie, the children were in class: he wouldn't have to cope with pointing fingers, staring eyes and tactless questions in his first five minutes back; except of course from the staff.

Nodding amiably to Charlie - Daniel was supposed to teach the boy but he saw much more of him in this corridor - he tapped the door and went inside to speak with Mr Chalmers. The man deserved to know that his school wasn't haunted, that reports of Daniel's demise had been premature.

Then he went to the library. There was an undertone of peering and whispering; he nodded amiably and logged on at the computer. He could have used the PC at home, but he had access to additional data here and it would be quicker. As well as giving him a reason to come.

He'd been working for ten minutes, the disturbance his arrival had created had subsided and the information he wanted was beginning to come in, when the whole enterprise started to go horribly wrong.

For once it wasn't Charlie who started the trouble. It was his sister Marilyn.

* * *

"Charlie Monroe has a sister Marilyn?" echoed Brodie faintly.

Daniel dried himself and waved a weary hand. "I know, I know. We're all so used to it now it doesn't even sound funny any more."

"What did she do?"

"I think she must have bunked off. She was there for registration, nobody saw her afterwards. Tricia Weston, who had her for PE, was trying to track her down. God knows why but she looked in the library."

"And she wasn't there?" Brodie still wasn't sure what he was telling her. But it was clear from the state he was in that whatever had happened had floored him.

"No, she wasn't. But a bunch of third-formers she hangs out with were, so Tricia went to ask them."

* * *

Tricia Weston had once played hockey for England. She didn't do anything discreetly. Her voice was trained to carry across sports pitches in the teeth of a gale - even when she was trying to obey the "Quiet in the Library" signs it had the penetrative power of a Cruise missile.

She leaned over the table where the girls were sitting. "I'm looking for Marilyn Monroe. Have any of you seen her since registration?"

They adopted the tactics which serve thirteen-year-old girls in the face of authority all over the world: they played dumb. "Marilyn, Miss? She isn't here, Miss. Doesn't she have PE, Miss? Didn't she turn up, Miss? No, Miss, we don't know where she is. Did you try the canteen?"

Tricia Weston breathed heavily. "Yes, I tried the canteen. It was full of Flappers practising their can-can for the end-of-term show. I tried the bicycle sheds, all four toilet blocks and the art room, and she wasn't in any of them. The last person who saw her, saw her with you four. Now where is she? Did she bunk off?"

"Don't know, Miss. We haven't seen her since first thing this morning, Miss. We don't know where she is."

The PE teacher was breathing heavily. Three laps of the running track didn't get her this hot under the collar. "I want to know. Where is she? I'm not leaving here until you tell me. Where is she? *Where is she?*"

Busy with their own confrontation, none of them saw Mr Hood's face drain to parchment and his eyes stretch as the words hammered at his brain. In an instant the book-lined room around him dissolved, leaving him cold, naked and blind, spread-eagled on a table, the same words fired at him like bullets, the agony of seared flesh the price of having no answer.

He stumbled to his feet, the library chair tumbling behind him. Tricia Weston looked round in surprise. "Daniel? Do you know where she is? Where, then? Where is she? Daniel?"

Backing towards the door, blind with panic, groping for it with desperate uncoordinated hands, he heard another, younger voice ask, with puzzlement and even genuine concern, "What's the matter with him then?" Then he was in the corridor, running.

* * *

"I couldn't get out," he whispered. "I got lost. I've worked there for twelve months and I couldn't find my way out. I kept running, and I couldn't seem to work out where I was. I just wanted to get outside. But I couldn't find a door. I tried every corridor I came to, and every flight of stairs, and I knew everyone was staring. They were calling after me. I even knew they'd help me get out if I could just stop running, but I couldn't. I lost it. I mean, completely. If you've ever seen a headless chicken ... "

But it wasn't a joke. There was nothing funny about it. Brodie said softly, "What happened?"

"I ended up outside the head's office again. There's a glass wall where the corridor overlooks the playground. Apparently" - he couldn't look at her - "I was trying to break it with my bare hands. The fact that it's on the second floor mustn't have occurred to me."

He swallowed. "Before he was a teacher, Des Chalmers was a Royal Marine. It's the perfect training for the job. He came out of his

210

office to see what the commotion was, saw me beating my head in against his wall and decked me. I came to my senses sitting on the corridor floor with Des Chalmers holding me and Charlie Monroe offering me the grubbiest hankie you ever saw because I was crying like a baby."

If it was OK for an ex-Marine it was good enough for her. Brodie steered him to the sofa, sat down beside him, put her arm round his narrow shoulders. He was still shaking. "And then you came back here? Daniel, you need help. It's too soon, it's all still too fresh."

"Des thought so too. He wanted to take me to the hospital. I made him bring me home instead. You only just missed him."

"You shouldn't be alone. Won't you let me call someone?"

He cast her a furtive glance. "I'm all right alone. It's other people I can't seem to deal with."

"A psychiatrist could - "

He wouldn't let her finish. "If I get into their hands I'll never be free of them. I can do this alone."

Brodie thought she owed him the truth more than kindness. "What happened today, Daniel - it will happen again. And again, and again."

He shook his head doggedly. "It won't. I'm not going back."

"What, never?"

"There's too much baggage. Too many people, and too many of them likely to be looking for one another too often." He forced a smile. "Maybe I'll join the Marines."

Brodie saw nothing to smile about. "Daniel, you're a teacher. You couldn't *lift* a submachine-gun. You like teaching."

"I'll have to find something else to like. I can't hack it any more. Whatever I do, it needs to be something I can walk away from if I have to. Without upsetting dozens of kids and having to be rugby-tackled by the head teacher. I can't be stuck in a classroom any more. Ah - " He caught his breath.

"What?"

Daniel looked broken, as if it were the last straw. "I left some stuff in the library. Unless somebody thought to shut me down I'm still logged on."

"I'll pop round for it," said Brodie. "I'll be back in fifteen minutes."

* * *

Mr Chalmers helped her. Pushing fifty now, he still looked more like a Royal Marine than a head teacher. When she explained her purpose he was full of concern.

"How is Daniel? I was most unhappy about leaving him in that shed but he insisted. He said if I tried to take him to hospital he'd get out at the traffic lights."

Brodie nodded her understanding. "Mules have nothing on my friend Daniel."

Mr Chalmers picked his words carefully. "He explained - before the incident in the library - a little of what happened during his absence. He didn't go into much detail. Would I be right in assuming you know rather more?"

"Perhaps. But I don't intend to swap notes with you."

He didn't take offence, just went on regarding her over his desk. "I'm worried about him, Mrs Farrell. If you'd been here forty minutes ago, you'd be worried about him too."

She sighed. "I *am* worried about him, Mr Chalmers. But you can only offer someone your help, you can't force it on him. Daniel's determined to deal with his problems his own way. I've given up trying to advise him: now I settle for helping him do what he wants to do."

The principal nodded pensively. "Stubborn little son-of-a-bitch, isn't he? When he first came here I thought the kids would eat him for breakfast. I mean, there's not much of him, and what there is doesn't shout authority. Then, when he'd been here about a week, there was an incident in the playground. One of the twelve-stone thugs who pass for fifth-formers round here pulled a knife. Daniel took it off him."

Brodie pursed her lips. "Was he hurt?"

"No one was hurt. Everyone was astonished."

They went to the library. The computer at which Daniel had been

212

working was still on line. Chalmers perused it briefly. "Suppose I print this stuff off? Take it to him, and if he needs anything else he can phone me. Tell him not to come back until he's ready. Tell him his job'll be waiting for him."

Brodie thanked him, gathered up Daniel's papers and left.

It wasn't until she was back in her car, propping the folders on the front seat so that they wouldn't spill their contents on the first corner, that she saw what he'd been working on.

Chapter 22

Brodie was too angry to knock. She stormed up the steps, the doorknob turned under her hand and she was inside before there was time to wonder if she had any right.

Daniel had fallen into an uneasy slumber, on top of the bed, still in his damp clothes. The rap of her footsteps on the wooden floor broke in on his sleep but there wasn't time for him to gather his wits. "Wha'?" He pushed himself off the pillow and searched myopically for the cause of the disturbance.

He saw the shape of her in the bedroom door but couldn't make out the details. "Who is it?" He groped on the table beside him but his glasses weren't there. "Brodie?"

His glasses must have fallen off the bed: she saw them on the floor. She neither passed them to him nor told him where to find them. Nor did she answer to her name. Later she would be ashamed of that. The last people who came in here without an invitation snatched him away to purgatory. Though his conscious mind knew no repetition was likely, the nerve-endings under his skin must have been alive with fear. She could have rescued him with a word. Even in her current mood Brodie didn't like herself for not doing.

Daniel's increasingly urgent search located the missing glasses and he crammed them on. "It *is* you. Brodie, you scared the life out of me! What - ?" He saw her face then, and the sheaf of papers in her hand. His expression stilled. "Ah."

"You want to explain?" she asked tightly.

"Yes," he said slowly. "But not while you're ready to hit me. I'll put the kettle on, let's - "

"Screw the kettle!" Brodie hurled the papers at him: they fanned out in midair, covering his legs and his bare feet like snow. "I want to know what this is about. You can't get this sort of information legitimately: you've been hacking into confidential sources, and the word for that is spying. Why? Because I said I might go on holiday with him?"

"No," said Daniel indignantly. He pushed himself upright at the end of the bed, coincidentally putting more distance between them. "Although - "

"No Although is the same as Yes," spat Brodie. "What the hell did you think you were doing? You think you can dictate who I see, who I go away with? Who I like?"

"Of course not. I just - I don't want you to make a mistake."

"Who do you think you are," she yelled, "my mother? It's none of your damned business! We were thrown together by circumstances, we're not even friends in any real sense A fortnight ago I didn't know you existed; another fortnight and you'll have gone back to what passes for your normality and I'll have gone back to mine. We both got hijacked by events beyond our control. Maybe I owe you something, Daniel, but not this - not a say in my life. You have no right to spy on someone I like because you don't approve of him!"

"That wasn't the reason."

"No? Jesus, Daniel, look at this stuff! If you wanted to know how much David Ibbotsen is worth you should have asked him - he'd probably have told you. What were you *thinking*? - that if he could afford to take me to the Caribbean he could buy you a new telescope? Were you trying to work out how much to ask for?"

She could hardly have said anything more hurtful. Daniel's jaw dropped and his eyes saucered behind the thick lenses. He was too astonished to deny it. Brodie took his silence for consent.

"God knows they owe you something, but at least have the courage to tell them face to face. This" - she flicked a disdainful glance at his research - "is like rooting round in the rubbish bins. Anyway, you won't get anything out of David. All the money belongs to his father. If it hadn't been this business would have been over as soon as it started, you wouldn't have got hurt, and you and I would never have met."

Daniel moistened his lips. "Neither would you and David."

"Me and David is nothing to do with you! Daniel, I understand that you resent him. That you hate them both. You have every right. If you want to change your mind and turn them in to the police, I won't try to stop you. But don't tell them it's over and then hack into

215

their personal data behind their backs. It isn't worthy of you. If you want to punish them for what they did, tell them. But don't use me as a stalking horse."

"Brodie, I'm not! You don't understand. This isn't about money - at least, not the way you think. You know I wouldn't lie about that."

"I don't know anything about you, Daniel! I know you say you don't lie - and then I find this." She gestured furiously at the print-outs. "You said you didn't want anything from the Ibbotsens. So what am I supposed to make of it? And incidentally," she added in her teeth, "I noticed that was another of those not-quite-denials. It's not about money, at least not the way I think. Well Daniel, I don't know *what* to think. I'm beginning to wonder if I've misjudged you completely. I thought you were a decent man who got caught up in terrible events."

"What do you think now?" His voice was low.

Brodie waved at the paperwork again. "That this isn't the act of someone who genuinely wants to put the matter behind him. There's one honourable way of getting even with the Ibbotsens, and this isn't it. What do you want? Tell me, and I'll tell them. But don't skulk round like a thief."

"I didn't. I mean ... " His voice ran up thin; he swallowed and tried again. "I was worried. Something you said, that I kept thinking about. I thought, maybe I was imagining it. I wanted to be sure. I didn't want to do something stupid. Say something stupid. I didn't want this to happen: that we'd end up shouting at one another."

"Something I said?" Confusion was undermining her anger. She went on looking at him, taking in the earnest nodding, the pale eyes, the gentle unremarkable face. A glimmer of understanding flickered in the fog. "Daniel - is this about us?"

"Us?"

"You and me. We've spent a lot of hours together this last week. We helped one another through some difficult times. It's been an emotional roller-coaster; there were moments it felt like you and me against the world. In those circumstances you can't *not* get close to someone."

Daniel nodded fractionally. "I suppose."

Brodie let her eyes fall shut for a second. So that was it. She really hadn't seen it coming. But she should have done. He'd had a close encounter with death: he'd come back to her voice and her face, and not much else. He had no family that she knew of, no friends who cared enough to find out what became of him. He had a job he enjoyed and an absorbing hobby; and one of them had got him into this, and the other was now a emotional minefield.

She was all he had left. She'd taken him into her life because he needed a friend and she needed to repair some of the damage she'd done. And he'd thought it was more than that.

"Oh Daniel," she sighed, sitting on the bed beside him, "I'm sorry. This isn't your fault, it's mine - I should have realised what you were thinking, how it must have seemed to you. I wanted to help, and instead I've managed to confuse you.

"What I said before: I didn't mean it. I hope we are friends. I hope we'll stay friends whatever happens between me and David. If anything does: dear God, I've known him even less time than I've known you!"

"Then, be careful," he murmured. "That's all I'm asking."

Her gaze was astute. "No, it isn't. You're asking me to make a choice: David or you. You're saying I can't enjoy his company and stay friends with you. Or - no, that's not quite it, is it? You think it's more than friendship. You think of you and me the way I think of me and David - not an item yet but with the potential to become one.

"I'm sorry but you're mistaken. I'm not in love with you; I'm never going to be in love with you. I looked after you because I felt responsible. My relationship with David can't come between us because there is no us, not in that sense. I'm sorry if anything I said or did misled you. I felt guilty about my part in all this and tried to make amends. I'm sorry if you took that for something else."

His voice cracked with distress. "Brodie, please - listen to me - !"

"No. Daniel, I understand that your emotions are in tatters: I keep telling you what to do about that but you won't do it. You won't talk to a counsellor, you insist on handling it your own way - but your way involves hacking into private sources of information and

217

driving a wedge between me and a man I like! I won't be manipulated like that - not by you, not by anyone.

"Get a life, Daniel. Stop trying to live mine." With that she turned on her heel and left.

* * *

Daniel went on sitting where he had been all along, cross-legged at the top of his bed, fighting back tears. He knew, if he was to have any kind of a future, he was going to have to master this tendency to break down when anything upset him. Being understandable didn't make it all right. *He* was tired of it, never mind anyone else. He clenched his jaw and shut his eyes, waiting for the weakness to pass.

When he heard footsteps and a knock at the door, he thought she'd got as far as her car, found herself regretting what she'd said and come back to hear him out. Still barefoot, he sprang from the bed and hurried to the door, flinging it wide. "Brodie - "

"Sorry," said Jack Deacon woodenly, stepping inside before the welcome could be withdrawn, "close but no coconut. Can I have a word?"

"Er - of course." Wondering, Daniel closed the door behind him. "Sit down."

Inspector Deacon did as he was bid. He made a considerable presence: it took a brave man to try and move him when he was standing in an open doorway. Seated, he had the same air of permanence as the Rock of Gibraltar.

He looked around him. "When did you come back here?"

"Last night."

"Got tired of being nannied, did you?"

"I thought it was time to start getting back to normal."

"Mm." Deacon nodded like a plush Alsatian on a parcel-shelf, giving as much away. "Any problems?"

"Problems?"

The policeman raised an eyebrow. "The first time you tried you stuck it just long enough for me to drive away. If Mrs Farrell hadn't given you a bed you'd have had to doss down with the drunks under the pier."

Daniel smiled faintly. "No. No problems."

"Mm," said Deacon again. "And so, emboldened by success, you thought you'd go back to work. How did that work out?"

Daniel regarded him for some moments before answering. "Inspector Deacon, you obviously know what happened at school this morning. I expect Mr Chalmers called you; I know he thought somebody ought to be looking after me."

"I thought somebody was. I thought Mrs Farrell had appointed herself to the task. Then five minutes ago I watched her stalk out of here radiating righteous indignation as if you'd goosed her. You didn't, did you?"

Daniel breathed steadily. "We - there was - It was a misunder-standing."

"What kind of a misunderstanding?"

"It was personal."

Under the tented eyebrow Deacon's pupil held a little red spark. "Sonny, this is a criminal investigation. There's no such thing as personal."

"It was nothing to do with your investigation."

"I'll be the judge of that."

They faced one another in a silence that lasted almost a minute. Neither man backed down or looked away. Finally Daniel said quietly, "No, Inspector, I will."

Deacon hid his surprise in a sniff. "You know, Danny, when this is over I'm going to have somebody behind bars. If it has to be you, so be it."

"You'll have to find something you can charge me with first. I don't think dislike is enough."

The policeman grinned wolfishly. "I don't dislike you, Danny. I just don't think you're being honest with me."

"I've told you the truth."

"Ah, but have you told me the whole truth?"

"You're the detective."

Deacon returned his smile, without the gentleness and also

without much humour. "Funny thing about that. People who say it never go on to add, 'So I'll give you all the help I can.'"

"Then I'll make your day," said Daniel. "Inspector Deacon, I'll give you all the help I can. Why are you here? Has something happened?"

Deacon pursed his lips and answered obliquely. "Being a detective isn't what people imagine. It's not often about fast cars and gunfights and leaping on suspects from a great height. Mostly it's about observation. You gather all the information you can about a crime and the people involved in it, and you look for things that don't fit. Things that could have happened the way you're being told they happened, but actually never would.

"There's a certain inevitability about events. People do things the obvious way unless they've some reason not to. Nine times out of ten what happened is what looks to have happened. There's always the chance that a one-armed man killed Mrs Kimble, but nine times out of ten it's going to be her husband."

"And you're observing me." It was a statement rather than a question.

"I am, Danny, I am. Any way you cut it, you're the key to this. You know more than you're telling me. The question is, how much more. Do you know who tortured you and tried to kill you? Do you know why? Have you worked out who Sophie is?"

"It's a common enough name, Inspector. Check the school register: it's one of those names that's been fashionable in recent years."

"Sophie's a little girl?"

Daniel felt himself flush. "I know of several Sophies under the age of about fifteen. One's a Rottweiler. I don't know any women of the same name. That doesn't mean there aren't any."

"And of these several Sophies, which one went AWOL?"

"I believe the Rottweiler did, once or twice. Inspector, why are you treating me like a suspect? If I could cast light on what happened to me, don't you think I'd want to?"

"You would think so, wouldn't you?" mused Deacon. He was patting his pockets, looking for something. Daniel watched with a kind of fascination. He had no idea what was coming next, only that

220

Jack Deacon wasn't a man to waste time on meaningless gestures. Everything he said and did was significant.

Finally he found the right pocket and pulled out a packet of cigarettes and a lighter. "You don't mind, do you?" It was clearly a rhetorical question: his thick fingers moved with a dogged determination that no amount of protest would have interrupted. He opened the packet, drew out a cigarette and tapped it slowly on the back of his hand. He put it between his lips and picked up the lighter. All the time his eyes were on Daniel's face.

Daniel's eyes were locked on the end of the cigarette, the snout of the lighter. When Deacon's thumb made the little flame shoot he started visibly. Even so, it wasn't the sight of the policeman lighting up that made the blood drain from his face. It was the smell. Hot and fragrant. The only thing missing was the scent of his own burning flesh.

Of course, he knew what Deacon was doing. It was only a cigarette. No one was going to hurt him. He leaned his head against the back of the chair and shut his eyes. "I don't have any ashtrays. There's a saucer under the plant-pot you could use."

Deacon drew on the cigarette and exhaled slowly in Daniel's direction. When he leaned forward for the saucer, Daniel shrank back.

Deacon smiled unkindly, but behind that was more respect than Daniel could have guessed. There was nothing casual about Deacon's cruelty: it was calculated and purposeful, but it hadn't achieved anything because Daniel Hood was a stronger, braver man than anyone ever gave him credit for. Deacon had met all sorts of people, both villains and victims, in the course of his professional life, and he still couldn't pigeon-hole Daniel Hood. It tasked him, as the whale tasked Ahab. He needed to understand, and he believed now that Daniel was deliberately thwarting him.

Yet still he recognised that he was dealing with a basically decent human being, and it bothered him that they always ended up like this, fencing with words and gestures until someone - no, to be honest, until Daniel - got hurt. It worried him that another kind of police officer could have gained his trust and got at the truth that way. But the only way he knew was head on, like a bull at a gate, and though it worked on thugs and cowards it didn't work on Daniel, only served to entrench the differences between them. Deacon regretted that, but couldn't seem to find a way round it.

He leaned back with a sigh and returned to what he'd been saying. "But then, you'd also think that someone who'd survived what was done to you would keep out of sight until those responsible had been caught. Instead of which you turn up at the general hospital and the school where you work: two places that anyone wanting to know if you were dead would be sure to look. And now you've come home. Danny, you're not behaving like someone whose life is in danger from unknown assailants. You're behaving like someone who knows the danger has passed."

"We talked about that."

"I know we did. You said you weren't prepared to spend the rest of your life running scared. It sounded pretty convincing at the time. Now I'm not sure. There's getting quietly on with your life and hoping for the best, and there's making a public spectacle of yourself."

Daniel's gaze dropped. "I lost it. I thought I could handle it, and I was wrong. Someone said - the wrong thing - and I lost it. Mr Chalmers had to knock me down and sit on me."

"That's how I heard it," admitted Deacon. "Not exactly discreet behaviour, you'll agree."

"Discretion wasn't my top priority right then."

"No. But you see, it should have been. You shouldn't have gone anywhere near that school. And if you had, you shouldn't have done anything to draw attention to yourself."

"It wasn't planned."

"Not the panic attack. But you deliberately exposed yourself to the circumstances which provoked it, and I still don't understand why."

Daniel shook his head wearily. "I'm sorry if you think I'm behaving oddly. You're probably right. But I still can't tell you anything you don't already know. If we're finished, I'd like to rest now."

Deacon went on watching him, his expression planklike, the thoughts condensing in his head battened down behind it. Of all the suppositions, possibilities, suggestions and inferences surrounding this case, he knew only two things. Daniel Hood had been the victim of an horrific attack; and he needed to rest now.

He stood up. "All right, I'll leave you in peace. I can't guarantee everyone else will do the same."

"Time's getting on. I think it's over."

The policeman eyed him in exasperation. "Danny, whoever these people were, at least one of them was a professional. I thought that before: now I know it. I've seen his portfolio.

"You weren't the first living canvas he's worked on. I've come up with three previous masterpieces I can definitely attribute to him, and four more that have everything but the signature. If we don't get him soon he'll die of lung cancer."

Daniel swallowed. Despite living with the memory for eleven days he still found it difficult to talk about. "Cigarettes?"

"Not invariably. Sometimes it's cigars, sometimes it's lighters; he's used a poker, and once it was a miniature blow-torch. You know, the kind that cooks use to finish off a crème brulée and put a nice crackling on pork. But always something hot and domestic. Innocuous. You carry a gun or a knife, even a pepper spray, and you'll have a lot of explaining to do if someone opens your briefcase. But cigarettes and a lighter? Even the blow-torch: drop in a white hat and a copy of Mrs Beeton's Cookbook and nobody'll give them a second look."

He didn't want to ask; he didn't want to know. Except that part of him did. "What - happened - ?"

"To the others? Dead, Danny, every one of them. The three definites and the four probables. He gets around, him and his smoker's compendium. One was in Aberdeen, another on the Isle of Wight. At least, that's where she floated ashore. She may have come off a boat. I say come off: I mean of course they threw her off. It was as good as shooting her. The shock of salt water on that many burns killed her before she could drown."

Daniel said faintly, "She ... "

"Oh yes," said Deacon briskly, "he's an Equal Opportunities torturer. A professional, like I said. And as far as we know, you're his only failure. Apart from those who paid him, the only living witness."

"I never saw his face."

"I dare say you'd recognise the voice again, though. I don't think you'll forget that in a hurry. He must know you're alive by now, and he won't be happy about that. It's the thing about professionals: they don't like leaving loose ends."

"I'm sure he has more to worry about than whether I'll ever hear his voice again. Unless he does a bit of television on the side, it isn't very likely."

"No," allowed Deacon. "But unlikely isn't the same as impossible. I think he'd be happier with impossible."

"Tell you what, Inspector," said Daniel, finally losing patience. "If he comes back here, you'll be the first to know."

Deacon shook his head grimly. "No, Danny, you will. I might be the second, but it'll already be too late. Your only defence against this man is to tell me who he is."

"I don't know who he is!"

"Who hired him, then."

"I can't tell you that either."

Deacon didn't believe him. He was still shaking his head as he tramped heavily down the iron steps. When he heard the door close above him he glanced back, and then he took the cigarette from between his lips and tossed it onto the shingle. He'd never got a taste for the things, even when he was young enough to want to.

Chapter 23

By the time she got back to the office Brodie had stopped fuming, was beginning to feel uncomfortable about things she'd said. She knew she'd over-reacted. So Daniel was behaving strangely: after what he'd been through it was no wonder. Her obligation to him didn't end because the mystery was solved, or because he'd developed a schoolboy crush on her. The fact that she now had more tempting demands on her time didn't change anything either.

She knew she should call and apologise. She was eyeing the phone askance, wondering what to say that wouldn't reopen either the argument or the wounds, when she heard the door. Immediately she thought of Daniel. She wasn't sure why he'd come - to apologise, to insist she'd jumped to the wrong conclusion or to profess his love - but she was glad he had. They'd survived too much to part like this. If he'd misread the situation she'd mishandled it, and he had more excuse.

But it wasn't Daniel, it was David Ibbotsen. For a moment Brodie couldn't decide if she was pleased or disappointed. In fact she was both. She was glad to see David, but right now she needed to see Daniel more.

David seemed to sense her ambivalence, a tiny frown pinching his eyebrows. "Is this a bad time?"

"Not at all," said Brodie, waving him in. "Do you want a sand-wich? - I missed my lunch."

He nodded, took the other chair and tucked into the tuna and mayo with gusto. Brodie regarded him with amusement and some affection. She was fairly sure that an hour ago he'd been tucking into sirloin with the Chamber of Commerce, or lobster with the Harbour Commissioners, or failing that Mrs Handcock's Star-Gazy Pie up at *Chandlers*. Lord only knew where he found room for a sandwich as well, but he wouldn't let her eat alone. It was a friendly gesture which she appreciated.

"How's Sophie today?"

Relief radiatied like sunshine from David's broad face. "Sophie's fine. She's still a little drowsy - I left her in bed with a colouring book." He chuckled self-deprecatingly. "It took me three attempts to leave the house. I kept nipping back to make sure she was still there."

"Has she said anything about what happened?"

He lifted a wry shoulder. "Nothing useful. Nothing that'll help us find the kidnappers. Actually, she seems quite confused about it. She talked about a man and a woman, and a cottage in the country, but I'm not sure how much she understood. I'm not even sure she knows she was kidnapped, and I don't like to press her because it's probably better if she doesn't."

Brodie was confused too. "Why does she think she was away from home for thirteen days?"

"Who knows what they think at that age? We're always doing something to them they can't possibly understand - we leave them at playgroup, we take them to school, we let people they don't know baby-sit, we let the doctor stick needles in them when we know it's going to hurt - we tell them everything's all right and expect them to believe us. And, not having much choice, they do. Maybe if the kidnappers told her everything was all right, she believed them. Maybe a fortnight in a country cottage with some people she didn't know didn't seem any stranger to Sophie than the time Mrs Handcock's niece took her pony trekking, or when my father took her to launch a new ship and left her with a crane-jockey all afternoon while he argued over the price of propellers."

Brodie laughed. "Paddy would *adore* spending all afternoon with a crane-jockey!"

"Great," said David, "that's her birthday treat sorted." They munched on, companionably.

But he hadn't come to be fed. Brodie waited for him to broach the real reason. When the sandwiches were gone and he still hadn't, she prompted him. "So what can I do for you today, Mr Ibbotsen?"

He cast her a shy look, uncertain how to ask. Brodie found his diffidence rather touching. He seemed genuinely anxious as to what her reply might be. "I wanted to know if you've given any thought to what we were talking about. The Caribbean. The four of us. We ought to - well - decide what we're doing."

"Yes, we must," agreed Brodie. "There are plane tickets to book."

"Actually, I've already booked them." He didn't give her time to object but hurried on. "Don't worry, that doesn't mean you have to say yes. Well, of course it doesn't, it's your decision. I'm not trying to put you on the spot, I just thought I'd get the tickets now rather than leave it to the last minute and have to sit at different ends of the plane. We don't have to use them all. I mean, I hope we will but we don't have to." He heard himself babbling and shut up.

"You won't get a refund. Not at this notice." There was a Puritan streak in Brodie. If someone promised her the moon she'd wonder if they shouldn't wait for the January sales.

David smiled again, a shade wanly. "You'd be amazed how obliging people are when your father owns a shipping line."

Brodie debated whether to say it. But he wasn't a client, she didn't have to massage his ego. "You could always walk away. Do something else for a living."

He looked at her as if the idea had never occurred to him. "Like what?"

"Like anything! Landscape gardening, interior design; get an HGV licence, be a cook; anything except being a rich man's son. You don't enjoy it so do something else."

He stared at the desk with its litter of breadcrumbs and clingfilm, his chin sunk on his chest. After a minute, without raising his head, he said, "I know you're right. I should have done it fifteen years ago. I think now - with Sophie, with the old man getting older - I've left it too late."

"David, you're - what, thirty-five, thirty-six years old? You've got most of your life ahead of you! Sophie's got all of hers. If you're unhappy with who you are and what you're doing, make a change. You don't need Lance's money. People with no family business, with no education, with no talents to speak of, still manage to make a respectable living and raise their kids. Feeling as you do, you have more to gain than to lose."

"And the old man?"

227

"The old man can make his own choices. I imagine he'd run his business for as long as he was enjoying it, then put in a manager. Don't buy the myth, David: the only power he has over you is what you allow him. You'd do fine on your own. All it takes is the decision."

He managed a rueful little smile. "You make it sound easy."

"It is - millions of people do it every day. Stand on their own two feet and take a pride in whatever they're able to do for their families. Whereas you have every material advantage and get no pleasure out of it. For pity's sake, do one thing or the other. Either enjoy being Lance Ibbotsen's son or tell him you're not dancing to his tune any more."

"He'd never forgive me," muttered David. "And it's not just my inheritance I'd be risking, it's Sophie's."

"Maybe," nodded Brodie. "Or maybe he'd be impressed as hell. He doesn't give you much credit, David, it might make him sit up and take notice if you told him where to go sometimes. Not," she added belatedly, "that it's any business of mine."

David laughed at that, relieved to have the searchlight of her scrutiny off his soul. "Are you always this ... ?"

"Opinionated? Yes, I rather suspect I am. People ask me what I think, and when I tell them they get this glazed expression - very much like yours - and I realise they didn't want to know what I thought at all, they just wanted me to agree with them. I'm not very good at that: falling into line for the sake of a quiet life."

"I am," murmured David. "But then, I've had practice."

Brodie made some coffee on the ring in the cloakroom. She'd forgotten he'd asked her a question, so eventually David had to repeat it. "*Have* you decided? About the Caribbean?"

Brodie started guiltily. "I'm sorry - *that's* what we were talking about before I started reorganising your life! Yes. You asked me to think about it and I've thought about very little else. I'm not sure how sensible it is, but I'd love to come. Or does that seem the height of hypocrisy?"

David didn't follow. "Hypocrisy?"

"Telling you to throw off the shackles of your father's money, but not until he's paid for our holiday in the Caribbean."

Chuckling, he shook his head. "I don't care if it is - we have it coming. You, me and the girls. Let's grab a bit of fun while we can. If the last fortnight has taught me nothing else, it's proved that we can't know from one minute to the next what the future holds. We get a shot at happiness, we have to take it." His eyes dipped again and he blushed. "I'm sorry, that must sound - presumptuous. A holiday: that's all we're talking about. A shared family holiday. It's just..."

He looked up then and his eyes glinted. "Brodie, you must be aware something's happening between us. Some chemistry. I feel I've known you for months. I feel you've known *me* all my life!"

She touched his hand across the desk. "David - don't try to look too far ahead. Starting how it did, the odds on this going anywhere aren't great. What we're feeling now, what we're enjoying - it might be real and it might last, but it might just be euphoria. We got through it, everyone survived, it's a natural human reaction to want to hug and kiss someone and neither of us has a significant other at home. I'm not saying that's all it is: I'm saying it might be.

"We need to go easy until our hearts stop thumping and there's time to weigh up if we like one another enough. If not, there's no harm done. We're two intelligent adults, we understand how a crisis throws people together. There's nothing wrong with that, it needn't stop us enjoying our holiday, it's just no basis for a lifetime's commitment. We need to get our breath back, get to know one another, and not ask where it's going until we know what we want."

David nodded acceptance. "That's good. That's - sensible. Only ... "

"Only?" echoed Brodie, one eyebrow raised.

"Only people don't go to the Caribbean to be sensible. Or, come to that, to be good."

* * *

When she got home, Marta had a message for her. Daniel knew both her office and mobile numbers, so he'd called Marta specifically to avoid talking to Brodie. She didn't mind. At least he'd made contact.

229

She wasn't going to meet a wall of iron silence when she tried to fix the damage they'd done each other.

But it wasn't going to be today. "He said he was going to London," Marta reported. "He said he'd be away a couple of days so you weren't to worry. He said he'll see you before you leave."

"How did he sound?"

Marta shrugged. "Troubled."

There was nothing Brodie could do about that. She was sorry if she'd hurt or disappointed him, but she wasn't responsible for his dreams. He had to accept she had a life in which he had no part. She'd gone about as far as she was prepared to in the cause of smoothing Daniel's ruffled feathers: it was time to consider her own needs.

Having made the decision to go, she had just three days to get ready. Both she and Paddy had current passports, but suitable clothes were another matter. Paddy had outgrown everything that fitted her last summer, and cruise-wear had been a low priority in Brodie's budgeting since the divorce.

She couldn't justify it now, either, leaving the business to an answering service and spending her savings on clothes with palm-trees on them. But she didn't care. David was right: she'd earned this. She'd worried about the business since setting it up, and she'd no doubt worry about it some more when she got back. But for the next two weeks she was going to have fun.

Wednesday morning she went shopping. She bought two suit-cases, a bright yellow one for Paddy, a bright red one for her, and set about filling them with absurdly frivolous clothes. A swimsuit she'd be embarrassed to hang on her line at home. Floaty wide-leg trousers and kitten-heel shoes that made her feel like Grace Kelly. Extravagant sun-hats for herself and both girls, and sun lotion you could distemper walls with. She went home poorer but thoroughly in the mood.

She hadn't told Paddy they were going on holiday. She did so this evening. The little girl listened in rapt excitement, then tried on her new clothes and posed before the mirror in her sun-hat. She and Brodie looked up the Caribbean in the atlas.

She asked about Sophie.

"Well, Sophie's daddy's a friend of mine. She's a year older than you. She's very nice. It'll be fun having someone to play with."

Brodie had debated with herself whether to say anything to Paddy about the last week's drama. But she was four, she wasn't stupid: in the course of a fortnight's cruise things were going to be said that she would pick up and knit together. Better that she know what they were talking about than be left to make up a horror-story of her own.

She didn't go into much detail. "Sophie's had rather a nasty time. She had to stay with some people she didn't like very much. She was glad to get home. Her daddy thought she deserved a treat, and he asked you and me to go too."

Paddy nodded absently. She seemed more interested in the sun-hat, but Brodie knew she was filing the facts away for future reference.

Just when she thought matters were settled, Paddy asked the question Brodie had been avoiding. "What about Daniel?"

Brodie caught her breath. "What *about* Daniel?"

"Is Daniel coming too?"

Brodie shook her head. "Daniel's gone to London for a few days."

"Won't he be back in time?"

It seemed an easy way out so she took it. "I don't think so."

"I like Daniel," the child said firmly.

"*I* like Daniel," said Brodie.

"Daniel had a nasty time too. Daniel got burnt."

"I know," Brodie said softly.

"Doesn't Daniel deserve a treat?"

"Of course he does. But darling, going on holiday with two little girls isn't *everyone's* idea of a treat. When we get back we'll take Daniel somewhere nice - how's that? Where shall we go?"

"The Museum of Farming," Paddy replied without a moment's hesitation. "I can show him the tractors."

231

Chapter 24

They were flying out on Saturday. Brodie spent Thursday and Friday tying up loose ends.

She drove to Newmarket with the owners of Flossie the pony, witnessed a tearful reunion and returned to Dimmock with a happy glow about her heart and a cheque in her handbag. On the way back she made another trawl of the Brighton bookshops, coming up with a small but profitable handful of the editions on her list. She broke the bad news to a man who was seeking to buy back his father's old Riley from a film company, that those scenes of it going off Beachy Head were not in fact special effects.

In between times she phoned those clients whose affairs could not be settled, explaining that she'd be away for a few days. Fortunately, time was not critical to any of them; still she gave them the option of instructing someone else if they preferred. No one did, although a couple couldn't resist the chance to grumble. She bit her tongue and made regretful noises. She wasn't in a position to offend any of them, even the unreasonable ones.

It was Friday evening before she'd done all she could and went home. Marta had fed Paddy, so Brodie got down to the packing. Laying out all their things made her laugh. Under the latest cruisewear they were both going to be wearing knickers so old they'd be lucky to last the fortnight. She refused to care. Where they were going, extra ventilation was a bonus.

A little after nine, with the job almost finished and Paddy fast asleep and dreaming of porpoises, the phone rang.

It was Daniel. "Can I come round?"

Brodie was surprised, found herself glancing at the clock. But she wouldn't tell him it was too late, not after how they parted. "Of course. Is everything all right?"

"I'm fine," he said; and though that was what she'd meant it wasn't what she'd asked, making her wonder what it was that was less than all right. "I'll be there in ten minutes." In the background she heard the distorted mutter of a public address system. He was calling from the station.

It didn't take ten minutes - at that hour there were taxis to spare - but it was time enough for Brodie to construct whole shooting-scripts as to what had happened to take him first to London and then, like this, back here. He said he was all right, which was reassuring. But something was going on that she didn't know about.

Brodie heard the taxi and had the door open before he could knock. "Daniel, before we say anything else, I want to apologise for what I said to you. It was unfair and unwarranted. I was going to call and say so, only then I got your message."

He shook his head, the bright hair dancing. "It doesn't matter." His manner perturbed her. He seemed distracted, avoiding her gaze. "Can we go inside? I've got something to show you."

Puzzled, Brodie waved him in. He was carrying his battered khaki rucksack, the only bit of luggage he seemed to own. He dumped it on the dining table, unaware of Brodie's wince, and took out two folders which for the moment he left unopened. He dropped his parka on a chair.

He seemed unsure how to start. He looked at Brodie and back at the table. "OK. Er - OK. Like I told Marta, I went to London. I had an idea to follow up, some research to do. The internet's great, but some things you have to do in person."

Brodie was watching him with concern. "Daniel, you look exhausted. You should be pottering round the park, not beating the mean streets of London. Have you eaten today?"

He spared that a scant moment's thought. "Probably. Yes, I'm tired and a bit sore, but I'm fine. I just - We need to talk about this. Let me explain, and then I'll eat all you like."

She nodded uneasily. "Go on."

One of the folders was red, the other was green. He opened the green one and took out a large number of photographs, fanning them across the table. There must have been thirty or forty of them, some coloured, some black-and-white. They were all of women.

Brodie frowned. "What is this? Who are they?"

Daniel chewed on the inside of his cheek. "Well, most of them are

233

perfectly nice, decent women that neither of us will ever have heard of. But it's possible that one of them kidnapped Sophie Ibbotsen. You met her - you're the only one who has. I'm hoping you might recognise her."

She stared at him in utter astonishment. "Daniel - how on *earth* have you got hold of a photograph of the kidnapper?"

He gave an awkward little shrug. "I don't know that I have; and if I have I don't know which of them it is. Sit down with them, take your time. I know she was muffled up to the eyeballs, but one of them may look familiar."

Not for the first time he'd succeeded in knocking the breath clear out of her. She had to sit down anyway: she did as he asked, sat at the table and started picking through the photographs. None of them meant anything to her. "Daniel," she said, her voice a plaint.

"Please. Just look. If it doesn't help, maybe I'm wrong. I'll have wasted a couple of days, you'll have wasted half an hour. Either way there's no harm done. I'll make you a deal: while you'll look I'll make something to eat."

She'd learned better than to argue with him. "Empty the fridge if you like, just leave me a pint of milk for breakfast. Anything left after that will spoil anyway."

"Ah," he said softly. "Yes."

So she looked. After a while a cup arrived with biscuits in the saucer. She sipped and she nibbled and she looked.

None of the women was known to her, but she started to form an impression of them as a group. They were all between perhaps twenty-five and thirty-five; all good-looking in their different ways; so far as she could judge from photographs, all with a certain amount of financial security. Some of the photographs had been taken out of doors, the women in cords and Barbours posed against rolling countryside, and others in nightclubs clad in expensive chic. Every picture was a portrait of the woman on her own. Wavy edges showed where another person had been cropped out of several. A couple included an extraneous hand.

"Who *are* they?" Brodie asked again, deeply curious.

"Can I explain later?" asked Daniel. "After we know if one of them was the woman you met in the wood?"

"I'm not sure I will know that. For obvious reasons, she didn't want me to see her that well."

Daniel nodded. "I know: the woolly hat, the scarf. Still, giving a description of someone is harder than recognising them. It's not just faces: it's the way people stand, the proportions of their bodies. All sorts of clues help us spot someone we know while we're still too far away to see a face. I know it's a long shot. But can we try?"

"I'm trying," protested Brodie, "I'm trying."

Like playing Solitaire, she arranged the photographs in an order that made some sort of sense to her. Some of them she was sure - she could not have said why - were not the woman she had met, and those she pushed aside. Some were slightly more promising, and others began to look vaguely familiar. "Some of these are of the same people."

"Yes," said Daniel.

"Do *you* know who they are?"

"Yes," said Daniel.

She drank more tea, ate another biscuit. She let her gaze wander over the table-top as the glass wanders over a ouija board. And in the same way she found it beginning to hang a certain way, gently tugging her towards particular photographs.

She separated these from the others and concentrated on them. After another minute she returned two of them to the discard pile and went on staring at the others, more closely as the field narrowed.

Daniel didn't join her at the table. He took his cup and a sandwich and lowered himself into an armchair, with his back to the table and no view of what she was doing. He didn't speak. He didn't eat or drink much either. He sat hunched in his chair, failing to fill it, and by degrees his head lowered on his chest. It might have been sheer tiredness, but it looked like dread at what was coming.

Finally Brodie straightened up. "It was dark and her face was covered. I couldn't make an identification that would stand up in court. I couldn't even put my hand on my heart and say I think this is her. But it could be."

Still Daniel didn't come over. "What did she say to you?"

Brodie frowned. "Why?"

"Listen to it in your mind. See if it goes with the face in front of you."

It sounded silly but she did as he asked. Certainly she had no difficulty remembering what that passed between them.

"Get out of the car and come up here."

"Come closer. You won't be able to see from there."

"Of course she isn't dead."

"The rope is tied in a slip-knot. One good yank and she drops like a stone."

"The last thing you'll hear will be the the first barrel of a double-barrelled shotgun."

The strangest thing happened. As Brodie rehearsed the words, the image in front of her moved. The body frozen by a camera shutter became vital again, the head moving in staccato irritation, the hands gripping to punch home the message, the chin rising at a challenge, dropping on an agreement.

Brodie took a couple of the discarded photographs and, turning them over, used the white card to mask off the upper and lower parts of the face. She was left with a pair of eyes, the bridge of the nose, cheekbones and a little fair hair escaping its knitted prison.

She took a deep breath and sat back. "I still couldn't vouch for it in court. Will I need to?"

Daniel shook his head. "I don't think so."

"Then, with that proviso, this is her. Who is she? How on earth did you find her?"

He stood up. It took an effort. He opened the second folder and leafed through its contents. "I followed a hunch." His voice was dead.

He found what he was looking for, passed her another photograph with a name on the back. "Melanie Fields," Brodie read aloud. The name meant nothing. "Is this her?" She turned it over.

Her blood ran cold. The iciness crept from her soul, up her spine and into her brain. She was very aware of her own breathing which was unnaturally soft and level. She put the picture down beside its partner, her gaze encompassing both, and fought for control.

Because she knew that if she lost it she wasn't just going to hurt Daniel's feelings, she was going to knock him halfway across the room.

When she believed she could say what she wanted to and nothing more she turned to face him. "You're sick. You know that, don't you? You're sick, and you're obsessed."

He wouldn't meet her gaze. "I didn't pick out the photograph," he muttered stubbornly.

"No. But you made it very easy for me to. What else have you got in there?" She took the red folder from his unresisting fingers, spilt its contents on the table. "Oh I *see*. So it really wouldn't have mattered which of these women I thought I recognised, would it?"

The folder contained another twenty or thirty photographs. Brodie shuffled through them, nodding. They were the same photographs, showing all the same women but this time in their uncropped state with the man who'd been edited out. By then even his identity came as no surprise.

Brodie pushed them away disdainfully. "Daniel, what are you expecting? That I'll shed a little tear and start unpacking? That I'll be so grateful at being saved from a terrible mistake that I'll fall into your arms and we'll live happily ever after? It's not going to happen. You played a trick on me, and I have to say it was a pretty low one. But that's all it was. A sleight of hand. This?" - she tapped the photograph with an impatient fingernail - "means nothing. I'm supposed to be shocked that David's had women friends before? I have news for you: I've had men friends before him. Damn it, we've both got children! Anyone seeking a virgin partner might have taken that as a hint."

"You're missing the point," said Daniel, chewing a thumb-nail. "None of the others matter. But you thought that was the woman you spoke to in the wood. The kidnapper."

Brodie breathed heavily. She wanted to slap some sense into him. "Having been involved in more court cases than you've done sums, I can tell you something about eye-witness testimony. It's the poorest

237

evidence there is. Honest reliable witnesses make mistakes all the time. They fail to identify the culprit; they pick out the solicitor's clerk instead; they get heights, ages, even colours wrong. People just aren't that good at recognising other people.

"Context is all. Tell a witness you've put together an identity parade and she'll assume that the man she saw will be there. She'll try to spot him. Random chance gives her odds of six-to-one. Backing racehorses at six-to-one, you'd get a fair number of winners.

"That's all this" - a disparaging flick at the litter on the table - "amounts to. You told me you might have a photograph of the kidnapper and asked me to pick her out. I did my best. The woman in that picture is like the woman I met. But we can go into any bar in Dimmock and I'll find you someone just as similar. It wasn't fair. Not to me, and not to her."

Her voice hardened. "Most of all, it wasn't fair to David. 'One of these women could be the kidnapper' - and they're all women he's known? Talk about loaded dice! How did you get these photographs, anyway?"

"From picture libraries in London. They supply shots of the rich and famous, to newspapers mostly."

"You asked them for photographs of David Ibbotsen with different women? What kind of a maniac did they take you for?"

"The kind who was paying cash," shrugged Daniel. "They really weren't interested in my motives. He's a public figure, they had photographs of him at various functions, they sold me copies of them. There was nothing underhand about it."

"You think not?" Brodie heard her voice soaring and capped it. "How far back do these things go?"

"Five years."

"Five years? You asked them for every photograph they had of David Ibbotsen with a woman taken in the last five years, and they didn't ask why? My God, it's true. There's somebody who'll do anything for enough money!"

When she heard what she'd said, the colour started rising from somewhere around her knees. Because it was true, there was. She'd given him into the hands of his torturer for money. The times he could have thrown that in her face and hadn't! Mortification struck her dumb.

Daniel took advantage of the silence. "I know how this must look to you," he said hurriedly. "You think I fancy my chances with you and for that reason, and others, I want to hurt David Ibbotsen. You're wrong, but I can see how you'd think it.

"And I know you can't make a firm identification of a woman you met once, in difficult circumstances, from a photograph. But you thought it was her - Melanie Fields. You can't want to leave it there any more than I do. To think that you may have identified the kidnapper of a five-year-old girl and never know for sure. Maybe if you met her in person?"

Brodie didn't answer. But when she'd thought about it her eyes said Maybe.

Daniel followed up the advantage. "Then, can we ask David to introduce you?"

"What?!!"

"I know - you think I'm mad and so will he. I don't care. He reckons to owe me something for what happened: well, this is it. I'm mad, I'm sick, I'm obsessed - but I want you and Melanie Fields to meet. That's all I want, if I get it he'll never hear from me again. Is it too big a price to ask? For peace of mind? For drawing a line under an unpleasant piece of family history?"

Brodie shook her head. "No," she said softly, "it's a bargain. If it's what you want, Daniel, I'll ask him. But I'm damned if I know what I'll say to the woman."

"You won't have to say anything. You won't actually have to meet. If David looks at you strangely and then sets it up, and Miss Fields turns up, obviously I'm wrong about this. I'll make my apologies and leave, and you can all laugh at me when I've gone. But if I'm right the meeting won't take place."

The thing was, he didn't sound mad. He looked tired and ill, and perhaps he was obsessed, but he'd gone to a lot of trouble and he'd come up with a photograph that said something to her. Brodie knew that if she threw him out she wouldn't forget what he'd said. And whatever his motivation, however misguided, she didn't think it was malice. He wasn't a malicious man.

"All right," she said in a low voice, "let's talk about this. What are you saying? That a woman that David loved and left got her own back by kidnapping his daughter?"

He blinked behind the thick glasses, then he nodded. "It's possible." His eyes on her face were intense.

Another question formed in the maelstrom of her mind and bubbled to the surface. "*Why* do you think this? You said, something *I* said ... ?"

"A few things," he said, "including something you said. There was the video tape. Remember the moment Sophie saw someone she recognised in the car?"

"But she didn't recognise the woman who had her by the hand."

"No. But there were two of them, and she *did* recognise the driver."

"What else?"

"The box of hair. You said that wasn't the act of a ransom kidnapper. You thought of the mother: it wasn't her, but it *was* someone who knew the child too well to want to hurt her."

"All right," Brodie allowed softly. "What else?"

"The exchange. It was designed to protect the kidnappers, but they also took care not to hurt or even frighten Sophie. As if she wasn't just a meal-ticket to them. Has anyone talked to her about what happened?"

"David did. She couldn't tell him much that we didn't already know. She talked about a man and a woman, and a cottage in the country."

"Was she able to describe the woman?"

Brodie shrugged. "She's only five. Everything that goes for adult eye-witnesses goes tenfold for small children. They forget things we can't imagine them forgetting; they confuse the real with the imaginary; they focus on irrelevant aspects of things. Ask a five-year-old to describe someone and she'll say she wore pink shoes. It's not wrong, it's just no help. She may have spent longer with her than I did, but you can't count on Sophie ID-ing her kidnapper either. Is there anything else?"

240

"Not really." Still Daniel's eyes didn't leave her face.

"It's pretty thin," said Brodie.

"It would be," he nodded. "Without the photograph."

"I told you about that. You asked the question that would give you the answer you wanted. Don't read too much into it."

"But if Melanie Fields refused to meet you ... ?"

"It still won't prove anything. If they're an ex-item, meeting with David and me is about the last thing she'll be willing to do! If my ex-husband asked me to meet up with him and his new wife I'd fetch him one with the poker!"

Thinking about it, a new demon came. Her eyes flew wide. "Daniel, we know what Lance Ibbotsen does to people he thinks have harmed him. If we throw this woman's name into the ring, can we be sure he won't do to her what he did to you?"

A shudder ran the length of Daniel's frame. "I won't let that happen. I'll tell Inspector Deacon everything before anyone else gets hurt."

Brodie pushed his theory round her head like Paddy pushing sprouts round her plate. It could be just so much kite-flying, and she could take refuge in that. He had nothing approaching proof. But proof was a legal hurdle; what mattered at this point was probability. Was there a realistic chance that, looking for a way to drive a wedge between her and David, he'd somehow stumbled on the truth? Identified Sophie's abductor in a way that explained the odder aspects of the case?

She made herself consider it in detail. If Melanie Fields felt about the Ibbotsens the way Marie Soubriet did, she might indeed have wanted to hurt both David and his father. But she knew Sophie; she was willing to use her but drew the line at hurting her. The little girl might well have been confused as to whether she'd been kidnapped or not.

Daniel's theory fitted the known facts too well for it to be safely dismissed as the figment of a troubled mind. He might still be mistaken but neither of them was in a position to judge. If they wanted to be sure she was going to have to meet this woman, and that meant involving David.

"All right," she said unsteadily. "It matters to you to know if an old flame of David's kidnapped Sophie Ibbotsen. I dare say he'd want to know as well. I'm not sure how I feel. I think, that as it stands right now everyone's safe and the worst is over. If we tell the Ibbotsens we suspect Melanie Fields took Sophie, that may not still be the situation tomorrow. You say you won't let her get hurt, but realistically the most you can promise is to tell the police *if* she gets hurt.

"Suppose you're wrong. If I'm ready to consider the possiblity that you're right, you have to think about what happens if you're wrong. I've got fond of David, but I'm not blind to his failings. The biggest of them is never standing up to his father. He stood by while Lance had you hurt, and even when he tried to kill you. He turned away, he threw up, but he didn't try to stop it. He couldn't stand up to Lance then and he won't now. If you're wrong you'll have set a mad dog on an innocent woman. Daniel, that won't make you feel any better.

"I hope you are wrong, because I don't know how it'll all end if you're right. You think it's going to come between David and me: well, maybe it will. But how much satisfaction is that going to give you? You're not a vindictive man, I can't see you getting any pleasure from making people unhappy.

"But it's still your call. It's a can of worms, but if you want to open it I won't stop you. Shall I call David? Or should I get Marta down here so we can pay him a visit?"

Daniel was white. A couple of times he seemed about to say something but then didn't. He reached for his parka and his photographs. "It's like the internet. Some things you have to do in person."

Chapter 25

The gates were shut. A dim bulb illuminated the intercom. Brodie pressed the button and waited.

After a minute a gravelly voice demanded, "What time of night do you call this?"

Brodie gave her name. "Is David there?"

"He's busy. With Sophie. Call him tomorrow."

Brodie felt her temper rising. She'd done too much for these people, been through too much, to be moved on like a brush-salesman.

Before she could vent the anger, though, Daniel leaned towards the microphone. "Let us in. We have information on the whereabouts of your money."

After the briefest pause, the gates swung wide.

As she drove Brodie cast Daniel a sidelong glance. "You don't know that."

"Neither does he. But he opened the gate."

"Has anybody ever told you you have a ruthless streak?"

Daniel considered, then shook his head. "No." He seemed neither pleased nor displeased so much as surprised.

Brodie drove round the back. The lights were on in the sitting room and the back door framed the rangy figure of Lance Ibbotsen. Already on edge, Brodie was prepared to be irritated by anything. "You own a shipping line, you shouldn't open your own door. They have staff, don't they?"

"I don't suppose they want to involve them in what's been happening," said Daniel quietly.

"That's pretty decent," said Brodie, mollified slightly. "They don't want to see them in the dock too."

"Decency has nothing to do with it. They don't want them selling the story to *The News of the World*."

They weren't up the steps before Ibbotsen began quizzing them. "You know who did this? Kidnapped Sophie?"

"Stole your money?" said Daniel, expressionless.

"You know?"

"Possibly."

"*Well?*"

"I need David to see a photograph."

The old man turned on his heel, ready to haul his son downstairs by the collar if need be, but David was in the hall. He smiled at Brodie. When she bit her lip instead of returning it, the smile died.

"What's happened?"

"They know who has the money!"

David's jaw dropped. "How?"

"Don't look at me," said Brodie indignantly, "I only do this professionally. Daniel does it because mysteries worry him. Give him an internet uplink and a return ticket to London and he'll tell you what happened to Lord Lucan, who was on the grassy knoll and how to start a room temperature fusion reaction!"

Daniel bit his lip.

David frowned. "What are you talking about?"

Ibbotsen turned the searchlight of his gaze on Daniel. "You know, don't you? You know what she's talking about, and you know who has my money."

"Possibly," Daniel said again. They moved into the sitting room. Daniel passed the photograph to David. "Do you know her?"

David's eyes flicked between the picture and Daniel's face. "She did this? Kidnapped Sophie?"

"I'm not sure. Do you know her?"

"I - we've met." His eyes went out sideways to Brodie and then dropped. "Well yes, actually I do. We went out for a time. But that's months ago. Her name's Melanie." His brow gathered. "Are you seriously telling me she's involved in this?"

"I'm really not sure. Do you know where she is now?"

"I think she went abroad."

"Where?"

"*I* don't know! We - parted, I didn't watch to see what she did next. I heard she'd gone abroad."

"So she could have come back."

"I suppose so."

244

"Is there anyone we could check with? Parents, a brother or sister?"

"She has a brother. I wouldn't know how to find him." Tiring of the cross-examination, he looked across at Brodie. "This can't be right. We parted amicably enough, and she isn't a vicious person."

"You mean she wasn't," said Daniel. "Months ago."

David looked down at him. "People don't change that much."

"No," agreed Daniel. "So you don't think we could contact her."

"I don't know how. Anyway, you'd be wasting your time. I told you, she wouldn't do something like that."

"Because you parted amicably. You stayed friends."

"If you like."

Daniel nodded slowly. He chewed on the inside of his cheek. He glanced at Brodie, and she saw neither disappointment nor relief so much as the burden of an unwelcome understanding. She wanted to ask him what he was thinking now but he looked away, his shoulders slumped.

Ibbotsen was watching too, his gaze switching rapier-like between them, impatience drawing the sinews of his body like bowstrings. "That's it? That's the great revelation? You thought it might have been my son's ex-girlfriend, only there's no proof and you don't even know if she's in the country or not? I'm missing *The Ten O'Clock News* for this?"

But Brodie knew him better. "Daniel, there's something you're not saying. I don't know what it is, but I do know it's time to put your cards on the table and never mind who gets hurt." From the way he looked at her then she knew it was going to be her.

Daniel swallowed and nodded. "All right. If no one else has anything they want to say." He waited a moment longer, carefully looking at no one in particular, but no one spoke.

He sighed, and looked for somewhere to sit. He chose the window-seat: he didn't want to sit next to Brodie or any of them, and he wanted something at his back. "All right. I don't know how much of this could be proven in court. Maybe all of it, maybe none; and maybe it doesn't matter. You can hardly go to court with it."

"Tell me who has my money," said Ibbotsen tightly, "and I won't need any court to get it back."

Still Daniel prevaricated. He might have been bluffing, stamping around at random in the hope of driving a rabbit out of the hole, but Brodie really didn't think so. His whole manner suggested that what troubled him was not the lack of an answer but the nature of the one he'd found. "I will," he said quietly. "If I have to."

Finally his gaze came to rest on David Ibbotsen. "Do I have to? Are you going to make me say it?"

David's expression was like boards, impervious and unyielding. His eyes smoked. "What do you mean?"

Daniel nodded, a Rubicon crossed. "Sophie was never in any danger from her kidnappers because she was never kidnapped. She was taken out of school by her father and his girlfriend. They said they were taking her on holiday, but within a few minutes David had switched to his own car in order to be home when the news came through." He glanced at Ibbotsen. "You were impressed at how quickly he thought up a lie for the school. But he'd had days, even weeks to plan what he was going to say.

"All he had to worry about was getting you to pay up quickly, and in fact that was the one thing he couldn't do. As it happened he knew his daughter was safe in the country with Melanie Fields and the young man who was probably her brother, but it would have been just the same if she really had been kidnapped. You weren't prepared to pay the ransom. Whatever your reasons, you were prepared to leave Sophie with her abductors rather than pay a sum of money you could lose through stock market fluctuations and never miss.

"I think that hit David harder than anything you'd ever done to him. He didn't embark on this lightly. He was in real financial difficulties - he'd made some bad investments, the sky was about to fall on him, he needed to get his hands on a serious sum of money ASAP. Still, you don't steal from your own father without agonising over it. He agonised, he looked for an alternative, but he couldn't find one so he decided to do it.

"And you had a quick think about paying the ransom and decid-

246

ed not to. David knew he was behaving appallingly. He was shocked to the core when you behaved worse."

Daniel's pale eyes left Ibbotsen and found his son. There was compassion in the quiet of his face. "You were trying to strike out without him, weren't you? To create a power-base independent of the Ibbotsen Line. But it turned out he was right - it's not as easy as it looks, just because he could do it didn't mean you could. You hadn't his skill or experience and you quickly found there are more ways of losing money than making it. You were close to losing everything.

"You could have asked your father for the money. He'd have bailed you out, to protect his own interests and Sophie's; but you'd never have heard the end of it. He hadn't much respect for you before - if he had to salvage you from the consequences of your financial ineptitude he'd have made you cry blood.

"And maybe you reckoned you had a right to it. That it wasn't just your inheritance, it was something you'd earned. That's something you'll have to hammer out between you. He might, in time, forgive you for taking his money. I'm not sure he'll forgive you the rest."

There was a longer silence then. Daniel was waiting for questions but no one asked any. No one spoke at all. Nor did they look at one another. To all intents and purposes, time stood still in the shabby, comfortable room.

Brodie was the first to find a voice, and a hollow, shaky thing it was. "You said we'd know, if we couldn't set up a meeting with Melanie Fields. I thought you meant, if she did a runner. But you didn't. You meant, if David prevented it."

"Brodie!" The point which had loomed for days had finally come, where even-handedness would no longer serve, where she had to believe in one of them at the expense of the other. David thought she'd chosen to believe Daniel. Shock and anger warred in his voice. "It's nonsense! A fantasy. None of it happened. You *know* what happened: you were there for most of it!"

She nodded slowly. "Yes. But nothing I saw or heard contradicts what Daniel just said. It makes sense, in the whole and in detail; and mostly when something makes that much sense it's the truth."

247

She looked at him with sorrow. "You say he's got it wrong? That it's a fantasy? Convince me. Please, David. Give me one reason not to believe him. One thing that happened that isn't consistent with what he says. One thing you did or didn't do that shows you didn't hold your own daughter to ransom. Just *one*. Please?"

Desperation was thumping through David Ibbotsen with the racing beat of his heart. He'd only get one shot at this and Brodie was the key to it. If he could persuade her, she would persuade his father. "Listen to me," he said urgently, leaning forward. "I know how it looks. I can see how he might come up with this - insanity - and how you might wonder about it. But I'm telling you, it didn't happen. You have to believe me. Brodie, I think I love you. You have to believe that I wouldn't lie to you, not about this.

"Damn it, you have to believe *me* before you'd believe Daniel! Look at him - he could give jumpy lessons to a grasshopper. His mental stability is on the point of meltdown. I know whose fault that is, and I'm sorry, but this is too important to humour him. You have to see what he's doing. He hates me, and he wants you to hate me too. He's put two and two together and come up with about fifteen."

She shook her head. "Daniel wouldn't do that. He's a mathematician. You may be right about his mental state, though I don't know how anyone in this house has the nerve to comment, but it isn't actually relevant. The known facts support his version of events. What are you telling me - it's a coinicidence?"

David came to his feet. For almost the first time she was aware how powerful a man he was: as tall as his father and twice as far round. And not all the bulk hung on the broad bones was business lunches - a lot of it was muscle. Two strides took him to the window. Hands fisted tight at his sides, he loomed over Daniel like an avalanche.

"Tell her you got it wrong," he ground. "Tell her."

Daniel shook his head. "You tell her I got it right. You owe her that much. You certainly owe her better than a Caribbean cruise."

Like a catapult when the elastic snaps, one of the big fists flew. It wasn't a punch: he backhanded Daniel across the mouth, knocking him off the window-seat onto his knees on the carpet. "Tell her!"

248

But he wouldn't, and Brodie knew he wouldn't. She rose swiftly from the sofa and tried to get between them. David pushed her aside, forcefully enough that she ended up back where she started.

The big hand fisted in Daniel's clothes hauled him to his feet. David's broad, handsome face was twisted with rage. "I'm sick to the back teeth with your spiteful interference. Who the hell do you think you are, to accuse me of kidnapping my own child? You think I'd put Sophie through that for money? You think I'd put my father through it?

"You're right, I could use the money. I could still use the money. But there are limits to what decent people do to get what they want. They don't use their own children for blackmail. And they don't lie to take women who wouldn't look at them twice away from better men."

"I'm not lying," gritted Daniel, pain in his voice. David's fist against his ravaged chest pinned him to the wall.

Brodie was on her feet again. "Get away from him. I mean it, David - back off. Or so help me I'll deck you!" She hunted the room for a weapon but nothing offered itself. No brass candlestick: the room was lit by wall-sconces and a standard lamp. Central heating meant no fire-irons. There wasn't even the regulation bag of golf-clubs in a corner.

"Not till he admits he made it up." It was no accident - David knew exactly what he was doing. He ground his knuckles into Daniel's flesh until the younger man whined and his eyes closed.

"Put him down," said Lance Ibbotsen in his teeth. "Now." He still sounded as though he was talking to the dog.

"Not until - "

He never finished the sentence. Ibbotsen hit him behind the ear with a piece of scrimshaw like a belaying-pin.

Scrimshaw only looks delicate: actually it's made from the bit that walruses fight with. David measured his length on the floor, rolled over once and lay still.

Ibbotsen returned the souvenir of his seafaring days to its home in the bookcase. He said heavily, "He never bloody listens." For the moment that seemed to be all he could cope with. He hadn't felled his son because of the allegation made against him. He'd done it because an order had been disobeyed.

Brodie sucked in a deep breath and went to Daniel, kneeling beside him. "Are you all right?"

His face was ashen. He plucked at his shirt-front with trembling fingers. "I think I'm bleeding."

Brodie ushered him towards the nearest bathroom. "We'll sort you out. Then we'll come back and sort him out."

* * *

The damage under Daniel's shirt wasn't serious. There was a little blood, and some seepage where blisters were protecting new skin, but all Brodie had to do was tidy up the dressings. She hadn't looked this closely since the lesions were a lot worse. She made approving noises as she smoothed and patted him back into shape. "You'll be as good as new."

"I wish," he said fervently.

Satisfied that she'd done all that was necessary, she rocked back on her heels and looked at him. Oddly enough, she felt quite calm. "What you were saying. About David. It's not just a theory, is it? You're sure?"

"Sure enough," he said honestly. "There are too many things you can't explain any other way."

"Like what?"

She wasn't arguing. She needed to know. He answered as best he could.

"There were two people in the car: the woman who got out and a driver we never saw. The woman was Melanie Fields. Sophie didn't want to go with her. If she recognised her, it wasn't a good enough reason to do what she must have been told a thousand times never to do - to go off with someone she didn't know really well. But when she got close enough to the car to see who was driving, all that changed. The driver *was* someone she knew really well."

"It didn't have to be David. It could have been - I don't know - the chauffeur?"

He regarded her with compassion. "Well, maybe."

Brodie gritted her teeth. "Go on."

"Sophie's five years old. She's not a baby. A five-year-old child may be useless as a witness, but she's pretty good at absorbing atmosphere. She knows the difference between people who care about her and those who look at her and see pound signs. I don't think she could have been kidnapped without realising it. She thought she was on holiday because from her point of view she was. She was happy enough to stay with Melanie Fields because David said it was all right. I expect he was phoning, maybe even visiting, whenever he could."

Then there was the box of hair. Brodie had thought it pointed to Sophie's mother, but it could equally well indicate her father. She nodded to herself. She didn't have to like it, but she knew the truth when it was put before her.

"And the timings were too - convenient," Daniel continued quietly. "The day you went to France. I thought, what will Ibbotsen say if the kidnappers phone before she gets back? But they didn't. But they *did* phone almost as soon as you returned and the decision had been taken to pay the ransom.

"And they asked for a woman to bring it. Why do that? Why not Lance, or David? Lance was the one with the money, David the father of the child. Why involve an outsider at all - and why stipulate a woman? It was as if they knew more about what was going on in this house, the alliances being forged, the confidences being established, than they had any right to - unless they had someone on the inside."

Brodie shook her head. "If David was involved, he'd have opted to handle the hand-over himself. It would have been both simpler and safer. If Melanie had insisted on doing the exchange with him, no one would have been surprised. It would be the obvious thing. David was the one with most lose, therefore the one most likely to do as he was told and least likely to get creative. If she'd said he was to come himself, no one would have argued."

But Daniel had worked that out too. "David needed to break his trail. As much as possible he wanted to stay in the back seat - avoid

251

meeting the kidnappers, avoid talking to them if he could, certainly avoid negotiating with them. That's why the woman always asked for Lance. Not just because he held the purse-strings but because David didn't want his fingerprints on the deal. If the arrangements were handled by his father, or by you, no one was going to think he'd given in too easily and wonder why. For ten years being side-lined by his father was a source of deep frustration to him. This time it was his alibi. It kept him safe from suspicion."

"Except yours."

Daniel didn't reply. He hadn't an answer that would make her feel any better.

She sensed evasion. "What made you suspect him? I can see how, once your suspicions were aroused, you had to check them out. You learned about his financial difficulties, and you got together some photographs of his friends from which I was able to make a tentative identification. But what made you suspect David Ibbotsen in the first place?"

Daniel's eyes dropped and he shrugged his clothes about him as if the bathroom was cold, which it wasn't. "He lied."

"About what?"

"What happened - here, outside. He told you he wasn't involved. But he was. From the start."

In the silence Brodie considered this. "He knew what they were doing to you?"

Daniel nodded.

"Maybe most people would have lied about that," she ventured. "He wanted me to think well of him. It's a long way from there to guessing that he kidnapped his own daughter. How could you know he was capable of that kind of - ruthlessness - when I didn't?"

"Brodie - it was David who shot me. Not Lance. He said that because he thought one of them was going to prison and he didn't want to deprive Sophie of her father. I suppose he thought I would-n't remember. But I do."

Brodie stared at him in horror. She was no longer wondering if it was true, only how it fitted together. "You're saying that he stood by and watched you tortured for information he *knew* you didn't have!"

252

Daniel gave an awkward shrug. "I suppose by then he was in so deep the only way out was confession. He thought his father would have turned on him. He would, too."

"So David watched you suffer for two days, and then he shot you?"

"Someone had to," Daniel said, almost apologetically. "David had the best reason to get it over and done with."

As Brodie's understanding grew, so did her sense of outrage. And not all of it was directed at David Ibbotsen. "You knew this. And you didn't tell me?"

"I was only sure today. When you recognised the photograph."

"I don't mean about the fake kidnap. I mean, that a man I liked and was going on holiday with - that I was taking my daughter on holiday with! - is a monster. A killer, except for the merest fluke of a frosty night. You *knew* he shot you and left you to die, and you didn't tell me."

His face twisted with regret. "Would you have believed me? You thought I resented him because you and he were getting close. If I'd told you then, without any kind of proof, the best you'd have thought of me was that I wanted it to be true. You'd have asked David, he'd have denied it and you'd have believed him. I needed evidence, quickly, before he drew you any deeper into the conspiracy."

"Drew - me - ?" she echoed faintly.

Daniel knew he was hurting her. So much of this he'd hoped he wouldn't have to say. He'd expected that David would come clean when he realised the game was up, or else that Brodie would guess or perhaps wouldn't want to know. But maybe, difficult as it was, it was better to have everything said. Open wounds look worse but heal better. Also, he hoped very much never to have to revisit this territory again.

"He was still covering himself. You're an intelligent woman, he knew if he ever gave you a reason to wonder about him you'd find the truth. He needed you on his side. He played on your sympathy until it started turning to something more. If he could make you fond of him, he could make you trust him. It didn't have to last forever, and of course it wouldn't have done. Melanie Fields didn't risk prison for the small change he'd have left after his debts were paid: she did it for him, and after what they'd done together he couldn't afford to offend her. They had to end up together, so at some point you had to be dumped. Any allegations you made about him after that would just sound like the spite of a rejected lover."

Minutes passed as Brodie reviewed the events of the past week in the light of Daniel's explanation. Twice she vented a sharp, hawk-like little pant; once she almost smiled. Finally, her tone still incredulous though her eyes believed, she said, "But - the *risk*! Maybe he thought he could fool everyone else, but Sophie knew. And Sophie's five years old. Sooner or later she was *bound* to spill the beans!"

Daniel shook his head. "Not really. Five-year-olds can keep secrets like their lives depend on it - if they couldn't there wouldn't be any abused children. If David told her never to speak of it, that he'd be in terrible danger if she did, she'd lock the whole thing so tight inside her it would take a psychiatrist to get it out.

"And she was never going to talk to a psychiatrist, was she? Or the police, or even her teachers. None of them knew she was supposed to have been kidnapped. And if she forgot her promise and talked about her holiday, so what? So she stayed in a country cottage when they thought she was on a Caribbean cruise. If they even noticed they'd think nothing of it.

"The only one who mattered was Lance. If she talked about it to Lance, he just might put it together. So David covered even that eventuality. He told you, so no doubt he also told his father, that Sophie was confused, that she hadn't realised she'd been kidnapped and he didn't want her to know. With that in mind, Lance would discourage her from talking about it - for fear of what he might give away, not guessing there were secrets he might hear.

"And suppose the very worst happened. Suppose she told Lance that she stayed with Daddy's old girlfriend and Daddy phoned her every day. She's five years old, she was drugged, it's already on record that she's confused about what happened: Lance would assume she was remembering something from way back and never suspect she was telling the literal truth. David's been his whipping-boy so long it's become a kind of shield. Lance wouldn't entertain the idea that his son might have taken him on and won."

Everything Daniel said was true. Everything accorded with what Brodie knew about the two men at the centre of it: what she knew from personal experience and what she'd been told. She groaned, and when Daniel looked anxiously at her explained huskily, "Marie. She *told* me, near as damn it. She said, 'At least Lance was an honest monster.' If I hadn't been - *feeling* things for him - I'd have heard the rest of it, the bit she didn't say. That David was a dishonest one."

"You couldn't have been expected to." Daniel was still trying to ease her way. "You needed to know what I knew; and I couldn't tell you. Not without proof."

Brodie took a deep breath and stood up. "Are you all right?" Daniel nodded. "Then we have to go back in there. We have to tell Lance."

* * *

But Lance already knew. He hadn't got to be a rich man without learning to read faces. What had been said, and how his son reacted to it, had told him all he needed to know. They returned to the sitting room to find him standing at the French window, his back ram-rod straight, tears streaming down his face. David was nowhere to be seen.

Brodie said, "What - where ... ?"

"He's upstairs. Packing. He leaves this house with what he can carry and nothing more. Except for Sophie: she's staying here. I'll call her mother in the morning, see what we can work out."

"You're throwing him out?" whispered Brodie.

The old man turned to her - and now he looked a very old man. "Mrs Farrell, David's my only son. My only child. The father of my only grandchild. I know he's not much of a man, but it didn't really matter. I was man enough for both us. I'd have left things so he couldn't make too much of a mess of them.

"But - this ... ! Not the money. Not even the fear, though it was like knives in my gut. But I could have forgiven him even that eventually."

255

He looked at Daniel, the pale eyes tormented. "But what he - made me do - "

Daniel shook his head. "Nobody made you do that. You could have handed over the money. You could have gone to the police. You did what you did to me because you like doing things your way. David's a liar and a thief; but torture isn't his style, it's yours. He was afraid to interfere because he was afraid what you'd do to him if you guessed why."

"I wouldn't have hurt him!"

"No? You thought I was using the child to extort money from you. He saw what you did to me. He thought if you found out it was him you'd destroy him. I think so, too. My God, you treated him like dirt just because he hasn't your head for business! No, Mr Ibbotsen, you can't escape your share of the blame for this. Your son is the man you made him."

Ibbotsen went on staring at him, too proud to hide the tears. "What are you going to do?"

"Nothing," said Daniel.

"Nothing?"

"Nothing at all." Brodie saw a tiny smile touch his lips. "I don't have to. Your life is in ashes now: anything I could do to you, anything the law could do, would only blow those ashes around. You're safe from me, Mr Ibbotsen, and so's David. But then, I never meant you any harm. I was just someone in the wrong place at monumentally the wrong time."

The sharp jaw rose like the prow of a sailing ship. "Go on, say it. Tell me I'm my own worst enemy."

Once Brodie had hated him, then she'd pitied him. Now he meant nothing to her. Not even enough to avoid stating the devastatingly obvious. "Not while your son's alive, you're not." Steering Daniel ahead of her she left the room, and the house, and never looked back.

Chapter 26

"Were we too hard on him?" murmured Daniel.

Eyes on the lamp-lit road, Brodie shook her head. "You can't be too hard on people like that. But most of the time you can't get through to them either. I'm with Marie: they're both monsters."

"They behave like monsters," agreed Daniel. "Actually, they're two deeply damaged people. A testament to the corrupting power of too much money."

"David didn't think he had too much money."

"He had, though. Too much ever to learn to stand on his own two feet. When it still wasn't enough, the only way he knew to get more was to steal it."

"From his own father." Her voice mingled wonder and disgust.

"Who else? He never learned to rob banks either. It had to be his father's money he took, in the same way that it had to be his daughter that he ransomed. The family is the whole of his life, the only part of the world he has any experience of. David's tragedy is that he couldn't raise his sights beyond the rôle created for him by his father's wealth."

"What do you suppose will become of him?"

Daniel smiled into the darkness. "I give them a year of long-distance odium. After that they'll be under the same roof again."

Brodie took her eyes off the road long enough to stare at him. "Never," she said with conviction.

"Neither of them has anyone else. Half a million won't last forever, not when most of it's already owed to other people. David's going to need someone to write cheques for him.

"And Lance needs someone to despise. If he despised the people he employs he'd have to sack them. He needs someone he can't get rid of, however much of a disappointment he is. The stars need night to shine and Lance needs David. Without him he's just a lonely old man with more money than he can spend."

Brodie was fascinated by his insight. It was almost as if he could see into the future and watch these consequences unfold. For a moment she hesitated, too proud to ask. But she wanted to know more than she cared what he thought. "What about Melanie Fields? Will she and David stay together?"

He shook his yellow head. "She joined him in this not because she was worried about his business losses but because she thought beating Lance would make a man of him. Right now she thinks they won. When she finds that nothing's changed, that his father and his father's money remain the hub of David's existence, she'll give him up as a lost cause. Melanie will get on with her life, and David will go home."

"Then it was all for nothing."

"I suppose it was. It didn't seem to be. You were prepared to risk your life for that little girl. The fact that she was never in danger doesn't alter that."

"It alters how I *feel* about it," she said resentfully. And then, after a long pause, her voice fallen to a murmur: "How do you feel? Now we know it wasn't even an honest mistake." She gave a brittle laugh. "If you know what I mean."

Daniel thought for a moment. "As far as Lance was concerned it *was* an honest mistake. He believed Sophie was in mortal danger and set about saving her the way that made most sense to him. It was his nature to fight rather than submit. I think I believe him when he says he'd have paid up if he'd believed it was the safest thing to do."

"I don't," growled Brodie. "He's good at convincing himself that what he wants to do is right. The bottom line is, he tortured you for two days rather than part with some of his money. It wouldn't have been much better if you'd been the man he took you for. In fact, not only were you not a kidnapper, but there hadn't even been a kidnap."

"He thought there had. He was afraid. Frightened people do stupid things."

She gave a disparaging sniff. "You're determined to see good in people, aren't you? All right then, what of David? He could have stopped it at any time. He didn't, because he wanted the money enough to watch you suffer. He knew Sophie was safe, you can't put it down to fear. It was greed, and that makes him evil."

"He *was* afraid," insisted Daniel. "He had no idea what he was getting into, and when Lance didn't react the way he expected he had no idea how to get out. Evil's too big a word for it. He was weak. He did what he's done all his life: followed the path of least resistance."

Brodie pulled in beside the sheds. The sea was a soft mutter of shingle further down the shore. She looked at the tall black buildings looming against the sky. "It's late. Why don't you sleep at my place tonight?"

But Daniel got out of the car. "It's over. I'm safe enough in my own bed."

"All right." The crunch of gravel startled her and she snatched up the torch. The beam found a man carrying a yellow bucket, who blinked in the sudden light and looked away.

"Bait-diggers," said Daniel.

"At this time of night?"

"Low tide." With a backwards glance and a shy wave he trudged across the stones towards his flat, an insignificant figure in an oversized parka. Brodie found herself smiling. He was a genuine original: an anorak with the heart of a hero. She headed for home.

She travelled a mile before the car slowed and coasted to a halt along the kerb. There was nothing wrong with it, she'd just stopped driving. Something was bothering her, and she at first she couldn't think what it was. Something he'd said, or she'd said, or something ...

Something she'd seen? It was dark, apart from some late night traffic they'd seen no one, only the bait-digger on the shore. Who was out at this time because he required low tide, and the tide followed its own agenda even more than Daniel did.

In a suit? He was digging bait in a suit?

He was on his way home. Working late in the office, found the tide out as he passed, grabbed his bucket and spade from the boot of his car and went to stock up on lug-worms or rag-worms or whatever bait people dug on Dimmock's stony shore. It was feasible. It was even plausible. There was no longer any reason to fear danger behind every door. The affair was over, its secrets told; the only one left with a reason to hurt Daniel was David, and he knew he'd have to answer to his father. Besides, she'd seen the man's face and it wasn't David.

Still somehow the car turned itself around and started back towards the shore.

She had no idea what she'd say when Daniel answered the door in his pyjamas. Something stupid. She'd said a lot of stupid things. She'd accused him of having a crush on her! He'd managed to avoid referring to that, but he couldn't have forgotten - it was going to be an embarrassment between them for as long as they knew one another. Almost, it was reason enough to end the friendship. To shake hands, part on good terms and let the wounds heal.

But not tonight. Uneasy as she was, Brodie wouldn't sleep if she didn't go back to check that he was all right.

The same impulse that had made her return made her park the car up the shore where its engine wouldn't be heard. And though you can't walk silently on shingle, something made her try.

She climbed the iron steps. The light inside the flat escaped through an imperfectly drawn curtain to illuminate her way. As she reached to knock she heard a man's voice. Not Daniel's: a voice she didn't recognise. Curious, she leaned closer.

The voice said, "... Call her. Ask her to come back." Then, "You will. It might take a little while, but you will."

The window beside the door, the one with the badly drawn curtain, was offset from the top of the steps. Brodie leaned over the rail, peering through the crack.

The man whose voice she didn't recognise was seated in the armchair, almost facing her. Daniel sat on the floor, his back against the man's legs. Brodie blinked. For a moment it looked so intimate that she almost tip-toed away.

Then she saw Daniel's eyes, stretched with fear, and after that she saw that his ankles were strapped together with lengths of bubble-wrap and duck tape. His arms were out of sight behind him: she guessed they too were tied. The man held Daniel against his

260

knees with one hand on his throat. The other was cupped close to his eye.

"You think you can refuse?" There was an arch, teasing note to the voice. "Daniel, we both know you can refuse me nothing. I know you too well. I know how to hurt you." The fingers of his cupped hand lit with a sudden rosy glow and Daniel convulsed in his grip.

"I will find her," promised the man. "You can't save her. You can just make things a little easier for us both." The cigarette lighter flared in his fist again. Daniel gasped as the flame licked his cheek.

I know how to hurt you; and *I will find her*. All the information Brodie needed was in those two sentences.

She'd thought all their enemies were neutralised, but she was wrong. This was the man Ibbotsen had dismissed as being too dangerous. He'd gone only after he believed Daniel was dead. When he learned he was alive he came back; and now Brodie had seen him too. Only for a second, by torchlight, before he averted his face. But people paid with their lives for seeing this man's face. He'd come back to kill Daniel, now he needed her dead too. *I will find her. You can't save her.*

Not daring to take a proper breath, Brodie considered her options. The car was a hundred metres away. The first fifty she'd have to be quiet, after that she could run. If she got away unnoticed the police could be here in ten minutes. Daniel had survived two days in this man's hands, he could take another ten minutes. Or fifteen, or maybe twenty, if she couldn't get Deacon, or couldn't get him to understand.

She was backing away from the door when she remembered the bucket.

* * *

"What's in the bucket?" panted Daniel.

Everything had happened so fast he wasn't sure when it had arrived. He'd heard a footstep outside the front door and thought it was Brodie mothering him again. With a tolerant smile, without even looking round, he called, "It's open." Then he was sprawling in one direction, his glasses cart-wheeling the other, and when his wits steadied the man whose face he had never known but whose voice was scratched on his soul was wrapping him like a parcel. And the yellow bucket was standing at the kitchen door.

The man scowled. "Never *mind* the bucket. I'll explain about the bucket in a minute. First, who's the girlfriend?"

Daniel said, "Your feet are wet." He could feel the damp where he lay against the man's legs.

"Daniel, your attention, *please*. Forget the bucket, forget my feet. Concentrate on this." He flicked the lighter again and Daniel flinched. "Now, I'm asking nicely. Who is she? You know I won't *keep* asking this nicely."

"It's just water, isn't it? Sea-water."

The man eyed him in disbelief. "Yes," he said, hanging onto his temper. "That's all it is. A bucket of sea-water. Happy now?"

"You won't get away with it!" The words came in a rush, broken with fear.

The man sighed wearily. "Of course I'll get away with it. I've been getting away with it for years. No one will even suspect a crime. They'll just think that the trauma of the last two weeks finally over-whelmed you and you chose to end the nightmare rather than live it. You took your own life while the balance of your mind was disturbed."

"The post mortem - "

" - Will find nothing inconsistent. I'm not new at this: I know they can distinguish between salt- and fresh-water drowning. And I know they'll check for ligature marks. Wonderful stuff, bubble-wrap. It's good for insulating greenhouses too," he added, as if Daniel might find the information useful.

"I have friends," gasped Daniel. "People who know me. Who know I wouldn't just walk into the sea."

Unseen behind him, the man raised a doubtful eyebrow. "Really? They haven't exactly been flocking here, have they? Not when you were missing and not after you came back. I don't think you have any friends close enough to argue with a coroner."

"Brod - " He stopped with the name half out of his mouth, but it was already too late. The man was a professional interrogator, familiar with all the tools of his trade. Sometimes pity worked better than fire.

"Brodie Farrell?" The man's voice soared in amused incredulity. "That's who it was - the woman who tracked you down? That's your idea of a friend? Dear God, Daniel, you're a sad case."

Daniel tried to struggle but the man held him with contemptuous ease. "Leave her alone! You hear me? She couldn't have seen you, there wasn't time. She's no threat to you. Leave her alone."

"You never saw me. Not in two days of intimate association. Most of the time you were blindfold; even when you weren't you hadn't got your glasses on. I've never seen lenses that strong. You couldn't have picked me out of an ID parade; you wouldn't have recognised me if I'd come up to you in the street. I'm not here because I'm afraid of you identifying me."

"Then - why ...?"

The man shrugged. "You're a loose end. I don't like loose ends. You might think they won't do any harm, but the only way to be sure is to tie them up and cut them off. I don't take risks, Daniel, even small ones. When I walk away from this, there won't be any loose ends."

"Please," whispered Daniel. "She has a child ... "

"How old?"

He wasn't sure why it mattered. "Four, I think." Understanding hit him like a blow, knocking the confusion off his face. "No!"

"Oh relax," said the man negligently, "four's way too young to represent even a tiny risk. She wouldn't have talked to a four year-old about this, and if she had a four-year-old wouldn't remember. I won't touch her, you have my word." Then, as if in the interests of honesty, he added, "Unless she's in the car at the time. Or the house, if I go for a gas explosion."

Daniel writhed furiously. The man slapped him across the head. "Don't get stroppy with me, sonny. Or - " He paused, considering. "Actually, nothing you do will have any effect on my actions." He got up from the chair and, linking a hand through Daniel's bound arms, dragged him through to the kitchen. Then he reached for the bucket.

* * *

The yellow bucket he'd carried up from the surf: now Brodie knew what it was for. A man can drown in four inches of water if somebody holds him down. Daniel had served his purpose, there was no longer any reason to delay.

He hadn't meant to betray her but he had. Now death stalked at her heels too. Close on news of his suicide - or perhaps ahead of it: his body might float around for a week before drifting ashore - would come reports of her own misadventure. A car crash or a gas explosion. Two suicides would raise eyebrows: this would be only an unhappy coincidence. The most they could hope for was an irascible question mark in Jack Deacon's notebook and an hysterical outburst in broken English from Marta. Unless the explosion killed her too.

Brodie's mind raced. Neither man knew she was here, watching, listening. She could get away, far away, save herself and her child, at least for now. Then she'd be where Daniel had found himself, living every day in the fear that this one, or maybe the next, she'd open a door and there he'd be. He wouldn't give up, he couldn't afford to. Daniel was right: it wasn't much of a life.

Even so it was more than he could expect if Brodie took advantage of the darkness to slip away. Ten minutes was the quickest she could hope to bring help. Daniel would drown in three.

Which didn't alter the reality that here and now there was nothing she could do for him. She couldn't take a professional killer with her bare hands. She backed silently away from the door.

264

Chapter 27

The bucket smelled of seaweed. Daniel thought, if he could knock it over …

But the man had thought of that too. He'd manhandled many desperate people in his time, most of them stronger than Daniel Hood. He knew how to. It wasn't only physical superiority that told, it was skill. When the time came to put out the light he prided himself he could do it as neatly as anyone in the business. He didn't leave it to others because he was squeamish. It was the loose ends thing again.

He raised Daniel's head by a handful of hair and looked him in the eye. Finally Daniel could see the man who'd ruled his nightmares for a fortnight. There was nothing remarkable about him. Average height, average build, perhaps a shade harder than average; aged about forty, a few grey hairs starting through the close brown crop; eyes somewhere between blue and hazel. An ordinary face, unmarked by the cruelty of the mind. He'd been doing this so long it had no moral implications for him. No emotion, no guilt. It was a job he was good at. The only thing that showed in his face was the assurance of knowing that.

"Now listen," he said. "The quicker we get this done, the easier it'll be. It's going to happen: you can delay the inevitable for a minute or two but that's about all. Accept it gracefully. You've done well. Now, know when to call it a day."

But it was Daniel's *life* he was talking about, and he'd tried so hard to hang onto it, to get it back when he'd almost lost it. He couldn't just give it up. He knew, as only a fool would not, that it would take something extraordinary to save him now. Still it was not in his nature to lie quietly across the tracks and wait for the train.

"Ibbotsen," he gasped desperately. "He'll know. He found you once, he can find you again. You're worried about loose ends? Worry about him."

If he was surprised that Daniel knew that name the man didn't show it. He frowned. "Why would Mr Ibbotsen care? He needs this as much as I do. Trust me: all Mr Ibbotsen will feel when your body washes up under Beachy Head is a huge sense of relief. He won't ask himself how or why, he'll just be glad."

"He'll know it wasn't suicide. He'll know who did it."

The man shrugged. "Who's he going to tell - the police? I don't think so."

"He owes me!"

The man laughed, not unkindly. "Daniel, whatever you think he owes you, whatever *he* thinks he owes you, he isn't going to put his neck in a noose to change the wording on your death certificate. If he was here now he wouldn't interfere to save your life. Mr Ibbotsen has more to fear from me than I have from him."

He emptied the bucket into the sink. Then he lifted Daniel bodily and slammed him face down on the worktop. With one hand in Daniel's belt and the other behind his head, he tugged him over the sink and pushed down hard.

Gasping with fear and effort, Daniel resisted with all his strength. It was nowhere near enough. He was both smaller and lighter than the other man, and trussed like a chicken. He tried to twist aside but the man jerked him flat and forced his head down. The stink of brine filled his nostrils: opening his mouth to snatch a breath he swallowed salt water. His throat burned, his heart thumped in his ears and he thought he was lost.

You can drown in four inches of water, but his ears were above the surface. In disbelief and sudden burgeoning hope he heard the rap of knuckles on his front door.

The hope vanished utterly at the words that followed. They didn't mean he wasn't going to die. They meant he wasn't going to die alone.

"Daniel, it's Brodie. Can we talk? Or have you gone to bed - shall I come back tomorrow?"

He felt the man above him waver, took advantage of the distraction to yank his face out of the water and grab a lungful of air. He tried to shout a warning, but everything after her name was just bubbles. "Hush now," said the man disapprovingly.

It wasn't just the arrival of another person that altered things, it was who was there. He couldn't both finish with Daniel and answer the door. If he continued with what he was doing the woman would go away: he'd have to look for her later, and risk not finding her until the discovery of Hood's body warned her of her danger.

When Daniel was dead, under the shield of night the man meant to carry him down to the water and launch him on his last journey. But tides are at once utterly constant and quite unpredictable: the same current might take him for a week's cruise around the Channel or deposit him on the shingle at his own doorstep. Brodie Farrell was the one who'd know he hadn't walked into the sea. Everyone else might believe it but she'd know to be afraid. If he was found in hours rather than days she'd take her child and run, and he could waste much time finding her. If providence had sent her to him it seemed churlish to turn her away.

"Just a minute." He hauled Daniel off the worktop, dropping him on the floor hard enough to wind him, and stuffed a dish-cloth in his mouth. Then he shoved him in a corner like a roll of unwanted carpet and shut the kitchen door.

"I'm coming." He glanced down but there was nothing alarming in his immediate appearance. By the time she wondered why he was damp it would be too late. He opened the front door.

He ran into the stock of an oar, jabbed into the centre of his face like a javelin. His nose didn't so much break as explode. His cheek bones snapped under the force, the centre of his face collapsing in a welter of blood and an odd, high-pitched yowling like a cat in a spin-dryer.

His own blood kept him from seeing her. If it hadn't he'd have been astonished at the fury, the Valkyrie that Brodie Farrell had become. Her eyes were like coals, dark and smoking and tinged with red. The naked savagery in her face would have startled him. The coiled-spring strength of her body might have alarmed even him if he'd had a moment to recognise what it meant.

But he hadn't. He was staggering back under the first blow, his hands going to his ruined face, when she landed a second in his abdomen immediately below his sternum. The air rushing from his lungs sprayed her with blood. Brodie paused just long enough to close the door behind her - two minutes ago she was praying for passers-by, now she wouldn't have welcomed them - then followed him as he scrabbled desperately, crablike, across the carpet.

Her voice was low, vibrant, ribbed with rage and infinite menace. "A car-crash, hm? A gas explosion? You don't threaten me, you sewer-rat, not if you know what's good for you. And you definitely never, ever, *ever* threaten my child!" She swung the oar again.

* * *

Try as he might, Daniel couldn't free himself. He couldn't get the rag out of his mouth. The best he could manage was to roll out of the corner and, half on his side like an inebriated caterpillar, make for the kitchen door. His lungs rasped and burned, and he thought he would choke long before he could influence the events beyond.

He couldn't open the door. He hadn't the strength to turn himself round and kick it: he butted it with his head. It rattled impressively; so did his eyeballs. He went to do it again.

The door opened inwards, pushing him gently across the lino. Afraid, his eyes clouding, he looked up; but the door masked whichever of them was still standing. Daniel held his breath. The next moments would tell if he would live or die.

Brodie looked round the door, located him on the lino. "Oh, there you are." She sounded numb. Her face, neck and breast were blazed with blood.

She saw the horror in his eyes, looked where he was looking, shook her head tiredly. "Not mine." She reached down and pulled the gag out of his mouth.

In two days the man had learned everything there was to know about Daniel Hood; but Daniel had learnt things about him too. Enough that he wouldn't have turned his back on him even if he thought he was dead. Enough that he wouldn't have *believed* he was dead if his head and shoulders were on opposite sides of a meat-cleaver. Somewhere he found the spit to shout. "Brodie, don't let him - !"

268

Brodie glanced round negligently. "Him? He's not going anywhere." She looked for the kitchen scissors, knelt beside Daniel and started unwrapping him.

When he was free she helped him to his feet; but Daniel made her stay in the kitchen while he went to investigate. Seeing what she'd done he understood her certainty. He reached an unsteady hand for the phone to ask for police and ambulance. But privately he thought the ambulance might have a wasted journey.

* * *

Detective Inspector Deacon saw Brodie first. She told him the truth, excepting only the involvement of the Ibbotsen family. That she'd taken Daniel home, seen someone loitering round the sheds and returned to learn of the attempt on Daniel's life and the threat to her own. With no time to get help she'd hunted through the rotting nets and old lobster pots stored under the flat for something to use as a weapon. The oar was the best she could do. Had there been a harpoon she'd have used that. If she'd failed to kill the man who purposed her death it was not for want of trying.

Deacon nodded slowly, non-committally. "Well, you didn't kill him, but he's going to need a good plastic surgeon. OK. I expect you want to get cleaned up. I'll have someone take you home. I'll need to talk to you again, but that'll do for now."

"You're not charging me?"

"Not at this time," said Deacon. Then he softened. "If this is the man who hurt Daniel, I doubt you have much to fear from the judicial process."

Brodie nodded. Reaction had caught up with her: she felt like a wet rag. "I don't know that for sure. I never saw him before. But if I hadn't gone back he'd have killed Daniel and then he'd have come for me. He said so: I heard him."

"Go and get some sleep. I'll talk to Daniel and then maybe we can draw a line under this."

Gratefully, Brodie did as he said.

Deacon was much longer with Daniel. He kept approaching the same area from different directions, and going over it minutely as if all the answers were there if he could only see them. Of course, he was right.

"It was the same man?"

"Yes," said Daniel.

"You recognised him?"

"I recognised his voice."

Deacon frowned. "He looked different?"

"No, he looked the same. Everyone looks the same when I haven't got my glasses on. You've seen one blob, you've seen them all."

Deacon held out his hand. "Show me."

"What?"

"The glasses. Show me."

Daniel passed them over. Without them he looked naked.

Deacon peered through them and quickly shut his eyes. It was like the start of a migraine, shapes distorted out of all meaning, colours that wouldn't keep still. He passed them back. "So you didn't recognise him when he passed you on the beach."

"I thought he was digging bait."

"In a suit?"

"I never noticed."

"Mrs Farrell noticed."

"She's a sort of detective. I'm a maths teacher."

"Hm." Deacon pondered. "So you're alive, and she's facing a murder charge."

Daniel's eyebrows rocketed. "How could it be murder? He was trying to kill me! Then he'd have killed her."

"Did she know it was the man who tortured you?"

"She may have guessed. She couldn't have known. I told her, afterwards."

"After she'd turned his face into steak tartare, broken three of his ribs and collapsed his lung."

"Yes. After that."

270

"So that wasn't why she did it."

"I told you. He was trying to kill me. He threated to kill her. He could have killed her daughter. It was self-defence."

"Self-defence *is* a valid plea," nodded Deacon. "The jury will take note of the fact that she's a woman and he was a strong and violent man. They may be less sympathetic when they learn that there isn't a mark on her and he's on life-support."

"It was him or us. There was no time for subtlety. If Brodie hadn't stopped him I'd have drowned. If she'd thought about it any longer I'd have drowned. You'd have had two corpses on your hands, and a killer who didn't wait around to answer your questions."

There was a long silence while Deacon considered. He knew he was getting the truth from these people; he also knew he wasn't getting the whole truth. When the man on the ventilator at Dimmock General recovered enough to be interviewed he'd join the conspiracy too. It wouldn't stop him going down - there was sufficient evidence to convict him of attempted murder here and murder elsewhere - but it wouldn't solve the mystery. Deacon wanted to know so much it hurt.

"I shall ask him, you know," he said. "When he wakes up, I'll ask him who Sophie was. Then I'll know what it is you're hiding."

"He won't talk. Whatever else the man is he's a professional. He won't tell you who employed him or why."

"Wrong answer, Danny," said Deacon with a grim smile. "The right answer was, I'm not hiding anything, Inspector. But you don't lie, do you? You don't mind misleading me, you're happy enough to keep back vital bits of the jigsaw, but you'll tie yourself in knots rather than actually lie. Did you think I didn't realise what you were doing? That I saw no difference between 'I don't know' and 'I can't tell you'?"

Daniel took a deep breath. His clothes were still damp and he was cold. "Inspector - "

"Oh, save it," snarled Deacon. "I know what you're going to say. That men you didn't know snatched you from your flat and tortured you for two days, and when you couldn't give them what they wanted they shot you. Then one of them found out you hadn't

271

died and came back to finish the job, only Mrs Farrell rearranged his features with the butt-end of an oar."

"Yes," said Daniel softly. "That's exactly what I was going to say."

"It's all you're going to say, too, isn't it?"

Daniel bit his lip. "Isn't it enough that the good guys won? That a man who takes money to destroy people is in custody and the people he came to kill are safe. There'll be no further repercussions: I give you my word. It's over. Can't you be satisfied with that?"

Jack Deacon felt a fury building under his breast-bone. He was a man who got angry easily, it didn't always mean much, often it subsided as quickly as it came like a storm that hurls and is gone.

This was different, a slow-rise flood of rage at how he and the law he loved were being treated. And not by the scum of the criminal sewer, who might try to take his head off at intervals but in fact respected him. No. By a quiet, gentle, decent young man in an honourable profession; a man who would be judged a pillar of his society by any reasoned assessment. A man whom, so far as Deacon knew, had never harmed a living soul.

A man whose stubborn pursuit of his own code undermined every principle Deacon believed in, struck at the foundations of who he was and the job he did.

Men like Fingers Molloy, the worst pickpocket in Dimmock, a man who couldn't open his own wallet without setting off alarms, might break the law with depressing regularity but at least they didn't try to rewrite it. They didn't try to argue that the law was wrong. Whereas Hood, who may never have broken a law in his life, didn't consider any of them binding. He complied with those he judged worthy. He thought his opinion of their merit was relevant. It was a deeply subversive attitude, more dangerous than outright defiance.

Deacon didn't shout. He kept his voice tightly reined. He leaned over the desk and thrust his face so close that Daniel recoiled. "Who the hell do you think you are? Who do you think *I* am - your hired help? You think I've been breaking my balls to get to the bottom of this out of regard for you? Because someone hurt you once and might do it again?

"Hood, I don't give a damn about you. If you'd died I'd have investigated your murder; since you lived I'm investigating the attacks on you. That's the sum total of what your existence means to me - the wording on a file. You're nothing. You can go to hell in a hand-cart, as long as you don't leave me to clear up the mess.

"Your word? You want to give me your word that everything's all right now, and you think that'll do? That I'll lick your hand and curl up in the corner and go to sleep like your big dumb dog? I'm a public servant, Hood. That doesn't mean I'm *your* servant."

Daniel blinked as if he'd had his face slapped. "I'm sorry. I didn't mean to suggest - "

"Yes," said Deacon furiously, "you did. You think the law exists to keep you safe. That once you're all right the whole tedious business can go back in the box until you need it again. Well, I have news for you. The legal system isn't a game, and it doesn't exist for your convenience. It's the difference between civilisation and barbarism, and that makes it more important than your little life and everything you've done in it. Give me your word? Your word isn't worth the breath it takes to get it out. The law keeps whole societies from tumbling into chaos. And you want to step over it because it's in your way."

"Whether you want it or not," said Daniel in a low voice, "I'm giving you my word that I haven't broken any laws. Mrs Farrell hasn't broken any laws. Nothing either of us has done is going to let the darkness in."

"Oh, you're so clever," sneered Deacon. "So well-educated. But all the education in the world wasn't worth a damn when somebody stronger than you tried to rip you apart for what you knew. I bet you were begging for me to ride to the rescue then! You'd have sacrificed babies to me and my law. Now you're safe you think you can pick and choose which bits you'll obey.

"Well, that's not the deal. I'll look after you, Daniel. I'll stop the men with the buckets and the cigarette-lighters from extracting what they want from you and throwing the dregs away. I'll protect you from the chaos if I have to risk my own neck to do it. That's what I signed up for, and I mightn't like it but I've never short-changed anyone yet and I'm not changing the habit of a lifetime for the likes of you.

"But it doesn't come free. You want my protection when you need it, you pay with your support when you don't. I don't want your word, Daniel, I can't bank your word. I want the truth. I want to know what you know - everything that you know. I want you to acknowledge that you have no right to withhold it."

Daniel's lips were dry. He moistened them with the tip of his tongue. Deacon was entitled to be angry. But he'd made a promise and he wouldn't go back on it. He regretted offending Deacon but he didn't think he had any choice.

"You think I'm ungrateful," he said. "I'm not. I have every respect for you and what you do. You want my support? - I swear to you, you have it. I just can't do what you ask. I can't explain why: if I could you'd understand. I can't tell you everything I know without betraying an entirely innocent party. Please don't hate me for that."

Deacon exploded with sheer exasperation. "Hate you, you arrogant little sod? You're not worth my hatred. I despise you. You pay a pittance on your income tax and you think that entitles you to a say in how I do my job. You think what happened to you was a kind of martyrdom, don't you? - that it bestowed some sort of divinity. You clothe yourself in your shining righteousness, you display your stigmata, and you think we lesser mortals will wave palm-fronds at you for ever more.

"Daniel, I'm not impressed by your scars. The first time I saw you, you were a mass of festering blisters and you stank of garbage. It's a bit hard to feel reverence for someone you've watched being cleaned up like an incontinent geriatric. You're alive because better people than you got on with their jobs and didn't give up when the going got tough. I don't know how you have the gall to ask me to leave my job half done."

"Because if you won't you're going to do a lot more harm than good," murmured Daniel.

"That's not your call!" shouted Jack Deacon, beside himself with rage.

Daniel's chin came up. "You think it's yours?"

"Maybe. Or my superior officers', or possibly the court's. There's a whole mechanism for taking difficult decisions in the public interest. And the funny thing is, Daniel, absolutely nowhere in the process does it come down to what a comprehensive school maths teacher thinks."

Daniel shook his head, trembling and obdurate. "You're saying I have no voice in whether it's more important to punish someone who hurt me or protect someone who never hurt anyone. I don't accept that. I have not only the right but the obligation to make a moral judgement. If I believe it's better to forgive than to repay one wrong with another, then no one - not you, not your superiors, not the Lord Chief Justice - is going to change my mind.

"Unless you can get the information some other way, this stops with me. If that's a crime, charge me. If it isn't, accept that I'm not going to tell you anything more."

Deacon regarded him for a long time before answering. He wasn't going to charge Daniel Hood with anything, he'd be laughed out of court. But neither was he going to forgive and forget.

"This isn't over," he said finally. "Yes, you're free to leave. No, I'm not going to arrest you. But one day, Daniel, you're going to regret making an enemy of me. You're going to need my help, or my understanding, or a word from me in the right ear, and you're not going to get it. I'm going to stand on a bridge somewhere and watch you drown. They say your whole life passes in front of your eyes: well, damn sure this moment will."

Daniel didn't know what to say. He'd never imagined fighting the forces of law and order. "Inspector, this isn't personal ... "

"Oh yes it is," snarled Deacon. "It's as personal as it gets. I tried to help you, stuck my neck out for you; and when the time came to return the favour, you didn't. Someday you're going to pay for that. I don't know how or when, but one day you're going to remember showing me two fingers and wish you hadn't. Now get out."

Daniel stumbled to his feet and made for the door, clumsily, as if through a fog, unsure of where it was. He got it open before Deacon spoke again.

"You can tell me one thing," he rasped. "And a refusal to answer will serve just as well. Does Mrs Farrell know who Sophie is? Does she know who hired the man she beat within an inch of his life?"

Daniel stood beside the open door. The corridor, the front steps and the street beyond beckoned. He dared not answer their siren call. He turned slowly and looked Jack Deacon full in the eyes.

He shook his head. "No," he lied. "She never knew, and I never told her."